Zodiac

Twelve tales

Cate Tyrrell

By the same author:
37 Songs
Parallel Lines

Text copyright © Cate Tyrrell 2017
Published by Cate Tyrrell 2017
ISBN: 9781973118701

For my friends

And for James – your sinful seven gave me the idea
for my twelve tales

Foreword

I had the idea for this collection of short stories when I was writing *Parallel Lines* in 2016. If you've read it, you'll know that a lot of the story centres around the filming of an adult movie. As I didn't have any direct experience of that, I had to do a lot of research. I happened upon some interesting behind-the-scenes videos on James Deen's website; some of them are well worth a watch, (the one where he duct-tapes Tommy Pistol to a wall is memorable), and I found them fascinating. There is a series of them where he describes his thought process behind the development of his Seven Sins sequence of films. I found some of the Sins themselves quite hard to watch, but listening to Deen speak so eloquently about his plan for the series got me thinking about writing a sequence of short stories. After meandering around several ideas, I settled on Zodiac – twelve short stories, one for each of the astrological signs.

Now, as often happens, the way this collection turned out bears little resemblance to my original plan. I thought that, with the short story format, I could write stories that were purely erotic, with little or no exposition. What I discovered about myself during the writing process is that I am, at heart, a storyteller. I love to develop characters and tell the reader all about them. So, instead of twelve stories about sex, we have twelve stories that happen to have some sex in them. And I must admit that it was a lot harder to come up with twelve completely different scenarios than I originally thought it would be. It's taken me a long time to write – over a year – but now it's done, I'm very glad it's finished, and I'm proud of the completed book.

I enjoyed playing with different genres. In here, you'll find contemporary romance, paranormal, historical, futuristic, polyamory, and post-apocalyptic tales. Writing them was a bit like Forrest's box of chocolates (I never knew what I was going to get), but I hope there is something here for everyone. My first attempt at Leo featured some characters from my first book, 37 Songs. Once I got going, I realised that it was going to be far more than a short story. I will be developing it as Rondo; book three of my Love Songs series. I did get to re-visit some old friends in Libra, though. Aquarius will also be developed into the first of what I hope will be a new series.

I have grouped the stories into their elemental categories; earth, air, fire, and water. You can read them in any order you like, but I think the sequence works well in the order I have used. I hope you enjoy reading my journey through the signs of the Zodiac; I'm going to enjoy going back to writing a full-length novel. As well as Rondo, I'm developing a new paranormal romance series. The first book in the series is going to be called *Queen of Fire*, and I'm looking forward to getting that one out to you.

EARTH

Taurus
Virgo
Capricorn

Taurus

Security, subtle strength, appreciation, instruction, patience

The alarm was buzzing like an insistent wasp. I struggled to wake up and reached over to shut it off, swearing as my shoulder reminded me that I'm not as flexible as I used to be. I'd had my running dream again; running freely through the long grass of my grandparents' meadow, then, as an adult, running on the roads in the city I had come to love. I used to be a runner. But that was a long time ago.

I sat up and swung my legs over the side of the bed. Pain shot up my right leg and into my back like always, and I sat there for a moment, waiting for it to pass. Two years ago, I had been happy, successful, fit and married to Toby. I still had enough of the arrogance of youth to believe that I was indestructible and that I had all the time in the world to appreciate how great my life really was. One moment of being in the wrong place at the wrong time put a swift end to all of that.

It was my thirty-eighth birthday, and I, my husband and a group of our friends had just left a restaurant. We were heading to a bar to finish the evening in style when a car mounted the curb and ran straight into our little group. I remember coming to and being relieved to see that Toby was okay and that the rest of our group were fine apart from a couple of scratches. Then I looked down at myself, and the pain started to radiate up through my body; my legs were trapped under the crumpled front bumper of the car. I was pinned to the concrete and blood was pooling around me.

Toby knelt on the hard ground by my head, and I remember having the bizarre thought that my blood would ruin his lovely, new jeans. He cradled my head and started to murmur soft words to me about how everything was going to be okay; that help was on its way. There was a small crowd of people gathering around us, and the girl who had driven the car into me was pacing nervously around, cell phone still welded to her hand, muttering that she was sorry, that she only took her eyes off the road for a second to check her phone.

After that, everything is a bit of a blur. In fact, the next six weeks or so are a bit of a blur. I remember being in the hospital and people coming to see me. I remember Toby taking me home and wheeling me into the house before lifting me onto the sofa in our living room and asking me if I needed anything. I remember thinking that he was acting a little strange – like we'd only just met and he was being polite.

So, it came as no surprise when, about six months later, I came home early from a physio session to find him and two of his friends loading his stuff into a hired van. "You were going to leave without telling me? Without saying goodbye?"

He looked stricken and put down the box he was carrying. "I'm sorry, Rhianna. I can't do this anymore. You're not the woman I married. This isn't the marriage I wanted."

I didn't blame him. I was more sad than angry, but I don't think I was surprised. I wasn't the woman he married. She had two legs and was able to run. I looked down at myself as I sat there on the side of my bed, breath coming in patchy gasps and memories assaulting my brain. My right leg stopped just below the knee. Both knees were painful, and my right hip was also aging far too fast. Tomorrow it would be two years since that fateful night. Two years since that stupid little bitch had thought that checking Snapchat was more important than concentrating on her driving. Two years since my life ended to all intents and purposes. And tomorrow I would be forty years old.

After the divorce was finalised, we sold the house, and I bought this little ground floor apartment. It's handy for work, and it's big enough for me. I have nice neighbours too; Mrs. Anderson across the hall is very sweet and Matt, my upstairs neighbour, is fun to have around. When I first moved in, I was still using the chair quite a lot because they couldn't get the fit for my prosthesis right. Matt started a weekly routine of Thursday movie nights which we still do every week. If there is nothing on at the cinema that we want to see, we order in and watch something we both like. And now, I consider him to be one of my closest friends. One of my few friends, to be honest.

A lot of the people I called friends in my old life had been Toby's first and, even though they all said the right things about staying in touch, as soon as he was out of my life, they all went with him. So, the people I actually called 'friend' are few and far between. Because of that, my odd-couple relationship with the young stockbroker who lives upstairs has become something I value. I know there is nothing I can't ask him to help me with and his youthful exuberance is a little infectious. The hours I spend with him on a Thursday evening always make me forget, if only for a little while, how crappy my life has become.

The pain had passed enough to move, so I reached for my crutches and hobbled into the bathroom for a shower. The first half an hour of the day is always the hardest, but by the time I'd showered, dressed, put on my leg and had breakfast, I was feeling more like my new/old self. As I was locking my door on the way out, Matt came down the stairs with a pretty, giggling blonde. I smiled inwardly; he had a lot of different girls up there. Sometimes, if the lady in question was particularly vocal, I could hear what they got up to. I heard them last night. She had screamed his name and begged him to fuck her. That seemed to be a common theme with his many lovers. I caught myself wondering if he really was as good as the many screaming orgasms I'd overheard would indicate.

"Good morning Rhianna. How are you today?" He gave me that twinkly smile, his blue eyes crinkling at the corners and I couldn't help but smile in reply. "This is Megan."

"Hi, Matt. And nice to meet you, Megan. I'm fine thanks. And it looks like you had a fun evening."

The girl blushed and giggled. She mumbled something about seeing him again, and he nodded saying he'd call her. I knew him well enough to know that meant he had very little intention of seeing her again. He kissed her cheek and stood next to me. "I just need to talk to Rhianna about something, babe. I'll see you soon." The girl looked confused for a moment, then realised that she had been dismissed and left. I felt sorry for her.

"That was a bit mean."

"What? I said I'd call her later."

"And we both know you have no intention of doing that."

He put his hands in his pockets and shuffled his feet, looking at the door through which his little plaything had just left. "Well … she was fun. But I don't think I'll be going for seconds."

"I heard the two of you last night. She clearly had a great time."

He closed his eyes and pulled a face that showed something I suspected was regret. "I can't stand the screamers, you know? I mean, I get it; they're having a great time sitting on my cock, but there's no need to make the windows rattle."

I couldn't stop the sound of disbelief that came out of my mouth. "Matt, you do know that women can fake orgasms, don't you?"

"Yeah. Of course. But she wasn't faking. I can tell."

"Of course, you can." I tried not to sound too patronising, but it was hard not to. He was so sure of his prowess; I found it kind of endearing. "Are we on for tonight?"

His face brightened, and he smiled at me before leaning over and kissing me on the cheek. "You know I wouldn't miss it – it's the highlight of my week. I downloaded 'What we do in the shadows' – thought it deserved another watch."

"Oh – great idea – I loved it when we watched it before. I'll order in some food. What do you fancy?"

He couldn't resist the suggestive eyebrow waggle in response to my question. He could always be relied upon to provide sexual innuendo in every situation. You knew where were with Matt. It was one of the reasons I liked him so much; no surprises.

"Okay. Thai, it is then. See you at seven."

He winked at me and took my briefcase. "You know me so well. I'll carry this out to your car."

"You don't have to do that, I can carry it myself, you know?"

"I know. I'm just being a gentleman. You bring that out in me." He winked again, and we walked out to the small carpark that was attached to our apartment building. When I had unlocked my car, he opened the passenger door and laid my case on the floor of the footwell. "See you later, Rhia. Have a good day."

I had my weekly physio session after work. Getting through it was always tough, and it was one of the reasons I looked forward to movie night every week. My instrument of torture today was the deceptively-named Norah. When I met her first, I'd been expecting a benevolent, older lady who smelled of lavender, but the reality wasn't nearly as pleasant. She was in her early twenties; a strong, black girl with a dry sense of humour and the unmistakable heart of a sadist.

She took me through my paces and, at the end of the session, she looked at her notes and rubbed her hand on her chin. "You should be further along at this stage. That hip seems to be getting worse. Are you doing your exercises?"

"Every day," I lied. I did them when I thought about it. I hated doing them because they hurt like hell.

She must have detected my untruth because she looked sceptically at me. "You won't get any better if you don't do your exercises." She looked at my notes again. "It says here you used to be a runner."

"Yeah," I said sarcastically, "I used to do a lot of things."

Norah put her hands on her hips and gave me a look I recognised as disdain. "You have a prosthesis that is designed for running. You should try it. The stronger we can make those leg muscles, the better your hip will be. It's all about support. Is there someone you can go for short runs with? A friend? Boyfriend?"

My head fell forward so that my chin touched my chest. The subject of boyfriends was a little sore. I had dated a couple of guys since the accident, but they both turned out to be total weirdos with a fetish for amputees. The six months or so I'd been signed up to Match.com, I'd realised that it is simply a huge hook-up site and I wasn't interested in that, no matter how much I was missing sex. And I was missing it. Badly. I was ashamed of the number of times a week I indulged in solitary pleasure. As I lay in my bed last night listening to the live broadcast of Behind the Green Door going on upstairs, I'd fantasised that some nameless, faceless hunk was fucking me senseless. It was always the same fantasy; I couldn't picture anyone real, or it was too shameful. The vibrator had whirred in my hand as I rubbed it up and down my pussy, bringing myself almost to the edge a number of times. I didn't want to come with the vibrator. I wanted to come with my cunt full of cock. I pushed my large, silicon dildo into my wet hole and started the slow, deep thrusting that I knew would bring me to my climax in a minute or two. As my orgasm rushed over me, I pulled the dildo out and pressed my thighs together, riding it out until the feeling subsided. Upstairs, the girl who I now know was Megan screamed out Matt's name, and I heard him groan as he followed her over the edge. As I lay there, panting and sweaty, I had pictured the two of them lying in a tangle; the three of us making some bizarre trio.

I was pulled back to the present by Norah asking the question again. "Is there someone you can go running with?"

"There isn't really anyone. I could try it on a treadmill?"

Norah nodded. "Yes. That might be better to start with anyway. Just don't try to do too much at once." She looked me up and down. "And you should get back out there and find a boyfriend – or girlfriend if that's your thing. You're young. You lost your lower leg, not your libido."

I was a little surprised by her frankness. I'd got used to friends and relatives avoiding the subject. My mother expressed her opinion frequently that I should probably forget all that and concentrate on getting well. I knew, though, that for my wellbeing, all that had to be a part of my life. I just didn't know how to go about getting it back and, the longer it went on, the further away it seemed.

I was just coming back from getting the Thai food delivery from the front door when Matt came down the stairs. He was barefoot and wearing ripped jeans and a faded tee-shirt, but his easy grace told of a human being who is comfortable in his own skin. Confident, uncompromising, predatory. He held up a flash drive. "Got the movie, and I can see you've got the take-out — so we're all set for a great evening."

He followed me into my apartment and went to set up the movie while I got some plates and cutlery. He wandered into the kitchen and opened the fridge, taking out two beers and opening them. "We're all set in there. Here, let me help you carry some of that stuff in." He picked up the plates and carried them and our drinks into the living room, where he put them down on the low table in front of the sofa. We spooned the fragrant food onto our plates and settled down to watch the movie.

"So, how was your date with the physio terrorist?"

"Norah. She could give the Marquis de Sade a run for his money."

"Hmm … I like the sound of her."

I laughed and poked him in the shoulder. "Yeah — she's just your type. And I don't think she'd be a screamer. In fact, I think she'd have you screaming — for mercy."

He pushed me gently in reply. "You're getting me hard, talking like that." He grinned at me and took a mouthful of his food. "So — what did she say today?"

"She suggested I started running again."

"You used to run?"

"Yeah. I ran marathons. I loved it."

"Wow. How come I didn't know that about you? Why don't you have medals and trophies and shit all over the place?"

"Reminders of my former glory? Of something I used to love but can't do anymore? Oh, let me think."

He looked sheepish at me. "Sorry – that was a bit thoughtless, wasn't it? But – and forgive me for asking a stupid question, but can you run? Don't you need one of those blade thingies for that?"

I smiled at his honesty. "I have one. I've never tried it."

His mouth opened with genuine shock. "What? Right. Tomorrow morning. You, me, sexy running gear."

I balked at his suggestion, but before I could say anything, he shook his head and held up his hand to tell me not to bother arguing.

"No – you're not going to say no. You're going to try it. If it doesn't work out? Then fine. But you're going to give it a go."

So that was how I came to be waiting outside my apartment door at stupid o'clock on the morning of my fortieth birthday. I'd retrieved some lycra running gear from the back of my wardrobe, and I felt self-conscious about how I looked. The running shorts ended just below my knee, giving the whole world a full view of my replacement lower leg. I was just thinking about ducking back into my apartment when Matt jogged down the stairs and saw me.

"Wow – you look amazing!"

For a moment I wasn't sure if he was talking to me and I looked around to see if there was someone else there.

"Rhianna. You. I'm talking to you. You look amazing." He gave me the once-over and, as his eyes moved to my lower legs, I felt myself cringe. "Is it wrong that I think that looks kinda hot?"

I looked at his face – his open, honest, young, handsome face and I felt the nerves fade. "No. It's fine." He always told me the truth and his honesty at that moment, helped me to relax. He didn't have an amputee fetish – he'd have been all over me within a week if he had – but he was letting me know that he didn't find it unattractive. A little flame of self-confidence, one that had been extinguished a long time ago, burst back into life.

Running wasn't easy. It took me a while to get used to the blade – it's one that's made for jogging, not speed, but it felt odd to start with. The extra friction made my stump sore, and my hip complained loudly, but I ignored it. We jogged slowly together and made steady progress. We started to run every morning and, after a couple of weeks, I was really starting to feel the difference.

Norah leaned back on the exam table with her arms crossed as I told her about my little running exploits. "See? I told you it would help.

Stick with it. You're a runner again. Maybe it's time you got the rest of your life back too."

I knew what she was talking about and I knew she was right. But every time I thought about it, I got that hollow, scared feeling in the pit of my stomach. Anyone I might want, probably wouldn't want me. I'd left it too late to do the whole married-with-kids thing and that, combined with my disability, meant that any man who looked at me as a possible partner was either a fetishist or just looking for a hook-up. And anyway, I wasn't sure if I was even physically able to have a normal sex life anymore. My body was improving, but my movement was still restricted quite a bit. I'd just have to reconcile myself to being alone and a monthly bill for C batteries that was more than the GDP of a small, African nation.

We were eating fish and chips with our fingers in front of the TV. The salty, greasy food was totally delicious. We hadn't had fish and chips for ages because the shop we used to get them from had been closed down for reasons that neither of us wanted to think about. But it had recently re-opened, under new management (a jolly-looking couple with Lancashire accents) and with a huge poster in the window advertising its faultless hygiene report.

When I'd finished all I could eat of my food, I gave what was left to Matt who polished it off before screwing up all the paper into a ball and launching it in the direction of the kitchen bin. He missed, so he got up and went to the open-plan kitchen to get more beer. "So – what did Norah say today? Is she pleased that you're running again?"

I got up to join him in the kitchen, washing my hands in the sink to get rid of the salt and vinegar smell. "Yeah – she did the whole 'I told you so' thing, but I'll let her have that one; she was right."

He washed his hands too then picked up two bottles of beer and followed me back to the sofa. "She sounds like a wise woman. What else has she told you to do?"

I felt myself blush. I didn't want to talk about this with my neighbour. "Oh – you know – the usual stuff about getting back into a normal routine, getting out a bit more, blah blah blah."

He turned to look at me. "You're blushing. What else did she say? Come on – spill it."

I looked at his expectant face and felt myself turn crimson.

"She told you to get back into dating, didn't she?"

I shook my head, but the look on my face probably told him everything he needed to know.

He sat back on the sofa and looked at me. "I knew it. How long has it been, anyway? I know you had a couple of dates with weirdos from Match.com, but you haven't said anything about dating in ages."

I felt very uncomfortable, but I knew he wouldn't let me drop it, so I just gritted my teeth and told him.

"It's been a long time, okay? I didn't sleep with either of those weirdos, by the way."

He sat forward, his eyebrows shot towards the ceiling and his mouth opened in shock. "What? Wait a minute – does that mean you haven't had sex in over a year?"

"Since before that. Toby, my ex, didn't want to hurt me, so we didn't do it after the accident. That was two years ago. On my birthday. The first day we went jogging was my fortieth birthday; the second anniversary of the accident."

He sat back again and blew out a long breath. "Two years? How do you manage? I mean – you must masturbate, right?"

I coughed and looked away. "Um – that's not something I want to talk about with you, Matt."

"Why not?" He looked and sounded genuinely confused. "Everyone masturbates. Hell, I do it all the time. Every morning in the shower, for a start."

Now I was intrigued. "What? You have sex nearly every day. You have a procession of pretty girls coming and going from your apartment."

"So? I could be having sex all day, but I'd still want to have a wank in the shower every morning. It's just natural."

"Oh." I didn't know how to respond to that.

"So – you do, right? God, I love the idea of you down here stroking yourself to oblivion while I'm up there doing the same."

"I – ah – I really don't know what to say to that."

He smiled at me and took a swig of his beer. "So – why haven't you found yourself some great guy to ease the ache." He clearly thought it was a legitimate question that didn't have an obvious answer.

I looked at him questioningly, but he didn't back down. "Well, for a start, I'm not exactly every decent guy's idea of a good time. I'm forty, and I only have three and a half limbs."

He shook his head. "I'm still waiting to hear a real reason why you haven't let yourself get back in the saddle."

He wasn't going to back down. And, if I was honest with myself, it felt good to be finally talking about this to someone I trusted. "Okay. Honestly? I'm scared."

"Scared? Of what?"

"Scared that any man who wants me only wants me because of this." I pointed at my prosthesis. "Or only wants me because he thinks I'm desperate and will take anything that's offered."

He nodded thoughtfully and took another sip of his beer. "I get that. There are some serious creeps out there in online-dating land, but there are a lot of great guys out there too. Not looking because you're scared, means you could miss out on something really good."

"It's not just that."

"Then what? Come on – tell me. I might be able to help."

I laughed. "I doubt that, very much."

"Why? What is it? Tell me, Rhia. You know you can trust me."

I could trust him; I knew that. He had been a friend through all this, and he'd seen me at my very best and my very worst. "Well – okay – I'm not sure I can do it anymore."

"Do it? What do you mean?"

"I mean, do it – have sex. My body isn't what it was. My hip is bad, and my back is bad. I have the knees of a sixty-year-old, and I have no clue as to whether or not I could do it, or what positions might work. There – I told you – happy now?"

He thought for a minute, rubbing his hand on his chin, then he looked at me and smiled. "You know? I think what you need is a night of no-strings exploration with a friend who's happy and willing to help you out."

I shook my head and looked at him, raising my eyebrows in an unspoken question.

"Would you feel better about starting a new relationship if you knew exactly what you can and can't do in the sack?"

I thought about that for a moment or two. "Well – yeah – I suppose so. But there's no point in thinking too hard about that – I mean, I don't know anyone who would be happy to help me find that out. Someone I'd trust enough to do it with."

As soon as his smile changed to that confident, sexy grin, I knew what he was going to say.

"Oh no – no, no, no, and a world of NO. I'm not going down that road with you."

"Why not? I've wanted to fuck you for ages."

"You have?"

"I have. You trust me, right?"

"Yeah …" I drew out the word, making it sound like a question.

"And this would really help you?"

"I think it might, yeah. But it's not going to happen. I don't want things to be weird between us."

He leaned forward and put his hand on my thigh. "It wouldn't be weird unless you decided to make it weird. Look – I need to fuck like I need food. You don't have any problem eating with me, do you?"

I couldn't see where he was going with this. "No – eating with you is nice. Fun."

"Good. So, fucking with me would be nice and fun too. No – forget that – it wouldn't be nice – it would be hot."

"Self-assured much?"

"No point in being modest. There are things I'm good at – poker, Call of Duty, my job, and fucking. You just need to decide to be brave enough to take me up on my offer. I promise to give you a night of fun. A night where you discover what you can and can't do in a completely no-pressure, relationship-nonsense-free, secure environment. Oh – and I'll make you come. You'll be screaming my name and making my windows rattle before morning. And when we're done? There'll be no weirdness. We'll still have Thursday movie nights and laugh and drink beer. And hopefully, before too long, you'll have a great guy in your life who can enjoy that with us."

My pussy was shouting at me to accept his offer. But my brain was listing all the reasons why it would be a bad idea. "I'm really touched by your offer – I mean, it's generous, and I can tell you mean every word, but I don't think I can do that."

He stood up, drained his beer and looked down at me. "I'm going up to my apartment. I'm going to leave the door unlocked. Think about what I've said. I hope you make the right decision." He walked to the door and turned to look at me. "I'll be waiting for you. Just don't overthink this." A moment later, he was gone, and I was left sitting on my sofa alone, trying to decide what the hell I should do.

I don't know how long I sat there. It was quite a while. I went over the pros and cons in my mind, stewing over them like I was trying to decipher the mystery of the ages. I knew what Matt had said made total sense; what I needed was to find out what I could do. But what was left of my self-esteem argued that sex without emotion was wrong. As soon as I'd made a decision, the other side would come back with a counter-argument; I was getting nowhere. Eventually, I decided to leave it to fate. I got up from the sofa and walked to the kitchen counter where I kept the pot for small change. I fished around and pulled out a two pence piece. "Right. Heads I go upstairs and tails I stay down here. I flicked the coin into the air, watching it turn over and over as it climbed to its highest point then began to fall. I let it fall to the floor, held my breath and looked. The Queen's head grinned up at me from where it had landed on the carpet of my living room, and I felt my heart leap up into my throat. Time to be brave.

He had left the door open, as he said he would. As I walked into his apartment, I was taken by how tidy it was. I'd never been up here before, and I hadn't known what to expect. I heard the shower turn off and a few moments later, Matt walked out into the main room wearing only a towel. When he saw me, he grinned and came to me, putting his arms around me gently. "Good decision. This is going to be fun."

"I feel sick." The words had left my mouth before I had a chance to try to stop them.

Matt laughed, the sound easing my nerves a little. "Well, I don't think I've ever had a girl say that to me before sex. There's a first time for everything, I suppose." He put his finger under my chin and tilted my face up, so our eyes met. "Look – don't worry. This is going to be fun. I think we're probably going to spend most of the time laughing. Relax. I'm not going to do anything you don't want."

It was at that point I realised that he was standing in front of me with only a towel around his waist. His body was beautiful. He isn't that much taller than me, but he has a swimmer's body; wide shoulders, narrow waist, and slender hips. His chest has a sprinkling of dark hair – a little darker than the hair on his head – which arrows down his belly as if it is pointing to his groin. As I looked down, the towel began to twitch as his cock went from flaccid to semi-hard under my gaze.

He smiled as he watched me looking at his body. "Oh yes. This is going to be great fun." He tugged at the towel, and it fell to the floor. "Ta-da!" He held his arms up and turned around, giving me the full three-sixty view.

"Oh …" It was all I could manage to get out. He was beautiful. His muscles were well-defined, and his skin had that blush of youth, unmarked by scars or tattoos. "You're … perfect." I dropped my head and looked down at my less-than-perfect body. "This isn't … I shouldn't have come." I turned, but before I could get to the door, he was there, enfolding me in his arms.

"Stop it. I want this. I want you. I meant it when I said I've wanted to fuck you for ages. You're a beautiful woman, Rhia. Let me show you." He put his hand under my chin and tilted my face up again. "And you've got to stop looking down all the time. All you see is what you don't have. Look up at what you do have and let yourself enjoy it."

It was probably the most profound thing that anyone had said to me since the accident. I looked into his eyes and felt myself relax. "Okay. I'll try."

"Good girl." He smiled again and, as always, I returned it involuntarily. I don't think I've ever met anyone whose smile was as infectious as Matt's. "Right – you get comfy." He indicated over to the bedroom. "Take off or keep on whatever you like. This is for you, not me. I'll go and open some wine."

He walked into the kitchen area and took a bottle of wine out of the fridge. He turned around and saw me standing in the same spot, so he made a 'shoo' motion with his hands. I obeyed, walking into his bedroom. It was simple – very masculine – a king-size bed taking up the majority of the space, which was decorated in classic blues and greys. I walked over to the bed and pulled back the duvet. My nose gave me a waft of freshly-laundered sheets. Part of me was relieved about that, knowing what he got up to in here on a regular basis. I found myself wondering how often he changed his bed sheets.

I was pulled back by the sounds of his voice behind me. "Here. Have a drink with me." He gave me a glass of wine, and I took a sip; the clean, crisp flavour washed over my tongue, and I smiled. "It's nice, isn't it?"

I nodded. "Very nice, thank you."

He looked amused, and I could tell he was trying not to laugh. "Okay. Let's stop with all the stiff-upper-lip stuff. I'm going to get on the bed, and you're going to get comfortable and join me. Alright?"

I nodded again. This all felt very strange and a little dream-like. Perhaps it was a dream? No – the swarm of butterflies that were currently fighting for space in my belly told me that this was real. "Alright." I put my wine down on the bedside table and sat on the edge of his bed. I felt the bed move as he sat beside me. I pulled my shirt over my head. I have no problems with the upper half of my body; my breasts are still firm, and my shoulders are nice. I have a bit of an expensive underwear obsession, so I knew that the dark red Agent Provocateur bra that I was wearing looked good.

I head Matt hiss in a breath, and then I felt his fingers on my shoulder. He brushed the back of his fingers down my arm and then over to my throat, stroking down between my breasts then moving up to push the strap of my bra off my shoulder. He bent to kiss my uncovered skin, and I felt myself relax. "You are gorgeous, Rhia. This bra is so sexy. Will you let me take it off you?"

I looked up at his face. His eyes were dark; the pupils dilated in the dim light of the bedroom. I nodded hesitantly.

"I need to hear you say it, Rhia. I don't want there to be any misunderstandings between us. If you want something, you have to tell me. And that goes double for if you don't want something. Okay?"

I started to nod in agreement then stopped myself. "Okay. I understand. Yes – you can take my bra off."

He placed a whisper-soft kiss on my cheek. "Thank you. It will be a pleasure." He turned his body and reached behind me, undoing the three hooks in a move that told me he'd done this many, many times. As the burgundy lace fell from my shoulders, he moved his hand around and cupped one of my breasts. "Look at me, Rhia." He kept eye contact with me as he explored my sensitive flesh. As his thumb brushed over my painfully hard nipple, I gasped, and he covered my open mouth with his, pushing his tongue into me with a stifled groan.

I let him kiss me, and my hand moved of its own volition to rest on the warm skin of his thigh. He groaned again and deepened the kiss, laying his hand over mine and directing it to the hot column of flesh that was now hard and firm against his belly. I ran my fingers tentatively up and down the length of his cock. "You're …"

"Seriously turned on." He laughed, and it broke the tension. "Can I help you take off the rest of your clothes?"

"My leg needs to come off first." I leant down and began to release the fastenings.

Matt moved quickly and knelt in front of me, watching as I released the prosthesis and removed the soft cover from my stump. He laid his fingers gently on my knee and stroked down towards the place where my right leg stopped. The skin was very sensitive, and I giggled. "Are you ticklish there?"

"I guess I must be. Nobody has ever tickled me there before."

He stroked his fingers up and down again, looking up at me, grinning as his gentle caress elicited more giggles. Then he stopped stroking and looked down at my leg. He bent his head and placed a gentle kiss on the skin just below my knee. I felt myself shudder and he looked back up to my face. "Now – let's get the rest of your clothes off."

I let him pull my leggings off, and he knelt back, looking at me. He sat forward and ran a finger under the lace of my knickers. "You have great taste in underwear. But can I take these off too?"

I knew I was past the point of no return now, so I nodded and said, "Yes."

I thought he would stay on his knees in front of me to do that, but he surprised me by standing quickly, putting one hand under my knees and the other behind my back so he could lift me and put me into the centre of his bed. I made a little squeal of delight, and he laughed, landing between my knees. He reached up for the waistband of my knickers, and I let him ease them over my hips and pull them off completely. He knelt back as if to admire his handiwork. "Wow." He reached forward and ran a finger gently through my pubic hair. "I'm going to have so much fun with you here." He grinned at me, cocking an eyebrow before leaning forward to place a kiss on my belly. "Now – I think you should get comfortable. Let's start with the position you lie in when you masturbate."

I coughed out a breath at his frankness. "Sorry?"

"Come on, Rhia. There's no point in being coy. Show me how you lie when you masturbate. That's got to be comfortable, right?"

"I guess so …" I wasn't convinced, but I positioned myself on his bed as I do when I'm lying in mine; propped up a little on a pillow, slightly on my right side with my left leg raised up and out.

"Good. Now show me how you pleasure yourself." When I didn't respond right away, he moved up to lie next to me, putting his arm around me to support my shoulders. "Come on – show me. Do you use your fingers or a vibe?"

I looked at his face. He wasn't at all judgemental, and I could see that he thought these questions were perfectly ordinary, not embarrassing or inappropriate. "I usually use a vibrator to start with; then I like to finish with a dildo."

"Okay. That's cool." He reached over to his bedside table and opened the drawer at the top. When he came back to me, he was holding a slim vibrator and a small bottle of lube. I watched as he opened the bottle and squirted a little of the clear gel onto the head of the vibrator before switching it on. It buzzed softly in his hand as he handed it to me, "Show me."

"Do I want to know why you have a vibrator in your drawer?"

He laughed at me and put the slim toy into my hand. "It comes in useful. And any man who hasn't tried rubbing one of these on the underside of his cock is missing a trick." He grinned again and kissed me softly on the lips. "I want to see how you pleasure yourself. It will help us work out what is going to work for you."

"Okay. That sounds reasonable." I couldn't quite believe what I was about to do, but I reached down, placing the head of the vibrator between the lips of my pussy, moving it around to spread the lube. I closed my eyes and tried to relax as the gentle buzzing began to stimulate my sensitive folds. As the sensation grew, my left leg fell outwards a little further, giving Matt a clear view of what I was doing.

"God, Rhia, that's so hot." I felt him move down the bed and he was kneeling between my legs again. I opened my eyes, and I felt powerful, watching this young, horny guy completely enthralled by what I was doing. "I've gotta get in there." He leaned forward and started to kiss my inner thighs, working his way up to my pussy. I let him take the vibrator out of my hand and replace it with his mouth. He licked and sucked at my outer lips for a minute or two then he used his fingers to spread me wide, exposing my clit and my hole. Matt made a sound of approval then put his mouth directly on my clitoris, sucking the engorged bud into his mouth and laving it with his tongue. He pushed a finger into my now wet hole, and I felt myself buck with the pleasure of that simple penetration. He pushed a second finger into me, turning his hand over and curling his fingers up to stroke my insides while he sucked harder on my clit. My orgasm came so quickly and was so powerful; I felt myself writhing on his hand as I tried to clench my thighs together. He held me open and continued to suck and finger me until it was over. Finally, he lifted his head and looked at me, cocking an eyebrow and grinning. "How was that?"

I was panting, trying to catch my breath. "Oh – you know – it was – fairly mediocre."

He laughed, a deep, rumbling sound that vibrated right down to my toes. "Well, we'll just have to try a little harder, then, won't we?" He reached over to his bedside table again and took out a condom. He ripped open the packet and unrolled it over his cock, without taking his eyes from mine. "I really need to fuck you now. Do you want to try the position you're lying in? Or do you think it's going to put too much pressure on your hip?"

I couldn't believe how considerate he was being. He was clearly very aroused and had just given me a seriously good orgasm; most men would be thinking only of their own needs right now. "Can we try it? I'm not sure if it will work, but I'd like to give it a go."

He grinned at me. "Absolutely. Now – if this hurts, tell me, and we'll stop." He positioned himself between my legs which straightened me, putting even pressure on both my hips.

I knew straight away that it wasn't going to work. Now that I wasn't leaning on my bad hip, it let me know it wasn't happy with a pain that shot right down my leg and echoed in the ghost of the foot that had once been there. "No – that's not going to work – sorry."

He moved quickly, letting me rest back to my original position. "You okay?"

"Yeah – I just need to be resting on this hip a little bit. Sorry."

"No need to apologise – that's why we're doing this – so that you know what does and doesn't work. Well – that and the fact that I really want to fuck you." We both laughed. "See? I told you we'd spend most of the time laughing, didn't I?" He stroked my face and kissed me. The kiss deepened quickly until our tongues were tangled and we were sharing the air from each other's lungs. When he finally broke the kiss, he moved so that he was behind me. "Let's try this."

I was lying slightly on my right side, leaning back against him. "This feels quite comfy."

He reached forward and lifted my left leg, pulling it back slightly over his hip. I felt the head of his cock moving against my pussy lips, and he groaned into my ear. "Put your hand down and guide me in. I need to be inside you. Please, Rhia."

I did as he asked, reaching down and placing the head of his cock so that he could push into me, which he did with one, hard thrust. I cried out at the penetration, his cock stretching me gloriously, and I arched my back, pushing my shoulders against him.

"Steady. Is that alright?" He was breathing heavily, and I could tell that he was trying to hold himself back, not moving until I told him it was okay."

"It's good. It's really good."

As soon as I'd said that, he pulled out almost completely, before thrusting back in with a groan. "God, Rhia. You're so fucking tight."

He was building up a steady rhythm now. "I'm trying to go easy, but I don't think I can."

"It's okay. I'm fine. I want you too." I felt his teeth bite into my shoulder for a moment then he began to piston his hips against me, and I knew that he was going to come soon. He let out a strangled cry and ground himself against me as he came.

I could feel his abdomen rising and falling against my back as he gulped in air. "Wow … that was fucking intense."

I could only nod and make a breathy noise in agreement. After a moment, I felt him withdraw his still-hard cock, and I heard him remove the condom behind me. Then his arms were back around me; his cock pressed between my buttocks. "So – that one works, then?"

I laughed softly. "Yeah. That one works." We lay together like that for several minutes, saying nothing. He was kissing me softly, licking at the skin between my neck and shoulder. I reached back and stroked his hip, and I felt his cock jerk against me in reply. "Are you ready to try something else?" I couldn't believe I was being that forward.

I heard him chuckle and he shifted away from my back and eased me down onto the pillows. He looked down at his erection, which was now twitching in time to his heartbeat. "Never readier. What do you want to try next?"

I looked at his gorgeous body and bit my lower lip. I knew what I wanted to say, so I took a deep breath and closed my eyes. "I want to try going down on you."

His face lit up, and he lay down, displaying himself with all the confidence of a creature who knows he's beautiful. "I'm all yours. How do you want me?"

"Stay like that to start with." I tried to get up onto my knees, but I just couldn't keep my balance like that. I fell over, face-planting on his belly, then rolled off and onto my back as uncontrollable laughter took me over. Matt joined in, and pretty soon, we were just holding each other, tears streaming down our faces and gasping for breath. When I'd calmed enough to speak, I looked up at him. "Okay – that isn't going to work. I can't keep my balance like that."

"No to worry. Sit on the edge of the bed."

I did as he instructed and he climbed off the bed and stood in front of me. My face was level with his belly button, and I gave in to the urge to rub my face in the soft hair that ran down from his navel to his groin. I looked up at him, and he smiled encouragingly before pushing his fingers into my hair and angling me down, letting me know exactly what he wanted me to do.

"That's it. Let me fuck your sweet mouth."

I licked up the length of his cock, lingering on the tight web of skin underneath the head. He shuddered, and his right leg twitched a little in response to my caress. I teased him with my tongue for a little longer then I took the head of his penis into my mouth, sucking gently but firmly on the soft skin. He made a low sound in his throat and gripped onto my hair again, this time with both hands. I let him move my head, directing me to pleasure him as he wished. I felt him push forward until he touched the back of my throat. He withdrew before my gag reflex had time to kick in then he did it again. I took in a deep breath through my nose and swallowed him.

He shouted out in shock and pulled out. "Where did you learn to do that?"

Now it was my turn to raise an eyebrow suggestively. "That's for me to know and for you to forever wonder about." I returned my mouth to his cock, and he took hold of my head again, thrusting into me until my jaw ached. I put my hands on his buttocks; his skin there was so soft that I just had to stroke it.

He was moaning and saying my name, shaking and thrusting into my throat. "Rhia – Oh god – I'm going to come – let me pull out."

I firmed up my grasp on his bottom and pulled him back towards me, not letting him withdraw. He'd brought me to orgasm with his mouth, and I wanted to return the favour. His body went rigid, and he went up on his toes as his cum flooded my throat. I swallowed, breathing through my nose as he emptied himself into me.

Finally, he pulled out of my mouth and fell onto his knees in front of me. "God, Rhia." He reached up and pulled my face down to his, taking my mouth in a rough kiss. "When you find your guy, he's going to be one lucky son-of-a-bitch."

I laughed at his honesty and pulled him back to his feet.

We lay back down on the bed, and he pulled me into his arms. "You have a seriously talented mouth." As if to reinforce his statement, he leant down and started to kiss me again. As before, the kiss soon turned into something wilder, and our hands were travelling over each other's bodies, finding new patches of skin to explore and caress. "You need to be able to do a position that has us face to face. I want to see your eyes as you come on my cock."

"Yeah. I'd like that. But the missionary we tried first just doesn't work, and I can't keep my balance on my knees, so I don't think I can ride you."

"You can if I hold you stable. Let's try it."

"Are you ready to go again?"

He gave me a look that said 'what do you think?' and nodded his head downwards. I followed his gaze to his cock which was completely hard again. "Ready and very willing." After a little interlude for more laughter and the retrieval of another condom, he lay back in the centre of the bed and took one of my hands. "Right – let's try this. Roll onto me, so you're lying on me."

I did as he suggested, lying on his strong body like he was a surfboard. Our faces were level, and he put the palm of his hand on my cheek, his eyes gleaming as he looked at me. "Hello, you."

"Hello, yourself." I couldn't stop the smile that broke out on my face in answer to his. "Now what?"

"Put your legs either side of my body." I moved my left leg first then tentatively tried my right leg. Without any weight on it, it felt okay. "Is that alright?"

"Yeah – it's fine actually. There's no pressure on it, so it's good. Not sure how long I can hold it like that, but let's find out."

"Ease yourself up onto your hands; take the weight onto your arms. You can lean on my chest if you need to."

I did as he suggested, easing myself up until both my arms were straight and my hands were flat against his chest.

"Right. Now I'm going to put my hands on your hips to hold you steady. When I've done that, try letting go with one of your hands."

I followed his instructions again. His strong hands holding me made me feel safe and secure; he wasn't going to let me fall.

"Good girl. That's right. Now – sit on my cock."

I looked at his face. His eyes had taken on the dark, intense look again. He was very aroused but managing to control himself for me. I reached down and took his cock in my hand, then I rose up a little and placed him at the entrance to my hole. I pushed down on him, taking his entire length inside me and my head fell back a little as I felt him fill me so completely. "Oh god, Matt. That feels so bloody good."

His reply was an incoherent groan. I looked down at him, and he was biting his lip, breathing heavily through his nose as he struggled to stay in control. "Touch yourself while you ride me. I want to see you come."

I felt brazen and bold, powerful and sexy. For the first time since the accident, I felt like a real woman, and it gave me the courage to do as he asked. I reached down and found my clit, swollen and ready. I began to stroke myself as Matt lifted me, helping me to move up and down on his cock. Our eyes never broke contact, and I could feel my pleasure building.

"That's it, baby. Stroke yourself and ride my cock. God – your cunt feels so good wrapped around my dick."

I squeezed my internal muscles, tightening my hold on him even more.

"Fuck – Rhia – do that again."

I did as he requested and felt a mischievous smile spread on my lips. "Do you like that, big boy?"

He started to sweat and lift his hips to get further into me. "Oh yeah. I like it. Screw the idea of finding you a man; I'm keeping you for myself."

I knew it was just the impending orgasm talking, so I put my head back and laughed. The action had the same effect on my internal muscles, and he cried out, begging me to come. I increased the pressure on my clit and looked into his eyes again. I wanted him to see me as I came with his cock buried inside me. His face was rigid, and his nostrils were flared as he held onto control by the thinnest of threads. As I felt the familiar sensation begin in my belly, I let it flow over me, falling onto my elbows so that our foreheads were touching. He cried out my name as he came with me, jerking his hips up to get the deepest penetration he could as he filled the condom with his cum.

We looked into each other's eyes, holding it for a few moments, then he brought up a hand and pulled my face to his, taking my mouth in a passionate kiss. It was all teeth and tongues and spoke of something neither of us had the words to say.

Finally, he put his hands back to my waist and eased me over onto my back, withdrawing his cock gently. I heard it leave me with a soft pop and I felt a rush of wetness follow it, oozing down between my thighs onto the bed. He put his hand down and felt where we had just been joined. "So wet. So fucking hot." He kissed me again then he removed the condom and dropped it into the small bin that had obviously been placed next to the bed for that purpose. He pulled the duvet up to cover us both and moved me so that we lay together, his front against my back, his arm around me in a tight hold. "So – that one works too."

"Yeah …" I said sleepily. "That one works really well."

"Go to sleep, Rhia." He kissed my neck and pulled me even closer to his body.

"Okay."

It wasn't weird. I was expecting it to be, but he was right – it was fine. The morning after our marathon exploration session, he made breakfast for us both, and we sat together eating in comfortable silence. When I'd finished my coffee, I got up and put my plate in the dishwasher. "I'd better go and get showered and dressed, or I'm going to be late for work."

He looked up at me, and I thought I saw a momentary emotion flicker there – disappointment? No, I must have mistaken it for something else.

"Leaving so soon?" He got up and came to me, putting an arm around me in an easy embrace.

"Yeah, I'd better go. I don't want to be late."

He pulled me closer and kissed my mouth. I was expecting a light, goodbye kiss, but he pushed his tongue into my mouth, stroking mine and encouraging me to respond.

I pulled away, breaking the connection. "I haven't brushed my teeth."

"Neither have I. I don't care." He kissed me again, and this time, I allowed myself to go with it. I could feel his erection pressing against my hip. "Call in sick today; I'm not done with you yet."

"I want to. But I can't. I have a meeting today that's taken a month to arrange. But if I didn't? I'd be staying here with you." He let me go, and I went downstairs to my own apartment to take a shower and get ready for work. I felt different. It was as though some little piece of me that had been dislodged had snapped back into place.

Over the next two weeks, we spent a lot of time together, and we found a lot more positions that worked. We discovered that the stool I had in my kitchen was the perfect height for face-to-face fucking. I arrived home a little later than usual to find him sitting on the stairs outside my door. He followed me into my apartment, saying nothing, closing the door behind him. I hadn't even got my coat off when he picked me up and sat me on the kitchen stool, slamming his mouth onto mine in a raw, predatory display of his desire.

"Need you, baby." He breathed against my mouth.

My body was singing in response to him, so I didn't resist as he pushed up my skirt and yanked my knickers off in one, quick movement. I heard a zip followed by the rip of a condom wrapper, and then he was inside me. It felt incredible to be doing this while we were still wearing nearly all of our clothes. He came quickly, calling out my name, then he fell to his knees and brought me to a swift climax with his tongue. As I started to come, he stood up and pushed his cock back into me.

I shuddered in his arms as my orgasm passed. "What are we doing?"

He pulled back to look at me. "I haven't had anyone else since our first night together."

"I know."

"I don't want anyone else, Rhia."

I shook my head and eased myself off the kitchen stool. I was hurting at the thought of letting him go, but I knew I had to. "It's got to stop, Matt. This isn't right for either of us."

He caught me by the wrist and turned me to look at him. "You don't really believe that."

"I don't want to," I confessed, "but look at us. Look at me. I'm not what you want."

"You're wrong, baby. I spent so long fucking every stupid little girl that crossed my path. Then we spent that night together. You squeezed my cock with your pussy, and I fell for you."

I shook my head again. "I'm trying so hard not to fall for you, but you're not making it easy for me."

He took a step forward and pulled me into his arms again. "So, stop trying."

"I can't. You're going to wake up one day and wonder why you're sleeping with an old lady with only one leg. I won't put myself through that. I won't let myself fall for you only to have to watch you grow to resent me."

He looked confused and shook his head. "What are you talking about? Are you telling me that you're not prepared to give us a go because you're scared it's going to end?"

"When you put it like that … but yes, that is what I'm doing."

"Baby – nobody goes into a relationship thinking it's going to end. But the majority of them do at some point. That doesn't stop us doing it."

I looked at him and bit my bottom lip. "I don't want to lose you as a friend."

"You won't. As long as we're both living in the same city, we'll have Thursday movie nights. I don't want to lose you as a friend either. But right now? We're way more than friends. You can't deny that's true."

He was right. I couldn't deny it. And I didn't want to.

"Let's enjoy this for however long it lasts. We started as friends; we will still be friends if this ends. But I'm not going to give up on you, so you might as well get used to the idea."

"I've really got to work on being able to disobey you."

He grinned and picked me up. He carried me to the sofa where he told me to get naked and suck his cock. Yeah. I've really got to work on the disobeying thing.

Virgo

Analysing, practical, reflective, observation, thoughtful

Jeremy Fitzwilliam opened his notebook, picked up his favourite pen and began to record the events of his day so far.

05:58 Woke up
06:10 Breakfast
- Two slices of wholemeal toast
- Two tablespoons of smooth peanut butter
- Two cups of coffee.
06:25 Bowel movement normal
06:30 Shower. Found a white hair growing on my chest
06:45 Shaved
06:50 Dressed
- White underpants
- Black trousers
- Blue shirt
- Navy tie
- Black socks
- Black shoes
07:00 Walked to train station
07:05 Caught train – was able to secure usual seat
07:25 Arrived at work
- Disinfected workspace
- Steam cleaned coffee mug
- 08:00 Started work

Jeremy closed his notebook and looked at the schedule for the day. His job as a lab technician at St. Edmund's Hospital was something he both despised and adored. Despised because it made him leave the safe confines of his home, travel on public transport (which is just crawling with every kind of bacteria known to man) and spend the day doing battle with the results of the despicable habits of other human beings. Adored because his work allowed him to exercise his need for absolute perfection. If one of his tests wasn't done as accurately as possible, then there were consequences. If he got something wrong, then there had to be punishment. That punishment usually took the form of denying himself something that gave him pleasure; no coffee for a week or no Big Bang Theory for six days. Or not being able to look at Delia until she smiles again. Delia never smiled.

As this thought passed through his mind, the subject of his obsession walked into the lab with a new batch of samples for him to test. "Hi, Fitz." She glanced at him before putting a medical cool-box on his bench. "A couple of rush-jobs in here – I've put them on the top."

Jeremy looked at the beautiful but distant woman who had been the subject of his fantasies for the last three years. "Thanks, Delia. I'll let you know as soon as I've done them."

"Thank you." That was all she said before she turned on her heels and walked out of the lab.

Jeremy reached for his notebook and wrote the number 16 against *Number of words from Delia*.

"Why do you always scribble in that little book whenever the Delia-demon comes in here?"

"What?" Jeremy was shocked out of his post-Delia euphoria by the voice of his lab assistant. Janice had been working with him for the last six months and he still had trouble sometimes remembering she was there, because he had worked solo for so long. "Just making a note of the time," he lied, "So that I can tell her how long it took." When he said it first, it didn't sound too bad, but as he thought about it, and watched Janice's face crease with an amused smile, he realised how lame his excuse was. He shook his head and put the book back in his pocket before unpacking the box that sat at the end of his bench.

Janice came over to take the less-urgent samples from him. "You know, you're wasting your time lusting after that one."

He looked up at her, surprised that she should say something so personal. She'd only ever talked about work matters before. "I'm not lusting after her." He looked at his assistant to watch her reaction to his claim and was dismayed to see that it was clear didn't believe him.

She raised one, pierced eyebrow and it almost touched the bright pink and purple of her fringe. The heavy eyeliner she applied made the pale blue of her eyes almost too startling to look at. "I've watched you. Every time she comes in here, it's like watching a fourteen-year-old lad ogling his best friend's hot mother. And, as I said, you're wasting your time."

He didn't want to engage in this conversation; Janice was far too observant for her own good, but she obviously knew something about the object of his desire, and the urge to add whatever it was to his secret vault of Delia facts was just too strong to resist. "What makes you say that?"

Janice fist-pumped the air next to her thigh. "I knew it. You do obsess over her."

"I never said that. I just want to know what you know about her, that's all."

She smiled and nodded knowingly. "Okay, Casanova; whatever you say. And if you ever ventured out of here to eat in the cafeteria, you'd see her there most days, holding hands with Marion Whistler."

"Holding hands with – wait – what did you say?"

"You heard me. Even if you could venture out of the safety of your little world here in the lab and speak to her, it wouldn't do you any good. You have quite the wrong frontal arrangement to be of any interest to dear old Delia." She gave a triumphant smile and pointed at the general area of his groin. "You have an outie where she likes an innie." Then she noticed the colour blanching from Jeremy's face and she felt guilty suddenly. "Sorry. That was uncalled for."

He lifted his eyes and forced a smile. "No need to apologise." He turned back to his bench. "Come on – we have lots of work to do today."

Janice put her keys in the glass dish, hung up her coat and flopped down on the sofa with a sigh.

Her flatmate, Roz, looked up from her phone. "Bad day? What did Mr Fitzweirdo do this time?"

"He's not that weird. He's just OCD, that's all."

"I stand corrected. So, what did Mr Fitzobsessivecomplusive do this time?"

Janice put her head in her hands and groaned. "He didn't do anything. It was me. I shattered his fantasy."

Roz laughed and put her phone down on the coffee table. "Don't tell me – you had to let him down gently – tell him that there was no way in hell that he'd ever get between your sweet thighs."

Janice looked up at her friend. "What? No. I told him that Delia is a lesbian." She sighed again and put her head down, covering her face with her hands once more. "You should have seen his face. It was just like when I told Ian that Father Christmas was made up." The memory of that day, when she had shouted out the truth to her younger brother to punish him for using her favourite lipstick as clown makeup, shot through her and filled her belly with a familiar feeling of dread. Then Jeremy's stricken face came into her mind too, and she couldn't suppress the groan that escaped her lips. "It was brutal. I had a suspicion that he fancied her, but he was devastated. He must be totally in love with her."

Roz got up and went into the kitchen, returning with a bottle of wine and two glasses. "But I thought you said she was evil incarnate."

"She is." She put on her best Dr Evil voice and continued, "Not the diet coke of evil."

Roz laughed out loud and joined in, "Does she run an evil petting zoo?"

"Perhaps she might like some O-RANGE SHER-BERT." They laughed together and drank some wine, then Janice went back to the subject of Delia. "She is though - she never even acknowledges I'm there when she brings samples into the lab."

Roz thought about that for a moment. "So – it's a shame that she's a lesbo then – I mean, it sounds like the bitch from hell and Mr Fitzweirdo deserve each other."

Janice couldn't really explain the sudden feeling of complete anger she felt towards her friend. She stood up and looked at Roz, feeling the unexpected rage bubbling up through her. "How can you say that? You've never even met Jeremy. He's a lovely guy. He can't help being the way he is – it's a disease. How would you feel if someone made fun of you for something you can't control? How about I tease you every time you do that thing with your nose?"

Roz stood up to face her flatmate. "Whoa!" She raised her hands in front of her, palms out, and took a step back. "Sorry – I didn't mean anything by it. I'm sure he's lovely. It's just you've only ever made him sound like a comedy character – I had no idea you felt like that about him. And – wait a minute – what thing with my nose?"

"I don't have feelings for him if that's what you mean. Though I wouldn't be ashamed if I did – he's actually quite hot, and he's sweet as honey once you get beyond the handwashing. I just don't like it when someone takes the piss out of someone else just because they're different. And you do this crinkling thing when you're thinking – it always looks like you're about to sneeze or something."

"Quite hot? You've never said that before. In fact, you've never even mentioned how he looks before. Girl – you can deny it all you want, but it sounds like you've got feelings for the guy. And I don't do a crinkling thing. You just made that up to make a point."

"I do not have feelings for Jeremy. I just … oh, never mind. It's late, and I'm going to go to bed. And yes, you do – when you're thinking hard or trying to remember something, you crinkle your nose and wiggle it like you're about to sneeze. I've seen you do it dozens of times." She turned to leave, not letting her stunned friend say anything else, and walked to the bathroom, closing the door behind her with a loud slam.

After her shower, she wiped the condensation away from the mirror over the sink and looked at herself. Without the mask of her makeup, she was just an ordinary looking girl. She knew that the piercings in her brow, nose and lip, along with her neon hair and goth-style make-up were a suit of armour she donned every day. They gave her the courage to step outside of herself and be the person she wished she could be without them; someone brave enough to go after the things she wanted and not care what anyone else thought.

When she'd finished brushing her teeth, she shut off the water, and the room was silent. She became aware of a muffled sound of weeping coming from the living room. Was Roz crying? Had their argument upset her that much? She looked at herself in the mirror again and cursed her reflection. "You bloody loud-mouthed bitch. Now, look what you've done." She blew out a long breath and opened the door, stepping out into the dark hallway of the flat. She listened carefully – yes, there it was again. She went to her bedroom and wrapped herself in her blue, fleecy dressing gown before tiptoeing as gently as she could back to the living room. Roz was sitting on the sofa, arms wrapped around herself, rocking backwards and forwards slightly and sniffing with the tail-end of what had obviously been a long, hard cry. Janice sat next to her, taking her hand. "I'm sorry. I didn't mean for things to get so heated."

Roz looked up at her with bloodshot eyes. "I'm sorry too. I shouldn't have said those mean things about your friend. As you said, I've never even met him."

"Please don't cry. I hate it when I make someone cry."

Her friend shook her head and squeezed her hand. "It wasn't you. I was crying because I was angry at myself. I always have to go too far – I try to be funny, and it always goes pear-shaped. I've pushed so many people away like that – I couldn't bear it if I pushed you away too."

Janice put her arms around Roz and pulled her in for a hug. "You're not going to push me away; I'm made of stronger stuff. And I'm sorry I got so angry. I think I reacted that way because … well … there's a possibility that you're right about how I feel about Jeremy and it was the first time I'd realised it for myself."

Roz sat up straight and looked her friend in the eye. "Really?"

"Yes. Really."

"I'm going to make us some hot chocolate, and then I want to hear all about Mr Fitzweirdo."

Ten minutes later, they were both holding steaming mugs of marshmallow-topped comfort. Janice stared into the fake flames of the electric fire and sighed. "I can't believe I only just saw it."

"What happened? I mean, something must have happened to make you realise what was going on?" Roz reached up and tucked a stray strand of hair behind Janice's ear. It was a protective gesture. "It might help to talk about it – you know – work out what's really going on here?"

Janice nodded. "Yeah. It might. Okay. Well – I can't deny that I found him attractive from the get-go."

"Really? You've never said that much about him other than to make me laugh with his OCD antics. I mean – writing down the number of times you go to the loo every day is kinda funny, even if he can't help it."

Janice laughed at the memory of seeing Jeremy's treasured notebook left open and unguarded on the workbench. It had detailed what time he had awoken, showered, what kind of bowel movement he'd had (this particular day had read *unfulfilling*) and what clothes he was wearing. She had no idea why he noted that because he always wore the same thing under his lab coat; black trousers, pale blue shirt, navy tie and black shoes polished till they shone. She had worked out that he must have numerous versions of this outfit because he always smelled of laundry detergent, so although he wore the same outfit every day, he didn't wear the same clothes more than once. After she had scanned the mundane details on the top half of the page, her eye had been drawn to an immaculately penned table near the foot of it.

Number of words from Delia
Urinations
Hands washed
Cups of coffee

Delia hadn't been in today, so there was no number written against her name. The other categories had little marks drawn neatly in groups of five – four uprights with a diagonal line to complete the group. So far today, he had peed six times, washed his hands thirty-six times and had drunk nine cups of coffee; which might explain the six pees. She was just about to go back to her work when she spotted her name written in Jeremy's characteristic, tiny handwriting.

Janice is wearing her purple leggings, black DMs, blue bunny sweatshirt. She smells of blueberries.

A very quick flick through the book told her that he made a note of what she was wearing and what she smelled of every day. Damn – this guy had the nose of a truffle pig.

She smells of raisins
She smells of bacon
She smells of blueberries
She smells of strawberries and blood (I believe she is menstruating)
She smells of oranges

Was he picking up on what she'd had for breakfast? That was just bizarre. And the blood one was a bit creepy.

She was pulled out of the memory by Roz nudging her arm. "Well – come on – spill – what's so attractive about this guy?"

"Well," She let her mind conjure up an image of her enigmatic colleague. "He's a bit older than us – I'd say he's probably about twenty-eight, maybe thirty – but he comes across as older because he's so uptight."

"Okay – uptight thirty-year-old – go on."

"He's quite tall – when I wear my platform DMs he's a couple of inches taller than me, so that would make him about six foot?"

"Right. Building a picture. Uptight six-footer."

"He's got dark hair – almost black, which he somehow keeps the same length all the time, and his eyes are almost the same colour as his hair. Really dark and … well … beautiful." The last word was almost a whisper as she realised just what she was admitting to Roz and to herself.

Roz took a sip of her chocolate and nodded in a sagely manner. "Beautiful eyes, huh? Sounds like you've got it bad for this guy. Any tats? Piercings? Facial hair?"

Janice shook her head. "No. Nothing. He's … perfect."

"Okay – so I've got an image in my head of Keanu Reeves in Sheldon Cooper's lab coat."

"Yeah. That's … not bad actually."

"Really? I was just kidding, but really? Girl … no wonder you think he's perfect." She took a long drink of her chocolate then she raised an eyebrow and smiled slyly. "Hey – do you think he's still – you know – perfect in another way?"

Janice looked at her friend and pulled a face. "I've no idea. He's never mentioned girlfriends, but then again, he's never really told me anything about himself. I don't even know where he lives." She got up from the sofa and put her empty mug down on the coffee table. "And whether he is still *virgo intacto* or not, really isn't any of my business. Or yours, for that matter. I'm going to bed now. Goodnight Roz."

"Goodnight Janice. Sweet dreams."

Jeremy couldn't sleep. He had gone to bed at the usual time – *watch News at Ten until the first ad break, brush teeth, empty bladder, wash hands enough times to make the daily count up to one hundred, apply moisturising hand cream and a fresh pair of cotton gloves to prevent contamination during the night, in bed with the lights out no later than eleven o'clock.* Tonight had been no different. But he knew the reason he couldn't get to sleep. Janice's bombshell about Delia had been like a kick in the gut. Even if he had managed to initiate stage one of his plan, she would never be his. She liked women. And he had an outie instead of an innie.

He remembered how Janice had looked when she realised what a devastating blow she had just delivered. She looked suddenly shocked and sad. Did she care that she'd upset him? He still wasn't sure of his psychedelically adorned assistant. She was funny and could be very kind. It was clear she felt awkward by his obvious reaction to her news, even though he had tried his best not to show it. Her pretty face had shown her feelings as sure as if she'd shouted them at him. She'd smelled of blueberries again this morning; it must be her favourite breakfast. She wore a perfume that was light and floral, but he could always detect a trace of what she had eaten in the morning. The image of her startlingly blue eyes, surrounded by their thick frame of black eyeliner, invaded his mind again and he cursed himself for allowing it to come forth.

Turning onto his back, he looked at the ceiling of his bedroom. Light from the street lamp outside was filtering through his curtains, making the distinctive shape of an arrow above his bed. He saw it every night. He had stared at it as he formulated his plan; a plan he had recited every night since as a mantra to ease into sleep. So – that was why he couldn't sleep – he hadn't recited the plan. It seemed pointless now that he knew it was a futile endeavour, but as the clock ticked on and the hours passed in sleeplessness, he gave in and spoke the familiar words to himself one last time.

Stage one: gain Delia's friendship and spend some time with her in a social setting.

Stage two: gradually introduce some romantic elements to the relationship.

Stage three: ask her to accompany me on a date for dinner at Moretti's.

Stage four: gradually become able to enjoy more dates in less familiar places without suffering from a panic attack.

Stage five: begin to engage in non-threatening physical contact, e.g. kissing.

Stage six: deepen the physical exploration with intimate touching.

Stage seven: lose my virginity to Delia

Stage eight: marry Delia

Stage nine: have children with Delia

Stage ten: live happily ever after

It was a ten-step program to pull him gradually out of his obsessive prison. He had devised it many months ago but hadn't even been able to achieve stage one. Now he knew the truth of where Delia's proclivities lay; he was glad that he hadn't put that much effort into it. Time for a new plan. As his mind finally gave up its grip on his consciousness, he felt himself drifting into longed-for sleep. And just before Gentle Morpheus claimed him fully, he could have sworn he smelled blueberries.

"Good morning Janice. How are you today?"

"What? Oh – yes – good morning, Jeremy. I'm sorry I'm a little late. I didn't sleep very well last night."

Jeremy looked at his watch. She wasn't late. She was bang on time. But she usually arrived ten or so minutes early, so he supposed that, by that measure, she was a little late. "You're not late, Janice. You're usually early, that's all. Make yourself a cup of coffee and get your breath back."

"Oh – okay – sure. Can I make you a coffee?"

"No thank you. I've just had one." She always offered and he always refused in the same way, whether it was true or not. Drinking a coffee that someone else had made (and that he hadn't watched them make) was something he just couldn't do. He was only able to buy drinks from the many coffee shops that had sprung up recently because if you stood in the right place, you could watch every step of the drink being made. He still didn't do that very often, though – only in dire need.

A couple of minutes later, Janice came back into the lab, wearing her white coat, clutching a steaming mug. She put the mug down on her bench and smiled wanly. "What's on the schedule for today?"

Jeremy looked at her. Her hair wasn't as neat as usual, and her makeup looked like she had applied it in haste. And she smelled of … coffee. She hadn't had breakfast. "Janice, is everything okay?"

"What? Yes – of course – why do you ask?"

"You don't seem to be quite yourself today. You didn't eat breakfast, did you? And – well – you're acting a little … weird."

She looked at him and both her eyebrows went skyward. "Weird? I'm acting weird. Says the man who logs every time he has a pee in that little book in your pocket. And how do you know I didn't have breakfast?" When he didn't answer, she continued, "You sniffed me, didn't you? You do it every day. And you have the nerve to call me weird."

"I didn't call you weird. I just said that you weren't like your usual self. I'm sorry … I …."

Janice let out a breath and held up her hand to ask him to stop talking. "No – I'm sorry. And you're right. I'm not myself today. I didn't sleep well – then I slept through the alarm – so I didn't have time for breakfast, which means I'm *hangry* and I have no reason to be mean to you again. I did enough of that yesterday. Please – can I just go out and come in again?"

Jeremy laughed gently at her simple admission. "No need for that. Go and get yourself something from the cafeteria – I don't need mistakes caused by your grumbling tummy."

She looked at him with those glorious eyes. "Thank you, Jeremy, – you're the best. Though – the sniffing thing is still weird."

"I apologise. I'll try to stop doing it from now on. And if it's any consolation, there must have been something in the air last night, because I couldn't sleep either."

"Really? Oh. And I didn't mean you have to stop the sniffing. It's kinda reassuring, actually. But that doesn't stop it being weird."

"Duly noted."

Half an hour later, Janice walked back into the lab. She saw Jeremy bent over the microscope and smiled. He looked perfect as always. Yes – she was definitely noticing him more. She decided to try out his extraordinary olfactory abilities, and maybe tease him a little, by walking close enough that she brushed against his ass where he bent over the workbench.

The sudden, unexpected contact caused him to stand upright so quickly that he nearly fell over backwards. When she saw his nostrils flare at her closeness, she gave herself an imaginary high-five.

"Sorry – I should have said excuse me. Didn't mean to frighten you out of your skin."

"Oh – you didn't. I was just absorbed in what I was I was doing – I didn't hear you come back in."

She laughed and winked at him. "That's because I'm a ninja; one who has now had breakfast and is feeling a lot more human. On that subject," she moved a little closer to him, "What did I have for breakfast?" She smiled playfully at him. "Come on – lean in and have a good sniff."

Jeremy looked at her warily, then he seemed to decide he wanted to play along and he leaned in closer to her. She closed her eyes – this was the closest she'd ever been to him – he smelled of shower gel and shampoo, though she couldn't identify the scent. "Well? What's the verdict?"

Jeremy gave one, last lingering sniff near her jawbone then stood up straight, looking at her closely. "You had a croissant with butter and blueberry jam. Blueberries are your favourite. You also had a glass of orange juice and a milky coffee – probably a cappuccino."

"Wow. How do you do that? That was exactly right – except it was a latte."

"You also smell of something floral. And you use Head & Shoulders shampoo."

Janice felt her jaw drop as she opened her mouth in surprise. "You could go on a talent show with that – I mean – it's freaky."

Jeremy laughed and stepped away. As he turned back to his bench, he looked at her again, and a satisfied smile lit up his face. "I don't know how I do it. I've always been able to – I just have a very sensitive nose. It's not always a good thing, though; a packed train in high summer can be a real trial."

"God – yeah – I can understand that. But you should be working making perfume, or something. It's a shame you're not using it for something other than freaking out your lab assistant."

He laughed at her again. "You're funny, Janice. I like that about you. And I'm quite happy working here."

He was happy working in the lab. He had stopped himself from adding 'with you' to the end of that sentence. He also didn't tell her about the effect her scents had had on him at such close proximity. He was glad for the loose covering of his white lab coat because the scent of her skin and the warmth of her body so close to his had given him an erection – one that was still throbbing some ten minutes later. The reaction had been instant and involuntary, and it had taken him completely by surprise. He was still in love with Delia, wasn't he? Surely, this tall, slender girl with the pink and purple hair and facial piercings couldn't be someone he could desire sexually. But his body seemed to have other ideas as he allowed his gaze to fall on her again.

"What are you staring at?" Janice's voice cut through the fog of his confusion.

"What? Oh – sorry – just lost in my thoughts for a moment.

Janice let her eyes follow the direction of his gaze to her chest, then she looked down to his lab-coat-covered crotch. The evidence of his thoughts was now pretty clear. "So I see." Her voice was uncharacteristically quiet, and she raised her eyes to meet his once more. "Jeremy – are you okay?"

Her simple question floored him. He had been caught red-handed (or perhaps red-eyed) ogling her. He had a tent in his lab coat from the strangely intimate act of smelling the skin of her neck and face, and yet she was concerned that he was okay. "Yes. I … I'm sorry … I don't know …"

She moved so quickly he barely had time to realise that she had moved from her bench. His reactions, retarded by the redistribution of blood from the brain to his cock, didn't engage in time to prevent what she did next. He was suddenly enveloped in her warm scent as she put her arms around his neck and hugged him.

He wasn't a hugger. Such intimate contact with another human being was something he had always avoided – even before his OCD had developed to its current levels, being so close to anyone was something that made his skin crawl. So why wasn't it crawling now? Why did he have the overwhelming urge to hug back? He wanted to put his arms around this woman who smelled of flowers and blueberries and hold on as tight as he could. He wanted it badly, but something stopped him. He just couldn't go there. There were stages to a relationship and hugging must be stage five or possibly six. He was shocked by a voice in his head that said *fuck the stages – hold the woman –* but as he was about to listen to his heart, she pulled away.

Janice stepped back and smiled at him. "Sorry. I couldn't stop myself." Her smile was genuine, and he found it oddly comforting. "Wow. I mean – that was awesome – I mean – sorry, I know you don't like to touch people. I should have asked you before I hugged you." She dropped her head and looked at the floor.

Jeremy's tummy did a flip. She was sorry she'd hugged him. "I'm not sorry."

"Excuse me?"

"I said I'm not sorry. That you hugged me, I mean. You took me by surprise, but I felt like I wanted to hug you back."

"So, why didn't you?"

"Hugging is a stage five thing." He gave her a pained look and was surprised when she relaxed and laughed.

"So – what stage are we at?"

She understood. He felt a tension release somewhere deep inside. "Stage one."

"Do you want to get to stage five?" She said it slowly, raising one, pierced eyebrow.

"Yes. I think I do."

"Good. So do I. I want it real bad, actually. So, how do we fast-track?"

Jeremy felt himself smile. "Would you like to have dinner with me?"

Moretti's was its usual, charming self. Jeremy had managed to get a booking at short notice, which was lucky. Janice looked up at him as they walked through the door into the warm, friendly atmosphere of the Italian restaurant. "This is lovely – I can't believe I haven't been here before."

He turned to smile at her, then Lucca Moretti greeted them and led them to their table. "It's good to see you, Fitz. I'll tell papa you're here – I'm sure he'll want to say 'hello'."

They sat down at the little table in the corner. The décor was predictable; red check tablecloths and candles in wicker-bound Chianti bottles, but Jeremy liked it. It was familiar because he had been coming here since he was a kid, so it was safe. He looked over the top of his menu at Janice. She was concentrating on the large, red, leather-bound volume but he didn't need to look at his because he always had the same thing.

Janice looked up. "What are you going to have – it all looks yummy."

"Ravioli Moretti. It's the house special. I always have it – it's delicious."

When Lucca came back, she ordered the same, then once the menus had been taken away, she took a sip of water and looked at him. "Delia called you Fitz as well. Is that a name you go by a lot?"

He nodded and drank some water too. "Yes – a lot of people call me that. You can call me Fitz if you like."

"I think I will. I like it. It suits you."

Their food arrived before they had the chance to discuss that any further. It was brought to them by the chef himself. "Mr Fitz! How good to see you, my old friend!"

Jeremy looked up at the red face of Papa Moretti. Everyone called him Papa. "Good to see you too. How's the family?"

The plump little Italian chuckled as he put the plates on the table. "All good, thank you for asking. Moira is well and the boys – well, you know the boys. Lucca is working here tonight, but he would rather be home making love to his Xbox."

Jeremy laughed at his friend's choice of words. "What about Carla? I haven't seen her in a long while. Is she still working in the city?"

The old man's face crinkled with a smile. "She is. And she is getting married. Adriano – he's a good man. They are very much in love." Papa Moretti looked at Janice and smiled. "Is this beautiful girl yours, my good friend?"

Jeremy blushed and looked over at his dining companion. "Uh – well – I .."

Janice grinned and looked at the friendly restaurateur. "We're working on it, aren't we, Fitz?"

"What? Oh – yeah – I suppose we are. One stage at a time."

Janice was smiling encouragingly. "One stage at a time." After Papa Moretti had gone back to the kitchen, she sat back in her chair and took a mouthful of the food. Her eyes rolled back in her head momentarily as the complex flavours burst on her tongue. "God, this is so good."

"I know, right? I always have it when I come here. It's the best." He took a mouthful of his food and felt himself relax. Familiar. Safe. Non-threatening. "You like it, then?"

Janice shook her head. "No – I don't like it. I LOVE it. We're definitely coming here again."

"We are? Does that mean we are going to have another date?" He tried not to take any notice of the sudden rush of adrenaline that was causing his heart to beat out a salsa. "Are we really going to do this?"

Janice put down her fork and looked at Jeremy. "I want to, yes. So, tell me about these stages."

"It's amazing that you don't think it's totally weird."

"I didn't say anything about not thinking it's weird. But I get it. You're a bit OCD. You need order. That, I understand. And I think I can probably get used to it."

"Oh. That's good, I think?"

"Tell me about the stages."

"What? Oh – yeah. Sorry. Well, I haven't done anything about it before. It's all theoretical at this point. But this is stage three."

Janice took another forkful of food and nodded. "Okay. Stage three. Sounds good. What does stage four involve?"

He thought about his plan and felt a sudden flare of courage. "We can come back to stage four. I'd like to go straight to stage five. Tonight." Kissing Janice was suddenly all he could think about. He knew her, knew that she understood him. He had smelled her skin, and now he wanted more. He reached over the little table and put his hand on her cheek. As he pulled her towards him, he moved too, and they met in the middle. His tie fell into his food, but he didn't care. Tasting this woman was all he wanted to do. His lips touched hers, so lightly at first, then she leant into the caress, and he tasted her for the first time. Oh god, she tasted even better than she smelled. His cock sprang into life, pushing against his fly painfully. The kiss only lasted for a couple of seconds, but he knew he'd be feeling the aftershock for the rest of his life. His first kiss. Had he ever imagined something so erotic?

Janice sat back in her seat, her eyes glistening and alight with excitement. "Wow. I wasn't expecting that."

Jeremy was filled with a sudden burst of uncertainty. "Was it alright? I'm sorry if you didn't want to."

In reply, she reached for his sauce-covered tie and pulled him towards her again. Her lips fastened over his, and she pushed her tongue into his open mouth. He'd never felt anything like it. His senses were working overtime as his nostrils flared, taking in her scent in all its glory and his tongue tasted her mouth. He wondered what her other mouth might taste like; the thought filled him with equal amounts of shock, shame and desire.

As they both sat back in their seats, a chorus of applause filled the small restaurant. Jeremy looked around to see that the other diners were all watching them and clapping. He looked over to Lucca who was pressing buttons on the CD player and, moments later, the opening lines of Dean Martin's *That's Amore* filled the room. The applause was replaced by good-natured laughter, and he reached over, taking Janice's hand in his. "Do you want to get out of here?"

They didn't say much on the journey back to Jeremy's flat. The air was so thick with expectation and desire that there hardly seemed to be room for words. When he opened the door and ushered Janice inside, the familiar smell of his home acted like Valium on his terrified mind.

She took her coat off and looked around the small, immaculate space. "I'm guessing this is the first time you've brought a woman here?"

He nodded and took her coat, hanging it on the hooks behind the door. "It is."

She smiled and walked around the small space. "So, you've never had sex before?"

He felt himself blush and his chin dropped onto his chest. A man of his age should have lost his virginity long ago. "No."

She came to him and put her finger under his chin, lifting his face so that her eyes met his. He had expected to see amusement or a mocking grin but saw neither. She was smiling sincerely, and she lifted her hand to stroke the skin of his cheek in a move that was both comforting and reassuring. "It's nothing to be ashamed of." She kissed him softly, rubbing her denim-clad hips against his erection. "So, what stage would losing your virginity be?"

"Seven."

She nodded and stepped away from him a little. "Kissing is stage five." She reached for the hem of her shirt and pulled it over her head, revealing a pair of beautiful breasts encased in a deep purple bra. "Fair warning, Fitz – I'm initiating stage six." She chuckled at the sudden look of complete shock on his face. She stepped forward and took his hand in hers, placing his open palm over the swell of her satin-covered breast so that he could feel the firm flesh and her nipple as it hardened beneath his touch.

Jeremy looked down to where his hand was pressed against Janice's beautiful body. She removed her hand, and he looked at her for further guidance, but she said nothing. She simply leaned into his touch, increasing the pressure of her hot globe against his palm. She held his gaze as she reached behind herself and unfastened the purple satin that was the only thing between his hand and her warm flesh. He watched, unable to look away, as she pulled the thin garment off her shoulders and dropped it on the floor.

His hand made contact with her hot skin, and he pulled it away as if he'd been burned. "I'm sorry. I'm not sure what I'm doing."

Janice didn't say anything, she just reached for his hand and placed it back over her breast, urging him to begin to stroke gently, moving his hand slowly over the landscape of her warm body. "Do you like that?"

His mouth was dry, and he didn't have the words to say what he was feeling, so he just nodded. He barely noticed that Janice had unfastened his shirt until her fingers began a slow journey over his chest and down his abdomen. Jeez, it felt like the whole of his blood supply had pooled in his cock, and that something was going to burst down there. He watched as her hands moved to unfasten his belt. His mind was racing; overloaded with new sensations and feelings. He still had his hand on her body, stroking her skin and he felt the urge to find out if she smelled the same all over. He bent his head so that his nose was millimetres away from the skin at the base of her throat. He followed a path down her sternum until he nuzzled against the soft curve at the top of the breast he still held in his hand. "You smell so good. I want to smell you all over."

"Okay."

"Is that weird?"

"A little bit – yeah – but I think it could be really hot. It would be easier if we were lying down."

"Yes. Of course, it would. Sorry."

"You've got to stop saying sorry, Fitz. And if you want something, say it. Never apologise for your desires. We're all made differently, and there is no right or wrong way to do things." She rocked her head from side to side as though she was considering what she'd just said. "Take that back – there probably are lots of wrong ways to do things, but half the fun is finding out. Now – come on – take me to your bedroom."

Jeremy took her hand and led her through the flat to the small room in which he slept. It held a double bed, one nightstand and a lamp. The fewer things in the room, the less dust they attracted and the easier it was to keep clean. It was how he lived – how he had always lived – but looking at his Spartan room now, adorned so beautifully by the girl with the pink and purple hair, he felt something inside him release. Like a coil that had been wound so tightly for so long, finally giving up its hold and releasing years' worth of tension. "Come here."

She came to him with an easy grace and settled into his arms. "I want you, Fitz. I know this is all new to you, but I'm not in any hurry. If there's something you want to do, then say it."

"Okay. Right now, I want to kiss you. Then I want you naked on my bed so I can see if you smell good all over." Was that his voice? Had he expressed his desires so easily to her? He pulled her up close to him and slanted his mouth over hers. The kiss started slowly, an easy exploration of her mouth with his, but as he deepened the kiss, pushing his tongue deep into her open mouth, that feeling of total release came over him again. Then he realised what was happening; he was going to come. Her scent filling his nostrils and the taste of her filling his mouth overwhelmed his senses. He shuddered as his cock jerked inside his clothes and he filled his underpants with semen. He pulled back from Janice's embrace and looked shamefully down at the patch of wet that was spreading out on the front of his trousers. "Oh god, I'm so sorry. I don't know wha…"

Janice put her finger over his mouth, stopping him from finishing the apology that wanted to spurt out of his mouth as surely as his cum had spurted from his cock moments before. "What did I say about apologising? It's perfectly okay. In fact, it's probably just as well."

"It is?"

"Yes. Now we've got that little crisis over and done with; you can relax a little bit and enjoy the ride."

"Oh." She had stunned him again with her honesty and gentle encouragement.

"Come on – let's get you out of these clothes."

Jeremy looked down as she started to unfasten his belt. The sight of her fingers so close to his cock made it spring to life again, and she grinned as she saw his reaction to her touch. She unzipped his fly and swiftly pushed his trousers and briefs down to his ankles and held them while he stepped out of them. She stayed on her knees, removing his socks and shoes as he pushed his shirt off his shoulders. "This is the first time I've been naked in front of anyone other than my mum and my doctor."

Janice looked up from her place between his feet and smiled encouragingly at him. "Relax. We don't have to do anything you don't want to do."

He reached down and cupped her cheek, stroking the soft skin of her face. "I think I want to do everything with you."

She stood up and kissed his mouth. "Good. Me too." She made short work of removing the rest of her clothes then she pulled the duvet off his bed and lay down. "I'm all yours. Put your amazing olfactory skills to work."

Jeremy stilled for a moment, but he knew what he wanted to do. He knelt beside her on the bed and dipped his head to run his nose along the base of her neck again. He felt her relax as his skin touched hers and he was emboldened to continue his journey down the length of her body. He nuzzled against one erect nipple then sealed his lips over it, sucking it into his mouth. He felt it harden under his tongue and a groan escaped his lips. Janice groaned too, rolling her hips and urging him to do the same to her other breast.

The taste of her skin drove him wild. His cock was now at full hardness again as he pulled his mouth reluctantly from her nipple, releasing it with a soft pop. He continued his journey down her abdomen – the scent coming off her warm body was incredible, and he knew where he wanted to go. Moving so that he was positioned between her open thighs, he bent his head again, hovering close to her pussy, and breathed in deeply. The aroma of her arousal, hot and spicy, assaulted his nose and another groan erupted from his throat. He knew what he wanted to do. "Can I taste you here?"

Janice looked down her body to where he was pushing the tip of his nose into her neatly-trimmed bush. "Yes," she panted, "Please. Lick me."

Jeremy couldn't hold it back any longer. He put out his tongue and pressed it against the swollen lips of her pussy. Her flavour hit him like a truck, and his cock begged him to bury himself in the warm, wet flesh he had just tasted. "God, Janice – you taste amazing." He returned to his licking; sampling her and allowing her scent to invade his senses. "I want to … I don't know what I want. I just need you."

She reached down and pulled him up so that they were face to face. "I think I know what you want." She took one hand from his face and put it between them, taking his cock in her hand. "I'm on the pill. And I'm clean – I promise. I want your first time to be skin to skin."

Before he had time to process what she'd said, he felt the tip of his cock nudge against her moist opening – the same one he had kissed just moments before. He locked his elbows, looking down at the glorious sight of Janice spread out for him. Her wildly coloured hair fanned out on his pillow, and her abdomen rising and falling as she dragged air into her lungs.

"Push, Fitz. Fill me up." She guided him to her, placing the head of his cock just inside her hole. "Push."

He did as she asked and – *oh god in heaven and all the saints* – her hot, wet flesh gripped him as he pushed himself into her as far as he could. Once he felt his balls touch the soft cheeks of her bottom, he stilled, looking down at her, trying to catch his breath. "Janice! Oh god! That feels incredible!"

She smiled slyly and started to rotate her hips, taking his cock with her as she moved in slow circles. "Good, isn't it?"

He tried to answer but couldn't make any noises that were more intelligible than grunts. Some instinct took over, and he began to thrust deeply into her. He could feel her muscles squeezing his cock as he ploughed her again and again, the friction working on him leading him to the point of no return. He was going to come inside Janice, and there was absolutely nothing he could do to stop it. The first warning shot pulsed through his cock, and he felt his balls draw up, tucking tightly against his body. "I'm going to come." It was all the warning he could give her before he felt it roaring through his body. He pushed into her as far as he could and cried out a sound that was maybe a strangled version of her name. He rocked into her as his cock emptied, then he fell helplessly against her, his head resting between her heaving breasts.

"Is that better?" She was stroking his hair gently off his forehead as he tried to catch his breath. "Was that how you imagined stage seven would be?"

He shook his head against her sweat-dampened breasts. "No. Not at all. It was way, way better."

He felt her chuckle, the vibration of it purring against his cheek. "Good. Your first time should be something you'll never forget."

The full meaning of what she had said hit him then. He raised his head and kissed her mouth passionately. "God, Janice. You're incredible. That was completely selfless. Show me how to do it so that you enjoy it too."

A broad smile broke out on her face, and she stroked his hair. "Who said I didn't enjoy it?"

"I … I just thought …"

"I didn't come, no. But it was a mighty fine effort for a first attempt. And we have the rest of the night for you to discover how to give me an orgasm."

"Really?" He got onto his knees, looking down at her soft body. As his eyes travelled the length of her abdomen, he watched as she bore down, pushing a steady stream of his cum out of her still-open hole onto the dark blue sheet of his bed. The sight was so erotic; he had marked her with his semen, and now, he wanted to do it again. He ducked down and ran his tongue along the length of her slit. He knew what his semen tasted like – he had often licked it from his fingers after masturbating and knew that the salty, musky flavour was guaranteed to inspire another erection. But he wasn't prepared for how it tasted when combined with Janice's sweet secretions. As the honeyed mixture spread over his tongue, he felt like his whole body was having an erection. "Oh, god, Janice. That is so sexy." He delved into her again, pushing his tongue into her slick hole as far as it would go.

Janice reached down and began to circle her clit with a damp finger. "Here. Lick me here."

He watched where her finger was stroking across the little nub of flesh then sealed his mouth over it, swiping his tongue back and forth.

Her body went into spasm beneath his caress, and she cried out, wrapping her thighs around his head, pulling him as close to her contracting hole as she could. "Yes! Oh god, Fitz! Yes!"

He continued to tongue her, letting her body relax under his hold, then he climbed up her body and claimed her mouth with his cum-covered lips. "I need to fuck you again." It was a breathy request, and he wasn't sure she'd heard him until he felt her hand encircling his cock once more, guiding him to her. As he pushed inside, he marvelled again at the sensation of the skin of his penis rubbing against her hidden flesh. That something should fit him so perfectly, give so much pleasure, was a shock and a delight. "Janice – I think I want to do to this with you over and over again. Please say you'll want me again. Please say I didn't mess this up."

She pulled his head down to hers and kissed him in a wild, open display of what she was feeling. When she broke away from him, she was panting, her breasts rising and falling in ragged judders. "Oh yeah. We'll definitely be doing this again. You've got a lot to learn, and I want to be the one who shows you." She kissed him again, then wrapped her legs around his waist, linking her ankles together across his back. "Now, fuck me, Fitz. Just go with your instincts. Do what your body is telling you to do."

His instincts were telling him all sorts of things, so he wasn't quite sure what to do first. But his hips seemed to have developed a mind of their own, so he answered their primal call, thrusting hard against her so that he felt the tip of his cock touch bottom.

She felt it too. "Oh fuck – you're as deep as you can be. I'm going to feel this in the morning."

Jeremy stilled for a moment as a sudden rush of an unfamiliar emotion flooded his brain. "Am I hurting you?"

"What? No! Just the opposite of hurting."

"Oh – when you said you'd feel it in the morning, I …"

"Fitz – it's fine – I want to feel it in the morning. There's nothing like going through the day enjoying the echo of the magnificent fuck you enjoyed the night before. Especially if you know that there is a very good chance you'll be getting the same again once the day is over."

He looked at her for a moment, then when he was sure she was okay, he gave into his instincts once more. When his cock was buried deep inside her, his mouth began watering to taste her again. He latched onto the soft patch of skin that marked the place where her neck met her shoulder. After licking and sucking her for a few moments, he surrendered his last ounce of control and sank his teeth into her soft flesh. He heard her hiss and felt her inner muscles clench around his cock as she began to climax around him. He didn't release his bite until she had stilled beneath him, then he loosened his hold and came up onto his elbows, giving himself more room to plough into her with everything he had. The bed was shaking and creaking, and the headboard was banging against the wall, but he didn't care. All he could think about was getting his seed inside this woman; marking her with it, searing her flesh with the hot spurts. He felt it begin; the familiar rush of pleasure that spread out from his balls as his orgasm built to its inevitable crescendo. "Fuuuuuuuck!" He drew the word out as he came long and hard, filling her again with his hot semen.

As the morning light filtered through the curtains of his bedroom, Jeremy stirred, waking the girl in his arms. It was real. He hadn't dreamt it. He had made love to Janice, and she was still here. "Good morning."

Janice yawned and snuggled into his arms. "What time is it?"

Jeremy looked over at the clock and squinted to see the time. "It's just after nine."

She sat up quickly, shocking him out of his reverie. "What? We're so late for work." She started to move, swinging her legs over the side of the bed and bending over to find her discarded clothes.

Jeremy pulled her back into his embrace. "Janice – relax. It's Saturday."

She sat still for a moment, then he saw her shoulders fall with relief. "Thank god for that. My boss is insufferable when I'm late."

He fastened his arms around her and kissed the tousled pink and purple cloud on the top of her head. "You've never been late." He began to stroke idle circles around her nipples, and she relaxed further, moulding herself to fit against him. "But let's say you were, what would you do to make it up to me?"

She didn't say anything, just smiled knowingly then climbed over him, straddling his legs. He had no idea what she was planning, so when she took his cock in her hand and leaned over to suck the tip into her wet mouth, he nearly came on the spot.

"Steady. Try to enjoy the sensation. Try not to come too quickly."

"That's far easier said than done." He pulled in a shuddering breath as she went to work on him once more, pulling his entire length into her mouth, opening her throat to take him as deeply as she could.

She sucked him tenderly, stroking the underside of his cock with her tongue until he had no choice but to give in to the incredible feelings she was eliciting. He thrust up with his hips, pushing himself to the back of her throat and came with a groan, spilling himself into her. She held on to him until he was done, then he reached for her, covering her lips with his, pushing his tongue into her semen-filled mouth. He tasted himself on her tongue, and he knew she was his. He was hard again within a minute, and he rolled her over onto her back and mounted her quickly, filling her pussy with the urgency of someone who needed to stake his claim.

"So, what comes after stage seven?" Janice was lying in his arms again, tracing little circles around his nipples with her fingertips.

"I don't think I want to think about the stages anymore. I wrote them down when I thought Delia was what I wanted. I don't want her anymore. I want you." He leaned over and kissed the top of her head.

"Good. I like the sound of that. But can I suggest something?"

"Go ahead."

"Stage seven and a half. A long, detailed exploration of giving each other as much pleasure as possible."

"Sounds good."

"I have some really filthy ideas."

"That sounds good too."

After she had demonstrated one of her filthy ideas, she lay back in his arms. "Fitz?"

"Janice?"

"You haven't washed your hands in well over twelve hours."

"I know."

"And they must be covered in all kinds of stuff."

"I know that too."

"Are you okay?"

"I'm perfect."

"Yes, you are."

Monday

05:58 Woke up with Janice
06:10 Janice made me come with her mouth
06:20 I made Janice come with my fingers and my tongue
06:30 Decided I don't need to write down the minutia of my day anymore. That was part of my life before.
06:45 Decided instead to write down a list of challenges for every day. Today's challenges are:

- Stop counting urinations
- Only wash hands when absolutely necessary
- Drink more water
- Fuck Janice as many times as possible
- Get an early night

Jeremy only managed two of his challenges on that first day. He drank a whole large bottle of water; the extra fluid had the predictable effect on his bladder. Urinations: eleven. He washed his hands many times, but at least he didn't keep count. And he didn't get an early night – he was far too busy working on the remaining challenge. He achieved that one to the best of his abilities and fell into a much-needed sleep with the taste of her juices still alive in his mouth.

Capricorn

Determination, dominance, persevering, practical, wilful

She was there again. The unseasonably warm weather had brought her outside once more. He'd seen her every day this week; sitting on the same park bench eating a deli lunch from a brown paper bag. Her couture suit, red-soled shoes and perfect hair told him that whatever she did for a living, she was high-up. Powerful. He felt the familiar tightness in his gut as he watched her eat the simple food. Would she relinquish her power to him? How would she look tied to his bed? How would she look with his cock down her throat?

He watched her finish her food, ball up the bag and launch it into the bin next to the bench. She took out her phone and appeared to be sending a text message. But she raised the phone – was she taking a photo of him? Perhaps his interest in her was mutual. She got up, brushed off her grey skirt and began to walk towards him. As she passed where he was sitting, a waft of some expensive perfume reached his nose. She smelled as classy as she looked. As she walked away, his eyes followed her; the subtle sway of her hips telling of lush curves and feminine grace that was concealed beneath the staid clothes. He got up from his seat, dumping the remains of his own lunch in a nearby bin and followed her. Today he had to know where she was heading.

She walked for several minutes. Purposeful strides, not stopping to gaze in shop windows, not pausing to talk or even smile at anyone else. He could see her easily, following the smart chignon in her dark brown hair. He imagined that he could detect the faint trail of her perfume as if it pulled him after her like an invisible, unbreakable thread. She turned into a smart building; black marble and tinted glass. So now he knew what she did and where to find her. She was a lawyer.

Sophia Anders walked into the cool air of her office and sat down at her desk. She opened her email inbox and looked at the messages that had come in while she was out to lunch. She was just about to begin typing a reply to one of her clients when her assistant, Jacqui, knocked on the open door and came in with the afternoon's post. "Thanks, Jacqui. I'll look at it in a minute."

The girl looked at her before closing the office door. "Well?"

"Well, what?"

"Was he there again?"

"He was."

"Did you get a photo this time?"

Sophia hesitated to answer. The last few days of sunshine had drawn her out of her office at lunchtime to eat in the pretty little park a few minutes' walk away. She'd seen him on the first day - a handsome, well-dressed guy sitting on the bench opposite hers. She had felt his eyes on her the whole time she sat there and when she walked past him on her way back to work, she had a distinct feeling that his gaze had followed her. Today was the fourth day that they had shared the same space for lunch and she'd be lying if the whole, bizarre episode wasn't giving her the tiniest thrill. She had told Jacqui about it yesterday, and the girl told her to try to get a photo so that she could see this silent enigma for herself. She had managed to take a photo while pretending to send a text message. If she showed it to Jacqui, the story would probably continue. If she didn't, she would never hear the end of it. Finally, she made the decision and pulled her phone from her handbag.

Her assistant clapped her hands and let out a little squeal of glee before taking the phone from her boss's hand and studying the image. She sat forward and turned the screen towards the light coming through the large window behind Sophia's chair. She used her fingers to zoom in on the image a little then looked up. "This is the guy?"

"Yeah. I may have overstated his appeal."

"No – you didn't overstate anything at all. But I know who this is." She raised an eyebrow and smiled conspiratorially. "How much is that little piece of information worth?"

"Not a thing. I'm not that interested. I only took the photo so that you'd stop banging on about it." Sophia took her phone back and looked at the image of the man on the bench. He had dark hair which was fashionably layered so that it brushed his collar. His navy suit had been made to fit him, and his black shoes gleamed in the sunshine. The only flash of colour in the whole picture was his purple silk tie. "And the weather forecast says it's back to cold and damp tomorrow, so I probably won't see him again anyway."

Jacqui pouted and slumped in her chair. "You're no fun."

Sophia looked up from her phone and gave the girl a slow smile. "You've worked for me for three months, and you're only just realising this now?" It was true. Fun was not a word that many people used in connection with her. She'd joined this firm three months ago, and she already had a reputation for being a humourless hard-nut. In truth, she suspected that was why she got the job. It wasn't really what she thought of herself – in her own mind; she was confident and self-contained. To people meeting her for the first time, this was often construed as coldness. But she had passion enough; it just had to be teased out by the right person.

Jacqui smiled and got up to leave. "Well, if you put it like that, I suppose I shouldn't be surprised. However, if you decide you want to know who your mystery guy is, just bring me a red velvet cupcake from Sweet Sensations and the info is all yours." She turned and walked out, closing the office door behind her.

The next day, it rained as the weather forecaster had predicted, so Sophia dashed out to the deli under cover of an umbrella to buy her lunch. As she walked past Sweet Sensations, something made her turn, and she went inside to buy a red velvet cupcake for Jacqui. She told herself that it was because she knew it was the girl's favourite and she just wanted to say thank you for all Jacqui's hard work with the case they'd just closed. It had absolutely nothing to do with the fact that she wanted to know the identity of the man in the park. No sir. Nothing to do with that at all. She was a little relieved to see that Jacqui was not at her desk when she returned from her damp shopping trip, so she put the little pink box next to the computer keyboard and returned to her desk to eat her lunch.

About half an hour later, there was a knock at the door, and Jacqui entered the office before Sophia had time to call 'come in'. She wafted into the room – a smug grin on her face – and placed a card with two words written on it on Sophia's desk. Then she wafted out again.

Sophia looked at the card. In her assistant's girlish, oversized handwriting was written, Paul Standish. She pulled up a Google image search on her computer and typed in the name. There he was, all tall, dark, handsome and expensive suit. She clicked on the link and went to the website. The Firenze Gallery website gave information about their latest artists and opening times. The about us page showed the image of Paul Standish and his business partner, Claire Marsters. The gallery's address was only a couple of minutes' walk from the park where she had first seen him. She went out to the small reception area where Jacqui sat at her desk. "Okay – you've got me intrigued. How do you know Paul Standish of The Firenze Gallery?"

Jacqui looked up from her typing, trying to look nonchalant. "I thought you said you weren't interested?" She took a deliberate bite of the red velvet cupcake. "Mmm … delicious."

Sophia crossed her arms over her chest. "I didn't say I was interested in him. But I am interested in how you know him."

The younger woman smiled, a small look of triumph crossing her face. "Well, your predecessor did some work for the gallery a couple of years ago. They were accused of trying to sell a fake, and we represented them. I just remember him. He is pretty memorable, after all."

Sophia had to agree she was right. Even if he hadn't been watching her so obviously, she would have noticed him. He was striking. "Well – thank you for solving the mystery. I think we can go back to normal now."

Jacqui grinned and took another bite of her cupcake. "Yes, Ms Anders."

Paul Standish looked dismally out at the grey sky, trying not to admit that what he was feeling was a disappointment. He tried to concentrate on the catalogue for the sculpture lots they had just acquired, but he was too distracted. He hadn't searched for her online, and he was determined not to. Nothing good would come of it. He looked back to the printer's samples for the catalogue then closed the folio with a sigh. It was no good. He already knew he was going to look for her, so he might as well get it over with. He typed in the name of the law firm he had seen her walk into the day before. The gallery had used the firm for that stupid business with the fake Julian Cox piece; they had been excellent. He typed in the words, not looking at his fingers, as if not watching himself type them might make his reasons for doing so less obvious. The company website came on the screen with photos of the senior partners. She wasn't among them. Of course, she wasn't; she was far too young. He clicked on the personnel page and there she was. He leaned forward to get a better look at the corporate photo of the smiling woman. Sophia Anders. So now he knew her name.

The rain fell every day for the next week. The last time he saw Sophia Anders sitting in the sun was an anchor point that was getting further away as the days passed. The memory wasn't diminishing though, despite the passage of time. In fact, it seemed to burn in his mind more brightly; every morning, he would wake with her image before his eyes and the faint memory of her scent in his nose. He admonished himself for letting a woman get to him so intensely. He was proud of his self-control, his self-containment. He didn't need anyone.

And yet, as the days passed, the memory became a fantasy, and the fantasy became a need. A real, pulsing, physical need that he felt in his gut every time he allowed his thoughts to stray in her direction. He knew he was in real danger of slipping into an obsession. He couldn't allow that to happen. Resolved, he got up from his desk and walked to where the company secretary was busy writing invitations to the new exhibition. "Jenna – add a name to the list, will you?"

Sophia looked at her reflection in the long mirror of the staff restroom. She had showered and changed into a short, black dress. Her hair was down, falling in soft curls around her shoulders and she had applied smoky eyeshadow to emphasise her eyes. She completed the look with her favourite pair of black Louboutin pumps. Their scarlet soles were the only hint of colour in her otherwise black outfit.

She looked again at the invitation. The front of the thick had an image of a modern bronze sculpture of a woman's torso against a black background. It was hand-delivered a week ago, and Jacqui had simply raised an eyebrow as she'd placed it on Sophia's desk. At first, she had dismissed it; she didn't have time for social events. But the spark of excitement she felt when she saw Paul Standish's confident handwriting on the card had spread. Fanned by a draft from her own imagination, that spark had flared into a full-blown blaze and, two days ago, she finally sent her RSVP. She had justified her decision with the fact that the gallery was a client; it would be good business to stay in contact with them just in case they ever needed the services of a high-powered law firm again. She had sent her RSVP as an email, and he had replied almost straight away:

I'm very glad you're coming to the gallery opening. After four days of sharing a lunch venue with you I had decided to speak to you, but the weather sabotaged my plan. I hope that you will let me get to know you a little better on Friday evening. I haven't been able to get out of my mind.

His candour had been a little surprising. She sent a simple email, replying that she was looking forward to the event and that she would be very happy to make his acquaintance in such an interesting setting. As she wrote the words, she told herself again that it was just because he was a client of the law firm. It had nothing to do with the fact that she hadn't been able to get him out of her mind either. She repeated this very credible reason as she left the restroom and walked back through the empty atrium. Jacqui had long since gone home, and she was grateful for that. The girl had dismissed Sophia's business explanation with a simple wave of her hand. "You just want to go and see Mr Mysterious." If Jacqui could see how much effort had gone into tonight's outfit, there would be no end to her teasing.

She walked into her office and sat down to log off her computer. On the keyboard was a small, black box which was sitting on a folded piece of thick, handmade paper. She took the note first, unfolding it carefully. There was a message from Paul Standish, written in blue-black ink, and in the same, confident script that had been on the invitation. *I saw you sitting in sunlight. I want to see you sitting in the moonlight. If you don't wear my gift tonight, I will understand that you are not interested in more than making my acquaintance. But if I see it on your wrist, I will take it as an invitation to get to know you much, much better.*

Sophia's heart was pounding, and she felt a little breathless as she opened the box. Inside was a pale blue jewellery box. Her fingers were shaking almost imperceptibly as she eased it open and took out a delicate bracelet. It was stunning and just what she would have picked for herself; a simple, classic design. She looked at her naked wrist. If she wore it, she would be telling him that she was available and interested. But what kind of man behaves in this way? He knew her name and where she worked. Why all the mystery? Was he some kind of deviant? Her mind and body warred furiously as she tried to decide. Her mind was saying, *No – you have no idea what kind of psycho he is. Go to the opening just to see him again, but don't risk anything else.*

Her body was saying, *Put the bracelet on. Allow yourself the chance to see where this goes. You wanted him the moment you saw him. Stop being so cautious.*

For once in her life, she allowed her body to win the argument. She carefully fastened the platinum chain around her wrist. The diamond drops spaced along its length sparkled in the bright, white overhead lighting of her office. Her heart began to beat fast again as she looked at it, and her mind had one last attempt to make her see sense. She dismissed it – not even letting it finish what it was going to say – and wrapped her soft, black shawl around her shoulders before stepping out into the night.

Paul Standish stood in the far corner of the gallery, watching the guests arrive. When his secretary told him that Sophia Anders had confirmed she was attending, his mind had raced, and he'd done something very out of character by sending her an email. He usually pursued a woman in a calm, collected way, following the usual rules of dating before taking her to his bed for their mutual pleasure. The seduction, however long it lasted, was as important to him as the act itself. But this woman was different. He was aching to touch her; impatient to skip over the pleasantries and initiate a sexual relationship that he knew would be intense.

He saw her then. She walked through the door, following an elderly couple he recognised from previous shows. She wasn't looking for him – or at least, she didn't appear to be looking for him – as she took off her black wrap and handed it to the girl on the door. As she raised her arm to pull the soft fabric from her shoulders, he saw her wrist as it sparkled under the white lights of the gallery. She had found it, and she had decided to wear it. His heart leapt up into his throat at the sight of his gift against the pale skin of her arm. Then his body below the waist began to warm as the realisation hit him; she was interested. If he managed to control the fifteen-year-old version of himself that had apparently taken up residence in his boxer-shorts, she could be in his bed by the end of the evening.

He decided to watch her for a while, so he stayed in his corner and observed as she took the flute of champagne that was offered but refused any canapes. He hadn't wanted any of the delectable little mouthfuls either – his stomach was roiling, and the only thing he wanted to taste was her. She wandered around the gallery, pausing to look at a few pieces before coming to stand in front of the centrepiece. He watched her closely as her eyes travelled over the bronze female torso and he imagined doing the same thing with her body. Finally, he decided it was time to speak to her. He walked over to the black marble plinth on which the bronze was displayed and faced her.

For a moment, she didn't notice that he was there. She took a sip of her drink then she raised her head, and their eyes met. Her pupils dilated, and her skin flushed. The wine glass in her hand trembled slightly, making the bubbles in her champagne speed to the top of the golden liquid and she swallowed before allowing a small gasp to escape.

"Hello, Paul." She looked directly at him now, her shoulders squared, her body language adjusted after that tiny slip to tell him she regarded herself as his equal.

He walked around the sculpture so that he was facing her. She held out her hand, but he didn't shake it. Instead, he took her wrist in his hand and ran his thumb over the fine platinum chain. "Hello, Sophia. Thank you for coming." He felt her pulse speed up under the soft pressure he was applying with his thumb. "You look very beautiful this evening."

Sophia's heart was racing; fluttering and beating out a rhythm so clear she was sure that Paul must be able to see it throbbing in her throat. He had said she looked beautiful. She knew she looked good, but it's always nice to have someone else tell you. He looked good too – formal black trousers and a shirt in the deepest green that was unbuttoned at the collar, showing the strong column of his throat. Her mouth was dry suddenly. "Thank you. You look …" she wanted to say beautiful as well, but she thought he probably wouldn't appreciate that, no matter how true it was. "You look perfect." She wasn't sure why that word was the only one that she managed to conjure. She hadn't felt so breathless around a man for many years. "Thank you for inviting me. And thank you for the beautiful gift. Though I'm not sure I can keep it."

He smiled at her, continuing to rub at the delicate skin of her wrist. "I'm glad you like it. And you will keep it. By morning, it will be the only thing you are wearing."

She heard a surprised gasp escape from her lips, followed by an unbelieving laugh. Did he really just say that? "You're very sure of yourself, Mr Standish."

He smiled, his eyes darkening, and the look reminded her of a predatory animal that has spotted a weak member of the herd. "You are here, wearing this," he stroked the fine chain again, "I'm not interested in playing games with you. I want you. If you don't want this to go any further, I'll give you one last opportunity. You can remove the bracelet and leave. If you do, I won't come after you, but please know that it will feel like a physical blow. You have the power, Sophia. The power to choose to explore this or to let it go. But as long as you're wearing this, you're mine."

Sophie looked at him, noticing for the first time the deep blue of his eyes. He was sincere. He might be arrogant and overbearing, but he wasn't trying to deceive her – the straight-talking, self-contained woman at her heart appreciated his honesty. She looked down at her wrist where his thumb still rolled over her skin and the fine chain of the bracelet. Her brain was screaming at her to reach over and release the clasp, but she had to be honest with herself about this. She didn't want to.

He saw the moment she made up her mind and his smile changed from predatory to victorious. "You have made the right choice, Sophia. Come with me." He moved his fingers so that he was holding her hand instead of her wrist and pulled her lightly towards a staircase that she hadn't noticed before. The wooden stairs led up to a smart apartment. He opened the door, which she noticed was not locked, and indicated that she should go into the apartment first. "I stay here when we have an exhibition running. I need to be on site. It's easier if I'm here."

She looked around at the large, open space of his apartment. It was furnished expensively; Persian rugs and leather chairs. Artwork of all eras decorated the walls, and the subtle lighting gave the oak flooring a golden glow. There was a faint smell of incense or something else that was familiar, and she felt her stomach tighten as the realisation hit; she was in his space, and her acquiescence was implied. "Won't you be missed at the exhibition?" Was that a last-ditch effort by her brain to try to take control of the evening? "Will people wonder where you are?"

He shook his head and his lips raised into an almost imperceptible smile. "No. Claire is running this show. I told her I might not stick around for all of it. She knows how much I hate having to be nice to potential customers." His frank admission shocked her slightly, and he smiled again at her reaction. "I'm good with the buying and selling to genuine customers. These evenings are more to try to promote the gallery – they rarely result in any significant sales. I just don't have the patience to make idle chit-chat with people on the off-chance that they might spend some money."

Sophie walked around a leather sofa so that it was between them. "No – you don't strike me as someone who likes idle chit-chat of any description." She was referring to his approach to seduction. "You like to get right down to business, don't you?"

In reply, he rounded the sofa and pulled her to him, sealing his mouth over hers in a forceful, demanding kiss. Her mouth was already open as she was about to speak again when he came to her so suddenly. She felt his tongue press into her mouth as he controlled the exchange. He was breathing through his nose, his chest heaving as his desire took control. She felt her body react to him – to his taste – her heart raced, and her breath came in desperate pants as she fought to stay afloat. She sucked on his tongue, encircling it with her own and she heard a groan escape from his throat. She didn't want him to stop, so fighting him in any way would have been deceitful.

Kissing Sophia Anders was a revelation. He knew he wanted her – had done since he saw her that first time in the park – but the way his body was reacting to her was unprecedented. He was in danger of losing the last, slender hold on his control. The blood had rushed from his brain, heading south, and now his cock was running the show. "I want you in my bed. I've wanted you in my bed since the first time I saw you sitting in the sunshine. I don't do hearts and flowers. I go after what I want. I don't see any point in wasting time on niceties. There'll be plenty of time for us to find out about each other. Right now, I'm going to take you to my bed, and I'm going to fuck you."

Her face showed shock for a moment, then, once again, he saw the moment she decided to agree. She wanted this as much as he did. "If I want you to stop at any point, I'll say, *Paul, stop*."

"You have my word. I want you to enjoy this. I know that once won't be enough for me, Sophia. If you're not enjoying what I'm doing to you, tell me to stop, and we will stop." He kissed her again, more gently this time. Then he took her hand and led her towards his bedroom. "Are you ready?"

She nodded. "Yes. I'm ready. I want you too – so much."

He smiled that predatory smile again and pulled her into the dimly-lit room that contained his bed and very little else. He pulled his shirt out from the waistband of his trousers and started to unbutton it, not taking his eyes from hers as he undressed. When he walked over to where she was standing, he was barefoot and wearing only his trousers and underwear. His arousal was obvious; tenting the fabric of his trousers as he approached her. Her eyes finally left him and he watched as her lips parted slightly. She liked what she saw.

Sophia looked at Paul's semi-naked body as he stood in front of her. She felt her heart speed up at the sight of him. His skin was golden in the dim light of the bedroom, and the muscles of his chest and arms were well-defined, showing that he took care of himself. There was a small patch of dark hair between his nipples, and a thin line of it ran down the centre of his stomach and disappeared into the waistband of his trousers. She let her lips fall open as she took in his beautifully male body, then she let her tongue run along their seam, moistening the skin which had suddenly gone dry.

He saw her reaction to him and smiled. "Well, that's encouraging." He had that predatory gleam in his eyes again as he reached for her, pulling her against him as he took her mouth in a rough kiss. She felt his hands move to the back of her dress and then he began to pull on the zip. She felt the cool air of the room brush against her skin and, when he had undone the zip completely, he reached up to the shoulders of the dress and pushed it off. The soft fabric floated over her arms and slipped to the floor in a soft pool around her feet.

She was about to bend over to pick it up when he stopped her. "No. Let me. Please." He fell to his knees in front of her and looked up the length of her body. "God, you're perfect." He helped her to step out of the dress before lifting the fabric to his nose and inhaling deeply. He folded it gently and reached back to lay it across the back of a chair. He looked up at her again as he slipped her shoes from her feet. He put them under the same chair and returned his attention to her body. He ran his hands up her legs, from her calves to her buttocks and, as he came up to his knees, he leaned forward and buried his nose in the damp silk that covered her pussy. She heard him inhale again and her hand moved forward so that she could run her fingers through his hair. It was soft and in perfect condition, like the rest of him.

She heard him make a soft moaning noise as she pressed his face into her warm mound, then he moved his hands to the sides of her knickers and began to pull them down. When he had uncovered her pubic hair, he pushed his nose into it, making the same, soft moaning sound. Then his actions changed speed. Her panties were pulled the rest of the way off, followed quickly by her hold-up stockings. He pushed her legs apart slightly and held her steady, one hand on the base of her spine, the other at the top of her thigh, his thumb just brushing the outer lips of her pussy. He leaned forward again and pressed his open mouth against her damp folds.

Sophia felt his mouth make contact with her aroused flesh and her knees dipped a little. Paul moved his hands so that he was holding her more securely. "Yes. I think I need to get you over to the bed now." He rose from his knees and stood in front of her. "Take off the rest of your clothes. Everything except the bracelet." As she pulled her silk camisole over her head, she heard him unfasten his belt buckle. When she looked again, he was laying his folded trousers over her dress on the back of the chair. She watched as he pushed his grey boxer-briefs down, releasing his erect cock. He was hard and magnificent.

His gaze turned dark as he stalked back to where she was standing. "Bra as well. And the rest of the jewellery." Before she could react to his demand, he was behind her, unfastening the hooks of her bra and slipping it over her shoulders. He pulled it off and threw it onto the floor under the chair.

She unclipped her earrings and took off the simple necklace that she was wearing. Now she was completely naked – except for the bracelet – in the bedroom of an equally naked stranger. Her mind delivered a hefty dose of reality, and she felt herself stiffen. What the hell was she doing? She knew nothing about this man yet she was on the verge of giving herself to him in the most intimate way. She moved, putting a little more distance between them. "I … ah … I can't do this … I'm sorry." She stepped forward to retrieve her clothes, the fine sheen of sweat from her arousal cooling quickly and making her shiver.

He stopped her by wrapping his fingers around her upper arm. "Sophia – wait."

She turned to face him, and he could see the fear that had suddenly bloomed in the depths of her eyes. "Paul. Stop."

He let her go straight away and raised his hands to let her know that he had no intention of pursuing it any further. "I'll phone for a taxi for you. Please, take your time." He picked up a landline phone and walked into the adjoining bathroom.

Paul stepped out of the shower and wrapped a towel around his waist. He walked out into the bedroom. She was gone. He saw the fine chain he had given her sparkling on the dark wood surface of the bedside table. "Dammit." He sat down on the edge of the bed and picked up the bracelet, running it through his fingers. "Too much too soon. You knew it was too much too soon." God, he had wanted her so badly; his balls still ached with the need to claim her.

He dressed and went back downstairs to the gallery. The exhibition was winding down, and most people had gone home. He walked to the area by the door where the girl had been collecting coats. He could see Sophia's black wrap hanging there – the only garment remaining. He pulled it off the hanger and lifted it to his nose. Yes, it was hers. He'd know her scent anywhere. He carried it back to his office and folded it gently. His computer was still on, so he opened the list of guests who had sent a RSVP. He found her name on the list and the email address he had used, but she hadn't provided a phone number. "Dammit."

Jenna walked into the office and heard him curse under his breath. "Is everything alright sir?"

He looked up and forced a smile for his assistant. "Yes, Jenna. Everything's fine. Well done for this evening. You can go home now. I'll see you on Monday."

"Yes, sir. Have a good weekend."

He thanked her and watched her collect her coat and bag, then leave. His partner, Claire, walked into his office a moment later. "That's the last of them gone. The caterers are just clearing away then we can call it a night."

He looked up at her. "Thank you. It was a good show."

She smirked at him and took a seat in front of his desk. "It was; though I'm not sure how you know that because you weren't here for most of it. We sold the bronze, by the way."

"Good. That's good news. At least the evening wasn't a total bust, then." He looked back down at Sophia's black wrap, and felt the desperate need to hold it to himself. He didn't, but he knew that if Claire hadn't been sitting there, he probably would.

Claire nodded in understanding. "She didn't go for the direct approach then?"

He looked up at her and his brow creased with suspicion. He never shared any details of his personal life with Claire. "I'm not sure I know what you mean."

She nodded at the soft, black fabric on his desk. "Well, I saw that come in around the shoulders of a really beautiful woman. That same woman disappeared with you up the stairs to your loft then reappeared a short time later and climbed into a cab. So, you were either very quick, or she knocked you back."

"I didn't realise you kept such a close eye on my social life."

She huffed out a laugh. "I don't. But when you ask me to take the lead at an exhibition and then disappear upstairs with someone who you requested to be on the guest-list – well – it's difficult not to be intrigued."

Shaking his head as if in defeat, he gave into the need to inhale her scent one last time. He picked up the wrap and held it to his nose. "I may have misjudged the situation somewhat."

Claire looked openly surprised by his admission. "So? Put it right."

It was a simple statement. Did he want to? The answer to that was probably yes. Did he have any idea how to go about it? That was an entirely different question.

The gallery was open as usual on Sunday morning. It wasn't open for business – though if someone wanted to buy something, they were always amenable – but the doors were open, should anyone passing want to come in and look around. Paul Standish wasn't usually at the gallery on a Sunday morning. He rarely stayed in the loft apartment over the weekend, but after Friday night's disappointment with Sophia, he just hadn't been able to work up the energy to go home. So, he was sitting at his desk again. Looking at her wrap again. Sinking into self-pity again.

He heard the front door buzz as someone came in. A moment later, Henry, the assistant who worked weekends, came into his office. "I've got a lady out here who left something after the exhibition on Friday. Do you know if anything was handed in?"

His heart leapt up into his mouth. There was only one thing left on Friday, and he had it in his hands. He got up and walked past the young assistant. "I've got this, Henry, thanks." He walked out into the brightly-lit space of the gallery and saw her. She was looking at the bronze again, and he took a moment to gaze at her – to take everything about her in and store the image away – before walking towards her.

She looked up when she heard footsteps approaching and when she saw him, the smile fell from her face. She had been expecting Henry to come back to her. "Paul – I wasn't expecting to see you here today." She looked down at his hands, where he held her lost garment. "Oh – you found it."

"Sophia – I'm so glad you're here. I didn't know how to contact you – I've been going out of my mind." It was true; he hadn't slept all weekend properly and he knew he looked dishevelled.

She looked at him, her eyes travelling the length of his body and he saw the colour drain from her face. "I'm sorry. I shouldn't have come." She turned towards the door and started to walk away from him.

"No. Please, Sophia." He caught up with her in two, easy strides and put his hand gently on her arm. He wanted to curl his fingers around her, but he didn't. "At least take your wrap – it's what you came here for, after all."

She turned to face him, and he could see something in her eyes; an emotion he couldn't read. "Thank you." She took the black wrap from him and, for a moment, they were both holding it. Her eyes connected with his and he saw that emotion again. "I don't want to keep you from your work."

His hand moved involuntarily towards her, and he lifted it to brush a loose strand of hair behind her ear. "You're not keeping me from anything. I want to see you. I want to talk to you – to explain and to apologise. Will you please let me do that?"

She dropped her head so that she wasn't looking directly at him. "There is no need to apologise. You were perfectly honest about your intentions, and I led you to think that I was happy to go along with it. I'm sorry. I shouldn't have done that. I thought I wanted it too – I really did – but when it came to it, I just couldn't." She looked up at him to see his reaction. "Thank you for holding on to my wrap."

She turned to leave again, and this time, he succumbed to his need to touch her again by wrapping his fingers around the firm flesh of her upper arm. "Sophia. Please. You don't have anything to be sorry for. I should have taken things more slowly with you. Please – don't go – let me make you a cup of coffee, and we can talk."

He didn't think she was going to agree. He was just about to loosen his grip on her arm when she turned and looked at him again. "Just coffee?"

He felt his face relax into a smile for the first time in days. "Just coffee. Come with me."

Sophia followed Paul up the stairs to his loft. Her mind was racing. *What are you doing? You ran from him – from this place – on Friday night.* That much was true, but when she had looked at him just now, she saw something that looked like sadness in his eyes, and she had followed him willingly. And she knew somehow that she could trust him. He had stopped when she asked him to, and he didn't pursue her – he let her go without trying to stop her. When he opened the door to the apartment, the large room was now flooded with sunlight and her nerves eased a little.

He ushered her inside and closed the door behind them. Then he walked into the open-plan kitchen and switched on a high-spec coffee machine. "What can I get you to drink?"

She eyed the machine and the various coffee pods stacked beside it. "Actually, could I have tea?"

He smiled and reached for the kettle. "I prefer tea as well. I only ever use this thing when I have guests." He busied himself in the small kitchen. "I have regular or Lady Grey."

"Lady Grey would be lovely, thank you."

She watched him go through the ritual of making tea; warming the pot, spooning the loose tea into it and adding the boiling water. He put it on a tray, with cups then sliced a lemon and put that on the tray as well. She smiled inwardly at the fact that he didn't ask her if she wanted milk – he just assumed that she would take her tea the same way he did – he was right, of course. He carried the tray to a low table in front of a leather sofa. There were no other chairs, so she would have to sit next to him. He poured the tea into two perfect china cups and added a slice of lemon to each; then he handed one of them to her. "I'm glad you're here. Let's start again – from the beginning." He sat back, kicked off his shoes and put his legs up on the low table, crossing his ankles.

Sophia sipped at her tea before putting it on the table in front of her. "I need you to know that I have never behaved like that with anyone else before."

He smiled and put his own cup down. "You don't owe me any kind of explanation. But, for what it's worth, I'm not usually in quite such a hurry either. You caught me off guard, Sophia. I wanted you the moment I saw you sitting on that bench. I still do want you."

She looked at him then, his face was open and honest, and her gut told her that he was telling her the truth. "Do you have a girlfriend or a wife?"

He laughed quietly at her question. "No – I don't have either of those things at the moment. He smiled, and his eyes warmed as he let his gaze drop from her eyes to her lips. "Please don't be angry with me, but I want to kiss you."

She spoke again before he had the chance to act on that desire. "Don't you want to know about me? Whether or not I have a boyfriend or a husband?" That hadn't come out quite as she had planned, and she knew she was in danger of starting to ramble.

"Do you?" He leant his head over slightly, and she got a distinct impression that he was humouring her.

"No. Neither." She reached for her tea again and sipped at it, refusing to meet his eyes. She was embarrassed. In the bright daylight of the apartment, the memory of what had happened before was becoming uncomfortable.

"Good. That's good." He shifted in his seat, turning to face her fully. "I still want to kiss you."

She raised her eyes to look directly into his deep blue gaze, and her tummy flipped at what she saw there; they were filled with raw emotion and desire. Her mouth was dry suddenly, and she ran her tongue quickly over her bottom lip to try to moisten it a little. His eyes followed her action, then he leant forward, taking her face in his hands as he sealed his lips over hers.

Kissing Sophia felt every bit as wonderful as it had done the first time. He went gently, not wanting to spook her again and when he finally pulled away, he kept his hands on her, holding her face gently, making sure she was looking at him. "Thank you for letting me do that. For trusting me to do that."

She didn't say anything, but she held his gaze as though she was searching for something. An answer to a question, perhaps? He was just about to say something else when she pulled him towards her and fastened her lips over his. He let her kiss him, forcing himself to leave the control with her. When she pulled away from him, her eyes were dark with desire, and she was panting softly. "Get undressed. I want to see you naked again."

He was so shocked by her unexpected request that he couldn't stop a look of surprise from passing over his face. He felt a momentary worry that she might be trying to manipulate him into a possibly humiliating situation, but he dismissed it. Her desire was real. He stood and began to remove his clothes. "If I want you to stop, I'll say Sophia, Stop.

She smiled as he repeated her words from two nights ago, and watched as he stripped out of his clothes in front of her. When he had completed his task, she nodded at the sofa, "Lie down."

His heart was racing in his chest, and he was sure she must be able to hear it. He sensed that if he questioned her or tried to take the lead, she would run again, and he couldn't let her do that. His cock was painfully hard. Her confidence and simple demand had caused his desire to ratchet up to such a level that he was shaking with need for her. He lay down on the sofa, his head resting on the arm with his knees raised.

She got up from her seat which gave him a little more room, so he relaxed his legs a little, but there still wasn't enough space for him to stretch them out completely. He watched in silence as she took off her clothes, his hand moving down to stroke his cock almost of its own volition.

"Stop that. The only person touching your cock will be me." Her words shocked him and sent a bolt of desire from his cock to the tips of his toes and fingers. She pulled his knees apart and climbed back onto the sofa, kneeling on the leather between his legs. "Don't move. You move, and I stop. Understand?"

He nodded, swallowing hard. "I understand." He wanted to touch her so much, but he forced himself to keep his hands pinned to his sides.

She bent her head and ran her nose up the inside of his thigh. He shuddered, and she stopped momentarily, raising her head to give him a warning look. She returned to her strange caress, brushing against his skin with the side of her nose, breathing him in as she moved up his body. She reached his groin and placed a light kiss on the underside of his erection where it pressed against his belly.

He couldn't stop a small groan and a tiny thrust of his hips to get a closer contact with her. He stilled, dreading that she would stop as she threatened, but she continued her exploration of his skin, moving up his belly and chest until her face was level with his. She dipped her head, sucking his lower lip into her mouth and biting gently on his flesh.

When she released her hold on his mouth, he couldn't stop a groan. "Please. Sophia. I'm burning for you."

In answer, she gave him a sly smile and kissed him again, thrusting her tongue into his mouth in a stroking assault. She reached down and grasped his cock in her hand, moving it so that the head rubbed between the wet lips of her pussy.

He was in agony now. If she didn't take him soon, he was going to lose it, flip her over and pound into her without being able to control himself. He was just about to beg her to mount him when she did just that, still holding his cock as she lowered herself onto him until he was seated completely inside her. He hissed a curse and put his hands on her hips to hold her in place. "Fuck, you're tight." He rolled his hips slightly, trying to ease the ache in his cock. "But you need to pull off me. I need to put on a condom."

"You'd better not come, then; because I'm not going anywhere yet. You feel too fucking good inside me." She rolled her head back on her shoulders and began to rotate her hips so that his cock moved deep inside her. She leaned forward, taking hold of both of his wrists and pushing them over his head. "And stop moving. If you move again, I'll leave."

"No!" The word escaped his lips before he had a chance to stop it. "No, Sophia, please. You're not leaving me this time. You can do what you like to me, but please, don't stop." He ceased moving and concentrated hard on staying still. Then he concentrated on not coming. Her inner muscles were squeezing him, and he knew he wouldn't be able to hold it for long. The sight of her moving over him, her beautiful breasts swaying as she moved her hips was enough to send him flying over the edge, but when she reached down and began to stroke her wet little bud, he knew he had to close his eyes. He cursed as he shut out the sight that wanted so desperately to see.

She must have seen his agony, and she laughed as she saw him close his eyes. "Oh, no you don't. Open your eyes. I want you to see me come as your cock is filling me up.

He obeyed her order, trying not to look at where her fingers were working her clit, but his eyes moved down her body, and he knew he was lost. "Please! Sophia! I'm going to come! Please, I can't stop it. You have to get off me."

With a victorious smile, she dismounted – not a moment too soon - as he came, shooting a thick stream of hot seed onto her belly where she bent over him. "You owe me now." She got off him, walking towards the bedroom, and he followed her on shaky legs.

Sophia felt a rush of erotic pleasure flood her belly as she watched him lose control beneath her. This cool, controlled man had broken into pieces as she rode him. She walked to the bedroom, knowing, without needing to look, that he was following her. When she reached the bed, she pulled the quilt off and lay back on the pillows, spreading her thighs. She felt the bed dip as he joined her and then she felt his hot breath on her pussy lips. "No – not yet – you need to clean me up first. You left your cum all over my skin. Lick it off."

He met her eyes for a moment; then he did as she requested, licking the cooling liquid from the skin of her belly, before moving up her body to kiss her forcefully, pushing his cum-covered tongue deep into her mouth as his fingers explored the lush, swollen folds of her cunt. "Do you want me to make you come with my fingers or my mouth?"

She was squirming beneath him, moving her hips in the same spiral that she had used when she was riding him. "Both. I want you to use both. Now."

He smiled and kissed her mouth again, before moving down her body to comply with her wishes. When his tongue touched the over-sensitive bundle of nerves between her legs, she felt a jolt of pure electricity shoot through her entire body, making her toes curl. He felt it and laughed against her skin as he pushed two, long fingers deep into her hole. "Tell me what you want me to do."

He was still letting her run the show, even though she was now lying beneath him. The knowledge that she had power over this magnificent male gave her another surge of pleasure. "Suck my clit. Fuck me with your fingers. Push them into me completely."

He did as she requested, latching onto her clit with his mouth and sucking hard as his fingers worked in and out of her. She felt her orgasm begin, firing tiny shocks through her inner muscles – taking her to the edge again and again but not letting her go over.

He must have sensed what was happening because he released her bud from his mouth for long enough to say, "Let it go, Sophia. I want you to come all over my face."

Hearing him express his desire was enough. As soon as he had sucked her clit into the warm, wet cavern of his mouth again, she flew over the edge. Her muscles contracted around his fingers as she lifted herself off the mattress, pushing her hips into his face as she came and came.

Watching Sophia lose control was the most erotic thing he'd ever seen. He felt her inner muscles squeeze his fingers as her orgasm tore through her, then she was lying in his arms, gasping for breath, her abdomen rising and falling as she pulled air into her lungs. As he felt her relax, he reached into the bedside cabinet and took out a foil packet. He was hard again, and he wanted to fuck her; wanted to push himself into her wet depths and claim her the same way she had claimed him on the sofa. He rolled the condom over his erection and positioned himself between her legs. "Now it's my turn."

She looked shocked for a moment; she was still coming down from the orgasm he had pulled from her with his mouth and fingers. Then she nodded and said the only word he wanted to hear. "Yes."

He pushed himself into her in one, glorious thrust, seating himself inside her as far as he could. He looked down at her face. "Is this okay?"

She nodded, panting and meeting his eyes with her own. "Yes. Do it."

He pulled out of her, leaving only the tip of his cock lodged inside, before pushing himself back in with a groan that he couldn't contain. "God, Sophia. I can't get far enough inside you. I just want to fuck you forever."

Now it was her turn to smile. "As long as you keep doing what you're doing, then that will be fine with me." She laughed, and he felt it through her inner muscles, squeezing him even more.

"Christ – do that again. Your cunt feels like a fist squeezing me."

She laughed again, and he knew she was glorying in the effect she was having on him. She pulled his mouth down to hers and kissed him roughly, pushing her tongue into his mouth. He met her thrust for thrust with both his tongue and his cock, pushing into her mouth and her pussy as deeply as he could.

She was driving him crazy with lust. He reached under the pillow for the long, silk scarf he had put there on Friday night. "I need to take control now. I'm going to tie your wrists. If you want me to stop, tell me, and I'll stop."

She looked up to where he held the strip of red silk over her head. She smiled and put her hands, permitting him to do what he wanted. He tied her wrists together then looped the ends of the scarf around the metal frame of the bed and secured it. "If I want you to stop, I'll say, Paul, stop."

He looked at her for a moment, she wasn't pulling against her bonds, but he needed her to do so. "Pull on the silk. I need you to look like you're trying to get free."

A victorious grin spread across her face, and she did as he asked, pulling and twisting against the soft fabric that bound her to the bed. The sight of it was enough to take him to where he needed to be. With a roar, he pushed her thighs open and lifted them so that he could press down on her legs and pound into her in a merciless rhythm. He felt her inner muscles clenching and looked down to see her mouth open in a mixture of shock and pleasure. It was clear she hadn't expected to reach orgasm again so soon. She cried out, shouting his name and sinking her teeth into the muscle at the top of his arm and he felt his release shoot into her as he called out her name at the top of his voice.

He untied her wrists and pulled her into his arms, kissing every patch of skin he could reach. "You're mine, Sophia."

She snuggled into the warm skin of his body, curling her fingers around his still-hard cock. "No – you're mine, Paul."

Over the course of the evening, they took possession of each other over and over again; both as happy to take control as to relinquish it. As she lay dozing in his arms, he reached over to the bedside table again and picked up the platinum chain. He fastened it around her wrist, and she turned her arm, making it sparkle in the dim light of the bedroom. "You're not taking it off again." He linked his fingers through hers and pulled her closer to him, breathing in the scent of her hair, her skin and the sex they had shared together. He kissed the top of her head and knew that she was already sleeping. "Goodnight, Sophia," he whispered. She had taken him completely by surprise with her aggressive claiming on the sofa, and he had been even more surprised by his willingness to let her take control. He knew they would be claiming each other again tomorrow, and that knowledge gave him an unfamiliar sense of contentment. He let it wash over him as he began to relax enough to fall asleep. For once, his mind was quiet as he let himself fall. He pulled his woman closer to his chest and slipped into slumber, surrounded by her scent and the warmth they had generated together.

AIR

Gemini
Libra
Aquarius

Gemini

Communication, indecision, inquisitive, intelligent, changeable

"Come on, sleepyhead. Time to get up or we'll both be late." Declan put his hand on his lover's hip and nipped at the warm skin of Jamie's shoulder. "You smell so good."

Jamie rolled, taking Declan with him so that he lay over him, pushing his legs apart and pressing his morning erection into the soft flesh between Declan's balls and ass. "Ohh ..." he groaned, taking Declan's mouth in a firm kiss. "Please tell me we have time for me to sink my cock into your delectable little hole?"

They both looked at the bedside clock and groaned with frustration. "Hold that thought." Declan pushed his lover onto his back. "We'll pick that up later." He walked naked towards the shower and turned when he heard Jamie getting off the bed to join him. "Uh-uh – you can use the shower in the guest bathroom. If you come in here with me, we both know what is going to happen. And if you wrap that sweet mouth of yours around my dick right now, we'll both be facing a warning for being late for work AGAIN."

Jamie grinned and walked off in the direction of the other bathroom, but not before turning to admire the retreating, naked buttocks of his soul mate. "We are definitely going to pick that up later." It didn't matter that they had been together since sharing a room at college - almost ten years now - looking at Declan's perfectly dimpled butt never got old. When they met, they had both thought they were one hundred percent heterosexual, but as their friendship grew, the inevitable time came when they had to acknowledge that the percentage was more like fifty/fifty. They had both had female lovers since – sometimes, they'd even shared the same one – but they always ended up together. Jamie climbed into the shower and soaped up, taking care of his morning wood with a few, swift tugs, and emerged into the kitchen, dressed and ready to go, a mere ten minutes later.

"Here – eat this." Declan put a slice of toast in Jamie's mouth and pulled him out of the door, unlocking the car so that they could both climb in. "If the traffic lights are with us, we should just about make it." He looked over to his lover. "What are you grinning about?"

"Nothing." He turned and grinned again. "I love you."

"Yeah … god, you've got me wrapped around your little finger."

"My little finger? I'd rather have you wrapped around my cock." He pointed to a gap in the traffic. "Drop me here – it'll be quicker if I walk the rest of the way. See you later – don't forget Carrie's birthday drinks – six o'clock in The Dick."

'The Dick' was The Dick Whittington – a bar that had been trendy when it opened in the 1980s, complete with sawdust on the floors and food served in wooden bowls. Now, thirty or so years on, it was rather faded and in desperate need of a do-over. But its regular clientele of office workers, who filed into the shabby watering-hole from five-thirty onwards, loved its quaint surroundings and its dogged determination to stay well and truly in the 1980s, where it belonged. And, of course, the endless double-entendre possibilities of talking about 'The Dick', never lost its appeal to the ever-replenishing supply of youthful interns and office juniors who frequented it.

Declan, Jamie and Carrie had been part of that youthful group some years ago. Hours spent propping up the bar, and downing ill-advised shots had cemented the relationship between the three of them. Before Carrie had met and married Pavel, the love of her life, she had shared their bed on numerous occasions. Happy to feed their occasional need for pussy of the female variety, in return for their incredible skills with cock and tongue. Now that they were all nearing the watershed age of thirty, the hours they spent 'Dicking around' were much reduced; but on birthdays, high days and holidays, the small group of friends, which now included Carrie's husband, met there after work and usually stayed until closing time. Tonight would be no different.

When Declan walked into the steamy atmosphere of the crowded bar, shaking the rain from his hair, he spotted the rest of the party already claiming territory in the corner booth. He waved at his friends and did the usual hand signals to ask if anyone wanted another drink. They all waved back that they were okay for the moment and Jamie held up a full glass of beer that he had already bought for his lover, so Declan walked over to the dark corner and sat down heavily on the deep red leather seat. "Hey everyone." He looked around the table at the familiar faces and was more than a little surprised to see a new one. Wedged between Carrie and Jamie was a new, rather beautiful face. He looked at her for a moment before turning to greet his man. "Hey, sexy."

Jamie grinned and breathed out a verbal caress that was meant for their ears only, before leaning forward to kiss Declan softly on the mouth. "You're late."

Declan leant over the table and hugged Carrie. "I know – I'm so sorry. Happy birthday, gorgeous girl!" He kissed her full on the mouth, knowing that Pavel didn't mind at all because he thought the pair was gay. "Sorry, I'm a bit late." He decided to pile on the camp a little bit for Pavel's benefit, though, if truth be told, he had looked forward to kissing Carrie all day. He loved – no, adored his man, but occasionally, there was nothing to match the soft, sweet taste of a woman. Almost of its own volition, his gaze travelled to the new person in the group. "And who is this stunning lady?"

Carrie laughed. "Declan – this is Elsa – a new friend."

Declan leant forward and kissed the girl on the cheek. She smelled of oranges with a hint of honey, and his cock twitched in response to the contact. "Hello, Elsa – I'll bet you're fed up with snowman jokes, huh?"

The girl giggled, and her pretty, hazel eyes sparkled in the dim light of the bar. "Just a bit. But you know, there's no point in getting uptight about it. I try to just let it go."

The table erupted into laughter, and Pavel got up to get another round of drinks. "Same again, everyone?"

Declan looked at Jamie. "Who's driving?"

"You are. I've already had two."

"God, you don't waste time!"

"That'll teach you for being late." He leant forward and claimed Declan's mouth in a rough demonstration of the passion they felt for each other. "And I've been thinking about doing that all day." He went in again and pushed his tongue into his lover's open mouth.

Declan had no choice but to go with it. When Jamie kissed him like that, he was lost. When the kiss finally ended, he looked up to offer an unnecessary apology to his friends. Carrie and Pavel had joined in the game, teasing each other with nips and licks. What surprised him – and aroused him in equal measure, was their new friend's reaction. Her eyes were gleaming, and her face was flushed. He winked at her and blew a kiss in her direction.

The rest of the evening took its usual, meandering route down various memory lanes. Tales of much drunkenness and poorly-thought-out trips to cold, British beaches were brought out again in honour of Carrie's birthday. By the time the clock had crawled around, and the landlord called for last orders, they were drowsily content and ready to go home to their beds.

Carrie pulled Jamie and Declan into a three-way hug. Slurring her words, she thanked them for coming to celebrate her birthday. "I love you guys."

Jamie kissed her passionately on the mouth. "We love you too, baby. Now go home with that gorgeous hunk of a husband and celebrate properly." He lifted an eyebrow and smiled at Pavel. "Take this beautiful girl home and fuck her senseless."

Pavel leant down and kissed his tipsy wife. "I fully intend to do just that."

"Good man." Jamie made a drunken lunge for the handsome guy and kissed him on the mouth too. "God, you're gorgeous. Has anyone ever told you that you're gorgeous?"

Before the shocked man could answer, Declan pulled his lover into his arms. "Come on, you. We have some senseless fucking of our own to do." He looked at the man in his arms, "Though, I fear the amount of booze this one has had tonight might mean we have to postpone that until the morning. Thank goodness tomorrow is Saturday!"

The group said goodnight with more hugs and kisses. Declan was secretly elated by how easily Elsa went into his arms for a goodnight hug, and he leant in for another kiss. She tasted just as sweet as before, and he knew he was going to have to explore something with her before too long.

The taxi arrived on time. Pavel took the front seat while Carrie and Elsa climbed into the back of the small hatchback and fastened their seat belts. When the car was on its way, and she was sure their conversation couldn't be heard over the late-night radio blaring from the car stereo, Elsa leant into Carrie and asked the question she had been dying to ask all night. "Are you sure those two are bi? They seemed pretty into each other from where I was sitting."

Carrie grinned and looked towards the front seat of the car. Happy that her husband was fully occupied by a conversation with the driver, she cupped her hand around her mouth and whispered loudly in her friend's ear. "Oh yeah – they both like a bit of lady-loving now and again. And they're very good at it."

Her friend looked shocked at what Carrie was implying. "You? Which one?"

"Both. At the same time."

Elsa's jaw dropped open so far; she thought it would crack. Aware of how that must look, she lifted her hand and used it to close her mouth. "Really? What was it like?"

Carrie's eyes misted over, and her face took on a dreamy quality. "Well – let's just say I never made any complaints."

Elsa sat back in her seat. "Wow."

Pavel must have sensed that the girls were talking about something spicy because he turned around in his seat and smiled warmly at his wife. "What are you two cooking up?"

The two friends adopted smiles so innocent they could give a couple of nuns a run for their money. "Nothing, honey. I was just telling Elsa how to make those muffins you love so much."

The man pulled a face, lifting an eyebrow which said he didn't wholly believe his wife, but he turned back around and continued his conversation with the driver.

As soon as his back was turned, the two women looked at each other and giggled conspiratorially. Carrie touched her friend on the hand. "You were a hit with both of them. Are you interested?"

Declan stretched and yawned, luxuriating in the warm comfort of the bed he shared with Jamie. There is nothing like waking up on a Saturday morning, knowing that the only tasks that need to be done are the ones you want to complete. He looked over at the still-sleeping form of his lover. The morning sun was sneaking in through the half-closed curtains, and a beam of light fell on the soft, blond head on the pillow beside him. Unable to resist, he reached up and ran his hand through the soft waves, brushing the floppy fringe off Jamie's face.

Jamie's eyes opened slowly, and he smiled. "Good morning."

"Hi." Declan continued to stroke back the hair on Jamie's head. "You're so beautiful when you're sleeping." He leant forward to place a soft kiss on his lover's forehead. "But you're even more beautiful when you're awake."

Jamie moved, placing his head on his lover's shoulder as Declan's arm came around to embrace him fully. He placed a hand on Declan's chest, reassured as always to feel the strong, steady beat of his heart. "I love you."

"I know. I love you too." Declan kissed the top of Jamie's head and pulled him closer into his embrace. "And I know it's not because what we have isn't enough."

Jamie sat up quickly and looked into the face of his soul-mate. "How do you always know what I'm about to say?"

Declan laughed and pulled his lover back into his arms. "Ten years, buddy. It's a long time. Long enough to get to know all your little nuances. And this time? I was going to say it too."

"Do you think she'd be interested?"

"I have no idea. She got seriously turned on when you and I were making out."

"You noticed that too, huh?" Jamie began to draw lazy circles on Declan's belly with the tip of his finger. "She made me think of … no, it doesn't matter."

"It's okay; I want to talk about her too."

Jamie and Declan had been lovers for about a year when they met Jenni. She knew that they were committed to each other and she had pursued them both equally. They both fell in love with her. The three of them were an inseparable unit for a while. They would make love together, spending each night in the king-size bed they had brought into the apartment they shared. They made a commitment to each other, wearing matching rings and going everywhere together as a 'triple'.

They adored her. She was smart and funny, and she didn't give a shit about what anyone thought of their unconventional way of life. Except for her family, that is; as far as they were concerned, she was Declan's girlfriend, and Jamie was Declan's best mate who happened to share their flat. But with their close friends, she was theirs, and they were hers. She would love them – separately or together – with all her mind and body, and they worshipped her curves and lush skin.

They lived together for nearly three years and, had fate not intervened; they probably would have stayed together forever. They talked about having children and decided that two (one fathered by each of them) would be the way to go. So, they tossed a coin and Jamie won. For the next six months, Declan wore a condom when he had sex with her.

When she didn't conceive, they all got tested. Both boys were totally fine, but Jenni's results revealed something else; she was ill. Very ill. She had ovarian cancer. Through all the chemo and radiotherapy, Jamie and Declan were right there with her. They tried to keep her positive, telling her their plans for the future; holidays they would take together and the fun things they would do. But the treatment had come too late, and the cancer had spread to the rest of her body.

One night, in her drugged state, she told her mother the truth about her relationship with her two lovers. Her family were horrified and closed ranks, refusing to allow Jamie and Declan to spend any of the last, precious hours of Jenni's life at her side, where they belonged. She died without their love surrounding her, and when they tried to attend the funeral a week or so later, they were turned away. Jenni's brother chased after them, calling them perverts. He went for Declan and Jamie tried to protect his lover; they both ended up with a black eye for their troubles.

They grieved for her for a very long time and agreed that any time spent with females from then on would be on a casual basis. Carrie was the first girl they took into their bed, a year after Jenni had gone. She was a mate – a fuck-buddy – they had a wonderful time together, but they weren't in love with her. There had been the occasional hook-up since then – temporary liaisons that scratched a necessary itch, but this was the first time they had both felt drawn to the same girl since Jenni. Were they ready to dip a toe into that pool again? Could they keep it casual, as they had with Carrie? Would Elsa even be interested in giving it a try?

"Hey, Declan." Carrie's voice was bright as always as she answered her phone after the first ring.

"Hey, Honey. It was really great to see you last night. Let's not leave it so long next time."

Carrie giggled down the line. "Agreed. I have a bit a hangover though."

"That would have been the Jaeger bombs." Declan tried to make his voice sound disapproving, but it wasn't working.

"Oh yeah? Well, if you hadn't been the designated driver, you would probably be in equally bad shape this morning." There's was a beat's silence, then Carrie's warm laugh came down the line again. "But you haven't phoned me to talk about drunken debauchery – you want Elsa's number."

Declan was so shocked by her correct guess that he nearly dropped his phone. When he'd got it back together, he tried to sound nonchalant about it. "Well, now that you mention it, we would quite like to get to know her a bit better."

"I knew you'd like her. If I'm honest, it's one of the reasons I invited her."

"Oh?" Declan wasn't quite sure how to take that. Did his friend think that his relationship with Jamie wasn't good enough?

Sensing that she may have touched a nerve, Carrie continued quickly. "I mean, she's just our sort of person, isn't she? I love her. She shares my sick sense of humour. And now that I'm off the market, so to speak, I thought you two might like another female friend."

"Oh – yeah. She's great." He tried not to sound too keen, though if he was honest, the thought of maybe being part of a triple again – even a temporary one – appealed to him. And he knew it appealed to Jamie too. "We both clicked with her."

"She really liked you two as well. And, for the record, if you two wanted to try being more than friends, I think she'd be interested in giving it a go."

"You told her? About us?"

Carrie knew that by 'us' Declan meant the three of them. They'd never really talked to anyone about that little arrangement before. She'd never told Pavel about it. "She guessed, so I told her how great it was."

"Oh. I don't know what to say. I mean – we were just going to get to know her a bit better – maybe see how it went – but if she thinks that's all we're interested in – well – I don't know."

"Shit," Carrie swore quietly down the phone. "I've fucked up, haven't I?"

"What? No – it's just ..."

"I'm sorry. Look – I'll text you her number. Meet her for coffee or something."

The coffee shop was pretty crowded, but Declan and Jamie had managed to snag a corner table. Jamie reached for his lover's hand and squeezed it reassuringly. "Don't worry – we're just going to have a coffee and chat."

Declan squeezed Jamie's hand in reply. "I know. I don't know why I'm feeling so nervous. I mean – she was lovely when we met her last week. And she clearly has no problem with us being together."

"I know. I'm as nervous as you are." Jamie looked at the handsome face of his partner and smiled. "And it doesn't really matter, does it? I love you, and that's never going to change." He was just thinking about going in for a quick kiss when a soft female voice came through the noise of the coffee shop.

"Hello – sorry I'm a bit late." Elsa was standing in front of their table, brushing raindrops from the sleeves of her jacket. "Can I get you two a refill?"

Both men looked up at smiled at their new friend. They stood and greeted her with a hug, then Declan indicated to the seat they had been saving for her. "No – please – sit down. I'll go. What can I get you?"

"Medium Americano please." She took off her damp jacket and draped it over the back of her chair before sitting down. "It's good to see you again. I was glad you phoned. But I've got to be honest; I'm really nervous."

Jamie smiled and blew out a relieved breath. "Me too. We were just talking about it before you came."

"So – is this a date? I don't know how this works." Her pretty face showed her uncertainty. "I haven't exactly done anything like this before."

Jamie reached over the table and took her hand. He hadn't meant to do anything like that so soon, but the connection he felt to this woman was so strong, he couldn't help it. "It's whatever we want it to be. And despite what Carrie might have told you, we don't make a habit of this either. But we both felt a connection with you last week."

Declan returned to the table with three steaming cups and a plate of cupcakes on a tray. "I wasn't sure if you wanted something to eat, but everything's better with chocolate, so dig in." He sat down and looked at his lover and their new friend. "What did I miss?"

Jamie took the cup of black coffee off the tray and put it in front of Elsa. "Not a lot. Elsa was just telling me she was a bit nervous about meeting us. And I was telling her that we were feeling the same."

Declan looked up, his eyes brightening as he smiled. "God, yes. And look – I know Carrie's told you some stuff about us – we're not deviants or anything – but we would like to get to know you a little better. We both felt that we clicked with you when we met."

"Yeah – me too. So, we can just spend some time getting to know each other?"

Both men answered together, "Absolutely."

Elsa felt herself relax a little bit. "Okay. Good. I really do like both of you, and I think we will get on well." She raised her coffee cup in a toast. "To new friends."

The two men echoed her, raising their cups and clicking them together with hers. Three hours, six cups of coffee, three toasted paninis and three more cupcakes later, the friendship was well on the way to becoming something special. Elsa seemed to fit into a gap that Declan and Jamie hadn't even realised was there. But by the time they had walked her to her bus and taken their own one home, there was no doubt in their minds about where they wanted this friendship to go.

"So, come on, where are they taking you tonight?" Carrie sat down next to Elsa's desk and put a cup of coffee down for her friend and co-worker. "You're wearing that silly grin again."

"I know! I can't help it." Elsa reached for the coffee and took a sip, enjoying the feeling of the strong brew slipping down her throat.

"It's going well, then?" Carrie had tried not to pry too much into what had been happening between Elsa and her two best friends for the past month, but the obvious joy the girl has been displaying over the last couple of weeks made it impossible to hold off anymore. "You look so happy lately."

Elsa nodded. "I am. We're having a great time."

Carrie raised her eyebrows and nodded, indicating that she wanted to know more. "Yeah?"

"Yeah. And you can stop fishing. Nothing has happened yet; we've just been getting to know each other and, having – well – fun. We've been having fun! It's weird, but I've loved every minute."

"Weird how?"

"I don't know. I mean, when you're dating a guy, it's all about making sure you look good and don't do anything stupid. I find all that really stressful."

Carrie nodded. "I know what you mean. It was such a relief when I got to the relaxed stage with Pavel. The first time I felt comfortable enough to fart in front of him was a real game changer."

Elsa laughed at her friend. "Well, we already reached that milestone!"

"You did?"

"Yeah! Mexican food. I overdid the refried beans." The two women looked at each other then laughed again. "I think I might be falling for them, Carrie."

"I think you might be too. And why not? They're the best."

"At first, I thought I might just want to be with Declan, you know? But now I get it."

"They come as a pair."

"I know. And I think I'm ready to accept that. And I feel the same way about both of them now."

Carrie finished her coffee and got up to leave. "I'm glad to hear that. I know that having you in their lives has made them both really happy. So – you never did answer my question – where are they taking you tonight?"

"They're not taking me anywhere. They're cooking me dinner at their place."

"Come in, my lady." Jamie bowed low as he opened the door to Elsa. He straightened and reached to hug her. "You look beautiful." He held her tight and inhaled deeply as his nose pushed into her soft fall of hair. "Mmmm … you smell beautiful too." When he pulled back from the embrace, his eyes were dark with excitement. This night was going to be a milestone for them.

"You look gorgeous too, Jamie." Elsa leant forward and kissed him lightly on the lips. They had begun to exchange these light touches over the past week or so. "Where's Declan?"

Jamie rolled his eyes. "He's doing a Gordon Ramsey in the kitchen. It's not safe to go in there right now."

"Don't listen to him, baby." Declan came into the living room, discarding an apron on the way, and enfolded Elsa in his arms. "So glad you're here." He kissed her softly then pulled away to look at his lover. "We're both glad you're here." He reached out to Jamie with one arm and pulled him into a three-way hug, before kissing him gently, licking at the seam of Jamie's lips. "My two favourite people in the world. I am truly blessed."

Elsa laughed at his dramatic proclamation. "Likewise. Now – something smells good – what's for dinner?"

Declan beamed with pride. "Oh, baby – I've cooked up a storm for you tonight."

He had, indeed, cooked up a storm. As Elsa put the last morsel of dessert into her mouth, she moaned with pleasure. "That was, without a doubt, the nicest meal I've had in a very long time."

Jamie grinned at her as he began to clear away some of the dishes. "He won't admit it, but he was working on that all afternoon." He dodged the napkin that Declan threw at him and walked towards the kitchen with both hands full of used crockery. "I'll put some coffee on. Why don't you stroke his culinary ego a little more while I'm gone?"

Elsa sat back in her chair and looked at the handsome guy who was sitting opposite her. "Where did you learn to cook?"

Declan leant forward and took her hand. "I don't want to talk about cooking." He lifted her hand to his lips and kissed the soft skin of her wrist.

"Oh?" Elsa tried not to sound too alarmed. The place where his mouth had touched her skin was tingling at the contact. "What do you want to talk about?"

Jamie came back into the room with a pot of coffee and cups on a tray. He sat down next to her and took her other hand, mirroring his lover's actions by kissing her wrist gently. "I think we want to talk to you about where we go from here." He looked at her, and his eyes were shining with emotion and dark with lust. There was no mistaking his intent.

Elsa tried to calm her breathing. "Okay. I think that is probably a good idea." She had no idea what to say to them. She wanted them both – had fallen for them both – but she didn't know how this worked. "I've not done anything like this before, so why don't you start by telling me what you'd like to happen."

The two men exchanged a look then Declan got up from his seat and led Elsa to the large sofa in their living room. Jamie followed, and the three of them sat down on the soft, red leather, Elsa in the centre. "Getting to know you over the past month has been amazing."

Jamie rested his head on her shoulder, breathing in her scent. "Yes. It really has. We love being with you, Elsa."

Declan stroked her cheek lovingly. "We both want you to be in our lives. And if all you can give us right now is friendship, then we'll take it – happily. But we want you to know that we want more." He looked over to his lover and nodded, asking Jamie to take over.

"Yes, baby. Our relationship is wonderful, but if you decide to be a part of it, it will be even more so. We've talked about this a lot over the last week or so. We want you to be a part of us. We have felt so much more complete with you in our lives."

Elsa took a deep breath and let it out slowly. "Wow. That was …"

"Honest." Declan kissed her lightly on the cheek. "It was honest. And that's what we'll always be with you, Elsa. That's a promise. So please be honest with us. If you don't want this, then say so, and we'll forget all about it."

Jamie chuckled. "Well, we may not be able to forget all about it. But we'll do our best. Whatever you want, Elsa. You're the one in control here."

Elsa needed some space from the two gorgeous men who were crowding her on the sofa, so she stood up quickly and turned to face them. "Right. Okay. Just give me a moment." She took a couple of breaths and then looked back to the pair who were now sitting together on the red leather a couple of feet in front of her. "I've been feeling the same." When they smiled and made a move to get up, she held up her hand to tell them to stay put until she had finished saying what she needed to say. "I haven't had that much experience with men. I mean – I've had boyfriends, but nothing's ever lasted very long, and I've never felt so comfortable with a man as I feel with you two. I keep telling myself that it's wrong to want both of you." Again, she held up her hand to stop any interruptions from the men. "But I don't think anything that feels this … this great is anything to run away from. But I'm all at sea, here. I have no idea what I'm doing. I'm going to have to trust you not to hurt me."

Nobody said anything for a few moments, then Declan and Jamie got up, moving together to stand either side of Elsa. Declan pulled her against him; her back flush with his chest as he bent his head to kiss the skin on the side of her neck. "You can trust us, Elsa."

Jamie closed the gap, and now she was sandwiched between them in an embrace so warm and loving that she could hardly breathe with it. His lips found hers, and he kissed her, starting with a slow, gentle pulling on her lower lip before increasing the pressure and slipping his soft, wet tongue into her mouth. Against her back, she could feel the evidence of Declan's arousal pressing into her bottom. As Jamie pressed further into her embrace, she felt his cock pressing against her belly. When he broke the kiss and looked at her, she let out a shuddering breath. "Oh boy."

Declan reached around and cupped her breast gently, rubbing his thumb over her hardening nipple through the thin layers of her dress and bra. "Tell us what you want, Elsa."

She turned around and captured Declan's mouth with hers, kissing him passionately. "I want to take this slowly. And I want to start by watching you two."

Jamie raised an eyebrow and smiled at his lover. "Really? You want to watch the two of us getting it on?" He looked at Elsa's face and watched her pupils dilate. "Oh yeah – you do. Well, you're calling the shots tonight, so your wish is our command."

The three of them left the living room and walked to the bedroom, which was lit with the soft glow of lamps. Elsa noted the huge bed that took up most of the room, but she wasn't nervous; far from it. She trusted them. And she wanted them. She realised suddenly that this felt more right than any of the small number of experiences she had had with her previous boyfriends. She felt a deep connection with these men. A connection that she knew they felt too. She watched as Declan pulled Jamie's shirt over his head then claimed his mouth in a raw kiss. Declan's shirt went the same way, and pretty soon they were both naked, kissing and caressing each other in a way that spoke of love and familiarity. These two had been together for a long time, and they knew each other's bodies and needs as well as they knew their own.

Declan looked over to where Elsa was standing by the bedroom door. "Come closer." He held out his hand, and Jamie turned to look at her as well.

Elsa stepped forward and touched Declan's outstretched hand. She looked at the naked bodies of the two men in front of her, and she felt an undeniable clench of desire in her belly. Her pussy was already watering at the sight of them together and the possibility of becoming part of the erotic scene. She was pulled into their embrace by Jamie who pressed his mouth to hers, groaning as he tasted her.

Declan began to undress her, easing the zip of her dress down so that he could push the soft fabric off her shoulders. It fell softly at her feet, and she stepped out of it. Declan picked it up and laid it carefully on the back of a chair, then returned to remove her shoes and the rest of her clothes. When she was naked, both men stood still and looked at her. She didn't feel self-conscious or ashamed as their combined gaze swept over her body from head to foot. This felt right; like something slotting into place.

Jamie tugged her towards the bed. "I know you said you wanted to watch us – and you will – many times – but I think I can speak for both of us now when I say we want to make love to you. We want you to be the centre of attention."

Declan nodded and walked to the other side of the bed, holding out his arms to encourage her to climb onto the centre of the mattress. "Yes. Let us love you, Elsa. We've been waiting a long time."

Elsa looked between her two guys – yes, they were her guys. Their cocks were hard, pressed against their tight bellies, and their skin was sheened with sweat. They looked very similar; a small patch of hair covering their pecs and a soft line of it ran down well-defined abdomens to a trimmed patch of hair that crowned their now-straining erections. The only difference was the colour; Declan's hair was dark as the hair on his head, but Jamie's was golden brown. "You're both so beautiful." She breathed it out and took in a shaky breath. "I can't believe I'm here. I can't believe I'm about to do this." She put one knee on the mattress, followed by the other, and made her way slowly to the centre of the enormous bed. Two pairs of very willing hands arranged pillows behind her head, and she lay down, sinking happily into the soft fabric.

"Relax, baby. Let us take care of you." Jamie's voice was a gentle purr against the skin of her neck.

She shook her head. "No – we take care of each other." She reached down and took one, glorious cock in each hand, caressing lightly.

Declan and Jamie groaned in unison and moved closer to her. Declan's mouth sought hers, and the kiss was searing; He seemed to brand her with it, fusing them together until her lips were swollen and tingling. Jamie latched onto one of her nipples, and he began to suckle with hard pulls that echoed deep in her pussy. Her hips moved involuntarily, and she groaned into Declan's mouth, squirming as their combined attention increased her arousal to an almost painful level.

Declan moved to take possession of her other nipple, pulling it into his mouth and licking around the areola with his tongue.

Jamie moved down her body, kissing his way south along her midline. He stopped to tongue her navel then continued further, moving so that he was kneeling between her legs. "You have no idea how much I've been thinking about tasting you." He dipped his head and ran his tongue along the seam of her pussy. The outer lips parted for him, and he pushed in further, licking the sensitive flesh of her opening. "God, you're so wet for us." He looked up to Declan and licked his lips. "She's glorious. She wants us." He continued to kiss her, paying attention to her upper thighs and the crease where her legs met her body. Then he pushed two fingers into her wetness, stroking across her clit with his thumb. "Does it ache, baby?"

Elsa could only groan into Declan's mouth as he kissed her, but she ground herself against Jamie's hand to encourage him to continue his exploration of her flesh. A thought flashed into her mind, chastising her for her wantonness. But the pleasure she was receiving from the man at her mouth and the other one at her pussy chased the fleeting thoughts away and replaced them with a relaxed acceptance of the luxurious experience.

Jamie felt the first, tiny spasms in Elsa's pussy; she was close. "That's it, baby. Relax and let us make you come." He continued to stroke her insides with his fingers, curling them up to stroke the sensitive spot against her pubic bone. "She's close." He looked up at Declan and smiled. "I'm going to make her come then I'm going to fuck her." He dipped his head again and latched onto her throbbing clit.

Elsa felt the hot connection of Jamie's mouth on her erect little bud, and it was enough to knock her over the edge. Her back arched and her mouth pulled away from Declan's kiss as her head pushed back into the pillows to let out a howl of release. As her orgasm washed over her, she could feel Jamie's fingers still stroking at her internal muscles, teasing even more sensation from her, and it seemed to go on and on, rolling through her like a tidal wave. When her body ceased thrashing, and she was able to draw a semi-normal breath into her lungs, she looked up into a pair of adoring eyes.

"You okay, there, baby?" Declan was grinning down at her, stroking the hair off her face where her thrashing had left it.

Elsa nodded and looked down her body to where Jamie was stroking her skin. His fingers were still embedded deep inside her channel, and he was smiling at her; his eyes twinkled with mischievousness. Leaning over to where Declan's hip rested against Elsa's he opened his lips and took his lover's cock deep into his mouth.

Declan groaned, rolling his hips so that Jamie could take him to the root. He turned to Elsa and claimed her mouth again, kissing her deeply while thrusting his cock into the mouth he knew and loved so well.

Jamie pulled his fingers from Elsa's wet hole and gathered up some of the fluid she had made to ease his way. He pushed Declan's legs apart and spread the lubrication onto the tight little gate that marked the entrance to his body. As he continued to suck Declan's cock, Jamie eased his fingertip into the hole, which relaxed and gave him entry. He eased in a second finger and pressed on through the tight ring of muscle.

Declan felt Jamie breach his ass and nearly spurted into his mouth. He loved having Jamie inside him; either his fingers or his cock. Their joining was more than physical. It represented how they each completed the other. And now there was another person to join with; to complete them. He felt Elsa's kiss become more urgent and knew that she needed something more. He broke away from her mouth and gasped as Jamie licked the underside of his cock and probed his prostate with his clever fingers. "Jamie, I think our girl needs more. You said you were going to fuck her. I think she wants that." He looked down at Elsa and asked the question with his eyes.

"Yes." It was whispered and shaky. "Yes. I need …"

Jamie released Declan's cock, taking one last lick of the trail of pre-cum that was leaking from it. He withdrew his fingers slowly, giving the stretched hole time to adjust to the loss. He reached over to the nightstand and took out a box of condoms and a bottle of lube. He took two condoms from the pack and gave one to Declan before ripping open the packet of his own and rolling the condom onto his length. He looked up at Elsa's beautiful face and reached to cup her cheek. "Are you sure? Once we do this, there's no going back. You're ours."

Elsa had never wanted anything so badly. Her insides were still twitching and churning from the orgasm that Jamie had given her with his fingers and tongue, but she felt so empty. She needed one of them to fill her, and the hunger was so acute that she could feel it flowing through her veins. "Yes, I'm sure. Please."

Jamie moved up her body so that he could kiss her mouth. There was no mistaking what he intended to do to her. Then he moved over to kiss Declan, who accepted his mouth and tongue with a groan. When the two men broke their kiss, Declan returned his attention to Elsa, locking his lips onto hers and pushing his tongue deep into her mouth.

Jamie positioned himself between her legs and pushed the tip of his cock into Elsa's wet opening. "God … you feel so …" He held himself there for a moment, then pushed on, filling her with himself so completely that it took his breath away. "Oh! Elsa." He rocked his hips, withdrawing a little before thrusting back into her hot depths. "Fuck … you're so deep."

Elsa felt Jamie's cock push into her, stretching her out to accommodate him. Once he was seated in her, he started to suckle on one of her nipples as Declan continued to kiss her mouth. Her brain was in danger of running into overdrive as the sensations of being loved by two, beautiful men at once overwhelmed her. She heard a strange whimpering sound and realised it was coming from her own throat. She lifted her legs and tried to wrap them around Jamie's waist, but they were shaking too much, so she just let them spread out on the bed beneath him.

Jamie felt Elsa try to lift her legs and smiled around her nipple where he was sucking her. Releasing her hardened bud with a soft pop, he blew on her heated skin, making her shiver. "It's okay, baby. Just let us take care of you." He looked up to where Declan was pushing his tongue as deep into Elsa's mouth as he could. "Your turn. Suit up." He picked up the unopened condom and tore it open with his teeth. He rolled it onto Declan's cock, thrilling at its hardness and the way he rolled into the caress.

Elsa felt Jamie withdraw from her body and made a quiet sound of protest.

Declan moved to take Jamie's place between her thighs and looked down at her body. "Look at you. You're ours now." He leant over and kissed Jamie where he knelt beside them. "I want you to put my cock inside her. Then, when I'm fucking her, I want you to fuck me."

The two men kissed again, then Jamie reached over and took Declan's cock in his hand. He guided it to its target. "She feels like heaven. And she's all ours." Jamie made sure his lover's cock was positioned at the opening to Elsa's sheath; then he pushed his hips to aid the penetration.

Declan felt Elsa's internal muscles welcome him and he groaned before latching his mouth onto the skin at the side of her neck. "Oh, god … Elsa … I've wanted this for so long." He began to thrust into her heat, glorying in the sensation of her clenching hole. Then he felt the cold glide of lube where Jamie was spreading it on his ass. He was still open and ready from where Jamie had fingered him earlier, and he felt his hole flex with anticipation. He loved being fucked by his lover. When Jamie's cock was buried in his hole, the three of them would be joined together. The deep symbolism and meaning of this first experience filled him with awe, and he looked back to watch Jamie's face as he penetrated the offered hole.

Elsa felt Declan's cock filling her every bit as well as Jamie's had. The two men were matched in size, and they had both stretched her. She would feel this for a long time; the idea of that was thrilling. She watched Declan as he looked back to see what Jamie was doing. She knew the moment he was penetrated because he stilled within her, then his head fell forward onto her breast, and he shuddered within her. Then the two men began to rock in unison and the wholly erotic nature of what they were doing made her spine tingle.

Declan kissed Elsa's neck and moved deeply within her. "Baby, I'm going to come soon. I can't last long when Jamie's cock is so deep in my ass. Please - are you close? I want us to come together."

"I am." Elsa could feel that familiar sensation; the one that told her she was climbing towards the goal of orgasm. "Oh Declan, Jamie; this is so good. I never knew it could be this good." She reached out both of her hands. Jamie grasped one, threading his fingers through hers, and Declan took the other, sealing their palms together in a hot, sweaty clasp. The three of them rocked together for a few minutes more, then she felt her climax begin.

Jamie felt his lover's hole begin to clench around his cock as the first spasms of his orgasm began. He looked down and watched as Elsa's face contorted with pleasure, her mouth opening wide so that she could drag air into her lungs. Her orgasm acted as the trigger; as her pussy clenched around Declan's cock, he came with a shout, the internal muscles of his ass clenching to milk Jamie's cock. Like a chain reaction, the three of them came moments after each other, then when it was over, they fell to their sides, still joined together, still gasping for breath, still one.

Elsa woke up slowly. Birds were singing, and there was a soft light coming through the gap between the curtains. She was wrapped in two sets of muscular male arms; one holding her from behind and one cradling her head on a warm chest. As her eyes became accustomed to the light, she could see that the hair on the chest that was acting as her pillow was golden. "Jamie."

"Yes, baby? Are you finally awake?"

"I think so, yes." She shifted a little and felt an erect cock pushing into her hip where Declan pressed himself against her body. She reached back and wrapped her hand around the solid column, squeezing in welcome. "Morning Declan."

The man behind her pulled himself closer to her, his hand coming up to stroke the skin of her breast in slow circles. "Good morning Elsa. How are you feeling?"

Elsa wriggled a little. A large amount of the moisture she had created was still sliding on the skin of her inner thighs, and there was a pleasant, though very definite ache between her legs. She had been wonderfully and thoroughly fucked. "I feel good. A little sore, maybe, but very good."

Jamie tucked his arm around her more tightly and kissed the top of her head. "Too sore for a little more?"

"I didn't say that. But can we maybe have some breakfast first?"

"Absolutely."

The three of them climbed out of bed, and Elsa walked towards the shower. "I really need to pee and get clean – so no following me in here, okay?" She heard the two men laugh as she closed the door on the small bathroom. She was finishing drying herself off when there was a knock at the door.

Declan's voice was warm and soothing. "There's a robe on the bed for you – and there's a brand-new toothbrush in the cabinet over the sink. Breakfast is ready when you are."

Elsa found the robe; a deep red, satin wrap that was embroidered with a dragon on the back. The label on the robe and the receipt that was with it in the bag told her that it had been purchased just two days ago. So – they had bought it especially for her. And she loved it. She walked out into the kitchen, her bare feet making no footfall. Her lovers didn't hear her approach, and she stood for a moment, watching them kiss and exchange words of love.

"I've fallen for her." Declan stroked his lover's face and pushed the shower-damp hair off his forehead. "I think I'm in love with her."

Jamie kissed Declan softly on the mouth. "I know. I feel it too. She's perfect for us."

"What if she doesn't want it? What if she decides that last night was a fun experience, but that's all she wants? I know we've only known her a month, but she's part of me now – part of you – part of us."

Jamie pulled Declan into his arms and hugged him tightly. "Then we'll carry on as before. It won't be easy, but I love you and you love me."

"And we both love her." They looked at each other for a moment, still unaware that she was in the kitchen with them.

Elsa's heart felt like it was going to burst when she heard them declare their feelings for her and for each other. They were a pair – as close as it's possible to be – and if she was going to be in a relationship with them, then it was going to be with both of them equally. A few weeks ago, her mind might have objected to the unconventional arrangement, but looking at the two men who had loved her so thoroughly last night, both her heart and her mind agreed on what she wanted. "And I love you too – both of you."

The two men looked up at the sound of her voice, and their faces changed from serious intensity to pure relief. Jamie held out his arms for her, "Hey, there she is. You look good in that robe!"

"I love it. Thank you for buying it for me."

"You're welcome." Declan pulled her into their joint embrace. "So – you heard what we were saying?"

"I did. And I'm in. This is right – whatever this is – and I'm not going to throw away something so good because a few people might raise an eyebrow. I don't care what anyone else thinks. What we shared last night was a revelation."

"Good." Jamie went back to tending the pan that held bacon and eggs. "I'm glad we're on the same page."

When the food had been eaten, and the coffee had been drunk, Elsa started to put the dishes in the dishwasher. "So – what I want to know is, how did you two get together?"

Declan put his arms around her from behind, pulling her ass into his groin so she could feel his burgeoning erection. "Oh, that's a story we definitely want to tell you. In bed. Come on." He took her hand and led her back to the bedroom, stripping her out of her robe and himself from the shorts and tee-shirt he had been wearing. Jamie joined them and stripped quickly, and they both pulled her back to the bed that they had shared so freely last night. When Elsa was comfortable between them, held tight between two, hot bodies, Declan sighed and kissed her hair. "You can blame that one. I was totally straight before he started wandering around our room naked. The sight of his gorgeous cock converted me."

Jamie laughed and reached over to stroke Declan's cock. "I never felt the need to flash my junk until I got sight of this beauty."

Elsa tried to look at both of them. "Seriously? You mean you were heterosexual before you met each other?"

"I guess not." Declan leant into his lover's caress. "I know it doesn't work like that. I must have always been bisexual, but it wasn't until I met Jamie that I realised it. After a couple of months of seeing him in his birthday suit, I just couldn't deny what I was feeling anymore."

Elsa turned to Jamie. "What about you? Had you ever had any feelings for another guy before Declan?"

"Not really. I mean – I'd watched some gay porn and got turned on by it – but doesn't everyone do that? I'd never done anything about it, and I knew I loved pussy well enough." He reached down to caress Elsa's pubic mound to reinforce what he was saying. "But I don't know – I just fell in love with the guy – what more can I say? And I suspected that he felt something for me, so I started to walk around in the buff – you know – display the wares, so to speak."

"So, who made the first move?"

Declan laughed, and the vibration of it travelled through all three of them. "Well – this one ignored the sock on the door and burst in on me fucking Lucy Tremaine."

"How many times do I have to say it – there was no sock on the door!"

"Whatever, anyway, the moment was kind of ruined, and she left in a hurry, leaving me with a hard-on and a serious case of the pissed-offs."

"What happened next?"

Jamie moved against Elsa, grinding his now erect cock into the flesh of her hip. "Well, there he was, all naked and gorgeous. He was so angry with me – it turned me on like a switch. I pulled off all my clothes, and he just watched me. I looked at him, and I knew I had him. I was so desperate to taste that cock of his; I jumped on him like a starving man."

Declan moved one leg so that it was between Elsa's, pushing them apart enough so he could get his fingers between the moist lips of her pussy. "He sucked me off, and I came down his throat like a steam train. We never looked back after that. We sucked each other every day for months; I'd never come so often inside another human being. It was incredible."

"When did you start fucking each other?"

Jamie laughed and stroked Elsa's face. "I'd been playing about with a dildo, so I knew I liked taking it in the butt. I begged him to fuck me. Then I begged him to let me fuck him. It didn't take us very long to realise that we could fuck as often as we liked. And we did. We even missed an exam because we were too busy fucking."

"Really? Wow." Elsa snuggled into their combined embrace a little more. "So, has it always been equal with that? Or does one of you … you know."

"You mean, is one of us the bottom more often?" Jamie nuzzled the hair that was curling into Elsa's neck. "No. We flip-flopped almost from the start. We both love to take cock."

"Have you always been together, or have you … you know?"

"Have we ever fucked any other guys?"

"Yeah – I guess that's what I want to know."

Declan pushed her over onto her back and began to suck on her nipple. "No. Jamie sucked off a guy once as a dare, but we've only ever had man on man sex with each other."

"A dare?"

Jamie chuckled. "Yeah. Wayne Harries – total jerk – total hunk of a jerk – found out that we'd been playing around and started calling us gay and fags. I dared him not to come if I sucked him off. He couldn't resist a dare, and he was so sure that he wouldn't even get hard. I wrapped my lips around his dick, and he got hard and came down my throat in less than five minutes flat."

Declan was rubbing insistently at Elsa's clit now. "We have shared a girl before."

"I know – Carrie told me."

"Not Carrie." Jamie kissed her neck again. "We did have sex with her quite a bit, but before that, we both fell in love with a girl called Jenni. We would have stayed together forever, I think, but she was taken from us."

Elsa sat up and looked at her two lovers. "I'm sorry. I didn't know."

"Why would you?" Declan lifted his arms and pulled her back into their joint embrace. "We both felt a connection to you – just like we did to Jenni – that first night we met in the Dick Whittington. Please say you'll give this a try – the three of us?"

"Yes. I've never felt like this about anyone – and you're like one person – I can't separate you in my head. When I'm with you, I'm with one person. One person who happens to have two of everything." She laughed as she said this and reached down to take a cock in each hand. "I just wish there was some way to have you both in me at the same time."

Jamie rolled his hips against her ass. "Oh, baby. There is. There are three ways, in fact."

"Really? Okay – I know I'm naive, and I can think of maybe two ways, but what's the third?"

Declan pushed her onto her back and rubbed the head of his cock up and down the wet slit of her pussy. "What are the two ways you think you know about?" He was teasing her, and she loved it.

"Well," she panted as the tip of Declan's cock rubbed against her clitoris, "I could have one of you in my pussy and one in my mouth."

"Yes. I like the sound of that." Jamie was rubbing himself against her hip as he began to suck her nipple. "What's the second way?"

"I could have one of you in my pussy and one of you in – you know – but I've never done that before, so I'm going to have to work up to that."

"One in the pink and one in the …" Jamie put his hand between Elsa's legs and pressed a finger against the tight hole of her anus. "We'll definitely be working up to that. We'll make it good for you – I promise. It hurts a bit at first, but once you get used to it, it's good."

Elsa wriggled against Jamie's finger, enjoying the illicit feeling of being touched there for the first time. "So, what's the third way?"

"Declan kissed her lips softly. "Well, going by how tight you felt last night, we're going to have to work our way up to that one as well."

Elsa's eyes flew open as she realised what he was saying. "What? Really? Both of you? At the same time?"

Declan laughed at her innocent reaction and stilled her with another kiss. "God, you're adorable." He went back to stroking her pussy with the head of his cock. "You can stretch here to give birth to a baby – I think you can probably take both of us together without too much trouble." He sucked her other nipple and groaned against her skin. "I'm aching for you, baby. Can I have the pleasure of fucking your beautiful, tight little pussy again?"

Over the course of the months that followed, Elsa did indeed 'work up' to taking both of them at the same time. Her first experience of anal sex persuaded her that the pleasure was well worth the small amount of discomfort, and when she was finally able to take both of them in her pussy, the experience was a revelation for all three of them. Their love for each other grew stronger and more tangible. Sometimes, the boys would make love to each other without her. Sometimes, she would make love with one of them only. But they always ended up in the same bed, sleeping together as a tight unit, joined as closely as peas in a pod.

On Christmas morning, they gave each other matching rings. It was a commitment they had all known was coming. They couldn't live without each other. When Carrie and Pavel arrived for Christmas lunch, they showed off their new jewellery to their friends, and the news was greeted with hugs and words of congratulations. Their true friends understood and were happy. And everyone else? As Jamie said so beautifully when he told Declan and Elsa daily that he loved them, "Here in this place, it's us three and nothing else matters. This is our own little piece of heaven. And the rest of the world can go to hell."

♎

Libra

Balance, justice, truth, beauty, perfection
Libra follows the story of two characters from my novel, 37 Songs.

I've known Christie all my life. She is the daughter of one of my parents' closest friends; her father was my dad's best mate at college, and they stayed close until Chris died before Christie was born. She is eight years older than me, but that never really mattered.

I remember the day she left for college. She looked so excited about the adventure she was about to have, and I thought she was beautiful then. Even my ten-year-old self recognised that this girl was always going to be an important part of my life. She had been there from the start; a friend and a co-conspirator.

I missed her when she was at college. Dad and I would visit her occasionally; St John's had been his college, so he liked to visit. And when she came home for the holidays, we would catch up with each other properly. I never felt like a little kid with her; she spoke to me like I was her peer as soon as I was old enough to hold a conversation.

I think the first time I realised that I loved her was when I was thirteen. She had graduated from Oxford and was going to study for a year in America. My grandfather is American; we never really had that much to do with him, but he helped Christie get the place at the college where he was Professor of Music. She came to our house to tell us the news, and I remember it like it happened yesterday. My first emotion was elation; she was so excited about it, I felt it too. Then the realisation hit; my Christie-bell was going to be out of the country for a whole year. I felt sick at the thought of not seeing her for so long. That was when I knew for sure.

We kept in touch that year. Social media and the odd Skype call. She came home for Christmas, and when she hugged me, I held on so tight, not wanting to let her go. The night before she went back to America, we had a gathering at our house. All my parents' friends and their kids were there. I noticed Christie slip out through the back door, so I followed her.

When she heard me, she turned around and smiled. "I just needed a bit of air. It was all getting a bit much in there."

I went to stand beside her; I was almost as tall as her now, and I put my arm around her shoulders. "I wish you didn't have to go, Christie-bell. I mean – I'm really glad for you, but I miss you so much."

"I know. I miss you too, Dominic." She pulled me into a tight hug. "You've always been my favourite member of 'the herd'. You know, mum reckons I'm going to fall in love with you someday." She laughed, dismissing the idea.

I laughed too, but I remember the feeling in my belly when she said that; something like the feeling you get just before you go over the edge on a roller coaster. "Really? Well ... I think I can get on board with that."

She looked at me a little askance. "Why's that?"

I thought about my answer for a moment. "You'll just laugh at me because I'm only a kid."

She looked serious for a moment. "I've never laughed at you – or treated you like a kid, have I?"

"No."

"So, tell me."

"Okay." I took a deep breath, and that roller coaster feeling returned. "If you do fall in love with me, we'll be in love with each other," I remember feeling the heat on my cheeks in the cold air as I blushed with embarrassment. My fourteen-year-old, hormone-filled body reacted to her of its own accord.

She didn't laugh at me. She just smiled and hugged me again. We went back inside, and it was time to say 'goodbye'. She left for America the next day, and she's been there for the last six years.

Growing up in the Quinn household was an interesting experience. My parents, Nick and Jess are, you might say, a little unconventional. On the surface, my dad seems pretty normal. He runs a choir that my mum sings in, and he plays the organ at our local church. He knows all about really old music; he tried to get me interested in it, and I used to sing in the church choir when I was younger, but I stopped when my voice broke. He was disappointed when I gave it up – people used to call me mini-me because I look so much like my dad. I have his red hair (mum calls it strawberry blonde), and I've also inherited his heterochromia; I have one green eye and one brown one.

When I was about eight, I was playing in my parents' room. I wasn't supposed to be in there; it was the only place in the house that was out of bounds to me and my sister, Lizzie. Of course, that meant it was the only place in the house we really wanted to be. I was digging around in the bottom of the wardrobe when I came across a large bag. It was heavy, and it clanked when I picked it up. Inside was all kinds of weird stuff that I hadn't got a clue about. Some of it looked a bit like things I'd seen on a school trip to the London Dungeon, and I had no idea why mum and dad would have any of that kind of thing in their bedroom.

Of course, I know now that my parents are into some seriously kinky shit. Throughout our childhood, Lizzie and I would go to stay with one of our extended families the first weekend of every month. After I had realised what was in the bag, I worked out why.

A few months after Christie had gone back to The States, I asked a girl at school out on a date. She was a year younger than me, pretty and smart; her name was Megan. She became a sort of replacement Christie for a while. We would hang out at either her house or mine. Watch TV, play Xbox and fool around. We went out together until I went to college and we're still friends. She studied Medicine at Manchester, and I followed my dad (and Christie) to Oxford. I didn't study music, though. I may look like my dad, but I have my mum's brain; I'm reading Maths at Magdalen. I'd just finished my second year, and I was getting ready to go home for the summer.

I was about to leave my room to walk to my job at The Coffee Shack when my phone rang. I looked at the screen to see who it was because almost no-one called me – we all used text messages. It wasn't a number I recognised, and I thought about not answering, but as it started to ring for the second time, I swiped to accept the call. "Hello?" I could hear something that sounded like sniffling on the other end. "Hello? Who is this?"

"Dominic? It's me."

Christie's voice flowed into my brain, and that old, familiar, roller coaster feeling came back with a rush of adrenaline. "Christie? I didn't recognise your number. Are you okay? You sound upset."

More sniffling. She was crying.

"My god – Christie-bell – what's the matter?"

"You haven't called me that in ages."

"You'll always be my Christie-bell. Where are you? Why are you crying?"

I heard her take a deep breath. "I'm alright. I'm just a bit upset. I'm coming home. I'm at Heathrow. Can you come and get me? I know it's a lot to ask, but mum and Andrew are on holiday, and I didn't know who else to call." She started to cry again, and some primitive part of me responded to the sound; I had to take care of her. I arranged for a friend to cover my shift at The Coffee Shack and I drove to Heathrow as fast as my little one-litre car could take me.

I saw her standing at the pick-up point for Terminal Three. Her shoulders were hunched, and she looked dejected; deflated somehow. As I got closer to her, I called out her name, and she looked up. My heart leapt as I saw her face, for real, not on a computer screen, for the first time in six years. She was as beautiful as ever. I watched her eyes fill with tears as she saw me and I ran the rest of the way. I put my arms around her and held on. She smelled the same as she always did and my heart began to thump in my chest as I inhaled her scent. It smelled like home to me.

She pulled out of my arms far enough to look up at me. "You're taller than me!"

"Well, that's got to be the greeting of the century." I laughed and hugged her again. Christie is tall for a woman – she follows her father for that – but in the last couple of years, I had got some tall genes from somewhere, and now I had overtaken her by about four inches. It felt good to hold her now; like a man, not a boy with a childish crush.

Six years we had been apart. Six years of emails, social media and occasional Skype calls. Six years of me being with Megan and a couple of others in Oxford. Christie was living with a guy in Washington DC where she was working as a music publicist. But none of that seemed to matter at that moment. She was home, and in my arms.

She didn't speak much on the journey back to Oxford. When I got onto the motorway, she reached over and took my hand in hers, curling her fingers through mine, and I felt my chest bloom with pride that she wanted to hold my hand.

I wasn't due to go home for a couple of days, so I took her back to my room. I put her suitcase down just inside the door; it was big and very heavy. "You've brought a lot of stuff. How long are you staying?"

"I'm not going back." Her answer was short and sad. "I fucked up over there, Dominic. I had to come home."

I made her a mug of tea and sat next to her on my bed. "Do you want to tell me about it?"

"Can we get something to eat first? I'm starving."

I ordered pizza, and we ate it in silence, watching TV, propped up on the pillows of my narrow bed. It felt like old times, but it also felt like something completely new. I wasn't a little boy anymore, and I had no idea where I stood with her.

When we'd finished eating, she swung her legs over the side of the bed and stood up, turning to look at me. "So, yeah – I fucked up."

"How? I thought everything was going well over there?"

She looked sad again. "It was. I had a good job. My mistake was shacking up with the boss."

I hadn't known that her boyfriend was also her boss. I could have probably guessed the rest, but the question came out of my mouth before my tired brain had a chance to stop it. "What happened?"

"He wanted to get married, have kids, the whole white picket fence bollocks. I liked him, but I wasn't in love with him, so I told him I was happy the way things were. He threw me out of our apartment. The next day, when I got to work, my desk had been packed up, and I was told there was a problem with my visa."

"What? How can they do that?"

"I didn't ask the question. I just wanted to get out of there. I got the super to let me into our apartment so that I could pack up my stuff, then I got on the first flight out of there."

I had a feeling that there was probably more to it than that, but I didn't press her on it. I just stood up, put my arms around her, and let her cry; which she did for a very long time.

That night will live in my memory for the rest of my life because it was the first night that the girl I love slept in my arms. After she had cried herself to sleep, I pulled the covers over us and held her close on my single bed, listening to her steady breathing. I was hard for her; it kept me awake for a long time. She stirred a little when I kissed her forehead, but she soon fell back to sleep, clutching at the material of my shirt. At some point, I fell asleep too, and we slept like that, curled together under my duvet until a dead arm and the need to pee woke me up just before dawn.

"It was very kind of Dominic to pick you up from the airport and bring you home." Mum was hugging me on the doorstep of our family house. "You know, we would have come home if you'd phoned."

I hugged her back. "That is precisely why I didn't phone you. And yes – Dominic was wonderful. He always is."

Mum gave me a look I recognised. "Yes. You've always had that boy wrapped around your little finger." She laughed and went back to the car to help Andrew with the luggage.

My step-dad put the heaviest suitcase down just inside the door and put his arms around me for a hug. "Hi, Peanut. It's so good to see you. I'm glad you're home."

I screwed my nose up at his use of my childhood name. "Andrew, I'm twenty-eight."

Mum came in with the hand-luggage and kissed me lightly on the cheek. "You'll always be my little Peanut." My dad – my real dad – had called me that in a video diary he made just after he found out that mum was pregnant with me. It had stuck, so I was Peanut to the whole family.

I didn't mind, really. In fact, if I'm honest, it made me feel loved and secure; being part of my loving family again after so long away. "I don't know why I stayed away so long." It was said quietly, a comment to myself rather than anyone else.

But mum has the hearing of a bat. She hugged me again, so tightly that it took my breath away. "You're home now. That's all that matters."

I was expecting the grand inquisition; questions about why I had come back to the UK without any warning, but my wonderful parents must have sensed that I didn't want to talk about it. They didn't ask any difficult questions. Mum said she was ready to listen when I was ready to talk. I'd been home about four days when it happened; we'd just finished breakfast and Andrew had gone to my brother Gareth's house to help with some decorating. "Do you want to know why I'm here?"

Mum looked up from the newspaper she was reading. "I said I would listen when you wanted to talk."

"I want to talk."

She took off her reading specs and closed the newspaper. "Okay. I'm listening."

"Tyler wanted to get married. I said no, and he threw me out."

Mum nodded and smiled. "I had a feeling it was something along those lines."

"Did Dominic tell you?"

"No. He didn't. He didn't need to. You haven't mentioned Tyler once since you've been home and your phone has been pretty quiet, so

I'm guessing he hasn't been trying to get hold of you." She looked at me and reached across the table to touch my cheek. "You don't seem too unhappy about that."

I shook my head. "No. I'm not." I had been upset when Dominic picked me up from the airport, but it was nothing to do with Tyler. I was angry that the decision to leave hadn't been mine and I was sad about leaving my friends and the home I'd made there. I must have been aware of that, but it hadn't sunk in fully until I spoke the words to my mother. "I didn't love him." I thought about the man I had lived with for nearly three years. "I'm not even sure I particularly liked him, now I think about it." He was an obvious choice; good-looking, charismatic, confident. "He was … boring."

My mother laughed. "Well, you're my daughter – mine and Chris's. Boring was never going to cut it."

I knew what she was alluding to. When I was eighteen, mum had shown me dad's video diary and told me the truth about how he died. He was murdered by mum's ex (who happened to be a gangster), and the whole thing was caught on camera. She told me the truth about that too; the house was wired up with cameras for reasons I still couldn't bring myself to think about. Like most people, I knew that my parents had sex, I just didn't want to think about it. And I really didn't want to think about them having kinky, on-camera sex. "Mum – please!"

"Okay, okay." She held her hands up, palms toward me. "I just know that, if you're anything like me, you need someone a bit more interesting."

I'm not sure why, but at that moment, I thought about Dominic. I thought about the two nights I had spent in his bed; I was very aware that he wanted me; his boyhood crush had grown up with him. The second night, I woke up too hot from being squeezed into a tiny bed with another warm body. I tried to move away from him a little, but he groaned my name in his sleep and pulled me tighter into the circle of his arms. I felt his erection pressing against my bottom, the heat of it burning through his boxer shorts and my PJs. Something wicked flared in my sleepy mind, and I moved against him, rubbing my backside against his hard cock. He rocked into me, groaning my name again, and I was pretty sure he wasn't asleep anymore. We rocked together like that for several minutes, and his hand came around and down, seeking the moist heat between my legs. The first touch of his fingertips on me, even though it was through a layer of fabric, was electric. I pushed back harder against his cock, and he moved his hand, finding the elastic of my waistband and pushing it down, baring my skin to his touch. I heard a rustling then felt his naked body against mine; he'd pushed his shorts down, and now his naked cock was rubbing between my bare buttocks while his fingers stroked the wet flesh between my legs. I was in no doubt now that he was as fully awake as I was. He made me come with his fingers and, moments later, I felt him ejaculate on my ass. It was one of the most erotic things I'd ever experienced, but we didn't talk about it. The next day, he drove us both home, and we talked about everything – the weather, his holiday plans, the music on the radio, but we both pretended that our mutual masturbation session hadn't happened.

All through that day, I couldn't shake the memory of that encounter from my mind. I kept thinking about his fingers on my skin, his groans as he ground himself against me and my own, quiet gasps as he made me come. Mum went to work at about ten o'clock, and I was left alone in the house, which just made it worse. And, as I was thinking about it for the fourth or fifth time, my phone pinged with a text message from Dominic.

I'm working at The Slug through lunch. Off at 4.00 – do you fancy doing something later today?

Dominic was working at the local pub, The Slug and Lettuce. I thought about him getting all sweaty in the kitchen, and my imagination started to fire again. We had to talk about what had happened. I had to know what he was thinking. Yeah, that would be great. I'll pick you up just after 4.00.

I got to The Slug a little before four o'clock and sat in the carpark waiting for him. As I looked at the dashboard clock of mum's car for the tenth time in two minutes, my mind was racing with a mixture of excitement and doubt. What the hell was I thinking? I'd grown up with Dominic – he was like a little brother to me. And I'd just come out of a long relationship. I was using him; I knew about his crush on me, and I was taking advantage to make myself feel better. Then I saw him walk out of the staff entrance and all those thoughts cleared. The sun shone on his hair, and he looked like he'd been sprinkled with gold. He wasn't a boy anymore.

"Hey, Christie-bell. Thanks for coming to get me." He climbed into the passenger seat and reached across to hug me.

"You smell of chip fat." I wrinkled my nose as the smell of the pub kitchen assaulted my nostrils.

"I know – sorry. Take me home so I can have a shower. Then we can decide what to do from there."

I drove the short distance to his family home. I parked up behind Dominic's little car, and he got out and unlocked the front door. The house was hot and stuffy, and it was clear that there was nobody home. "Where's your mum and dad?"

"They're on holiday. We've got the place to ourselves. Make yourself comfy – I'd love a cup of tea if you fancy making one – and I'll go and have a quick shower."

She was downstairs, looking and smelling lovely. I turned the temperature of the shower down to almost freezing to try to get rid of my hard-on, but the memory of what we had done that last night in Oxford wouldn't go away. The moment I came on the hot skin of her ass I was lost. I'd started a hundred conversations about it in my mind; I just hadn't managed to say anything out loud. And the longer we didn't talk about it, the harder it was going to get. Not that I could actually get any harder. I sighed and started to rub my cock; I couldn't go downstairs with a huge erection. In my mind, I was sliding my dick in and out of Christie's sweet little cunt. She was moaning and begging me to fuck her.

Then my fantasy took a turn that was becoming familiar. I had her tied down, and she loved it. Her wrists were bound above her head, and her feet were tethered in a spreader as I ploughed into her and she was crying out my name, whimpering that she wanted to come and asking me for permission to do it. In my head, I heard her beg for it, and it tipped me over the edge. I spilt myself against the glass door of the shower enclosure, unable to stop the moans as my balls pulled up, and my cum hit the glass in six, hot spurts.

After washing away the evidence of my solitary climax, I dried off quickly and walked the short distance to my bedroom with a towel wrapped around my waist.

"Well, that sounded like you were having fun in there." Christie was sitting on my bed, sipping at a steaming mug of tea.

"Fuck! Christie – you made me nearly jump out of my skin. How long have you been sitting there?"

She grinned at me and looked down to where my cock was obviously stirring again, before looking back up to my face. "I brought your tea up about five minutes ago." She pointed to my bedside table and the mug she had brought for me. "Long enough to hear you having some quality alone-time in the shower."

I wasn't sure what kind of demon was riding me. I knew I should clutch the towel closer to my body, grab my clothes and go and get dressed in the bathroom. But I didn't do that. I looked directly at her and felt my body respond in its usual way; my cock stood to attention against my belly, and I grinned at her and dropped the towel. "Why didn't you come and join me. You know it's much better with two."

Her mouth opened in shock as she took in my naked body for the first time. "Dominic … I think we'd better talk about what happened in Oxford."

I walked towards her and stood directly in front of where she was sitting on my bed. My cock was virtually level with her face, and I reached over, cupping her cheek with my hand, stroking the soft skin with my thumb. "Yeah. I suppose so. I'll go first. I'm glad it happened, and I want it to happen again. I want more. I want you. I've always wanted you. You know that. So, the decision is yours. If you get up and walk away, I'll know you're not interested in exploring this thing between us."

She didn't get up and walk away. She looked up at me, and I watched her pupils dilate as she inhaled the scent of the pre-cum that was now oozing from my cock. What she did next took my breath away, and I'll never forget it. She leaned forward, took my cock in her hands and wrapped her lips around it, pulling the head into her mouth. She sucked at me and stroked the underside of my dick with her tongue, and my knees went weak.

I fisted her hair and pushed her further onto me, forcing her to take me to the back of her throat. "Yes! Do it, Christie – it's yours – do what you want with it." I tipped my head back and opened my mouth to try to breathe as the sensation of her hot mouth on my cock flooded through me.

She continued to suck me, hollowing her cheeks as she pulled me into her. When she began to roll my balls between her fingers, I knew I had to pull out, or I'd come down her throat.

"No. Not yet. Your turn." I flipped her onto the bed and pushed her little skirt up over her hips. She didn't resist me as I pulled her panties off and I couldn't miss the distinctive scent of her arousal. I took the damp lace underwear and wrapped it around her wrists. She looked shocked at first, then her face relaxed, and she let me bind her. "Hold your hands above your head and don't move them."

She lay back and put her bound hands over her head, holding onto the metal frame of my headboard. I heard her sigh as she arched her back and spread her thighs to me. She looked down her body and got eye contact with me as I climbed between her legs and pushed them further apart.

I held her gaze as I dipped my head and pressed my mouth to her hot centre. I swirled my tongue against her pussy and grinned when I found out how wet she was. After lapping softly at her for a few moments, I gave into the need to put my mouth on her properly. I'd only done this a couple of times before – and both times, the girl I was with had been embarrassed by it, trying to close her legs, but there was no embarrassment this time.

Christie groaned and spread her thighs as far as she could. "Yes – Dominic – I need it!" She was squirming, and she started to undulate her hips, driving the contact between us.

I put my hand on her belly and stopped the movement. "No. You'll take what I give you. Keep still." I put my mouth on her again and pushed my tongue into her hole. I felt her inner muscles clutch at me for a moment, then she relaxed and allowed me to invade her as deeply as I could. I reached up and pressed my fingers into the damp skin above where my nose was pressed against her. After stroking around for a few seconds, I found the hard, little bud of her clitoris. When I flicked it, her body jerked, and she cried out, so I knew I'd found it. I worked it back and forth, using her moisture as lubrication, while I continued to fuck her hot hole with my tongue.

I was going out of my mind with pleasure. The sensations that Dominic was creating with his tongue and his fingers were coursing through my mind and body, leaving me a gasping, helpless mess. "Oh god … Dominic … Please!"

He raised his head and looked up my body, meeting my gaze and holding it. He had a wicked gleam in his beautiful, odd eyes as he continued to torture my clit with his fingertips. "Please? Please, what? Tell me what you want, my love."

It was exhilarating. Tyler hadn't liked dirty talk and, although he loved it when I sucked his cock, he almost never returned the favour, even when I asked him to. But here was Dominic, eating me out and making appreciative sounds as though he was enjoying a gourmet meal. "I want you to make me come with your mouth. I like it."

"Good. I want you to look at me as you come. Scream my name. I want to hear you say it as I make you fall apart." He lowered his head and connected with my body again, pushing his tongue into me. But he didn't drop his gaze. All the while, those mesmerising eyes maintained contact with mine.

His tongue was deep inside me, stroking me, and his fingers were flicking and circling my clit in a maddening rhythm when I felt my climax begin. It spread out and consumed me. I felt my thighs press open as far as they could go as the pleasure washed over me, and I looked down to where Dominic was hunched between them. As the pleasure crested, I locked my gaze onto his and screamed his name. "Dominic! Oh, fuck! Yes – don't stop – please, don't stop!" I heard and felt him laugh against my skin; then he gripped my thighs hard as he coaxed the last of my climax from me.

I felt him move and watched as he got up onto his knees, looking down at me. His cock was rigid against his belly, and there was a steady line of clear fluid oozing from the narrow slit in the inflamed head. He held eye contact with me as he reached down and began to stroke himself, using his pre-cum as a lubricant. "I want to fuck you. But I don't have any condoms, so this will have to do. But be warned, Christie; as soon as I've rectified that situation, I am going to fuck you – over and over again."

There was something so incredibly erotic about what he was doing and what he was saying to me, I felt my body warming again, even though it was still coming down from the orgasm he had just torn from me with his mouth. I got up on my knees in front of him and put my bound hands over his where he was stroking himself. "I don't have a problem with that." I grinned at him and licked my lips, then I reached between my legs to scoop up some of the copious amount of moisture that was leaking from my pussy. Once my fingers were covered in it, I put them on his cock and began to rub it into the silky hot skin of his shaft. "Here – let me help you with that."

"Be my guest." He removed his hand and gripped my hips, pulling me closer to him. His eyes fixed on mine as I stroked him and he began to rock his hips into me as he thrust into my clenched fists. His breathing became laboured, and he began to moan, then he made one, last thrust through my slick hold and he came. His semen sprayed over my belly and dripped down into my pubic hair as he ground himself against me. He shouted my name and reached for my face, pulling me to him so that he could cover my mouth with his.

I tasted my musk on his lips, and I realised that it was our first kiss. We had performed oral sex on each other, and this was the second time we had made each other come, but until that moment, we hadn't kissed. Somehow, that felt oddly appropriate.

Christie was dozing in my arms, her face pressed against my chest, and her dark hair spread out over my arm like a heavy piece of silk. I'd kissed her. Why hadn't I kissed her before? We had done all kinds of things to each other, but I hadn't kissed her before. God, she felt right lying on me like that. My cock started to stir again as I remembered how she tasted and how it had felt when she came on my face. I couldn't wait for her to come on my cock too.

Then the niggling little voice started. *You know she's only using you, don't you? She's just having some fun with you to get over what-his-name. She sees you as more of a brother than anything else.* I giggled a bit at the last one; if she saw me as a brother and thought it was okay to wank me off, then we were in big trouble.

At the sound of my quiet laughter, she lifted her head and looked at me through a curtain of tangled hair. "What's so funny?"

There was no point in lying to her; she always could see right through me. "My inner monologue said something daft, so I was laughing at it."

"Huh?" She sat up and looked at me. She was still wearing her tee shirt, and her skirt was hiked up around her hips. "So, what did it say?"

"It said that this is probably just a distraction for you. That you see me as more of a brother than a lover."

She gave me an incredulous look, her eyebrows nearly meeting in the middle. "Well, if you think that I'd do what we just did with a brother, then we might need professional help."

"That's what I said."

"What?"

"Nothing. It doesn't matter." I pulled her back down to my chest and ran my fingers through her hair to get out some of the tangles. "But I think I do need to know something. We haven't really talked much about what's going on. And I think I need to know where I stand."

Christie sat up again and looked at me. "I think I know what you're going to ask, but go ahead."

I sat up too, my eyes met hers, and I felt that roller coaster feeling in my tummy. What if this was just a bit of fun for her? "You know how I feel about you?"

"I think so."

"I've been yours for as long as I can remember. I know I was just a kid, but I knew you were the girl for me – I just knew it."

"I know that." She smiled and stroked my cheek with her fingers.

I leant into her touch and kissed the palm of her hand. "But if this is all you can give me, then I'll take it." It cost me to say that. I didn't feel like that at all really. I wanted to yell at the top of my voice that if she left, it would break me. But I didn't. I didn't want to freak her out.

She looked serious, her face changing from the familiar, teasing grin to something I hadn't seen for a long time. She dropped her head so that her chin was almost resting on her chest and I watched her draw in a long breath then exhale it just as slowly. When she lifted her face again, she looked at me. "I love your eyes."

"What?" I wasn't expecting that. "Okay. Thank you. I love yours too."

"And you have grown into a beautiful young man."

"Again, thank you. I think you're beautiful too."

"I don't want to hurt you."

So, there it was. She was telling me that this was it. "I see. Well, thank you for being honest with me. Please tell me it's not going to be weird between us now. I couldn't bear it if we stopped being friends."

She smiled and took my hand. "I promise it isn't going to be weird."

But it kinda was. We didn't see that much of each other over the rest of the summer. She got a temporary job, and I was working a lot at the Slug. We texted a lot, and it felt the same, but I knew it wasn't. The night before I went back to Oxford, my parents had a party for all our friends. Christie came with her parents and Gareth.

My sister came too. Lizzie had always been able to read me like a book, and she never shied away from letting me know what she was thinking. She leant against the kitchen doorframe where I was standing, watching Christie. "Still got it bad, for her, huh? If you want my advice, you'll go back to Oxford, find a gorgeous girl of your own age and fuck her brains out."

"I don't want your advice, Lizzie, but thank you for that nugget of wisdom." I looked back over to where Christie had been standing, but she was gone. Then I felt a tap on my shoulder and looked over to see her standing right beside me. "Stealth moves – cute."

She smiled and stood on tiptoes to kiss me on the cheek. "Have a great year. I expect I'll see you at Christmas."

"You could always visit." I heard the desperation in my voice as I said it and kicked myself. "You know if you're not busy or anything."

"I'll bear that in mind."

At the end of September, I was offered a job in London as a publicist with a record company. Tyler had set up the interview, and I almost didn't go because of that, but I needed a job. He said he felt bad about the way things ended, and for some reason, that made me happy. The night before I was moving to the city, I sat in the kitchen drinking wine with my mum. Andrew was working a night shift, so we were on our own.

Mum refilled my glass and looked at me. "I'm a bit worried about you, love. You've been – I don't know – sad, all summer."

I didn't want to talk about it. "Yeah. I guess the whole thing with Tyler just caught up with me." I picked up my phone as it pinged to tell me there was a message. When I saw the name on the screen, I smiled involuntarily.

Hope moving day goes okay tomorrow

Thanks – I'll be glad when I'm there and settled in

When do you start your job?

Monday. How's uni?

Oh – you know – uni-ish. I miss you.

Mum tapped me on the sleeve. "Give Dominic my love."

"How did you know it was him?"

She raised an eyebrow and smiled. "I know it's him because he's the only one who inspires that particular look on your face."

"What? What look?"

She took a sip of her wine and studied my face for a moment. "The look that says you're really happy but deeply miserable at the same time. You've been sad all summer, Peanut. Do you want to talk about it? Is it Tyler?"

"No – it's not Tyler." I looked back down at my phone and signed off, telling him that my mum sent her love.

"Then it is Dominic." She blew out a breath and shifted in her seat. "Something clearly went on between you two not long after you came home. Do I want to know?"

I shook my head and looked at her. "Probably not. It was nothing. We … fooled around a bit is all."

"And, let me guess, he wanted more, but you didn't?" She looked for my reaction, but I didn't say anything – there was no need. "He's always been all about you, Christie – how could you lead the poor lad on like that?"

I felt tears start to burn behind my eyes. "I didn't mean to. And the thing is – oh mum – I think I might have really fucked it up. And it's making me miserable, because – oh bugger, I don't know!"

"I think you do." Mum put her arms around my shoulders and let me cry. "Follow your heart, Peanut. Just follow your heart."

The next morning, mum and I loaded my stuff into the back of her car; I was only taking clothes as the studio apartment I was renting was fully furnished. I hugged Andrew and my brother Gareth, who had come over to see me off. I was just about to climb into the car when Dominic's mum and dad arrived. As I watched Nick get out of the car, the sun caught his hair, and it struck me that I knew exactly what Dominic was going to look like when he got older. The resemblance was striking, and that made my heart ache, just a little.

Jess climbed out of the car and reached into the back seat for a bag. The two of them came over to where I was standing, and Nick put his arms around me. "I thought we might have missed you, gorgeous girl." He kissed my hair and pulled me closer. "You get more like your dad every day. He would be so proud of you." As he released me from his embrace, he stroked my hair and smiled at me. His lovely, odd eyes had laughter-lines, and his hair was just beginning to show the odd flash of silver amongst the golden red.

Jess came over and hugged me. "We wanted to give you a housewarming gift. Open it when you get settled in."

I looked inside the bag. It held several wrapped parcels and a bottle of my favourite wine. "Thank you so much. You didn't need to do this, but I'm glad you did – thank you."

"You're very welcome, gorgeous girl. Let us know when you're ready to receive visitors."

"I will. You're welcome to come and see me anytime." I meant it, too. These people had been there from the very start, offering love and support to mum and me.

One more round of hugs and I was in the car on my way to London. We didn't talk that much during the journey; we sang along to our favourite songs and I watched the scenery go by. Pretty soon, we were pulling up outside the studio apartment in Clerkenwell that I had rented. It didn't take very long to unload the car and, far too soon, I was sitting alone in my little room. I felt a sudden wave of sorrow mixed with loneliness as I looked around my cramped quarters. Then I remembered the wine that Nick and Jess had given me, so I found a glass in the tiny kitchen and opened the bottle, before reaching into the bag for the rest of the parcels.

There was a large parcel that contained a huge, soft bath towel. The note stuck to it said, *you can never have too many towels.* I smiled as I heard Nick saying that in my head, then the voice changed slightly and it was Dominic's voice I could hear. The next parcel contained a pretty glass vase. The note, in Jess's neat handwriting, said, *Every home needs at least one of these – fill it as often as you can afford to.* I smiled when I remembered how many vases of flowers there always seemed to be in the Quinn household. Nick bought flowers for Jess every week. They were such a great couple.

Finally, I unwrapped a framed photo. It had been taken a couple of days after I got home from America; mum and Andrew had thrown a party, and nearly everyone was there. The group photo showed us all looking relaxed and happy; I was seated in the middle, with Dominic behind me, his arms around my waist. There wasn't a note stuck on this gift, but there was an envelope addressed to me.

Dear Christie

We're so happy that you've come home to us and that you've got a whole new life to look forward to with your new job. We thought you might like to have a copy of this photo. You are loved very much by everyone in it.

Call Dominic when you're settled in. He misses you so much.

Love, N & J xx

I put the note down and looked at the photo. That empty feeling returned as I looked at the image in my hands. I wanted to feel Dominic's arms around me again like they were in the photo. Why do I always realise what it is I truly want when I've missed the chance? Mum's words came back to me then; *follow your heart, Peanut; just follow your heart.*

I'd just done a double shift at The Coffee Shack. It was late, and I was tired, so I went straight home to my room, refusing the offer of a drink with Amelia. She'd been flirting with me since I started back there a couple of weeks ago. She was nice enough; pretty and smart. But I didn't want her. I still only had thoughts for one person.

When I'd had a shower, I checked my phone for messages. There was one from dad about Lizzie's upcoming birthday, and there was one from Christie.

Hey, you – I'm all settled into my palatial (tiny) new flat. It's absolutely gorgeous (bearable) with a stunning view (of the bins behind Tesco Express).

I looked at the time she'd sent the message – nearly six hours ago. "Damn it."

Sorry, I only just saw this – just worked a double. Your new pied a terre sounds divine. I can't wait to see it.

I wasn't expecting a reply as it was so late, but about a minute after I'd sent my message, her reply came.

What are you doing at the weekend?

My stomach turned over. I missed her so much that I could almost taste it. But if I went to her, I'd want to touch her, kiss her. I couldn't do that again. Who was I trying to kid?

Well, it looks like I'm coming to see you xx

She was right; her flat was tiny. She had one room, which had a small kitchen area, a bed and a sofa, and a bathroom, which wasn't big enough for two people to be in at the same time. Once she'd given me the tour, we sat together on the sofa, and she talked about her new job. She was talking really quickly, and she had a thin sheen of sweat on her upper lip. "You're nervous."

She looked at me and bit her lip. "Yes."

"Why?"

"I'm worried that I screwed things up with you."

"You couldn't ever do that, Christie-bell." I put my arm around her, and she came into my embrace easily. I kissed the top of her head and stroked her back. Aware that I was in danger of getting carried away, I pulled back. "Sorry. I just can't stop myself when I'm near you."

She looked up at me, and I could see tears brimming on her lashes. "I don't want you to."

"You don't want me to what?"

"I don't want you to stop. Kiss me, Dominic."

I pulled away from her completely and stood up and turned my back on her so she couldn't see me fall apart. "I'm sorry, Christie. I can't do this again. If I kiss you, I'm going to want to go to bed with you. If I go to bed with you, I won't ever want to stop being with you. And you don't want that. You made that pretty clear last time." I heard a shuddered breath, and I turned around to see that she was standing beside me. "Christie – I'm sorry, I shouldn't have come." I turned towards the door, but I felt her hand on my arm.

"Please – Dominic – don't go. I need to explain." She looked so stricken, and I never could refuse her anything.

"Okay." I went back to the sofa and sat down. "I'm listening."

She paced for a while; then she turned to look at me. "I know you're in love with me."

"That's not exactly news, Christie."

"Please. Let me finish. I've practised what I want to say."

"Okay. Sorry. Go on."

She took a deep breath and started again. "I know you're in love with me. When I came home from America, I was in turmoil. I wasn't upset because I was in love with Tyler – far from it. I was relieved it was over because I didn't love him. I was upset because the decision hadn't been mine. I was thrown out of a life I thought I wanted and I hadn't had any say in it. That night in Oxford, I don't know what was going through my mind. I needed something, and you did too. In the morning, I thought I would feel guilty or like I'd made a mistake. But I didn't. And that just confused me even more. Then we nearly had sex – I have to admit, what you did to me? It was the hottest thing I've ever experienced. If you'd had a condom, there is no doubt that we would have had sex. And I wish we had, because then maybe I wouldn't have been such a stupid bitch." She stopped to take a breath and looked at me.

"Okay – I'd like to hear why you think you were a stupid bitch."

"When I told you that I didn't want to hurt you, I was using my stupid head. I wasn't brave enough to use my heart. I'm nearly eight years older than you. My head was saying that I couldn't possibly make you happy."

"So, what does your heart say?" I couldn't stop the feeling of hope burgeoning in my chest.

"My heart is saying that I should just admit what I feel for you and that the age difference doesn't matter."

I got up and went to her. "So, what's it to be, Christie? Head or heart?"

She flung her arms around my neck, and I lifted her off her feet so that she was eye to eye with me. "My heart knows the truth. I know you're in love with me. And I feel the same way about you." She kissed me on the mouth, and it felt incredible.

Bizarrely, I was reminded of the time I dislocated my shoulder playing rugby – when it slotted back into place, everything stopped hurting. And that's how it felt to have her back in my arms; like something that had been dislocated was back in place, and the hurt went away. I kissed her back, a desperate meeting of mouths, biting, sucking, licking and groaning. "I need you."

She put her head back, baring her throat to my mouth as I let her drop to the floor. "I need you too. Being in your arms feels … I don't know …"

"Like home. It feels like home."

She nodded and reached up to cup my cheek with the palm of her hand. "Yes. I think that's it." Her eyes met mine, and she smiled. "You know, we're going to get a lot of flak from everyone? They're going to say that I'm too old for you and that I'm just taking advantage of your boyhood crush."

I covered her mouth with mine, kissing her deeply. Then I pulled back and looked at her. "I don't care what anyone says. And this isn't a crush – I don't think it's been that for a very long time. Do you care what people think?"

She thought about it for a moment; then she shook her head. "No. No, I don't. The people who matter will know the truth."

I thought back to the last conversation I had with dad about the subject. He'd caught me moping at home a few days after Christie and I had almost had sex. *Be patient, son. If it's meant to be, it will happen. When I first met your mother, I fell headlong in love with her, but she was still with Uncle Adrian. I waited, and she came to me in the end, because it was meant to be. You and Christie will find your way.*

"They already do." I smiled and kissed her again. "God, I love kissing you. I'm never going to want to stop kissing you." I watched her walk towards the bed. "So, you liked what I did to you before?"

She gave me a sultry smile and pulled the covers off the bed. "I really did. Everything. I liked it when you tied my wrists together with my knickers – I've been fantasising about that ever since."

I made it to her in two, long strides and pushed her down onto the bed. "Good. Cos, you should know that I intend to do that again."

She laughed, then looked serious. "Do you need it?" She didn't sound worried, or judgemental.

"I think so, yes. Not all the time. But sometimes? Yeah. I think I may have inherited a kinky gene or two."

Her eyebrows shot up. "Nick and Jess? Into kinky stuff?"

"Yeah. One day, I'll tell you about the bag of stuff I found when I was a kid."

"Wow ... you never really know someone, do you? My parents – mum and Chris – they were into some pretty filthy shit too, by all accounts."

"Then there is no help for us!" I laughed and knelt on the bed, straddling her hips with my knees and holding her arms above her head. "How about we agree to not talk about our parents when we're fucking?"

"So, you do intend to fuck me this time?"

I reached into my pocket and pulled out the pack of condoms I'd been carrying around in the hope that I'd get another chance with her. "Oh, yes."

We were really going to do this. Dominic was kneeling over me, his erection straining against his jeans, and I was so aroused by nothing more than his presence, that I could smell the tell-tale musky dampness between my legs. "Tell me what you want." My vision dimmed as my pupils dilated.

Dominic released my wrists and pulled his shirt over his head. His skin was flawless and dusted with freckles. A patch of fine rose gold hair on his chest continued in a soft line that disappeared into the waistband of his jeans. "I want your mouth on me. And I want my mouth on you. Strip." He climbed off the bed and removed the rest of his clothes.

I wriggled out of my clothes, not even trying for finesse, and returned to the bed to lie next to him. His mouth was on mine before I had the chance to say anything, plundering me with his tongue. I responded – I didn't have any choice – my body, as always following its own rhythm when he touched me. He cupped one of my breasts with his hand, and I felt my skin respond; my nipple hardened under his touch and gooseflesh broke out on my arms and neck.

Dominic laughed softly as he pulled his mouth from mine. He sat up and turned so that he was facing my feet. "Gotta taste you." He gripped my thigh and pushed my leg up and out. He positioned himself so that his mouth was level with my pussy; then he put his mouth on me. I felt his tongue pushing into my hole.

"Fuck! Dominic! Nobody has ever done that like you!" It was true. I could count the number of times a guy had given me good oral sex on the fingers of one hand. Dominic was about to show me his skills in that area for the second time.

He pushed my leg further out and rubbed his chin against my inflamed clitoris as he fucked me with his tongue. As he did this, he pushed his erection towards my face. He took his mouth off me for a moment. "You know what to do with that." Then he was back on me – devouring me like a starving man.

I groaned with pleasure as he returned his mouth to my wet flesh, then I turned my head to face his cock. It was hard and glistening. I ran my tongue around the ridge before taking him into my mouth as far as I could. He made a low groaning sound and thrust into me, and I swallowed as much of him as I could. I loved the taste of him. This was something I had done for other guys, but between the two of us, it felt different- more intimate somehow. I tasted his pre-cum and felt a flutter of intense desire flow through my belly.

He was writhing against me now, his one leg bent, foot on the bed, giving me as much access to him as he could. He groaned as I stroked his balls then pushed my hand further along his perineum towards his ass. "Oh god, Christie. I want you to play with my ass so much, but if you do, I'm just going to come."

His confession surprised me a little. Whenever I'd indulged my fascination for this little game, I'd enjoyed it far more than the guy I was doing it to. But here he was, groaning and telling me he wanted it. I ignored his pained request, removing my mouth from his cock just long enough to suck my finger until it was wet. Then I sucked his cock back into my mouth, scraping my teeth on the velvety skin as I pushed my damp finger towards its target. As I circled his butthole with my finger, he groaned again, rotating his hips in time with my stroking.

"Fuck! Yes – do it." He lifted his leg to give me better access, and I pressed my wet finger through the tight ring of muscle. It went in easily, and I felt his muscles clench against the intrusion.

Then I felt his fingers delving into my pussy, and it was all I needed to push me over the edge. I started to come, squeezing his fingers with my inner muscles. He cried out, and I felt my own finger being squeezed as his anus clenched and pulsated as he came down my throat.

We stayed in that position for a few minutes, before he straightened and came up to face me. "That's the third time you've made me come, and I still haven't fucked you." He kissed me, and I tasted myself on his mouth; it was strange and erotic.

"We're getting around to that." I kissed him back, pushing my tongue into his mouth. "So, you like a bit of ass-play, then?"

He grinned and reached for my fingers, kissing them. "Oh yes. Been playing that game for a long time. I have an Aneros – that's a prostate massager – that can make me come hands-free."

I felt my belly warm at the thought of that. "I want to see that."

"Oh, you will. But now – there is something a little more pressing we need to take care of." He rolled me onto my back and pushed my legs open with his knee.

"Already?"

"The stamina of youth, dear lady. I can – and will – fuck you for hours."

I felt my muscles go lax and I put my arms up over my head.

"No – not this time – I want your hands on me when I'm inside you." He got up on his knees and reached for the packet of condoms he'd put on my nightstand. Tearing into a packet with his teeth, he rolled it on easily, and it occurred to me that, despite his youth, there was a strong possibility that he was more experienced than I was. "Are you ready?"

"Yes." It came out as a breathy sigh. I was more than ready. "I think I've been waiting for you."

"Waiting for me to grow up?" He laughed and raised his eyebrow teasingly. "Well, I'm a big boy now."

I looked down his body. He was beautiful, and my body was agreeing wholeheartedly with what he'd said. "Yes, you are." I reached for his ass and pulled him towards me. I felt the tip of his cock nudge against my pussy-lips.

He looked down to watch as he penetrated me. "Fuck, Christie – that's so hot." He continued to watch as he moved with shallow thrusts, pushing a couple of inches of his cock into me before withdrawing and then pushing in again.

I let him enjoy the view for a few moments, but it wasn't long before I needed more. I needed all of him. "Enough teasing. Fuck me. I want you deep inside me."

Dominic looked up at me, his glorious, odd eyes flashing with desire. Then he gave me a wicked smile as he thrust into me at last. And I knew then, that wherever he was, wherever we were, as long as we had this, we had a home.

Aquarius

Knowledge, humanitarianism, serious, insightful, duplicitous

For Jay

Ashleigh Goldman put her head in her hands, leaned her elbows on her desk and sighed. She was exhausted. She hadn't asked for this responsibility, and she still wasn't sure how or why it had been given to her. But here she was – de facto leader of Station Eleven, code name Aquarius, one of the survivor hideouts under the city.

A year ago, Ashleigh had been living and working happily in London. Her job as a translator for the French Embassy suited her down to the ground; interesting enough to keep her occupied during working hours, but not too taxing that she didn't have energy left at the end of the day to take advantage of living in such a vibrant city. She had a gorgeous apartment within walking distance of Soho, and she'd just started a relationship with a cute French guy called Remy. Everything was rosy in her little world. And then her world – and everyone else's for that matter – had ended in one, horrific day.

The sign on the Embassy wall said, 'Danger Level High', which meant you should find somewhere safe and stay there until it passed. But there had been warnings like this every day that Ashleigh could remember; if you took any heed of them, you'd never go anywhere or see anyone. And anyway, how bad could it be? Since the leaders of every country with nuclear capability had signed the agreement to disarm fourteen years ago, the threats were localised at best. She remembered the worldwide celebration that followed the signing of the agreement, and the televised destruction of amassed weapons. Everyone had felt such hope for the future. But Man will never change.

Now, the world had split into East and West, and a war of words had been burning slowly ever since; like the embers of a fire, waiting for the right wind direction to leap into life and cause untold destruction.

"Are you going straight home?" The voice of her colleague, Marin, pulled Ashleigh from her memories.

"What? Oh – no – I'm having supper with Remy at his place."

Marin shook her head and looked at the glowing warning sign on the wall. "Well, be careful out there."

That was the last time she saw Marin. Or any of her colleagues at the Embassy. She left Remy's flat close to Midnight; he had begged her to stay the night, but she needed sleep, and she knew she'd get precious little of that in Remy's bed. So, even though her lady parts complained at her for leaving her skilled lover in favour of a solitary night, she walked to the Underground to catch a train home to Soho.

Hampstead Underground Station is the deepest in the city, and that was probably why the small number of travellers who had been waiting on the platform survived what happened next. Ashleigh was texting Remy, letting him know that she was safe and waiting for a train. She felt the first explosion before she heard the rumble of it, then successive ones as they got closer, then faded away again. Alarms started to wail in the tunnels of the Underground and everyone on the platform watched in horror as the small space in which they were standing was shut off from the rest of the world by steel doors that dropped into place as blue lights flashed.

She felt her phone vibrating in her pocket and saw Remy's name on the screen. Swiping to accept the call, she could hear his frantic voice before she'd finally got the thing to her ear.

"… okay? Ashleigh – where are you?"

"I'm okay. I'm on the Underground – Hampstead."

"Stay where you are!"

"I don't think I have any choice; the whole place has been shut off with big, metal doors. What's going on? Was that an explosion?"

She heard Remy pacing around his room as he spoke to her. "Nobody knows what's going on. The city is under attack I think. But there is no damage – I can't see any fires or anything from my window – it's weird."

That was the last she heard from Remy. When she tried to call him an hour later, the phone said, 'no service'.

In the days that followed, the twelve people that had been thrown together by a tragedy got to know each other very well. There were six Brits, an American, a German, two Poles and two Swedes. As Ashleigh was the only one who spoke more than one language proficiently, she was unofficially made group leader. The vending machines were full of drinks and snacks, so the first thing she did was gather all the supplies together and work out a plan for rationing. When the food and drink started running low, they decided that a scouting party should climb the spiral staircase in search of more from the floors above.

They drew straws, and Ashleigh was one of the four people to begin that long climb, eight days after they had been trapped. There was no news from above because none of their technology was working. As they reached the lower concourse, the smell of death hit them. There were several corpses – most of which looked like they had just sat down and died without a struggle.

Ashleigh looked around at the disturbing scene. "What the hell happened here?"

Max, the German architect, looked up from his phone. "I've got a signal."

The news that was available was patchy, but after fifteen minutes of searching, they had a pretty good picture of what had happened. The city – and, apparently, most densely populated areas in the West, had been subjected to a biological attack. The gas had been buried in explosive devices which were timed to explode at the same time across the world. The virus, or whatever it was, was airborne and, once infected, a person lost the ability to make decisions for themselves. With nobody to tell them what to do, or even to breathe, most had just found somewhere to sit and die.

In retaliation, the West had deployed nuclear warheads that it claimed it had destroyed. In a matter of hours, the world was in ruins.

Lilia looked around the sorry scene in the concourse. She muttered something in Swedish, and everyone else looked to Ashleigh for a translation.

Ashleigh nodded and said something to the girl in her own language. Then she looked back to Max and Jonas, the American journalist. "She said it looks like they just sat down and waited to die."

Max looked back to his phone and started searching again. "It says that the pathogen has cleared and it is safe to go up to the surface."

"God only knows what we're going to find up there." Jonas looked towards the stairs. "But we're going to have to go up – there's nothing we can use here."

He was right. There were no vending machines on this level. Ashleigh thought for a moment then decided. "Okay. I'm in favour of going up. If you don't want to come, you don't have to. But if you do, I'd be grateful for the company."

Since that first expedition to the surface, the group had grown in number. Survivors had found them through the maze of tunnels that formed the city's underground railway. Hampstead station, now known as Station Eleven, code name Aquarius, had been repurposed as a secure living space. On the first level, which had been the ticket hall, there were storage areas for the goods that scouts found on a daily basis. On the next level down, in an area called The Basement, were communal areas for relaxing and kitchens for preparing and eating food. One level down, on the lower concourse, was Ashleigh's office and her sleeping quarters.

There was also a comms room, and sleeping quarters for couples, as well as a large area where everyone could gather for meetings. Finally, down on the platform level, the tracks had been covered over, and there were bunks set up for single people to sleep in one, huge dormitory. They had rigged up the station's emergency generator, which kept essential technology running and a water purifying system to collect and clean surface water. It was a life – not a great one – but it was a life.

The underground station kept them safe from the jackals. About a month after the attacks, the first news of infected survivors started to filter through. A small number of people had been infected by the pathogen but didn't succumb to it in the same way as everyone else. They had become extremely aggressive, even cannibalistic, and trips to the surface were often cut short because they were around. Tales of unfortunate survivors being caught, killed and eaten by the jackals came through the news network nearly every day.

"Remember all those zombie movies and TV shows that were on when we were kids?" Jonas was standing behind Ashleigh in the comms room.

"Yeah. My folks loved them when they were kids – made us watch the re-runs all the time." There was silence between them for a moment. "If you'd told me then that I'd be holed up in some London tube station, hiding from god only knows what, I would have probably laughed at you."

They looked at each other for a couple of seconds; then it was back to business.

"Ashleigh – you need to come to the comms room." Max stuck his head around the door of Ashleigh's room, "Libra's been hit."

Libra – Station Seven was another of the colonies of survivors that had made their home in the underground. Ashleigh had never met any of the people there, but she felt like they were friends. She communicated with Pejman, their leader, nearly every day and he probably knew more about her than anyone else. She made it to the comms room in under ten seconds and put on the headset. "Pej – talk to me – what's happened?"

There was a crackle of static; then she heard his voice come through. "They got in – god knows how – the jackals got in."

"How many have you lost?"

"Fourteen. God, Ashleigh. I've never seen anything like it. They ripped them to shreds."

"How many are you now?"

"Twenty-three."

Ashleigh turned to Max, who had become her right-hand man. "Can we accommodate twenty-three?"

Max nodded. "Somehow – it'll be a squeeze, but yes."

Ashleigh pulled Max into a quick hug and kissed him on the cheek. "Okay." Then she spoke again to Pej, "Can you get here? Through the tunnels? We can accommodate you."

"Thank you. God, thank you."

Three hours later, they heard the knocking on the great door that blocked off the tunnel. The twenty-three survivors of station seven had made it through the underground to Aquarius. Soon, they were sitting in the Basement, wrapped in blankets, drinking tea and eating a hastily prepared meal of toast and jam. Pej came to stand next to Ashleigh. "Thank you."

Ashleigh looked up at the tired, tense face of her friend. "You're not anything like I imagined."

Pej smiled and looked back at Ashleigh. "I could say the same thing."

She looked at him again. His Iranian heritage had given him dark golden skin and hair that shone blue-black in the artificial light of station eleven. That hair looked like it hadn't been cut since before the attack. He had it tied back in a sleek ponytail that ran from the back of his head down to between his shoulder blades. In the tight fabric of his black tee shirt, his muscular chest and arms looked impressive, and she could just see the hint of a tattoo climbing the strong column of his neck. He looked … lickable. Pulling herself out of the reverie, she walked off in the direction of the stairs.

Pej watched Ashleigh walk away and disappear down the stairs to the concourse, where he knew her room and the comms room were situated. Damn, that girl – he'd listened to her honeyed voice for months now, fantasising about what kind of face and body might go with it. He'd imagined all sorts; young, old, fat, slim, tall short, ugly, pretty. But nothing compared to the actual thing. She was stunning. Tall, strong, nice tits. Red hair that looked natural caught up in a band and hanging in a ponytail down to her waist, and pale skin, that from lack of sunshine, was almost translucent.

He spent several hours making sure his people were going to be comfortable. There were bunk beds down at the track level for most of them. The one married couple of their group who had made it through had taken the room next to Ashleigh's. "Good. I think we're all settled."

"What about you? Where are you going to sleep?"

Pej turned as he heard Ashleigh's voice behind him. "Oh – yes – I suppose I do need somewhere. I'll go and see if there are any bunks left down at the bottom." He started to walk towards the stairs, but Ashleigh's voice made him stop in his tracks.

"I've got a spare room. It would make sense for you to be close to me and the comms room."

He turned to look at her. "Yes – I suppose it would. Alright. I'll get my pack."

They got along okay. Ashleigh's spare room was actually just half of her room which had been divided off with a makeshift screen made of cardboard. When the original members of the Aquarius group had insisted on her taking one of the larger suites, she had agreed only on condition that the room was divided up in case anyone else needed it. With such a flimsy partition between them, Pej could hear pretty much everything she did at night. He listened to her sleeping, heard her soft snoring and her frequent nightmares. Once, he had heard her muffled cries as she brought herself to orgasm with her fingers. When he heard the tell-tale sounds coming from her side of the room, he'd given into the need to rub himself to oblivion, only just managing to keep his own cries from giving him away.

By day, they worked together to make sure their people were fed and cared for. By night, they shared a tiny living space and tried to pretend that they weren't attracted to each other. There was far too much going on to allow for any distraction. There were too many people depending on them to spend any time thinking about their own needs.

And so, it continued. After three months of living together, Ashleigh had finally become used to sharing her space with Pej. She got up at least an hour before he did, and went to bed at least an hour earlier so that she didn't have to watch him doing simple things like showering or dressing. She knew that, if she did, if she let herself look, she probably wouldn't want to stop.

It was very early in the morning. Ashleigh had been in the comms room for about an hour, and there was nothing to hear; no news, no chatter, everything was quiet. Max pulled his earpiece out and looked at her. "Why don't you get a scouting party together and go out. Everything's quiet up there – it might be a good time to go and look for a pharmacy that hasn't been emptied yet. We could do with some more meds."

Ashleigh looked at her friend. The big German had become one of the most important people in her life. They'd been thrown together, but she knew she would trust him with anything. She smiled at him and put her headset down. "Yeah. That's probably a good idea. I'll go and tell Pej. We'll get a scouting party together." She walked the short distance to her room and was about to call out Pej's name when she heard the shower running. Her conscience told her to turn around and leave him to his ablutions, but something stronger made her feet walk towards the sound of running water.

The small bathroom they shared was just an area of the bedroom that had been sectioned off with a wall of glass bricks, through which she could see Pej's outline as he stood under the spray. As she watched, he turned so that he was side-on and she could see his erect penis and the hand that was rubbing it frantically back and forth.

Ashleigh knew she should walk away, knew she should leave quietly so that her roommate didn't hear her, or know he'd had an audience for his solitary erotic pleasure. But her body had other ideas. The sight of his defined body hunched over as he pleasured himself, along with the groans that were audible over the sound of the water, had her taking a step further into the room. She wanted to watch. She wanted to share this experience with him.

And so, she watched. As he grew ever closer to his moment of release, his groans became louder; curses and sounds that might have made her think he was in pain if she couldn't see what he was doing. As his semen flew from his body in a wide arc that splashed against the glass that separated them, she heard him shout out, "Fuck! Yes! Leah!"

Leah. He had begun to call her Leah very soon after he had arrived here at Aquarius. It suited her well. Pej finished cleaning himself under the warm spray of the shower and thought some more about Leah. He'd been able to think about precious little else for the last few days; his attraction to her was bordering on obsession. As always, thoughts of his red-haired roommate had him hard in an instant, and he gave into the need to take himself in hand.

As he allowed images of her to invade his imagination, his favourite fantasy rose to the surface. In his mind, he was fucking her with long, deep thrusts, his cock finding her centre again and again as he ground himself into her yielding flesh. She cried out in ecstasy as he took her, bringing her to orgasm before taking his own pleasure. He felt the familiar spasm; the tell-tale pleasure-pain and the irresistible need to thrust. He tightened his fist around his cock and imagined that it was her sweet cunt squeezing him and, as his cum shot from him, he cried out her name. "Fuck, yes! Leah!"

A sound like a gasp pulled him from his fantasy, and he turned to look through the glass wall that separated the shower from the rest of the room. She was there, her hand over her mouth to stop the sound, but it was too late; he had heard her, and now he had seen her. Through the steam and the distorted view through the glass, he could clearly make out the flush to her skin and her breasts rising and falling as she breathed deeply at the sight of him. She didn't move.

Pej couldn't move either. He stood facing her, his cock still hard as the last of his cum oozed out and dripped onto the floor of the shower. The moment seemed to go on forever, stretching thinner and thinner until it threatened to snap. Just then, he heard Max's voice at the door, and Ashleigh answered, taking one last look at him before turning to leave. When she reached the door, she turned back and shouted to him, "We're going up top. Be ready in five minutes if you want to come along."

Five minutes later, he was climbing the spiral staircase that led to ground level. The scouting party included three of his own people; Bo, the wiry teenager who could apparently get in and out of almost anywhere, Charlotte, the loud-mouthed girl who had an uncanny knack of upsetting everyone, and Kenny, the easy-going Jamaican who could run as fast as the wind. From Ashleigh's people were Jonas, the American journalist who had become an expert in picking locks, Tan, the Chinese ex-restauranteur who could make a decent meal out of whatever was brought to him, and Eric, the big Swede who rarely spoke but noticed everything.

"We'll head towards the Royal Free Hospital. There may still be some meds there we can use." Ashleigh was giving out bottles of water and telling the group where they were heading. "Once we've checked out the Royal Free, we'll go up towards Belsize Park. Don't split off from the group – we stay together. Is that clear?"

There was a murmur of agreement among the small group, and they set off, following the main road towards the empty shell of the hospital. When they got there, the pickings were slim, but Bo managed to find a storeroom that was still locked. Jonas made short work of the lock, and the heavy door swung on its hinges, creaking in disgust at being opened after such a long time. Pej went in first; it wasn't a medical supplies cupboard, but there were things they could use. "Looks like cleaning supplies. There's hand-sanitiser in here – a lot of it – we can use that." Soon, two of the shopping trolleys they had brought with them were filled with things from the store-room; hand sanitiser, towels, soap, disinfectant. It was a good haul.

In the basement, Ashleigh found some green scrubs. "I like these – they'll make comfortable pyjamas."

As she started to put the packs of folded cotton into a trolley, Pej allowed his mind to wander for a moment. Leah in pyjamas. Not green, cotton ones, but red silk that clung to her creamy skin. Red silk that he could peel from her before laying her out, naked and warm, on his bed.

"Pej?"

"What?" he was pulled from his fantasy by her voice. "Sorry – I was miles away."

"So, I see. I said I think we've pretty much got everything useful that we can carry. We'll come back another time to see if we can use any of the equipment."

"Okay. Yeah – sure. Lead on."

Ashleigh led her scouts along the road, past the burned-out shell of a Premier Inn hotel and the ransacked ruins of a petrol station. As they approached the impressive building that had once been a centre for the performing arts, Eric raised his hand and stopped, indicating for the rest of the group to be quiet. "I hear something."

Pej sniffed the air and looked around. Then he heard it too; the faint shuffling that sounded like something was following them.

"Jackals!" The sound of Bo's high-pitched warning pierced the air, and they all turned to see a group of about a dozen of the wretched creatures loping towards them. "Run!"

The group split, running in all directions. The Jackals were strong, but they were not fast. If you could run, you stood a good chance of getting to safety. Pej grabbed Ashleigh's hand and pulled her back in the direction of the ruined hotel. "Come on – run!"

Ashleigh took one, last look at their loaded trolleys then turned on her heel and ran as fast as her legs could carry her. Pej pulled her into a side street and up the black and white tiled steps of a once-grand building. As they passed through the doorway, she noticed that Pej was gripping a large spray bottle of disinfectant in his other hand. She was about to ask him why he'd brought it with him when he pulled her behind him and started to spray the strong-smelling liquid to cover their tracks.

"That should keep them off our scent." He continued to walk backwards into the house, spraying the floor and the air where they had been. By the time they made it to the foot of a grand staircase, the air was heavy with the artificial pine smell of the fluid. On the third floor, they found a room where the heavy door had not been pulled off its hinges and Pej pushed her inside. After spraying around the door, he closed it, and the two of them pulled a heavy chest of drawers across the doorway.

Ashleigh could hear her heart thumping in her ears as she struggled to get her breathing under control. She walked around the edge of the room towards a window that faced out onto the road. Carefully, so as not to be seen from the road, she looked out into the fading light. She heard a noise and looked down; a pair of jackals were leaving the house and making their way back towards the main road. "I think your spraying worked," she whispered, "They're all going back the way they came."

Pej came to stand behind her by the window and looked out onto the empty street. "Good. We'll stay here until dark just to be safe."

Ashleigh could feel the heat coming off his body where he stood behind her. Adrenaline was coursing through her system from their flight from danger, and the relief of safety made her head spin. She turned to look at him, but before she could say anything, she was pushed against the wall, Pej's body pressed against hers, his breath hot against the skin of her neck. She could feel his heart beating against her.

"Leah." The word sounded like it gave him pain to say it. "I could have lost you."

She felt his arms tighten around her waist as he pressed himself closer to her. He ran his nose along her jawline before covering her mouth with his.

When she sighed into him and opened her mouth, he groaned and pushed against her, getting as close to her as he could. "I saw you watching me this morning. You watched me come."

"Yes." She breathed out the word as Pej moved his lips down to suck on the tender skin of her neck.

"You heard me call out your name." He pushed his thigh between her legs, almost lifting her off her feet. "And now it's my turn to hear you call out mine." He found the button of her jeans and flicked it open before pulling the zipper down. As he pushed his hand inside her underwear, he kissed her mouth again. "Your mouth tastes sweet. When we have more time, I will taste you here as well." He pushed his hand between her legs and parted her folds with his fingers. "You're wet for me?"

Ashleigh nodded and tried to breathe. The huge amount of adrenaline she still had coursing through her veins was ramping up her arousal to an almost unbearable level, and when she felt him push two of his long fingers into her wet flesh, her knees almost gave out beneath her.

Pej chuckled as he felt her response to his touch. "Oh no, you don't." He pushed his thigh between her legs again, holding her up as he plundered her. "I'm going to watch you come on my hand." With his other hand, he lifted her chin and forced her to look at him. "Don't take your eyes off mine. I want to see your face as you come."

Ashleigh was shaking now; her body, which had been hers alone since that fatal night, consumed Pej's touch like dry earth consumes rain. She felt his questing fingers delve inside her and his thumb rub over her clitoris in maddening circles. She wanted him. She wanted him in her bed, held tight between her thighs. But here and now, she just wanted him to finish what he had started. She reached down and placed her hand over his, steering him, directing him to bring her to a swift climax.

Pej felt her muscles begin to clench around his fingers as her orgasm began to crest. "Look at me! Leah, look at me. Let me see you come."

Ashleigh lifted her eyes. As her climax swept through her body, she met his gaze and held it, and when the wave of pleasure finally ended, she pulled his face to hers, claiming his mouth with a groan. "Pej …"

"And now we're even." He smiled wistfully as he pulled his fingers gently from her hot core. He lifted a finger to his mouth and sucked it, savouring her taste. "When we get home, I'm going to taste you properly."

They left the house when darkness fell. The trolley with the loot from the hospital was overturned, but nothing had been taken. Jackals were only interested in things they could eat, so they'd left most of the stuff where it had fallen. Ashleigh and Pej gathered up the spilt scrubs and packed them back into the trolley. Ashleigh's body was still humming from the erotic encounter in the upper room of that once-grand house. Their escape from danger had heightened every sense in her body; Pej's touch had lit a fire in her belly that was still smouldering. It hadn't been enough. She wanted more of him, and she intended to take it as soon as they were alone.

They were almost within sight of Aquarius when Pej heard a soft moan coming from behind an overturned wheelie bin. "Did you hear that?"

Ashleigh stopped in her tracks and looked towards the bin. "Yes. I did." She looked at Pej, and something unspoken passed between them. "There's someone hurt back there."

"It could be an injured jackal."

"It could be a trap."

"Or it could be a person. We have to find out." Pej began to walk towards the bin. "Who's there?"

The groan got louder as if someone was trying to answer.

"Bo?" Pej's voice took on the edge of panic as he began to run towards the bin. "Is that you?"

When Ashleigh joined him, she looked down in horror at the bloody mess that still held a scrap of familiar humanity. The boy had been felled in the alley, and his thin body had been torn open. Ashleigh could see bone, muscle and blood – lots of blood. He wasn't going to survive this.

Another shared glance then the two of them were on their knees. The concrete was wet with the boy's blood and Pej could feel it seeping into the fabric of his jeans. "Okay, buddy. We're going to get you out of here."

Bo winced in pain as Pej lifted him up. "Where's Charlotte?" Forcing the words out cost him dearly, and he slumped against Pej's shoulder.

Ashleigh looked at the boy, then back to Pej. She shrugged her shoulders and shook her head to tell him not to say anything. "Don't worry about Charlotte. We'll find her."

"She ran. Drew them off me."

"Don't talk anymore, buddy." Pej started to walk out of the alley with Bo bundled in his arms. "We'll find her. I promise."

Bo stilled in his arms and slipped from consciousness.

"Leah?"

Ashleigh turned to look at Pej. He had tears forming in his eyes, and she could feel the sorrow coming off him in waves.

"I think he's gone."

When they got back to Aquarius, Ashleigh signalled for the lift to come and get them. They rarely used the lift because the sound of it could be heard from ground level and it used a lot of precious electricity.

Lilia came up to meet them, and when she saw the bloody bundle of flesh and bone in Pej's arms, she lifted her hand to cover her mouth, tears filling her eyes. "We went out to look for him but couldn't find him. Charlotte made it back here and told us he was down."

"Where is Charlotte?" Pej laid his precious cargo down gently on top of a pile of boxes. "What did she say?"

Lilia nodded sadly and pointed to a long shape on the floor of what had once been the ticket hall. It was wrapped tightly in a sheet with a wreath of paper flowers laid lovingly over it. "She'd lost an arm – they must have just ripped it off her – we couldn't stop the bleeding in time." She bowed her head. "I'll get some more people to come up and get Bo ready. We can take them through the tunnels to the river. We'll burn them there." They had done this once before; a child had come through the tunnels and found them. He was covered in rat bites from having slept in the underground labyrinth for months, and many of them were infected. They had used some of their precious antibiotics, but it wasn't enough. He died ten days after he arrived and they had wrapped his thin body and carried it to the river. The jackals never ventured to the river, so it was the safest place to set up a pyre. It had taken about six hours and every scrap of wood they could find to burn him.

"No. It would take too long, and we don't have the time to gather the wood. We'll bury them on the Heath." Hampstead Heath was nearby; it would be easy enough to dig a shallow grave and bury the teenagers together. Or it would be if it wasn't somewhere that the jackals liked to prowl. "Tell Max we're going to need his guns."

Pej insisted that Ashleigh stayed behind. "No, Leah. If something happens out there, these people will still need you. You're their leader."

"I never asked for that job." Ashleigh slumped down onto her mattress. "But I suppose you're right. Just be careful out there, will you?"

"I will. We will. I promise. We'll go through the tunnel to the Heath. We'll get everyone together to remember Bo and Charlotte in the morning. I think we need to do that." He reached down and ran his hand through the tangled red curls on Ashleigh's head. "Get in the shower – it'll make you feel better." He bent to kiss the top of her head and then he was gone.

Ashleigh sat in the dark and quiet of her room for a few minutes, then she peeled off her bloodstained clothes and stepped under the warm spray of the shower. As the water soaked her hair and cascaded over her body, she felt a wave of relief mixed with grief crash into her. Grief for her lost friends, relief that she was safe. But she knew she wouldn't be able to rest until Pej was back safe and sound. As her mind filled with images of him, her hand moved down her body, as if it had a mind of its own, to trace the path of his hands on her. When her fingers pressed through the damp folds between her legs, the evidence of the orgasm he had pulled from her with his fingers slicked her hand, and she felt herself blush.

Then the emotion of the day overwhelmed her, and she collapsed against the glass wall of the shower, gasping for breath as sobs wracked her body and tears became indistinguishable from the water flowing over her. She stayed like that for a long time. When the storm of grief had passed, and the water was beginning to run cold, she hauled herself up and washed her hair and body before drying off and falling onto her mattress, pulling the covers over her.

Pej shovelled the last of the soil over the grave they had dug in the soft earth under a huge tree next to the lake. Anywhere near water was a little safer because the jackals seemed to stay away from it. "Okay. That's it. Let's go."

"Aren't you going to say something?" Max turned from where he had been standing watch with his rifle.

"Like what?" Pej looked wearily between the big German and the three guys who had helped him to bury Bo and Charlotte. "Here lies Bo the street-thief and Charlotte the loud-mouth? They were kids. Just kids." He felt a fury rise within him; one he'd been suppressing for too long. "Someone is responsible for this. Someone thought it was just fine and dandy to kill millions of people – and for what? There's nothing left of our world. It's all gone to shit! And these two?" He dug the tip of his shovel into the soft mound of earth that was covering them, "These two are probably better off out of it."

The small group of men stood in silence for a moment then they gathered up their things and started to walk back towards the station where they would follow the tracks back down into the tunnels and home.

Pej gave one backwards glance as they left the burial spot. He'd had enough of death for today. What he wanted – no, needed – was to get back to Ashleigh and claim some kind of life. Enough waiting and dancing around her. He'd wanted her since that first day when he'd emerged from the tunnel and saw her standing under the harsh light. She knew, and she hadn't run. She'd watched him masturbate in the shower, and she'd let him frig her today as they hid from the jackals. When he got home, he was going to make sure she understood.

The room was dark, and he could hear Ashleigh's soft breathing as he closed the door. He stripped off his clothes, which were covered in a mixture of Bo's blood and the soil with which he had buried him, and felt his way into the shower stall without turning on the light. He washed quickly and was glad that he couldn't see the grim evidence of his day washing down the drain. When the smell of blood and earth had been replaced with the smell of mint shower gel, he turned off the water and dried himself on the towel that Ashleigh had left to dry on the rail. It smelled of her, and he felt his cock stiffen.

The thin cardboard partition that separated their mattresses gave little resistance as he lifted it to the side of the room. He pushed his bed the short distance to Ashleigh's and lay down beside her.

"Pej?" Her voice sounded sleepy; then she turned over to feel that he was lying beside her. "Oh! You're safe – I had such horrid dreams!"

"I'm here. Are you properly awake?"

"What? Yes – I am now – why?"

He didn't speak. Instead, he lifted her covers and moved over to her side of the bed. As he felt her warm, naked skin make contact with his cooler, damp body, his already stiff cock became as hard as a rock. As he placed himself between her legs, he threw the covers off them so that he could have full access to every part of her body. He lifted her thighs, pushing them out to expose her hot hole to him and he sank into her, covering her intimate flesh with his mouth.

Ashleigh wriggled in surprise at the sudden invasion of his mouth and tongue. "Oh!" Her back arched off the mattress as a wave of pleasure took her by surprise, and she heard Pej chuckle.

He broke contact and replaced his mouth with his fingers. "Do you like that, Leah?"

"I do … oh god, please!"

"Please what? What do you want, Leah?" He knew he was torturing her now and it filled him with a sense of power he hadn't felt in a long time. "You have to tell me what you want, or I'll just do as I please."

He dug his fingers into the soft flesh either side of her cunt and dipped his head to lick her again. "Well?"

Ashleigh was panting, and he could tell she was trying to hold back. "Finish it – make me come."

"How? How do you want me to do it?"

"I … I don't know …"

"Come on, Leah; this isn't the time to be shy. Tell me what you want." When the only answer he heard was a long exhalation of breath, he came up to his knees and flipped her over. "Well, if you can't tell me what you want, you'll just have to take what I give you." He slapped her loudly on the bottom which made her jump. "If you don't want to do that, tell me now." He slapped her again, and her response was a groan. "You like that?"

"Yes." She was panting

"You're mine, Leah. You've been mine since you opened your door to me." He reached under her and rubbed her clit with his fingers. "You're so wet, Leah. Is this for me?"

"Yes. All for you."

"All those times I heard you rubbing one out – trying not to make any sound – who were you fantasising about?"

"You. I wanted you as soon as I saw you. No – I think I wanted you before that – just from talking to you."

Pej grinned in victory. "My girl. My beautiful red-haired girl." He put his hands on her hips and pulled her towards him. In one, easy movement, he buried his cock up to the hilt in her wet pussy.

Ashleigh felt his hands on her hips and knew what was coming next. She wanted it; she felt empty, and she was so aroused that her hole was aching with need. She arched her back, pushing her backside towards him and she felt the head of his cock nudging at her. Then he was inside her, filling her, and her body responded to him, taking him in and clenching around him, holding him as tightly as she could.

"Fuck, Leah! You're so tight. God, I just want to fuck you. I've wanted this for so long." He pulled back so that only the tip of his cock was left inside her; then he pushed back in again. He filled her completely, claiming her with a need that he could barely control. "Feel that? Oh, fuck, Leah, you're driving me crazy. Tell me you feel it."

Ashleigh looked back over her shoulder. In the dim light that filtered into the room from the landing outside, she could see Pej's face. He was sweating; eyes shut and mouth open as he gasped for air.

"Yes, Pej. I feel it. I feel your cock filling me – it's mine!" She was panting now, her whole body seemed to be singing with pleasure, but she wanted more. "I want to see your face while you fuck me."

Pej groaned at Ashleigh's demand. "Fuck, yeah." He pulled out of her reluctantly, his cock and balls letting him know they didn't appreciate being removed from the wet warmth of Ashleigh's body. Quickly, he gripped her hips and flipped her over onto her back. "Like this? Or do you want to be on top?"

"Like this. I want to ride you, but right now, I want this." She pulled him back towards her, reaching down to guide his cock back inside. "Don't hold back, Pej. I need this."

"What do you need? Tell me." He ducked his head and began to suck on the tender skin of her breast. "I need to hear what you want, Leah."

Ashleigh felt as though every nerve-ending in her body was racing towards the hot, needy hole between her legs. Her skin was hypersensitive and burned where Pej's body touched hers. As he pulled her nipple into his mouth, an involuntary groan escaped her lips. "I want to feel your mouth all over me. And I want your cock – as deep inside me as it will go."

Hearing Ashleigh voice her desires so freely stoked the fire of Pej's lust till it threatened to consume him. His balls felt so tight that they were almost aching, sending the message that he was going to come soon. "I'm going to come so hard in you." He reached for her wrists and pushed them up, holding them together above her head as he continued to thrust into her.

Ashleigh lifted her thighs and spread them as far as she could to take him. "I'm so close, Pej. Don't stop. Please, don't stop."

Pej pushed her wrists further into the mattress as he screwed her with every ounce of energy he had. He put his mouth on her neck, sucking then biting the soft flesh. He heard her cry out as he bit her and felt her cunt clench around his cock, pulsing with her climax as she began to milk him with her inner muscles. "That's it – come on my cock. Get used to it because you're going to be getting it as often as I can get you alone." He stifled her cries with his mouth, sucking her bottom lip before plunging his tongue inside. He was claiming her; filling her mouth with his tongue, her pussy with his cock and holding her down so that he could fuck her as hard as they both needed.

Two more thrusts and he was spilling himself inside her. He went up on his elbows, pushing himself into her in one, last thrust as he emptied himself into her. His cock continued to twitch and pulse within her even after he'd finished coming; the force of his orgasm left him trembling above her, gasping for breath. He pressed his forehead to hers as she lay beneath him, panting and shuddering. There was so much he wanted to say to her, but he didn't have the words.

Pej rolled them onto their sides, sighing as his still-hard cock slipped from her body. Pulling her into his arms, he kissed the top of her head and gently brushed the hair out of her eyes. They lay like that for a long time, not speaking, just lost in the intimacy of the moment. When he heard her breathing slow and change to the tell-tale rhythm of sleep, he kissed her hair again and held her close to his chest. His body was still awake and needy – he wanted her again – but he let her sleep.

Ashleigh woke up from the best, unbroken sleep she'd had in months. She was very warm, and it took a moment for her to awaken fully and realise that she was still held tight in Pej's arms. He was snoring quietly, and the sound was soothing. As she moved slightly, his hold on her loosened, and he rolled onto his back. As their bodies separated, the scent of sex filled the air. Her pussy ached deliciously, throbbing with the memory of Pej's cock thrusting inside her. She wanted him again.

A wicked idea began to take root in her mind. She said she wanted to ride him, and here he was, lying on his back, his long hair ruffled and his beautiful body hers for the taking. She sat up and eased the covers off, revealing him fully to her. His cock was soft, and she could see it in the dim light, nestled against his leg, crowned with a dark patch of hair. Ashleigh reached down and laid her palm over his penis. His skin felt like warm silk against her hand, and as she began to stroke him with her fingers, his cock started to fill again, rising slowly until it was standing hard against his belly.

He was still asleep. Ashleigh couldn't quite believe it; she had aroused him with her hand, but he hadn't woken up. He made a quiet sound and drew in a breath through his nose as she moved her thumb over the moist crown of his cock, but he didn't wake up.

Ashleigh felt a thrill go through her. She was going to take what she wanted. She moved slowly, straddling his hips, before taking his cock in her hand so that she could impale herself on it. As she took him inside her, she felt her body sigh with pleasure. She pressed down onto him until she felt her swollen pussy-lips brush against his soft pubic hair. She couldn't stop a gasp of pleasure as she felt the head of his cock touch the opening of her womb.

Pej opened his eyes and, as he came to and realised what was happening, they widened with surprise as he looked at her in the near-darkness of their room. "Leah – what the fuck are you doing to me?"

"I told you I wanted to ride you. Now lie back and let me do it." She laughed quietly, leaning down to take hold of his wrists, which she pushed up and over his head, holding him down as he had done to her. "It's your turn to lie there and be fucked." She began to move her body, going up on her knees before pressing down again. Soon, she had a steady rhythm going and Pej was thrashing beneath her.

"Leah – please – I want to touch you!" He was straining his body, trying to push his hips up to make even more contact with her. "Please."

Ashleigh took her hands off his wrists and sat up fully. "I want your hands on me too."

Pej sat up and put his hands on her hips, pushing her down fully onto his cock. "This is so right. This is where I belong." He moved forward and captured one of her aroused nipples between his lips. He sucked the sensitive nub hard, and Ashleigh's back arched in response. "I could suck on these for hours." He switched to the other nipple and was rewarded with another groan of pleasure.

"Promise me you'll do that someday." She was rocking faster on him now, and she reached her hand down, pressing the tip of her long, middle finger against her clitoris.

"Oh, I will, I promise." He pulled her nipple into his mouth again and used his teeth on her, nipping at her with just enough force to make her moan.

Ashleigh ground herself down onto him as the first waves of her climax began to pulse through her body. "Yes – oh god, yes – I'm going to come." She began to gyrate her hips so that Pej's cock rotated inside her. The feeling was so intense, it tipped her over the edge, and she came with a cry, falling to lie on his chest.

Pej brought his arms up and held her to him as he started to come. "Oh god, Leah. I just want to come inside you forever."

When the storm had passed, and their breathing had returned to almost normal levels, Pej eased Ashleigh over so that they were lying on their sides again. Their bodies were damp with sweat which cooled quickly in the dry air of their room. He pulled the covers over them again and held her close to his chest as they both gave themselves up to sleep.

The sounds of the morning were drifting in, announcing that the day was beginning and it was time to get up. Ashleigh could hear Max's deep voice as he spoke to someone on the landing outside. She felt Pej stir and looked up to see that he was awake and looking at her. "Good morning." She smiled and kissed the skin of his chest where she lay against it.

"Good morning. You okay?"

She nestled into him, enjoying the warmth that their bodies were generating. "I'm good. You?"

"Yeah … I had the strangest dream that some sexy bitch was riding me like a succubus." He giggled and kissed the top of her head.

"Really? Was it good?"

"It was fucking amazing." They remained silent for a minute or so; then he pulled her as close to his chest as he could. "I should have used a condom. I'm sorry. I got a bit carried away."

Ashleigh laughed at his understatement. "A bit? Crikey – if you ever get completely carried away, I won't be able to walk for a week!" She rubbed her nose against the skin of his chest, enjoying the warmth and his scent. "I've got a coil, so we're okay."

Pej felt a moment of relief, then something else. "My inner caveman is disappointed." He tried to make it sound like a joke, but a very real part of him was indeed disappointed. Images of Ashleigh's belly swollen with a child that he had put into her filled his mind. He shook his head to erase the thoughts; this world was no place for children. But somehow, that fact just made it all so much worse. The enormity of their loss, of everything that had been taken away from them, hit him like a steamroller. He pulled a shaky breath into his lungs and tightened his grip on her.

Ashleigh felt the change in him and looked up at his face. "Hey now – what's this?" She watched as a tear spilt over his lashes and left a wet trail down his cheek. "Pej – what's the matter?" She brushed the tear away and sat up so that she could pull his head against her breast.

"I think it all just hit me. Everything we've lost. They took it all. They had no right. This life. This existence. So many things I always thought I'd do, and now I can't."

"I know." She felt her heart swell, empathising with her lover and feeling sorrow for herself. "We could have had such a different life."

"A life where we probably wouldn't have met."

"That's true." She kissed the top of his head and rocked them both in a soothing rhythm. "So, it isn't all bad then." A soft chuckle escaped her lips. "I wouldn't have wanted to miss that stellar fuck for anything."

They made love again; quietly, gently, rocking into each other until they were both gasping. As his seed poured into her again, Pej took Ashleigh's hand, linking their fingers together. "You're mine, Leah. And one day, I will put a child in your belly. One day, when we can leave this place, we'll find somewhere in the country. We'll find a doctor to take that thing out of you, and I'll fill you up."

When they finally made it to the comms room, damp from the shower and glowing from their lovemaking, they were met with sly smiles and laughter. Max looked over his shoulder from where he was studying a computer screen. "Sleep well?"

"Very well, thank you." Ashleigh smiled and looked at Pej. "The best sleep I've had in ages."

"Good. Everyone else on this floor says they were kept awake half the night – sounded like a couple of animals rutting, apparently. I don't suppose you two know anything about that do you?" He grinned knowingly as he looked at them.

Pej put his arm around Ashleigh's shoulder and pulled her towards him so he could kiss her hair. "No. We must have slept through that. Can't think what could have caused that kind of noise." He could hardly contain the grin that was spreading on his face. "Can you, Leah?"

Ashleigh blushed and tried to suppress a giggle. "No. No idea."

Max lifted his chin and grinned at the pair. "I have a feeling we'll be hearing it again."

"Highly likely." Pej pulled Ashleigh against his chest and smiled at the big German. "I think there's a real possibility that you'll be hearing it again before too long."

This story will be developed in a forthcoming series of novels

FIRE

Aries
Leo
Sagittarius

Aries

Active, demanding, determined, effective, ambitious

"Yeah, baby – suck it. Suck it hard."

I looked up from my position; kneeling on the floor in front of Max Endsleigh. His cock bobbed in front of my nose, and I knew from the look on his face that he was too far gone to realise that I wasn't really into what we were doing.

I had been dating Max for about three months. He'd pursued me for months before that and I'd finally given in. He was nice enough, but he wasn't really what I wanted. I was settling for something less than perfect, and I knew it.

A groan from above reminded me of where I was and what I was expected to do. I had a choice; I could either let him fuck my face go on believing that everything was hunky dory between us, or I could get off my knees and leave. The first option was the easy way out. I was tired and wanted to go to sleep. Option two would mean I wouldn't be able to do that anytime soon. It turns out I wasn't as tired as I thought.

Max's face was a mass of anger and confusion. "What the fuck is going on? You get me all fired up then you just get up and say you're not into it? What kind of game are you playing, Izzy?"

I turned back to look at him, my coat half on my shoulders. "I'm not playing a game. Well, not anymore, anyway. I don't want you, Max. I never did. I thought it would – I don't know – develop or something. But it didn't. You don't do it for me and you never will. And I like myself enough to want something better than second best."

He managed to tuck his wilting cock back into his jeans before he came at me. I could feel the fury riding him – coming off him in waves, but I wasn't scared. I probably should have been, but something stronger than his pathetic ego was growing inside me. "Second best?

What the fuck are you talking about? I'm the best you've ever had, and you know it." His face creased into a sneer and I saw his true self for the first time. The easy-going, handsome guy that I'd been sleeping with had the heart of an arsehole. He reached for my arm, but I pulled away.

"Don't. You lay one finger on me, and I swear to god, I'll take you down."

I must have looked like I meant business because he backed off, holding his hands up as a sign of peace. "I just don't get it. What's changed?"

"Me. I've changed." I cringed slightly at the cliché, but it was true. "I don't want to settle for anything subpar anymore."

"Subpar? What the fuck are you saying? I'm not one of your sales reps – I've been fucking you for months, and you've been enjoying it. Are you seeing someone else? Is that it? Some new guy with a big dick giving you what you need?"

I shook my head and felt my top lip lift in disgust at his words. "No. There isn't anyone else. I just don't want you – it's as simple as that. And before you say anything else? Subpar is exactly what I mean. You think you're some kind of stud but you're pathetic."

I watched the colour blanch from Max's face and his mouth open and close like a goldfish stranded out of the water. "Pathetic?"

"You come too quickly, and then you fall asleep. Most of the time I end up rubbing myself off while listening to you snore. And if you seriously think you're the best I've ever had then you have no understanding of what a woman wants from a man. You're not even in the top five. I'd place a night with nothing but my own hand higher on the list than a night with you." His look of abject horror should have told me to stop, but I was on a roll. "And I truly doubt that you've been the best that anyone has had unless you were the only one they'd had." I finished putting my coat on. "I'll see myself out."

As I closed the door behind me, I heard a thud from somewhere inside Max's flat. Had he just fallen over? I was considering checking on him when the door opened, and the small bag that I left there with toiletries and a hairdryer came flying past my head and fell with a crash on the landing. "That'll save me having to come back for it," I muttered to myself before picking up the bag and its spilt contents and making my way down the stairs. Relief. The overwhelming emotion I felt was relief. I should have done that weeks ago.

Meilin perched herself on the corner of my desk and gave me that look. "Are you okay, hun?"

I didn't need sympathy – especially not from my best friend who should know better. "I'm fine. I told you I was fine yesterday – and the day before that."

She tilted her head and pouted her lips a little. "I know – but breaking up is hard to do."

"Someone wrote a song about that. But – like I told you yesterday and the day before that – it was a relief. I should have done it weeks ago. No – scratch that – I shouldn't have started going out with him in the first place. He was an arse. And he couldn't have found my g-spot if it had bloody GPS and Siri was giving him directions." I looked at her, then we both started to laugh. "That's better. Now – leave me alone – I have a ton of work to do."

"Okay. Still on for drinks after work?"

"You betcha. I'll see you in the Bells when I'm done here – shouldn't be later than six."

I watched her walk off and then put my head back down to concentrate on the spreadsheet in front of me. I didn't need any of this shit. Time to start concentrating on me – and what I wanted out of life – instead of singing along with the song that everyone else was singing just because it was the easiest thing to do. Max had been a verse in that song. I hate that song. Time to write a new song.

One month later

"What is this band called?"

"What?"

"WHAT. IS. THIS. BAND. CALLED? You can't hear a word I'm saying, can you?"

"Too loud – I can't hear a word you're saying."

The band was called Unstable. They were a tribute act for a band called Disturbed. I'd never heard of Disturbed, let alone imagined a tribute act, but Meilin loved them, and she'd dragged me along to a gig in a sweaty basement on a Friday night. After half an hour or so (and once my eardrums had lost some of their permanent function) I was beginning to enjoy it. The throaty vocals and driving beat were compelling – almost sexual.

About halfway through their set, I noticed the drummer. Wow. He was obviously high on something (I tried to convince myself it was life) and his acrobatic playing was mesmerising. He was built – muscular arms and chest showed off to fantasy-inducing proportions by the skin-tight tee shirt he was wearing. His shoulder-length dark blonde hair was flying around his head like a halo as he moved to the rhythm he was pounding out, and I could see the sweat flying off him. By the proportions of his upper body and arms, I guessed he was tall.

I shook my head to clear the impending lust. Come on Isobel – a drummer in a rock band? What are you, fourteen? But the driving beat and the image of the guy who was providing it was beginning to have a very real effect on my lady parts. They finished a particularly loud song and the lead singer signalled with his hands for the crowd to quieten down – which they did.

"Okay, you lot. You're a great crowd." There was a loud cheer from the audience, and he signalled for quiet again. "Right – this one is really special to us, and it's been requested a lot."

The stage went black, and then a single spot shone down on a stool in the middle of the stage. The singer climbed onto it, and he was all I could see. There was a gentle piano introduction that was oddly familiar, and then he started to sing; low down in his register, the pure, deep sound was hauntingly beautiful. The room went quiet as we all listened to him and it transfixed me.

"Hello darkness my old friend, I've come to talk with you again." As the strains of 'The Sound of Silence' filled the dark room, you could almost feel the expectation in the air. It was thick enough to taste.

He was accompanied by a keyboard and guitar only – drummer boy wasn't visible in the darkness, but it was possibly one of the most beautiful things I'd ever heard. I looked over at Meilin, and tears were falling down her cheeks.

When the singer got to the verse that starts, *and in the naked light I saw*, he went up, an octave and more lights came up on the stage. There he was – drummer boy – standing at a pair of timpani, holding the beaters, ready to start. I watched him – my initial thought that he was tall was apparently correct – he was bent over the drums waiting for the beat, then he started to play. Oh god … my body started to send *lady-part crisis* warnings to my brain, which my brain summarily ignored. Lust flooded my body like a river that had broken its banks, and I knew there and then that I would be replaying this image over and over later that night.

Two more numbers and the band were done – I had to admit it had been a hell of performance, and it made me want to listen to some of the music by the band that had inspired it. But most of all, I wanted to get home and ease the ache between my legs.

Meilin hugged me when we got the street where we had left our cars. My ears felt like they were full of cotton wool from the volume of the performance I had just experienced. "Thank you for coming with me – they were just great, weren't they?"

"Yeah." I was surprised by how much I had enjoyed the music, but there was no way I was going to share my teen-level response to the drummer with her – she'd never let me forget it. "They were great. I want to find out more about the actual band now."

"Oh, my god!" Meilin looked like she was about to burst. "I knew you'd love it! I've got all their albums – I'll copy them and bring them for you on Monday." She hugged me again, and we said goodnight.

Back in my flat, I poured myself a glass of wine and logged on to Youtube. I had no problem finding the video of Disturbed singing 'The Sound of Silence', and I watched it a couple of times. Then I looked for 'Unstable' and found a grainy, poor quality video that had been filmed on a phone. The music was something unidentifiable, but I could see the drummer working himself up into a frenzy, his muscular arms flailing around and his hair fanning out around his head. It was enough to start the slow burn of lust again, and I watched it once more before going to bed.

I pulled the duvet over me and lay back in the dark. The cool, cotton fabric of my bedsheets brushed against my over-sensitive skin, and I knew that there was no way I was going to get to sleep without easing the ache between my legs. I reached down and shivered as my fingers brushed through my pubic hair and ventured into the damp, swollen folds of my pussy. The image of the drummer came into my mind, and I imagined that his wild, blonde head was between my thighs, licking at my overheated flesh. I dipped my finger into my wetness then circled my clit with it, torturing myself by not applying enough pressure to bring me to climax. I wanted this to last.

I conjured up the image of drummer-boy again and reached down with my other hand, pushing two fingers into my hot hole. In my fantasy, he was over me now, his strong arms bracketing my body as he pushed himself into me, murmuring filthy words of encouragement. It didn't take long for me to come. I felt the first warnings and pushed my fingers as far into my cunt as I could, and then it broke; my back arched and my legs spread as far as they could as the waves of pleasure flooded my whole body.

When it was over, I lay in my bed panting and sweating, waiting for the feeling to pass. It took a very long time. When I was finally coming down, I looked down my body; I had thrown the duvet off at some point, and I was now lying naked and shivering in the dim light of my bedroom. Max's bitter words came back to me. *"I'm the best you've ever had, and you know it."* I started to laugh. The combination of post-orgasm euphoria and relief that the sexual tension of the evening had been released made me laugh so hard that tears ran down my cheeks. "Yeah, Max. Not even in the top five." I knew I was talking to myself, but it made me feel better somehow.

Three weeks later, I was sitting in a restaurant with Meilin and her new boyfriend, Ash. He was just her type – pretty in a masculine kind of way and very smart. One whiff of him had told me that his cologne was as expensive as his immaculate suit. He was classy. And he'd brought us to a classy place to eat; a French restaurant that I'd always dismissed as an option because I knew I couldn't afford to eat there often. But Meilin had been so excited that he'd managed to book a table, I gave in to her insistence that I had to go too. "Ash really wants to meet you. And it will be amazing. They have live music there – a proper orchestra – it's going to be so posh."

It was posh. The waiter pulled my chair out for me and placed my linen napkin in my lap. One look at the menu had me wincing in expectation of the bill. "Um – this all looks wonderful. But I'm not that hungry actually – I think I might just have a starter."

Ash smiled and reached for Meilin's hand. "Didn't you tell her?"

Meilin blushed and leaned over to kiss her man on the cheek. "No – I forgot – sorry."

"Tell me what?" I tried not to sound annoyed. If these two had set me up for something, I was going to be pissed off.

Ash turned his very white-toothed smile on me. "I did some work for the owner. This meal is on the house – so please, order what you like – I'm certainly going to."

"Oh." I felt myself blush. "Okay. What kind of work do you do?"

He took a sip of his water (which had come in a very expensive-looking bottle). "Employment law. They had an illegal working in the kitchen. They'd checked him out but not well enough, and they were caught out. I got them off with a caution."

"Wow. I had no idea. Meilin didn't tell me that much about you." That wasn't strictly true. She had gone to great lengths to describe how good he looked without his clothes and how skilled he was with his tongue. Looking at him now, all sharp suit and handmade shoes, I felt myself blush again remembering her lurid description of their first night together. "Okay then – I'll have the filet mignon."

Our main courses had just arrived when a soft, lovely sound began to drift over from the far corner of the restaurant. Ash looked over my shoulder to where the sound was coming from. "Oh good – the band is here. I know a couple of them. They're mostly music students – but they're good, aren't they?"

I let the relaxing and familiar notes of Pachelbel's Canon flow over me like warm water and closed my eyes to listen properly. When they had finished playing, a gentle patter of applause ran through the restaurant, and I turned around to look. There were two female violinists, a young man on viola and an older woman playing a cello. Then my eyes moved to the young man at the piano. He was dressed in black, as the others were, and his dark blonde hair was pulled back into a smart ponytail. Even though I hadn't thought about him in weeks, I would have known him anywhere. Sitting at the piano, looking very different to the last time I saw him, was drummer boy.

By the time we were enjoying our coffee and cognac, the musicians were starting to pack their instruments away. Something was tugging at my conscience to go and talk to drummer boy – say something – anything – the attraction I had felt on that first night was back with a vengeance.

Meilin looked over at me. "You okay, Izzy? You look a bit distracted."

"What?" I snapped my attention back to my friend. "Yeah – I'm cool. Just getting a bit tired I think. It's way past my bedtime for a school night."

Ash and Meilin both laughed, then Ash looked up and smiled at someone approaching the table. I assumed it was the restauranteur coming to check that everything was okay with the meal, but he stood up and greeted whoever it was with a fist bump. "Hey, Nate – dude – you were good tonight. Love that thing you played last."

I felt a pair of hands land on the back of my chair as their owner leaned over in the crowded dining space to talk to his friend. I turned around and looked up into the smiling face of drummer boy. I felt the colour drain from my face as I inhaled his scent – fresh sweat and sandalwood. "Hi."

Nate looked down at me and smiled. "Hi."

Ash watched the exchange, and I saw him nudge Meilin's shoulder out of the corner of my eye. "Mate, this is Meilin, my girlfriend."

Nate broke eye contact with me and looked over to Meilin. Then he stretched his arm over my shoulder to shake her hand; his muscular arm touched the side of my neck as he did it and I felt a tingle spread out from that brief contact point. He pulled his arm back and returned his hand to the back of my seat. "And who's this?" He was smiling at me again.

"I'm Isobel. Meilin's friend. It's good to meet you." I turned around as far as I could and put my hand out.

He took it in a firm handshake and held on for longer than necessary. "Lovely to meet you too." There was a moment's awkward silence then the people at the next table got up to leave. Nate grabbed one of the chairs they had vacated and aimed it at the space next to my seat. "Budge up." I moved my chair over as far as I could, and Ash did the same, making room for his friend at our small table. He sat down and grabbed the water bottle and my glass, filling it then downing the cool liquid in one, greedy gulp. "That's better."

My plan to go home flew out the window. This was too good. "How do you two know each other?"

Nate looked at me, then his friend. "We were at college together."

Ash reached over and poked his friend in the arm. "Yeah – but this guy dropped out after two years. Studying law was making too much of a dent in his extra-curricular activities." They shared a look that told of affection and more than a few shared secrets. "He's a really good musician though – have to give him that."

The waiter came over to ask if we wanted some more coffee and Nate replied for everyone. "Yes, please, Pascal. And another bottle of water. And can I have something to eat? Whatever's in the kitchen."

"You play here quite often?" It was an obvious question, and I kicked myself for asking. He clearly knew everyone here, and his request for food and drink was met with a smile.

"Yeah – my dad is the owner. He kind of has dibs on my free time at the moment. I don't do every night though – I play in a band as well."

"Unstable?"

"How did you know that?"

"Meilin and I came to one of your gigs a few weeks ago – at The Cave – it was great."

Meilin looked over at me with surprise. "I didn't think you enjoyed it that much – I mean – enough to remember anyone from the band. I'm impressed!"

I didn't say that I wouldn't be able to identify any other members of the band in a line-up. "I never forget a face."

Just then, a man who looked like an older version of Nate came to the table carrying a plate of food and a bottle of water. He put the things down on the table and put his hand on Nate's shoulder before speaking to Ash. "I hope everything was to your liking?" His French accent was gorgeous. "And I see my son has ingratiated himself on you." He tweaked his son's ear affectionately. "Pascal is bringing your coffee now."

Ash stood up and shook his hand. "Monsieur Masson. Good to see you again. The meal was really good – thank you."

"You are most welcome." Then he squeezed his son's shoulder, "Nathanael, eat your food before it goes cold. And don't bore these good ladies with your college stories."

It was nearing midnight when we finally decided to call it a night. I couldn't stop the yawn that forced my mouth open wide enough to crack my jaw. "Oh – god – sorry! I'm about to turn into a pumpkin."

Nate grinned at me. "You'd look cute as a pumpkin." He took my hand and wound his fingers around mine.

Ash and Meilin were making their way to the door, and I knew I had to follow because they were giving me a lift home. But I didn't want to leave. *Come on Isobel – if you want something, ask for it.* I looked back at drummer boy – his eyes looked as tired as mine. "I'd like to see you again." The words fell out of my mouth before I'd had a chance to stop them, followed by some equally ill-thought-out friends. "I haven't been able to stop thinking about you since I saw you at The Cave."

He looked shocked for a moment.

"Sorry." I dropped my head and looked at the floor. "You probably think I'm a crazy bitch blurting that out. And I'm sure you already have a girlfriend. Forget I said anything. But it was great to meet you." I turned to join my friends, but a firm hand on my upper arm pulled me back.

He turned me to face him. "I like a woman who knows what she wants and isn't afraid to ask for it. I don't have a girlfriend at the moment. And I'd like to see you again. Soon." He leaned forward and touched his lips to mine. It was a gentle exploration; a first kiss that held the promise of more if I wanted it.

I'm not very good at waiting for things. I wanted more. I put my hands up and wound my fingers into his hair, dislodging it from the tidy band at the back of his head, and slanted my face to kiss him properly. A sound of cheering from my friends brought me back to my senses, and I pulled back, licking my lips to enjoy the remnants of his taste in my mouth.

His pupils were dilated, and his face was flushed. "Wow. I wasn't expecting that." He reached into his pocket and pulled out a card that advertised the piano quartet that had entertained us in the restaurant. "The number on this is mine – call me – soon." He let go of my arm and pushed the card into my hand. "Bonsoir Isobel." His accent was perfect, and I felt my tummy flip.

"Goodnight Nate." One more look back and I was walking away from him, towards my waiting friends.

Meilin gawped at me as she gave me my coat. "What the hell was that?"

Ash grinned at his girlfriend and put his arm around her shoulder, ushering her out of the door. "I think that was Izzy making a stand for equality." He turned and winked at me. "Go, girl – Nate's a great guy."

"Have you called him yet?" Meilin was perched on my desk again, clutching a coffee and trying to look like she hadn't been out till past midnight the night before.

"It's only nine o'clock. I don't think musicians are morning people. And right now, I don't think I am either."

She pulled a face at me that I knew very well. It was her *you're going to chicken out, aren't you?* face.

I replied with my *what the hell was I thinking?* face. "I think I might have made a fool of myself last night."

Meilin made a noise and said something in Chinese that didn't sound very complimentary. "Izzy – you put your tongue down his throat."

I groaned and covered my face with my hands. "I know …"

"And he kissed you back – I was watching – girl, he gave as good as he got. And then he gave you his number. Add that to the fact that he was flirting with you from the moment he sat down; this is a no-brainer. Call him. Before lunch. You don't want me to nag, do you?"

I really didn't want that. I had been subjected to Meilin's nagging once before, when I'd signed up for yoga classes with her then didn't go. She bombarded me with texts and left post-its all over my desk –

every day for a whole month until I finally gave in and went to yoga. I lasted two sessions before I gave up, but at least she left me alone. "No. I don't want that. I'll call him. I promise."

"Make sure you do – I want details." She finished her coffee and left her mug on my desk before leaving me to my work.

The morning dragged. I didn't want to call him too early or appear to be too keen – although, Meilin's reminder that I'd played tonsil hockey with him already made that sound a bit ridiculous. Finally, just before noon, I plucked up the courage to do it. I walked to the breakroom to make a coffee and dialled his number. He picked up after one ring.

"Hello? Izzy, is that you?"

"Yes. Hello." I tried not to sound too surprised by the fact that he's answered so quickly and that he'd guessed it was me. "How are you?"

"Better now. I've been waiting for your call all morning. Been driving my boss crazy by pacing up and down. He's worried I've worn a line in the carpet."

I hadn't thought to ask him if he had another job – I cursed myself for not thinking about that and groaned inwardly at my stupidity. "What do you do? Sorry – I should have asked you last night."

I heard a little exhalation on the line that made me think he'd just smiled. "You thought I was a starving musician, didn't you?"

"Not starving, no." I laughed a little with relief at his playful tone. "You obviously eat well enough at your dad's restaurant. But yes, with both of your music commitments, I didn't think you'd have the time or energy to do something else."

"I work at Booktique."

The small, independent bookshop on the high street was a place I hadn't visited in a couple of years. Like the rest of the world, I buy most of my books as e-books for my Kindle. But thinking about how it had been the last time I saw it, I could see him there; it fitted him. "Cool. I haven't been there for a couple of years."

"Do you like reading?" He sounded like he wanted to know and wasn't just making small talk.

"I love it – I read a lot. But mostly ebooks."

He laughed softly, and the sound of his breath over the phone made my tummy flutter. "I'm supposed to reprimand you for that – lecture you about why you should buy books from an independent store – but I'm the same. I love the convenience of downloading books. It's great that you read – a lot of people don't."

"I know – and I can't understand that – but I wouldn't have thought you had much time to read – what with your music and your job."

"There's always time to read." There was a moment's silence then I heard him chuckle again. "I didn't intend for this conversation to be about our reading habits."

"Oh? What did you intend?"

"I want to see you again. Tonight."

The nerves that had been stirring up my stomach into a bad case of IBS disappeared the moment he said that. I can't explain it – it just felt right. "I like the sound of that. What do you fancy doing?"

"Well, I've got a gig at The Cave again – but we're sharing the spot, and we're on first. Should be finished by nine. How about you come along to the gig, and then we go out to have something to eat afterwards?"

I couldn't think of a better way to spend a Friday night. "I'd love that. I've wanted to see your band again."

"We're going to be doing a bit more of our own material tonight. I'd like you to hear it." I heard him speaking to someone; it sounded like a customer asking about a book. "Izzy – I've gotta go. I'll leave your name on the door – we're on at eight. I'll come and find you – stand near the bar. Can't wait to see you."

"Me too. See you later."

What the hell do you wear to a heavy rock concert that will also look okay for a meal of some kind afterwards? After trying various options, I settled on black skinny jeans and a red silk shirt. I pulled on my favourite boots and a jacket I had only worn once before. It had been an impulse buy – a black leather jacket with a glorious phoenix embroidered on the back. I looked at myself in the mirror and, at the last minute, I pulled the band out of my hair and let it fall around my shoulders. "You'll do." I nodded at my reflection before grabbing my bag and heading out.

The Cave was pretty full when I arrived just after seven thirty. I saw him straight away, setting up his kit on the stage and I took the chance to watch him unobserved. Torn jeans and a tight, black tee shirt. I let out a little whistle of appreciation when he bent over showing his very fine ass to the crowd. I imagined clutching at it with my hands as he thrust himself …. Whoa! Where did that come from?

As if my ogling had transmitted a signal across the room, he looked up then and saw me standing, as instructed, near the bar. He grinned, and his eyes lit up, then he bounded off the low stage and pushed his way towards me. "Hi – so glad you came." He leaned in to kiss me on the cheek.

Something about this man makes me do crazy things. The kiss at the restaurant was completely new territory for me, but I knew, as soon as his woody, male scent filled my nose, that I was about to do it again. "Glad you asked me." I put my hand up and pushed my fingers into his hair before pulling him down to me. I took possession of his mouth, pushing my tongue between his open lips and the taste of him set my blood alight.

He groaned into my mouth and pulled me closer to his body. I could feel the hard ridge of his cock pressing against my hip.

There was a sound of clapping and cheering coming from the stage, and I ended the kiss with a sly smile. "Hold that thought. It looks like you're needed up there."

He looked over to his friends and waved, taking their teasing in good stead. Then he turned back to me and kissed me quickly, sucking my lower lip in and biting it softly. "Stay right here. As soon as we've finished, I'm coming back for more." One, shining smile and he was pushing his way back through the crowd to take his place on stage.

The gig was good. I liked the songs they said were their own. About ten minutes before their set was due to end, the lead singer did the *pipe down* signal with his hands, and the crowd went quiet, waiting to hear what he was going to say. "Okay, you guys – this is a bit of a treat – our very talented drummer wants to serenade a very special lady in the audience tonight. So get close to your nearest and dearest – coz he's gonna sing you a love song."

There were whoops and cheers from the crowd, and I felt my cheeks redden as I watched Nate move from the drum kit, pick up a beautiful acoustic guitar from the back of the stage and take a seat on the stool that the lead singer moved into place for him. He looked across at me then started to play. I recognised it straight away. My parents had listened to a lot of James Taylor and, as a teenager, I claimed to hate it. But when I moved out, I bought my own copies of the CDs. The beautiful guitar introduction to one of my favourite songs floated across the room and, when he started to sing, the hairs stood up on the back of my neck. He was playing the guitar like some kind of god and his voice was pure and beautiful.

There's something in the way she moves
Or looks my way, or calls my name
That seems to leave this troubled world behind
If I'm feeling down and blue
Or troubled by some foolish game
She always seems to make me change my mind
And I feel fine anytime she's around me now

As he continued to sing the song – which was so unlike anything else that they had played that night – the atmosphere in the crowded space filled with something that was almost tangible. Couples in the crowd were holding onto each other – standing together watching my guy pour his heart out on stage. And when he'd finished, and the last notes died away from the guitar, there was a moment's silence before the audience erupted into loud cheers and whistles. Nate looked over at me and smiled.

Wait – did I just call him *my guy*? Whoa …

The lead singer reclaimed his place at the front of the stage and spoke into the mic. "Well, boys and girls, that was kinda special, wasn't it?" There was a loud agreement from the crowd; then he looked at Nate who was back in his seat at the drums. "And dude – I think you are so getting laid tonight." The crowd was laughing and cheering, and my embarrassment soared up to expert level. I was glad that no one could see me in the dim light of the bar.

Their last number was a loud, crashing song that I didn't know. I watched Nate as he beat the drums, raising his arms to get the most impact, his hair flying around his head like a sweaty crown as he moved it in time to the rhythm. When it was over, the audience stomped and cheered, and the band took their bows. A moment later, Nate leapt off the stage and made his way towards me.

The crowd parted for him, and my embarrassment level grew even higher. He stopped a foot or so away from me, waiting to see my reaction. Was he unsure of himself? I found that endearing. But I found the sight of him, sweaty and fresh from his performance, thoroughly delicious. I couldn't stop myself; I stepped towards him and threw my arms around his neck. I claimed that beautiful mouth again and tasted him as deeply as my tongue would go.

He groaned into me and put his hands down to cup my buttocks. He lifted me up, and I wrapped my legs around his waist, enjoying the feeling of his muscular body between my thighs. When we finally broke our mouths apart, to the cheering of the crowd, he rubbed his nose against mine and said, "Let's get out of here."

"I want you naked and on my bed." I couldn't believe I was saying the words that were coming out of my mouth. I'd never been the aggressor in a relationship before; always letting the guy take the lead and call the shots. It was just easier that way. And it usually got the whole thing over and done with as quickly as possible.

Wait! Does that mean that I haven't ever truly enjoyed sex with any of my previous lovers? Whoa … (that was a total, Bill & Ted *whoa* by the way).

So, what was different this time? I looked over at the grinning, gorgeous boy who was currently struggling out of his clothes. He was different. I wanted him. And by the size of the bulge in his jeans, it was mutual.

His shirt landed in in a crumpled heap on my bedroom floor, and I could see that his skin was still glistening with sweat from his exertions at the concert. "I need to shower. I'm all sweaty from the gig." He looked over at me, his eyes dark with lust. "Join me?"

I shook my head. "Uh-uh. We can shower afterwards. I don't mind fresh sweat. And I intend to make you lose some more before we're done. Now – I thought I said something about naked?"

He raised an eyebrow and grinned at me again. A look passed between us that said game on, and he began to wrestle with his trainers and socks. When he was naked, he walked to me and grabbed a handful of my shirt fabric, pulling me into his embrace. "So – you have me at a disadvantage. You've still got all your clothes on. Shall we do something about that?"

I pushed gently out of his embrace. "Get on the bed. Prop yourself up on the pillows and watch me. And don't even think about touching that gorgeous cock of yours – that thing is all mine." Where the hell was all this stuff coming from? Had this woman always been inside me, waiting for the right inspiration? Or was she a new arrival? I had no idea, but the effect on Nate was obvious, so I decided to continue. I pulled at the buttons of my shirt, and soon, it joined Nate's clothes in a pile on the floor.

His eyes were fixed on my breasts, still encased in the lacy balcony bra I had chosen. He was already fidgeting on my bed, and I was in the mood to make him squirm. I lifted my hands and squeezed my lace-covered globes together. "Do you want to see them?"

Nate was breathing so hard that his answer came out as a croak. Then he nodded and moved his hands to his body. He was teasing a nipple with one, and the other was cupping his balls.

"I'll take that as a yes." I reached behind and unfastened my bra, then let it fall to the ground. I'd never felt so wanton or powerful. I took off my jeans and boots – I toyed with the idea of leaving my heels on, but my prey was clearly already close enough to the edge, so I shucked them off. I left the lacy panties on and went to the bed, climbing on it, straddling Nate's thighs. I wanted him to touch me everywhere at once; I was so aroused, I could feel my juices oozing out onto the red satin that covered my pussy. I scooted a little higher and put my arms around his neck. Before I went in for the kiss that would take this further, I had a sudden dose of reality. "You still with me, baby?"

Nate's smile widened, and he reached for me, enfolding me in his muscular arms. "Oh yeah. I'm with you all the way. Tell me what you want me to do."

"I want your mouth on me." I wanted it so badly; I was aching for it. My whole body was tingling with the need to feel his lips caressing and licking my skin.

He didn't say anything. He pulled me closer with his arms and dipped his head, taking one of my aroused nipples into the warm, wet welcome of his lips. As he sucked on the hard bud, my hips began to move as though someone else was controlling them. It felt so good, and I needed to relieve the ache between my legs. He switched his attention to the other nipple, and I ground myself on his thigh. "Christ, Nate, what have you done to me? I'm acting like a she-cat in heat."

He laughed against my skin, and even that small vibration was enough to spark another flare of lust in my body. The sight of his silky hair falling around his face and the smell of his skin was driving me insane. He removed his mouth from my nipple and started to tease it between his thumb and forefinger. He looked up at me. "I know what I'd like to do to you."

"Tell me."

His hands moved to my hips, and he began to push my panties down. "I want you out of these."

I moved so that he could push them down further. I was impatient to be completely bare for him; my pussy was dripping with the need for his touch. So, I climbed off him for a moment and pushed the sodden fabric to the floor. I picked them up and tossed them at Nate. He caught them in one hand and raised the fabric to his nose.

His eyes closed and he groaned as he inhaled my scent. "God, Izzy. You are incredible. Come back here. I need to touch you now."

I did as he asked, climbing back to my original position astride his legs. His cock was almost upright and pulsing in time with his heartbeat. I wanted to taste him. I'd never felt such an overwhelming need to claim a man before. I bent over and sucked the head of his penis into my mouth. He let out a shuddering breath and tried to move, but I put my hand on his chest and pushed him back down onto the pillows. I was going to drive. I reached down and cupped his balls with one hand, and I curled the fingers of the other around the base of his shaft. Then I sucked more of him into my mouth, stroking the sensitive underside with my tongue.

Nate was trying to hold still, but his hips began to move as he tried to thrust into my mouth. "Oh god! Izzy – please – I can't stop …" He gave one last thrust and filled my mouth with spurt after spurt of hot cum.

I held on, sucking him till his cock had stopped twitching, then I raised my head and wiped my mouth triumphantly. "Good boy. Did you enjoy that?"

"I … Izzy … oh fuck, that was awesome."

I felt that unfamiliar power and confidence flooding my body again. I reached for the pillows behind his head and pulled them away, forcing him to lie flat on his back. "Good. Now it's my turn." I'd never done this before. Never straddled a man's head and taken pleasure from his mouth in such a daring way. My mind flitted to the last time Max had tried to make me come with his mouth. He had made it clear that what he was doing would mean that I owed him big time; that it wasn't something he bestowed on me without expectation. After five minutes of reluctant licking, he had given up and fucked me.

I shook my head to clear it of the unwanted memory and looked down at the expectant face of the man between my legs. He was panting, and his tongue darted out to lick his lips. He wanted this as much as I did. I moved up, positioning my wet slit over his mouth.

Nate groaned and put his hands on my hips, pulling me down onto him. He didn't wait for me to ask or give instructions – he began to lick me in strong, even strokes that went the length of my opening, pausing to concentrate on the hard, little bundle of nerve endings at my apex, before returning for another stroke. I felt so powerful as I ground myself into his face and the sounds he was making told me that he was enjoying the ride as much as I was.

I felt my inner muscles begin to clench as the first wave of an orgasm washed over me. He felt the change in me and increased the pressure of his tongue on my overheated flesh. As the full force of my climax took me over, I threw my head back and howled. I reached back and took hold of his cock, which was now steely hard again, and I felt it pulse against the skin of my palm as my inner muscles clenched and throbbed with the power of my release. I'd never felt anything so powerful. Top five? Forget it. I had the feeling that whatever I shared with this guy would wipe all my other experiences off the board.

I eased back down Nate's body until I was straddling his chest and I looked down at his handsome face. He had my juices smeared over his lips and nose, and he was grinning like the Cheshire Cat. And I'd never seen anything so beautiful in my entire life. "Hi." The word came out with a laugh of relief.

"Hi." His grin widened, and he reached up to pull my face down to his. I could smell myself on his skin. "You look like a goddess when you come. I'm going to need to see that again before this night is over." His mouth sealed over mine and he was kissing me, thrusting his tongue deep into my mouth. When our lips parted, his eyes were dark with lust. "Can I fuck you, my goddess?"

I could feel his erection pressing between my buttocks where I knelt astride him and, even though I had just come in the most powerful way, I felt that empty ache in my cunt. I was aroused, and I knew what I wanted; his cock, buried in me, balls-deep. "Yes. I want you inside me. Fucking me."

His face turned serious, and he put his arms around me, flipping me easily onto my back. I could feel the strength in his muscles and wondered at the restraint he had shown as I had claimed him twice – once with my mouth on him and once with my pussy on his mouth. "God, Izzy. What the fuck have you done to me? My cock has been hard since I smelled your hair in the restaurant last night."

My puzzled look was involuntary.

"When I leaned over you to bump fists with Ash, I caught the scent of your hair. It went straight to my cock. And I knew I had to have you." He leaned down and took a handful of my damp hair, lifting it to his nose. He inhaled deeply, and I felt the instant effect it had on him as his cock twitched against the skin of my belly. A sound escaped from his lips – something between a groan and a growl – and he began to kiss and lick the skin under my ear. His caress moved down my neck, leaving a moist trail of desire that burned into my skin. When he reached my breasts, he paused, using his hands to push them together so that my taught nipples were only a couple of inches apart. He began to nip and suck at them, moving from one to the other, lavishing them both with attention that had me panting and writhing under him. "I think I could make you come just by doing this."

I responded with a clenched moan and moved my hips to try to get some contact. I needed him inside me now, more than I'd ever needed it. "Please …." It was all I could manage to gasp out.

Nate grinned at me and climbed off the bed, reaching for his discarded jeans. I watched as he took something out of the pocket, and I heard the sound of something being torn open. Then he turned to face me, holding my gaze with his dilated pupils as he sheathed his cock with a condom. "I want to fuck you skin to skin. But we're new. So, for now, we'll have to make do with this." He walked slowly back to the bed, his easy gate reminding me of some beautiful, sleek, big cat stalking its prey. "I will love you slowly another time. Now we're both too desperate for that. Get up on all fours."

His command was hypnotic, and I didn't stop to question it. He was right. There would be time for a slow, sensual joining. But now we both needed something else: the raw, frantic mating that was about to happen. I pushed up onto my hands and knees and positioned myself in the centre of my bed, my back turned to him. I felt the bed dip as he joined me on the mattress and then his hands were gripping my hips.

"Put your head down. Open yourself up to me."

I did as he instructed, crossing my arms and resting my cheek against them. I felt his fingers dip into the sodden well of my pussy and heard him whistle in appreciation.

"You're mine. I'm yours. This night – this," He pushed his cock into me in one, hard movement. "This is yours. And this," He reached under me with his hand and cupped my mound, pushing one, long finger into me, stretching my already full hole with the intrusion, "This is mine." He began to rock his hips, taking me hard in an erotic rhythm and he withdrew his finger, moving it to find the hard nub of my clit which he rubbed in time to his thrusts.

I tried to say something equally meaningful, but all I could manage was a rhythmic groan as his fucking pushed the air out of my lungs. It was intense, and I knew I would be feeling the echo of it for a long time to come. I also knew that this was more than a wild fuck; it was a beginning, a launch into the unknown.

Nate was shaking now – I could feel it against my thighs when he reached full penetration. He was mumbling something I couldn't quite translate; then I felt him bend over my back so that his lips touched the skin of my shoulder. What happened next was shocking. I felt him open his mouth and take the soft flesh between my neck and shoulder between his teeth. As he started to come, he bit down. I felt the skin break as he teeth found purchase and the sudden shock and pain triggered an orgasm, the like of which I had never experienced before.

He held on, groaning as he emptied himself inside the warm, wet grip of my clenching innards. When it was finally over for both of us, he relinquished his hold and, as he withdrew his teeth from my flesh, I felt a soft trickle of blood travel down between my breasts where they hung beneath me. He had marked me. I felt my pussy tighten around his wilting cock at that realisation.

Nate withdrew his cock from me, and I saw the knotted condom, and its plentiful contents fly towards the waste-paper bin beside my nightstand. He flopped down on the bed, rolling onto his back and moved to pull me into his arms. Then he saw the blood between my breasts. "Shit! Izzy – I'm so sorry! Jeez – we've got to get that cleaned up."

I could feel his panic, and it bothered me. I wanted him to enjoy the amazing post-coital glow I was feeling. "It's okay – it was amazing – I've never come like that before."

He was kneeling over me now, looking into my eyes. "Really? You're not mad that I did that?"

"No." I laughed softly and stroked his hair. "How could I be mad when you just made me see stars?"

His face eased into a broad grin that I was beginning to recognise and adore. "Stars, huh?"

"Don't let it go to your head lover-boy." I pulled him to me, and we kissed. A deep, licking and tonguing that seemed to validate what we had just done."

He let me kiss him for several, breathless moments, then he pulled away and looked at me. "But seriously – we need to clean that. Human bites nearly always get infected. I can't believe I went so hard on you. Come on."

He pulled me up from the bed, and my legs complained as I put my feet on the floor and tried to follow him to the bathroom. He felt the inertia and turned, lifting me easily, showing me again that his muscles weren't just for show. He deposited me gently on the toilet and walked away towards my small kitchen. I appreciated the view as he walked away from me; his easy strides flexing the muscles in his ass, giving me a world-class view that I would remember forever. I heard him clattering about in my kitchen and, a few minutes later, he returned with a steaming bowl, which he put down on the vanity unit next to my inelegant seat.

"Do you have any cotton wool?"

I lifted my chin to indicate the cupboard over the sink, and he opened the mirrored door and retrieved the pack of cotton pads I kept in there. He dipped one in the bowl and let it soak through the white fibres. "This is hot, salt water. It might sting a bit." He applied the warm, wet pad to my skin and I felt it burn slightly. He took another pad and repeated the movement. "Press hard on this."

I did as he instructed and stood up, facing the mirror over the sink. When I eased the pad away from my skin, I saw the clear outline of his bite. It made me tingle. I'd never felt like this before. Something primeval took hold of me, and I reached for him, pulling him into my arms and between my legs as I hitched myself up to sit on the vanity unit. "You've marked me."

He looked crestfallen. "I know – Izzy I'm so sorry."

I pulled him closer, and he looked confused. "Now I'm going to mark you."

His eyes widened as he realised what I was saying and I felt his cock stiffen, going from semi-hard to fully erect in a heartbeat. He reached behind me and opened the mirrored cupboard once more, retrieving the pack of condoms I kept in there. "Good job you have these. I only brought one with me."

"One? I smirked at him and took the box from him, retrieving a slim packet and ripping it open with my teeth. "You're not leaving here until neither of us can walk straight." I reached down and sheathed his cock with the condom. Then I opened my thighs as wide as I could, bringing my feet up to rest on the on the cool surface of the vanity. I felt wanton and open in front of him as my pussy lips parted as I stretched out for him.

Needing no more encouragement, he pulled me as far forward as I could go and put his hands underneath my buttocks, steering me towards him. I felt him. I was slightly sore from the wild fucking he'd given me on the bed and the mild smart stirred something in me. I cried out his name and wrapped my legs around his hips, pulling him into me. Our eyes locked as he began to rock inside me and I knew this was going to be as fast and furious as the first time. He reached down and started to rub his thumb in circles over my clit as he pushed his cock into me. "You know what to do."

I did know. As I felt the first sparks of my climax ignite in my belly, I pulled him forward and sealed my mouth over the hard ridge of muscle that formed a bridge between the column of his neck and his shoulder. As he felt my teeth take possession of his flesh, his movements increased, and his cock burrowed into me so I couldn't tell where he ended and I began. I felt it then; the primitive reflex that had been passed down to me by every woman since the dawn of time. As my muscles clenched, binding me to this male between my legs, I bit down on him.

"Yes. Izzy, yes. Do it. Mark me." Nate's hands pressed harder into the flesh of my buttocks, and I felt the shape of his fingers digging into my skin. He was close.

I bit down on him, applying all the force I could manage, and I felt the muscle beneath my tongue contract as the pain hit him. I felt something give way, and then I tasted blood in my mouth; the warm, metallic tang of it filling my senses and spurring me on to reach the height of my orgasm. As my internal muscles clenched around him, I threw my head back and shouted his name as I milked his cock until he stilled inside me.

He rested his head on my shoulder and stayed there until his ragged breathing returned to some kind of normal rhythm. Then I felt him withdraw from me, his softening member slipping from my wet hold. I winced as he left me; I was sore from his pounding, and I was going to feel it for some considerable time. I could feel the ghost of his cock in my open channel, and I gloried in the knowledge that he had left his impression so deep inside me. I watched him remove the condom and dispose of it in the bathroom bin. Then I looked up to where my mouth had marked him. "We'd better clean that up." I tried not to smirk, but the look of pure pleasure on his face made the smile I was trying to conceal widen into a grin.

The sun was beginning to rise, and we lay together on my bed, legs entwined and tangled in the sheets that were stained with a heady mixture of my juices, his cum and our blood. I caught myself wondering idly if Vanish would work, then laughed as I imagined myself doing one of their TV ads. "Blood and cum? No problem."

Nate kissed the top of my head. "What are you giggling about?"

"I was imagining being on an advert for Vanish, showing how cum and blood covered sheets were no match for its magical cleaning abilities."

He was silent for a moment; then I heard him chuckle. "You're weird."

"Yeah. I am." We were silent for a few minutes then I felt his fingers stroking the skin of my arm. "I think you might have wrecked my pussy."

He kissed my hair again. "Are you sore?"

"A little bit. Yeah."

"Me too. It's good."

"Yes, it is." More silence. Comfortable, companionable silence. Then I turned to look at his face, the shadow of a golden beard covering his jaw. I wanted to feel the scrape of it as he kissed the skin of my belly. "How do you know that James Taylor song?"

He looked down at me. "We just shared the most erotic, depraved night of our lives and you want to know how I know a James Taylor Song?"

"Yeah." I snuggled into him, inhaling deeply, taking his musky scent into my lungs. "I liked it."

"Really? I'd never have guessed." I felt his body tremble with laughter. "I used to do a JT tribute act in college. The older guys loved it. Which begs the question, how do you know a James Taylor song?"

I kissed the skin around one of his small, tight nipples before sucking the hardened nub into my mouth. I heard him groan and I released it with a soft pop. "Well, you should probably know I'm actually fifty-three years old. I've had a lot of plastic surgery."

I heard him laugh. "I always did fancy the idea of a cougar."

I sat up slightly and slapped his chest with open fingers. "My parents had all of his albums and I secretly loved them. The one you sang is one of my favourites."

"So, that's why I got the world-class fuck? I'd better re-learn some more of his stuff."

"No. I think I'd already decided that we were going to have sex. But don't let that stop you. I'd love to hear you sing some more."

He pulled me tight into his embrace and kissed my mouth in a gentle exploration that reminded me of the first time his lips had touched mine in the restaurant. Had that been only hours ago? "That, my sexy little cougar, would be my pleasure." He kissed me again, then pulled back slightly, his brows creased with an unspoken question.

"Yes. I was kidding about being fifty-three. I'm twenty-nine. The same age as Meilin.

He let out a laugh and lay back on the pillow, looking up at the ceiling, watching the morning light as it crept higher up my bedroom wall. "Do you know what?"

"What?"

"I don't think it would make the slightest bit of difference."

Leo

Ruling, warmth, generosity, faithful, initiative

I have followed Richard for more than half of my life. I supported him and his mother when they plotted to usurp his father, King Henry. I followed him to Jerusalem on the Holy Crusades; I bought the Manor of Fordleigh from him to help fund his endeavours. And I followed him here, to Normandy. We've been at war with Philip of France ever since, and I'm tired of it. I'm tired of war, I'm tired of Richard, and I just want to go home. Perhaps this battle will be the last one I have to endure. Perhaps I can go home to Fordleigh and the life I have imagined there; managing the land and the peasants who farm it. I dream of raising fine horses and fine sons. This life as a warrior was sweet to me once; now it is as bitter as gall. I have seen my king for the hopeless dreamer he is. I will not be named a traitor – he is my king – but if this battle should be the end of his campaign, then I won't pretend to be sad.

"Sire? Are you awake? Sire? Can you hear me?"

The voice was insistent, and it carried through the fog in which I seemed to be trapped. All around me, fog and silence. Like a blanket, it shrouded me with pain and fractured memories. I saw the battle; the final assault on the castle at siege – a battle fought because my king coveted a treasure that would never be his. And then I saw Richard, shouting at the enemy and daring them to leave their fortress.

Then another fragment; I was on a boat, crossing an angry sea. I remembered the ceaseless rolling of the boat on the waves and the sickness that had held me prisoner, even as I drifted in and out of consciousness.

And now? Where was I now? The voice was familiar – my squire, Thomas – he was here with me. But where was here? And what had happened after I watched that crossbow bolt find its mark on the shoulder of my king? The blanket of fog won the victory and my consciousness lost ground. I submitted to it, allowing it to wrap me in its hold and take me to oblivion.

"The wound is healing. There is no more we can do for him. Take him home – his life is in the hands of God now."

I looked up and saw the face of my squire and another man – a priest. So, I was with the Hospitallers of St John. I opened my mouth to speak, but my lips and throat were too dry, I couldn't form words.

"Sire, please don't try to speak." Thomas looked frantic.

"Thirsty." I managed to get the sounds out through my parched lips.

The priest looked at me and then spoke to my squire. "Let him drink. The small beer is safer than the water. Give him a little of that."

I felt the warm, sour brew flow into my mouth as my squire held my head up so I could drink. I swallowed hungrily until the wooden ladle was empty, then I let Thomas lay my head back down on the straw-stuffed pillow. "Where am I?"

"Dover. You wanted to go home to Fordleigh, but this is as far as I could get you. You've been here, with the order of St John for near a fortnight."

"I don't remember what happened." The words came hard, like pulling a deep root from the soil. "Were we victorious? Does the king live?"

I watched as Thomas's face fell. "No, Sire. The king took a bolt in the shoulder. He died soon afterwards. You were wounded in the battle that followed; you were run through with the point of a halberd. It pierced your armour and went into your leg. I tried to get you home, Sire, but you succumbed to a fever on the boat." He reached for another ladle of the weak ale, and when I nodded, he helped me to drink it. "I have been tending you e'er since."

"Help me to sit up, Thomas. I want to see what ails me." My young squire put his arm under my shoulder and helped me into a sitting position. I looked down my body. I had shrunken during my time in this narrow cot. "Is my armour ruined?"

"Yes, Sire. I have it all, and the blacksmith may be able to repair it."

"No. It's for the best. It would be far too big for me now." I looked then at the large bandage that covered my left leg from hip to knee. I could see the site of the wound as there was a spot of fresh blood that had made its way to the surface. "God in heaven, it looks like I came close to losing my cock." The wound was at the very top of my leg. "An inch to the left and I would have been a eunuch."

"Yes, Sire." Thomas chuckled and helped me to lie back down. "Do you think you can travel?"

"By the gods, yes. Take me home."

Three pain-filled days later, the wagon in which I was travelling drew to a halt at the top of a hill. Thomas helped me to sit up, and I saw the gentle slope of the hill that led down to Fordleigh. I had spent just one week at this Manor before leaving for the Crusade, and that had been nearly nine years ago. But looking at it now, my whole mind and body recognised it as home.

"We're home, Thomas. We're home."

"Yes, Sire. It's but a mile further. We'll be home by nightfall."

The wagon continued on the last part of our journey. One of my men rode ahead to let the house know we were coming, so when we approached the gates a while later, they opened for us, and we trundled into the courtyard before coming at last to a halt. I felt my whole body relax with relief as the wagon finally ceased its swaying.

"My lord! What joy!" An elderly man who I vaguely recognised rushed out through the great door of the manor house, wiping his hands on a cloth that was hanging from his belt. "Oh, God be praised that he has brought you home safe to us after all these years."

"Thank you – it's good to be home." Thomas and another of my men, Gerald Baliol, began to lift the litter on which I was lying off the wagon. The pain went through my leg like a hot blade. I winced and tried not to cry out.

"Sire, please, be at ease." The old servant, whose name I now remembered was Hugh, went ahead of the litter, opening doors and leading the way to the narrow stairs which led up to the solar. "I have sent a girl to fetch Lady Lovell. She will be here shortly."

"Lady Lovell? My mother is here?" I must have looked as confused as I felt about this. My mother, last I heard, was happily married to her fourth husband and living with him in Wales.

Hugh laughed nervously. "No, Sire. Lady Emma Lovell. Your wife."

"My wife? Oh – yes, of course." The seventeen-year-old girl had come as part of the deal I struck with Richard for Fordleigh. The Manor had been in her family for generations but some debt to the crown – real or otherwise – had led to it be offered for sale. The girl's father had insisted that I marry her so that she could stay in her family home. I had not objected – she was pretty enough – and the likelihood that I wouldn't return from The Holy Land was fairly strong.

I remembered the wedding day. A cold, wet day. Only her father, the old servant Hugh and my man Gerald Baliol witnessed the ceremony – it would be easy enough to have the marriage annulled. I was a little surprised that she had not already sought that on the grounds of desertion – I had been away from the marriage bed for nearly nine years, after all. This led me to thoughts of the marriage bed. The consummation of our union was witnessed by my man, and the local midwife – on the insistence of her father. Not the most romantic of ways to start a marriage. She was scared to death, and I could barely get a cock-stand, but we managed somehow, and the old woman had inspected the bed and Emma's bloody thighs and declared that the marriage was true in the eyes of God.

When we were to ourselves, she smiled at me and stroked my cheek. I remembered that now; she had hair and eyes the colour of warm honey and her skin looked like the cream the dairymaids took from the top of the churn. I ploughed her for a second time and, because she felt no pain, she welcomed my body into hers. The next morning, I climbed on my horse and left to follow Richard on his Crusade. When I looked back, she waved.

Alas, I must confess that I gave her scant thought after that. There were always women in the camps, and I availed myself of their wares many, many times. I like to fuck – especially if the woman is willing. I'm not enamoured of the reluctant virgin types, though I know a lot of my comrades enjoy that. I like a woman who enjoys cock and isn't afraid to show it.

A woman like Sabrina. Oh yes, Sabrina. The dark-haired beauty I had spent many nights with in Jerusalem had no problems showing me how much she liked to ride my cock. She would often wake me in the night by mounting and riding me like a horse.

"Here we are, Sire. You should be comfortable enough here. I'll bring you something to eat."

I was pulled from my thoughts of Sabrina's wicked thighs by Hugh's voice. I was laid in a large bed. I recognised the heavy drapes; this was the bed in which I had spent my wedding night.

"Is there something special I can get for you, Sire?"

"What? I'm sorry – my thoughts were elsewhere."

"Of course. Do not worry. I will bring a tray with a selection of things from the kitchen, and you can choose what you'd like." He turned around and left me alone.

I don't know how long I slept. I woke from a fevered dream, crying out to dead men in the horror of a battle relived in all its bloody glory. A cool hand on my forehead brought me around, and I stilled, breathing heavily, and looked up into a pair of honey-coloured eyes.

"Be still, my lord. You are home and safe now." Her voice was like honey also, and she smelled as sweet as a garden in summer. "I'll get you a drink."

She got up, and I looked across the bed. Had she been sleeping beside me? I tried to pull myself up but failed, slumping back against the pillows. Emma returned a moment later, and I saw her lithe body outlined beneath her nightgown as she stood with her back against the light from the fire. She had grown up since I saw her last. Her hair was held back in a large plait that reached past her waist. The neckline of her simple gown, gathered with a silk ribbon, dipped low enough to reveal the promise of a bosom worthy of some attention.

"Here. I'll help you sit up." She put her arm under me, and I felt her strength as she helped me to sit up against the pillows. "I brew the ale here myself. This small beer is refreshing but not strong enough to upset your stomach."

I took the cup from her and sipped at the weak beer she gave me. It was good. Much better than any I had drunk for a long time. "This is good. Thank you."

She blushed a little at my compliment; in the dim light from the fire and the lamp she had lit, I could see the pink flush spread down her neck and into the soft valley at the top of her breasts. She watched me drink then took the empty cup. "Can you eat something? You were asleep when Hugh brought the tray, and I didn't like to wake you."

"Emma."

"Yes, my lord?"

"My name is Danyell. It would please me to hear my name on your lips."

She bowed her head. "I'm sorry, my lo – Danyell. You have been gone such a long time. Perhaps we need to get to know each other again."

I lifted my hand and stroked her cheek. I don't know why I felt so tender towards her. Hours ago, I had entertained thoughts of having our marriage annulled, but something in her sweet countenance was making my belly clench. She was mine. "We knew each other well enough. Seeing you now, grown to womanhood, makes me regret not being here to watch it happen."

She blushed again but held my gaze. "I have missed you, Danyell. I am very glad that God brought you safely home to me."

"Aye. A little broken and battered, but I am home. With you. And I'm planning on staying this time." I tried to move a little and winced as the pain in my leg increased. "Right now, though, I need to get to the garderobe. Can you help me?"

She shook her head. "I'll get you a pot. I don't think I can lift you." She went around to her side of the bed and picked up a large, clay pot. She put it on the floor and began to ease the bed coverings off me. "I'll help you sit up."

I let her help me, though it injured my pride to need her assistance for this most basic of needs. She held the pot for me, and I lifted my shirt far enough to get a hold of my cock to aim. She watched me take myself in hand, and I looked at her. She was beautiful. I felt a sudden shot of desire go through me and I cursed my body for not being able to act on it. Another desire filled me then; the desire to heal and return fully to my life here at Fordleigh.

Weeks passed, and I healed. My wife took care of me, helping me bathe and dress. I grew stronger by the day. I learned that I was married to a remarkable woman. When John's men had tried to sabotage the crops of the tenant farmers, she brought in sheep and goats. When nobody would buy the wool from the sheep, for fear of retribution from John, she filled the old Saxon great hall that stood in the courtyard with looms and spinning wheels. The women from the farms on the estate came every day to spin and weave our wool into the fine fabric that Emma sold directly to traders in the nearby city. Fordleigh was flourishing, despite the best attempts of the King.

We were walking in the herb garden – I had been able to take short strolls with her for a few days now. I looked at her; the sunlight made her hair glow like gold. I would have to have her soon. "How many times have John's men come?"

She stopped walking and held her face up to enjoy the soft sunshine. "They come every year. It's always the same. They say that the land is forfeit because the debt was not paid when you bought it from my father. Each time, we go to the Assizes, and I show the document that proves you bought Fordleigh and that my father's debt was paid in full."

"You stand at the Assizes yourself?"

"Aye. There is no one else who will do it. I must defend my land and my people. And when they attacked the Manor once, I helped to defend it then, too." She smiled knowingly. "I can shoot a bow as well as any man."

I saw her for what she was; my wife was a woman of courage. Ready to stand against attacks on those she cared about. For she did care. The work she had created in the weaving house to keep the peasants fed, and the many loaves baked in the kitchen every day that were sent out to stop the children crying with hunger were proof of that. "You are a remarkable woman. I am fortunate to have you as my wife. Your father was right to insist that you were part of the debt."

She looked at me, scrutinising my face. "There was never any debt, you know?"

I nodded my head. "I know. Richard needed money for his campaign, and I was happy to go along with it. Why were you so happy to go along with it? You needn't have married me."

A sly smile crossed her lips. "I wanted you the first moment I saw you. It was I who suggested the marriage to my father. Does that surprise you?"

I reached out and touched her face. "Emma, after everything I have learned about you, I don't think anything could surprise me." I leant forward and kissed her. "Methinks I followed the wrong Lionheart all these years."

She laughed and stepped away from me, continuing our walk amongst the herbs. "Methinks you are right! But you are home now. And I am glad of it." She took another step then turned again. "If for no other reason than we should be spared John's attention now that you are back. And we can start to get Fordleigh back to normal." Her laughter echoed through the walled space as she skipped away from me.

"Your bath is ready, Sire."

"Thank you, Thomas. You may go. Lady Lovell will assist me." Emma had helped me bathe several times, and I liked her gentle touch. She had been shy at first; turning her head away when she washed me. But the last time, she had gazed at my nakedness without blushing.

The bath had been set up in the usual place, in front of the great hearth in the solar. When I entered the room, I saw her; she was bending over the wooden tub, adding some sweet-smelling oil to the water. "You wish to make me smell like a flower garden, my love?"

She looked up at me and smiled. "The lavender helps with the healing. And I like it when you smell like a flower garden." She swirled the water with her hand. "The water is hot. Come, husband. Let me help you undress."

I walked to her. Unaided by the stick I had been using, I felt like a complete man in her presence for the first time. And I realised that was as much to do with her as my healing body. I let her help me out of my shirt and boots. She stood back to allow me to unlace my breeches myself as I had done every time before. But I straightened my back and looked directly at her. "No, my love. Tonight, it would please me if you undressed me."

I saw a moment of indecision pass over her face, then a quick nod of her head. She knelt before me and reached for the laces that held the two halves of my breeches closed. I watched her slender fingers pull at the fine leather strands, and I gave in to the temptation to push my fingers into the soft curtain of her hair. She raised her eyes to me and a sly smile formed on her lips. Without breaking eye contact with me, she continued to unfasten my breeches before pushing them down so that I could step out of them. She sat back on her heels and looked at me. "Husband, you are healing fast. And I do believe your armour will fit you again afore long." She reached out and brushed her fingers over the puckered, pink skin of the newly healed scar at the top of my thigh.

I heard a groan escape my lips as her fingers caressed me and I leant into her touch. Unable to stop the desire that was now coursing through my veins, I laid my hand over hers and curled her fingers around my thickening cock.

She gasped and looked up at me for assurance. Then I felt her brave fingers cupping me of their own accord, and she licked her lips before leaning forward and placing a whisper-soft kiss just below my navel.

My cock leapt in her hand, and I heard her chuckle with amusement. I stroked her cheek again, her smooth skin warming my palm. "Aye, my lass. Name me as husband again for it pleases me to hear it."

"Husband." She smiled and turned to kiss my palm, "You have come home to me. I intend to make sure you stay." She stood up and took my hand. "Now, let's get you into this bath before the water turns cold."

I reached for her and turned her around so that I could begin to unfasten the ties at the back of her surcoat. "There is room for two in that magnificent tub. Join me, wife. For I long to see you."

She turned her head, and I thought she was going to object, but she said nothing, just nodded and allowed me to continue. After I had (with her help) stripped her of various layers of clothing, she turned to face me. She held one arm over her breasts, and the other was laid over her belly so that her hand covered the soft mound between her legs. She shivered a little in the golden light from the fire, and her eyes asked an unspoken question.

I took hold of her hand – the one she was using to cover her womanhood – and lifted it to my lips. "You are beautiful Emma. You do not need to cover yourself when we are together." In truth, I had never stood completely naked before another human being since my mother last bathed me as a child. But Emma's shy gaze emboldened me to want to experience this state with her and to experience it often. I saw her relax a little at my words and she let her other arm fall to her side. As her breasts came into view, I felt desire pool in my belly like a hot liquid. "Come, let us bathe together. For I am anxious to have you in our bed."

She turned away from me and walked towards the steaming bathtub in front of the fire. I watched her hips sway as she walked; she had blossomed into a fine woman.

I caught up with her and put one arm around her, pulling her against my body so that I could kiss her neck. Then I reached down with my other hand and cupped the soft flesh of her buttocks, pushing between them until I came across plump lips that were slick with her desire. She was wet for me. My cock surged against her back at the discovery, and I heard her sigh.

Emma helped me into the fragrant water and stepped in after me, settling behind me so that I was cushioned against her body with her legs holding me tight. She reached for the washing cloth and the precious cake of soap that we had bought at the market the week before. She reached around me and washed my skin gently, smoothing away the aches I hadn't realised I was feeling.

When her soapy fingers edged towards my cock, I stopped her going any further. "No, my love. If you touch me there again, I will shame myself in front of you."

Emma stood up behind me and moved around to sit down astride my legs. She lifted the washcloth and soap and began to rub them in slow circles around her breasts. My cock stood to attention, and I saw her smile as if in triumph.

I was hit by a sudden wave of doubt. The girl I had deflowered all those years ago had been a willing lover once our audience had departed, but she had shown no knowledge of the act itself, or indeed of how to encourage my desire. Yet, here she was, straddling me like a tavern whore and caressing herself for my enjoyment. I grabbed her wrist and stopped her. "Where did you learn how to do that?"

She looked at me with shock. "Wash myself? I have known how to do that since childhood." She pulled herself out of my hold and sat down quickly at the other end of the bathtub, crossing her arms over her breasts to cover herself. "What are you asking, *husband?*" The last word was emphasised with a note of accusation.

I stopped myself from saying anything to make the situation worse. The look of abject misery on Emma's face was enough to bring me to my senses. I shook my head and looked away from her. "I don't know. I'm sorry. It's just that …"

Tears were beginning to run down her pretty cheeks now. "You doubt my fidelity?" She sounded incredulous, as though I had accused her of something terrible. "I … I'm sorry." She stood up, covering herself as best she could with her arms. I watched the water stream off her lovely body as she stepped out of the bath and reached for a drying cloth. "I will ask Thomas to come and assist you. I will leave you in peace."

I felt her grief; misery was pouring off her along with the bathwater. "Emma – please – I didn't mean to make it sound like that. Please – don't leave."

She turned to look at me. "I can't imagine how you meant it to sound, then. I have been faithful to you all these years. Can you say the same?"

I couldn't, and the look on my face probably told her that.

"As I thought." She wrapped the drying cloth around her and turned to face me again. "I sought simply to try to encourage you to become my husband again. That night we spent together has stayed with me all this time. I fell I love with you, and I have longed for you. I saw how you reacted to my body. That is all." She turned and picked up her clothes before walking through the solar and leaving.

I didn't call after her. I just sat there in my cooling bathwater like the idiot I was.

Two days later, I was sitting in the late autumn sunshine, looking over the ledgers for the Manor. Emma had stayed out of my way since the bath; I had seen her at breakfast and supper, but she had not spoken much, other than to answer the questions I asked about her welfare.

Gerald Baliol came to sit next to me on the stone bench. After a moment, he looked at me. "Danyell, I have been with you for many years, and I've watched you do some stupid things. But this? You are a pillicock."

My first thought was to shout at him for insubordination. We may no longer be fighting men, but he was still my man. But he was also my friend, and I knew he was right. I was indeed a pillicock. I sighed and looked at him. "Yes. I do believe I am."

"So, what are you going to do to put it right? You have a beautiful woman who's just desperate to have her husband back. She's up in the library, sobbing. And what are you doing?" He took the ledger from my hand and looked at it. "What is this?"

"It's the accounts for the Manor."

Gerald took a closer look at the pages covered in small, neat script. "This says you're a rich man."

"I am. And it's all Emma's doing. She is an extraordinary woman."

He sat back and blew out a breath. "Go and talk to her. Tell her you're sorry – for whatever it was you did to upset her."

"I accused her of being unfaithful."

There was a silence that seemed to stretch on and on, then finally, he spoke again. "I'm not going to comment on that because I have no idea what caused you to think it. But I know you – and I know that there was barely a night in the last nine years when you didn't have your cock buried in some wench. You two didn't know each other when you married. But if you were to meet her now, would you want to marry her?"

"Yes!" It came out in a rush before I had time to think about it. "Yes, I would."

Gerald stood up and handed the ledger back to me before laying his hand on my shoulder. "Tell her that, Danyell. Go and find her and tell her just that."

I found her in the library, just where Gerald had said she would be. When she heard the heavy, wooden door open, she looked over. And when she saw me, she quickly wiped her eyes and looked back to the leather-bound volume she was pretending to read. I walked over and sat down next to her. "What are you reading?"

She answered without looking up. "This book belonged to my mother. It is a breviary. My father gave it to her as a wedding gift."

I looked at the brightly illuminated pages. There was an image of the Virgin Mary and the Angel Gabriel; the Annunciation. "Tis very beautiful."

She said nothing, keeping her head down. I watched as a large, wet drop fell from her downcast eyes and landed on the vellum page.

"Emma, I'm so sorry. I don't know why I said what I did. You have every right to be angry with me."

"I'm not angry." It was said so quietly that I barely heard her words.

"You're not?"

She looked up at me then, and I could see that her eyes were rimmed with red. She had been crying for some time. "No. I'm not angry. I'm hurt and sad."

That I had made her feel that way caused an ache to bloom in my chest. "I very much regret the way our bath ended. You gave me no cause to suspect you. And, as Gerald so kindly pointed out to me, I had no right to do so either."

The first hint of watery smile arrived on her lips. "Gerald Baliol?"

"He called me a pillicock."

She smiled truly then. "I would agree with that." She looked at me for a long time; scrutinising my face. "I was faithful to you all those years."

"I know. But I wouldn't blame you if you hadn't been. I was away for so long. And Gerald made me realise something else too."

"What was that?"

"He asked me if I was to meet you now, would I want to marry you?"

"And what did you say?"

"I said yes. In fact, the word came out of my mouth before I even had a chance to think about it. You are remarkable as well as beautiful. Please say you'll let me show you how much I mean that."

She closed the book and laid it carefully on the reading desk in front of the bench where we were sitting. "I won't ask you if you were faithful to me while you were fighting with Richard. I can't believe for a moment that you were. But if you are going to be my husband, you will honour the vows we took from this day on."

I didn't need to think about it. I wanted the life that was within my grasp here at Fordleigh and that included the woman whose tear-stained face was tilted towards me. "You have my word." I took her hand and raised it to my lips. "Did you really fall in love with me after just one day?"

She blushed, the pink flush spreading down her face and neck. "I did. I thought you were the most beautiful thing I'd ever seen."

"And what do you think now?"

She looked me up and down, scrutinising my appearance. "You need to put some more flesh on your bones. But you're still the most beautiful thing I've ever seen."

I couldn't hold back any longer; I reached for her and sealed my mouth over hers. She opened her lips with a sigh, and I plundered it with my tongue. I could feel her heartbeat where her breasts pressed against my chest. When I pulled away from the kiss, her skin was flushed again, and she shuddered as she let out the breath she'd been holding. "Will you come back to our bed this evening? I have missed you."

She stood up, and I thought she was going to reject me, but what she said next left me speechless. "I do not wish to wait until this evening." She took my hand and pulled me up, so I was standing next to her. "Our bed is made and waiting for us now." She gave me a coy smile and tugged on my hand.

I pulled her back into my arms and kissed her again. She came willingly and kissed me back, tangling her tongue with mine. I lifted my hand and caressed her breast through the fabric of her gown. I could feel her nipple beading against my palm even through the layers of linen and fine wool she was wearing. Every part of me wished I had my full strength; I wanted to lift her into my arms. "I promise that when I am back to my old self, I will carry you to our bed. But for now, I'll have to be satisfied with your hand in mine." I took her hand, and we walked as fast as our feet could carry us towards the solar.

The bed was indeed made, and there was a girl laying the fire. When she saw us come into the large room that served as our living quarters, she got up, bobbed a curtsey and left quietly. I reached for Emma and began to unfasten the ties at the back of her gown. She aided me, and soon she stood before me in just her linen shift. I put my hand into her hair and kissed her again. "You are so beautiful. Had I known such riches were waiting for me here, I would not have tarried so long." It was true. In the past weeks, I had fallen desperately in love with my wife.

Emma smiled and began to help me out of my clothes. The sight of her elegant, long-fingered hands on me caused my blood to stir. I let her undress me. She told me to sit on the bed, and I followed her direction like a loyal hound. I let her pull my shirt over my head. When I'd been with her on our wedding night, I had kept my shirt on, and none of the women I had been with since had seen my body completely bare. But she had helped me bathe, and so the sight of the many scars on my chest and back were nothing new.

"One day, I'm going to ask you how you got these." She reached forward and ran the soft pad of her finger along the jagged white line of a scar that ran from my shoulder to my navel.

"And one day, when I'm not so desperate to get my dick inside you, I'll tell you the story of every one of them."

She smiled and fell to her knees to relieve me of my boots and breeches. My cock leapt to attention as she bared me completely; the sight of her kneeling between my spread legs had me harder than a frost in January. "Please," the words were strangled, and I barely recognised the voice as my own. "Please, Emma. Touch me. I am desperate for you."

She reached out tentatively and circled my cock with her soft fingers. "Tell me how to touch you. I do not know how."

I placed my hand over hers and curled her fingers around my shaft before working her hand slowly up and down as though I was pleasuring myself. "Taste me, Emma."

Her face lifted to meet mine, and she looked unsure. "You wish for me to kiss you here?"

"More than a kiss, my love. Taste me with your tongue. I long to feel your mouth on me."

She still looked unsure, but she leant forward and ran her tongue up the underside of my cock. I shuddered with the pleasure of it, and she repeated the action, more slowly this time. By the time she had licked me from root to tip, I was shaking with desire for her. "Come here, Emma. Let me help you disrobe." I stood and helped her to her feet before turning her around so that I could untie the laces of her shift. As the fine linen garment fell to the floor, I felt gooseflesh rising on the skin of her arms. "Yes, it's a little cold. We disturbed the girl before she could light our fire." I walked to the fireplace and struck a flint onto the kindling the maid had left. The dry wood caught quickly, and the fire leapt into life. I returned to my wife and finished undressing her.

When she was naked, she crossed her arms over her breasts before turning to face me. She looked unsure of herself, and it made my heart ache.

"Do not hide from me, my love. You are mine, and you are perfect."

She looked up at me and tears began to fall down her pretty cheeks.

I lifted my hand and wiped the wet trails from her skin. "Now, what's this? What ails thee?" I pulled her into my arms, and she put her cheek against my chest. I felt her tears wetting my skin. "Have I hurt you in some way?"

I felt her shake her head against me. "I have kept something from you, husband. And I am ashamed."

I eased her away from my body so that I could look at her. She looked stricken, and I felt a sudden panic rise in my chest. "Tell me, Emma. I promise I will not be angry. I meant what I said – if I were to meet you now, I would want to wed you. So, it doesn't matter what you have to tell me." I sat down on the edge of the bed and pulled her onto my lap. I reached for the soft woollen blanket the was folded at the foot of the bed and wrapped it around us, enclosing us both in its warmth. "Tell me, my love." I kissed her cheek, turning her on my lap so that she faced me, putting her thighs either side of my hips. I could feel the moist warmth of her sweet cunt mere inches away from my cock.

I watched her as she gathered herself. Whatever it was she needed to tell me; it gave her pain to think of it. She nodded and began. "Three years ago, John's men came to Fordleigh. We turned them away at the gate like we always did, but one of them broke through and got into the house. I ran for the stairs, planning to lock myself in here, but he caught me."

I felt the skin on the back of my neck prickle with rage, but I managed to hold myself in check. I needed her to tell me the rest of the story. "Go on; please tell me."

She nodded. "He pulled me down to the ground and ripped open my gown. He saw me naked. He would have done more if one of his comrades hadn't pulled him off. Danyell, I was so ashamed."

I wanted to get up, find the man and kill him – slowly and very painfully. But I managed to keep my anger in check. "You have nothing to be ashamed about, Emma. Who was this man?"

"It was Piers Griffin."

"Henry Griffin's son?"

She nodded and laid her head against my chest again. "He died of the fever last winter. God forgive me, but I rejoiced at the news."

"He is fortunate that fever took him. For if it hadn't, I would have made sure he suffered hours of pain before he finally met his maker."

We sat there for a while, silent in thought. I rocked her against my body as her tears ceased. When she had quieted, and all I could hear was our breathing and the crackling of the fire, I lifted her face to meet mine and kissed her mouth gently. "Thank you for telling me. I meant it; you have no reason to feel ashamed. And I want you to feel at ease showing me your body, for it is very beautiful." I let the soft blanket fall off her shoulders, and it fell onto the floor. I reached to cup her breast, and she shifted to give me better access. My cock stirred back into life and pushed up into the soft flesh between her legs.

Emma groaned a little and kissed me, pushing her wet, little tongue into my mouth. "All these years, Danyell; I have ached for you." She moved against me, rubbing herself against the crown of my cock, smearing it with her honey.

My body was screaming at me to flip her onto her back and fill her with one, long thrust. But I knew that would not give her what she needed. What a woman needed hadn't been much of an issue in bed sport for me in times past, but this was different. I wanted more than bed sport with Emma; I wanted a true joining. I put my hands underneath her full ass cheeks and lifted her a little so that she was positioned directly above me. "Take me then, love. Ease the ache."

She looked confused for a moment, so I rotated my hips so that the head of my cock worked its way between the outer lips of her cunt. She nodded and leant forward to kiss me while she pushed herself down, and I felt her envelop my cock in her wet warmth.

"Oh, sweet! You feel so good. How have I stayed away from you for so long?"

She smiled slyly at me and began to move, riding me gently. "And how have I gone so long without feeling this?" She groaned softly as she pushed herself onto me again, impaling herself on my shaft.

"Here, love. Let me give you more pleasure." I licked my thumb and put my hand between our bodies, seeking the sensitive little button that Sabrina had taught me to tease. I found it and began to rub it gently, back and forth, then in circles. I felt a gush of wetness on my fingers as she smeared them and my cock with her juices.

Emma groaned and put her head back, opening her mouth to pull air into her lungs. "Danyell! What are you doing?" Her thighs were shaking, and I knew she was going to spend soon.

"I can feel your pleasure, my love. Let it come. Do not try to hold back."

She threw her head back again and cried out. I could feel her insides squeezing me, and I couldn't hold my seed any longer. I let go with a shout and pumped into her over and over until my balls had nothing more to give.

She laid her head on my shoulder, and I could feel her laboured breaths against my neck. I pulled us both over so that we were lying on the bed, side by side, her leg over my hip and my cock still buried in her wet sheath. I kissed her mouth and pulled her closer. I was still hard, and I knew it wouldn't be long before I would want to plough her again.

When her breathing had ceased to be so ragged, she looked up at me. "I do not know what just happened between us." She blushed, and the pink colour spread down her neck, heading towards her breasts.

I kissed her again, cupping the flushed mound of her breast in my hand. "Only what God meant to happen between a man and a woman." I began to thrust gently into her. "And it will be happening again very soon."

She still looked slightly dazed as she turned to face me. "After you left me, I spoke to several married women. I asked how they could bear to be away from their husbands. Most of them said it was a relief and that what happened in the marriage bed was a chore, not a pleasure."

"You disagreed with them? Emma, we only had one night together, and I confess I did not pay you the attention you deserved."

"It hurt the first time. And it was humiliating because they were watching. But after they left us alone? I saw your body, and I felt mine warming." She wriggled in my hold, and I felt my cock push further into her as I became fully hard again. "I felt pleasure the second time. But nothing like the pleasure you just gave to me."

I could sense that she was concerned; a lady shouldn't be so wanton. I could only imagine the conversations she had had with the matrons; they had told her that lying with their husbands was something to dread. "My love. Our bodies were made to fit together." I punctuated what I was saying by pushing up into her as far as I could. "And our bodies were made to take pleasure in that. Yours as well as mine. If those women told you otherwise, then their husbands clearly do not know how to pleasure them. Now, enough talking; I am anxious to take you again." I rolled her over onto her back and pulled out of her wet warmth reluctantly so that I could gaze on her naked body laid out before me.

She laughed, and I watched as the action pushed a pool of our juices out of her body onto the bedsheet. She felt it and stopped laughing. "Oh!" She sat up and tried to cover herself, as though being full to the brim with my seed was something of which she should be ashamed.

I pushed her gently back down and ran my finger through the wetness she had just expelled. "This is nothing to be ashamed of, sweet Emma. You are full of me. And you will be full again; many, many times." I dipped my head and kissed the soft swell of her belly. I longed to taste her fully, but I knew that if I went straight to the place I longed for, I might frighten her, so I eased my way down her body with soft kisses.

Emma moaned quietly at my caress and moved her hips, letting me know that she was becoming aroused by what I was doing. There was far more I wanted to do, but as I looked up her body, her hard nipples called to me. I had not paid them any attention yet, and I knew we would both enjoy it if I did. So, I left the hot junction of her legs and moved up, kissing her skin as I went. I cupped her breasts with my hands and closed my lips around one, hard nipple, sucking the sweet flesh into my mouth.

Emma's back bowed as she pushed herself further into my mouth. She was so responsive to my loving; I cursed myself for having stayed away from her for so long. I sucked and licked at her, then moved over to pay the same homage to her other tit. She was firm and sweet. "Forgive me, wife. I should have been here. I should have given you children to suckle on these dainty teats. Know that I intend to make up for lost time where that is concerned."

Emma placed her hand on my head, directing me back to her tender flesh. "You have left me empty for nine years, husband. I hope you have the strength to keep your promise." I could feel her squirming beneath me as I sucked on her nipple.

After torturing her with my mouth for a few more moments, I gave into the desire to follow the hot, musky fragrance that was rising from her body where it had joined with mine a short time ago. I kissed a line from her breastbone to her hip, before pushing her thighs apart, revealing her wet centre to me. The lips of her sweet hole opened to my gaze, and I answered their call by kissing the sensitive skin either side of them.

Emma wriggled in my embrace. "No – Danyell – it is not proper."

I laughed softly at her modesty. "Sweet, I just had my cock buried deep inside you – are you saying that I am not permitted to kiss you here?" I was teasing her, and I was enjoying it. "I am your husband, and I will kiss you where I please." She stilled, and I felt a slight unease run through my veins. "But I will only do so if you want it. If you wish for me to cease, then say so, Emma. I will not take what is not freely given." I had seen men who did that; I'd seen the evil in them as they took what did not belong to them and I had vowed never to become one of them. Bed sport was much more enjoyable when the woman was willing.

"I … want it, Danyell. But everything I have ever been told about the work of a wife would make me believe that wanting it is wrong."

I cursed quietly. When would it be seen as a proper thing for a husband and wife to enjoy each other equally? "My love; does not the Bible tell a husband to love his wife?"

"Yes. It does say that."

"Then I will show you that I love you by kissing you everywhere. Including here." I dipped my head and placed an open-mouthed kiss against her entrance. She shivered from the touch, but she did not try to stop me. She tasted good, and I let her scent and taste flood my nose and mouth. When I felt her relax, I increased the pressure of my mouth, finding her tender hole with my tongue and pushing inside.

"Oh … Danyell!" Emma wriggled in my hold as the new sensation washed over her. "Please, I …"

Whatever she was about to say to me was interrupted by a loud thumping on the door of the solar. I felt rage flow through me like a swollen river, and I was just about to yell at whoever it was when the thumping began again.

"Sire, I'm so sorry, forgive the intrusion." Hugh's voice sounded thready with panic. "There are men approaching. John's men. They will be here within the quarter hour."

I looked at Emma and saw her face fall. She reached for a blanket to cover herself. "I had hoped they would stop now that you are home."

I reached for her hands and held them tightly. "I promise, my love, this will be the last time." I wrapped a sheet around my waist and walked to the door. When I opened it, I saw Hugh, pale and scared. "Thank you, Hugh. You did the right thing. Tell Gerald Baliol to get the men ready and meet me out in the courtyard as soon as they are able."

"Yes, Sire." He dipped his head in a short bow and scuttled off in the direction of the stairs.

When I turned around and walked back into the solar, Emma was standing in her unlaced gown, trying to pull her hair back enough to get it under a wimple. "Help me with my ties, please?"

"What are you doing? You're staying right here. And as soon as we've run those bastards off the land, I'll be back to finish what we started."

She shot me a steely gaze, and I knew the argument was probably futile. "Husband, I have dealt with every attempt by John's men in the last nine years. I am not going to just lie down like a scared virgin and wait for you to come back from another battle. We do this together, or not at all."

I smiled at her and nodded. "My beautiful Lionheart." I helped her to finish tying the laces of her gown and smiled again, knowing that she wore nothing underneath. "I meant what I said about finishing what we started. As soon as they have gone. I will be unlacing this gown again."

"As you wish." Her smile told me that would not deny me. "Get your boots on, husband; we have visitors to deal with."

The sun was beginning to set as we gathered in the courtyard. I gave instructions for the gates to be opened and, moments later, a group of a dozen men on horseback rode in. I looked around at my men and the household folk who had all turned out to stand with them; we made a formidable sight and outnumbered our visitors by two-to-one. But the most formidable sight was my Emma. The wimple she had pulled on so hastily gave her a demure look, and she stood with her back straight, facing the enemy, as brave as any man I had fought with in Palestine or

Normandy. I took hold of her hand, and she looked up at me. What I saw were strength and determination.

The man at the front of the group of riders removed his helmet, and I recognised him as Henry Griffin. I felt the blood rise in me as I remembered how his son had assaulted my wife. He would be paying for that very shortly. I let go of Emma's hand and stepped forward, my hand on the hilt of my sword. "Dismount so that we can speak eye-to-eye."

Henry Griffin looked around to his men then slipped his feet out of his stirrups and slid to the ground. He looked past me and addressed my wife. "Good day, Mistress. I see you have some extra support of late."

I went for my sword, but Emma laid her hand on my arm. She looked at me and shook her head before stepping forward a little. "My husband and his men have returned from fighting for the King in Normandy. You have no reason to be here. Turn around and leave. And never return."

Henry's mouth curled into an ugly smile. "Oh? And why would I do that? This land belongs to the King – the rightful King, John. And you are part and parcel of the deal. My son told me how sweet you were; I have come to complete his claim and take you and your house for myself."

I could bear to hear no more. I stepped in front of Emma and raised my sword. "Your son assaulted my wife. You should be grateful that a fever took him, for if he were still alive, I would flay him and use his skin as a doormat." I took another step towards him, but he didn't back down.

"I have no quarrel with you, Lovell. Stand aside. You have no real claim to this land or this whore. Leave now, and I will see to it that you receive recompense from the King."

He looked so arrogant; I wanted nothing more than to swipe that grinning head right off his shoulders. But I knew that if I were the aggressor in any fight we had, I would lose my Emma forever. I had to wait for him to make the first move. "You dare to call my wife a whore? When your own wife cuckolded you more times than I could count?" It was a jibe, but it was true. Eliza Griffin had been mistress to one of Richard's men; he had told me of it himself while we fought side by side against the Saracens. "Rafe Du Buisson told me many stories of rutting on your wife while you drank yourself into a stupor, so you didn't have to listen to her crying out for him to fuck her harder."

I heard a gasp from behind me and stifled laughter from Griffin's men. The humiliation in front of his men was more than his mean, little heart could take. He raised his blade and ran for me. I parried with him, deflecting several blows, letting him think he was getting the upper hand. He pushed me down and raised his sword over his head. "Are you ready to meet your maker, Lovell? One of us will be warm between your wife's thighs tonight." He raised his arm higher, and I pursed my lips, letting out the whistle that was a signal to Gerald Baliol. From his position up on the roof, he heard me and, moments later, I heard the tell-tale whine of an arrow heading directly for Griffin's chest. It landed squarely, the bodkin point slicing easily through the mail coat he wore.

Henry Griffin stopped in his tracks, sword still held high over his head and looked down to where the wooden shaft of the arrow protruded from his chest. He looked back to me, trying to drag air into his lungs. Then he coughed, spraying me with blood, before dropping to his knees then falling on his face at my feet.

There was a moment's silence while Griffin's men looked between each other. Then I heard Emma's voice rising clearly in the Autumn air. "We have archers positioned on the roof. Enough to send you all to hell in the blink of an eye. Take this with you." She stepped forward and kicked the bleeding corpse of Henry Griffin. "And never return. I have proved my ownership of this land over and over again at the Assizes. You have no legitimate reason to come here. And now we are protected by an army big and skilled enough to fight you and win."

My heart swelled with pride at my woman standing so bravely against these intruders. And I felt my cock swell with desire for her again. I looked back to Griffin's men – they were muttering amongst each other, then one rode his horse so that he was in front of the others. He removed his helmet and slid from his horse, walking towards Emma and me where we stood next to the body of his erstwhile leader.

I stood straight and faced him. "Everyone here witnessed what just happened. Henry Griffin attacked me and would have killed me but for the action of one of my archers." I didn't want to disavow Emma's statement about our archers – we had one archer, Gerald Baliol, but they didn't need to know that. "Leave now, and there will be no more bloodshed. But raise your swords against us, and you will all enjoy the same fate as this man." I toed the ugly body at my feet and watched as his heart's blood ran freely towards the drain in the centre of the courtyard. A fitting end for his vile life.

The man nodded. "We are in agreement. To continue with this endeavour is pointless. We have no claim to this place. Henry was determined to take it from you. He said he was acting on instructions from the King, but I have never seen any real evidence of that." He turned to face his men who were now nodding in agreement. "Do what you wish with his body – we don't want it. In my opinion, the dung heap would be too good for him." He turned to face Emma. "Forgive me, Lady."

Emma smiled as she looked at the young man. "It was you; you pulled Piers off me when he would have raped me."

The young man bowed to my wife. "It was, my lady. Dunstan Marchmaine, at your service."

I reached for the young man's hand and shook it firmly. "You have my thanks. My wife told me of your actions." I looked over to the group of men who were waiting for their new leader to return to them. "Are these your men now?"

"Aye, my lord. Though I have little to offer them now that my allegiance to the Griffins is broken."

I looked at him, then his men, then spoke in a voice loud enough for them all to hear. "There is always a place for good men here at Fordleigh. If you find there is no other place for you, come back to see me."

There was a general murmuring among the men, and Marchmaine looked to them for an answer. He nodded and turned to face us again. "We will return on the morrow, and we will be glad to give you our allegiance." His gaze travelled between Emma and me, and I knew he was taking in our hastily dressed appearance and my cock-stand, which was now becoming quite painful against the stiff fabric of my breeches. "It would seem that our arrival interrupted more than your peace. Forgive us." He bowed, and when he straightened, I could see he was smiling knowingly. "I wish you and your wife a peaceful night."

I closed the door of the solar and watched Emma walk into the room. She stopped to add logs to the dying fire, which burst into life again, filling the room with a soft light and the fragrance of applewood smoke. When she reached the bed, she turned to look at me.

"Husband, I believe there is something you neglected to finish before we were so rudely interrupted."

I covered the ground between us so quickly; I made her gasp. Without saying a word, I captured her mouth with mine, kissing her deep and hard, pushing my tongue into her in the way I wanted to push my cock into her; rough and determined. I lifted her in my arms and laid her on the bed; the combination of fear and elation from the recent conflict filling my veins with a strength I'd forgotten I owned. "I cannot wait, Emma. There will be time for tenderness later."

She reached for the hem of her gown and pulled it up to her waist, baring herself to me. "I am desperate for you, Danyell. Take what is yours."

I tore at the laces of my breeches and opened them enough to release my aching cock. "Open yourself to me, my love. For I am burning with lust for you." I reached for her thighs, helping her to spread them as wide as she could. I caught the unmistakable scent of her arousal, and my brain and body joined in their response. I positioned myself between her spread thighs and pushed my cock into her. As I reached the end of her channel, filling her wet hole with my cock, I cried out with pleasure. "Oh, Emma! I am so deeply in love with you!"

She reached for me, locking her lips with mine. "Husband; I am yours entirely."

I began to thrust into her. "Forgive me, Emma. I need to fuck you. I will be gentle later, but at this moment, my balls are so full they are aching." I began to slam into her, our bodies making a loud slapping noise as I pushed my cock into her without finesse.

Emma was panting and holding onto me, taking my battering and groaning with pleasure. She linked her ankles together around my waist and sank her teeth into my shoulder.

The shock of her bite had me spilling myself deep inside her, and I felt her cunt begin to clench around me as she spent herself over my cock.

We lay together for a long time, not speaking, not separating. When my breathing had finally settled, I lifted my head and looked at my beautiful wife. "You are mine."

"I am yours. And you are mine."

"Always. My Lionheart. I will follow you to the ends of the earth."

She laughed, and I felt the vibration of it squeeze my cock where it was still buried deep in her sheath. "Oh no, Danyell Lovell. You are not going to the ends of the earth again. You have come home to me, and this is where you're going to stay."

Sagittarius

Philosophical, motion, experimentation, optimism

What makes up a person? Is it a body; arms and legs, the ability to walk or run? It can't be – what about Stephen Hawking? He's very much a person, but he can only move one of his eyelids or something. It must be the mind, then. The mind is what makes a person; their intellect, knowledge and sense of humour. That must be it. You could take the mind of someone (if such a thing were possible), put it in a computer and you'd still have a person you could recognise. Perhaps I should try to find out if that's possible.

Okay, so I wouldn't have a body, but right now that seems like a good thing. Let's weigh up the pros and cons.

Pros: NO PAIN.

Cons: I'd seriously miss laughing. And chocolate. And wine. And orgasms.

But, let me review that list of pros again: NO PAIN. Yeah. I'm going for the brain in a jar option. Where do I sign?

My mind was spinning again, and I was thinking stupid thoughts. It was the painkillers; they didn't seem to be doing much about the pain I was feeling, but they were doing a mighty fine job of screwing with my mind.

"Hello, Vicky – how are we doing today?" It was that bloody annoying nurse again. Nobody calls me Vicky. I had told her that – at least I thought I had – it was possible that I had hallucinated it.

"Tori."

"I'm sorry, what?"

"My name. It's Tori. I hate Vicky. It makes me sound like I've just rubbed myself down with menthol."

"Ah! You're getting your sense of humour back – that's great!" She started fussing with my drip then she did my blood pressure. "You'll be on your feet again before you know it and a positive attitude is what's going to help you more than anything."

What I wanted to say was that my sense of humour was probably seared into the tarmac somewhere on the Edgware Road, and that the thing that was going to help me more than anything else right now was a large dose of morphine. But I didn't have the energy to say it. So, I just gave a weak thumbs-up with the hand I could still move. I'd discovered that the gesture seemed to make everyone who visited feel better about my situation, so I used it a lot. I felt bad enough about it; I didn't need to feel the undiluted pity coming in waves off everyone who came to see me. I just didn't.

My situation did suck pretty badly, to be honest. Some disillusioned kid blew himself up during the morning commute, and I happened to be one of the many people who were within exploding distance of his last, idiotic action. I heard him shout something; dedicating his pointless death to something equally pointless, then I was on my back fighting to breathe. I'm not sure how long ago that was – the days have all merged into one. I've got broken bones in nearly every part of my body and burns to my left side. I pressed the button for more pain relief, and a cold shot of my new best friend came through the cannula in my hand. I sighed with relief as I drifted off into blissful oblivion. I knew it wouldn't last long, but I took what I could get.

That summer was one of the hottest I'd ever known. I was coming to the end of my first year at uni, and I'd just left my final shift at the campus burger joint. I had to pack my room up because my dad was coming to pick me and my stuff up in two days.

The lift was out again, so I took the stairs; the halls I had called home since last September were old and in dire need of refurbishment. But I'd been happy there and would be sorry to say goodbye to it. I'd already arranged a house-share with four friends for next year, and I knew it would be a lot easier living somewhere with a kitchen and a room where we could all hang out together. But my new house would be missing the one key ingredient that had made living in halls so enjoyable; I wouldn't be living next door to Richie Callahan.

Richie Callahan looked like an ex-member of a boyband who now made his living making pornos or winning surfing competitions. He was a total wet-dream for me, and I had secretly lusted after him since the day he moved into the room next to mine. We'd always been polite with each other – saying 'hi' and 'how's it going?' whenever we passed on the stairs – but there had never been anything else between us. Except in my fantasies, of course. In my over-active imagination, we had got up to all kinds of dirty stuff.

Richie was just unlocking his door as I came down our corridor. He had a towel around his waist, and another slung over his shoulder, and he smelled fantastic. Freshly-showered Richie Callahan was even better than the regular sort. That image was going to rock me to sleep in the dry, Richie-less months ahead. "Hi, Tori." He opened his door and looked at me as I approached mine. "Are you all ready for the move?"

"Hi, Richie. Yeah – just about – a bit more packing to do. Gonna miss this old place."

"Me too." He grinned and winked at me. That was new. He'd never done that before. "It's been fun living next to you."

"It has?"

"Oh yeah." He grinned again, and I got the feeling he was hinting at something, but I had no idea what. "You know – you're very loud when you masturbate."

I felt the colour drain out of my face. "I ... What?"

"I hear you. You call out my name when you come. How about you come in here with me, and I'll give you a taste of the real thing?"

The dream was a mixture of a memory and a morphine-induced hallucination. Richie had indeed told me that he heard me shouting out his name, but he hadn't been draped only in a towel when he did it. And he did offer me a taste of the real thing; I had run into my room and locked the door as fast as I could. As the drugs took over once more, I had a feeling that the memory and the fantasy were going to part company in a big way.

Richie slowly removed the towel from his damp skin, uncovering his hips. He held the wet material with one hand, covering his cock. He looked at me, smiling, then he looked down at himself. I watched, mesmerised, as the towel twitched under his fingers. His cock was growing hard as he looked at me and his breathing slowed. "You've got me hard just thinking about you fingering your pretty little pussy." He let go of the towel – it hung there for a moment, caught on his considerable erection, then it slipped to the floor with a soft thud.

"Oh, my." He was gorgeous. His cock was thick and long, and his balls were big. My mouth began to water at the very thought of it, and I felt a familiar warm ache between my legs as my pussy joined in.

Richie reached for my hand and led me into his room. It was the same as my room – right down to the bedding and photos on the wall. My brain just accepted it – we must have come into my room instead. "Good. That's just how I want you."

I looked down at my suddenly naked body. When had I taken my clothes off? Or had I been naked standing out in the hall? I felt bold and wanton standing in front of this gorgeous, naked man. "What do you want to do to me?"

He reached for me and pressed himself as possible. I could feel his cock pressing against my belly and his breath on my cheek as he put his arms around me. "I want to eat your pussy; then I want to fuck you."

"That sounds like a plan." Where was this coming from? I've never spoken to a man like that in my life. Sex for me had always gone just as the guy had wanted; my needs had never really been taken into consideration.

Richie lay down on his bed and pulled me over to him. "Sit on my face. I want you to grind your sweet cunt into my mouth. Take what you need."

I straddled his head and lined myself up with his mouth. I could feel the juices running from my hole, making my thighs wet, I was so turned on by him.

"That's it. Give it all to me." He put his hands on my hips and moved me slightly so that he could push his tongue up into me without having to crane his neck.

The moment his lips and tongue made contact with my wet pussy, I went off like a rocket, crying out and gasping.

I woke up crying out and gasping, my insides churning with a very real orgasm. I'd had a sex dream, and it had made me come. I was almost sorry that I'd come so quickly – I would have loved to see where it was going to go. I willed myself to go back to sleep and re-enter the dream, but the pain in my legs and back had returned, so now, I was as awake as my drug-soaked brain would allow.

Days passed. The annoying nurse insisted on calling me 'Vicky' and I gave up trying to change it. Friends and family visited, I even had a visit from a TV news film crew who wanted to update the good people of the UK on how the survivors of the bombing were doing. It was then that I learned how many people hadn't survived; information that my visitors and carers had refused to give me. That stupid, selfish little bastard had taken six people with him, including a kid of twelve. I cried when they left. I'm not sure who I was crying for, but I think if I'd been honest, I would have known I was probably crying for myself.

Days became weeks and then the day I had longed for arrived when they told me that I could go home. I was still in a lot of pain; my legs were going to be in plaster for a while yet, but I had both my arms back, and the skin graft on my body had taken well. There would be daily visits from healthcare workers, and my three sisters were going to take it in turns to stay with me.

The first thing that hit me as I was wheeled into my house was the smell. After weeks of hospital smell filling my nose, that comforting, familiar scent of home was the most wonderful thing I had experienced in a very long time. It made my heart clench, and I began to sob quietly as I was wheeled into my living room.

"Hey now – what's this?" My sister, Helen crouched down so that she was at the same level as me. She brushed my tears away gently and made cooing noises which were oddly comforting.

"Just so glad to be home. I'm alright."

"Okay. Let's get you into bed." There was a brand-new adjustable bed sitting beside the window that looked out onto my garden. It was the same as the one I had just left in hospital, except this one was made up with pink, floral bedding - my bedding. The sight of it made me ache with wanting to lie in it. I knew it would smell of my laundry detergent and I wanted the comfort of that.

The paramedic who had accompanied us to my house helped me get out of the chair. I'd started some physiotherapy, so my arms were getting quite strong. I could put weight on one of my legs, but the other one had been so badly shattered by the blast that I had metal pins sticking out through the plaster, attached to a frame. It would be a long time before I could trust it to bear any of my weight.

I slid my bottom onto the bed and Helen helped me to lie back and put my feet up. She gave me the remote control, and I got myself as comfy as I could, raising the bed up so I could see what was going on in my garden.

"Here's the TV remote. I've rigged up a baby monitor, so you can call me in the night if you need to. We've got a commode for you here – everything you need. It's so good to see you home."

I looked out of the window onto my back garden. I wasn't a great gardener, but I kept it tidy. It was woefully overgrown and messy. "The garden needs a bit of TLC."

Helen looked out of the window. "I know. Don't worry. I was talking to your neighbour, Margaret, this morning. She said that her son said he would come around and sort it out for you. He's got a landscaping business – said he thinks he remembers you from uni or something."

"I don't think I can afford to pay a landscape gardener, Helen. Can't we just find someone to mow the lawn and cut the hedge?"

She smiled patiently at me. It was a look I recognised from childhood – when I said something daft, she would give me that beatific smile and correct me gently. "He's offering to do it for free, Tori. People want to help you. You need to let them."

"What's his name?"

"I can't remember. Margaret did mention it, but she was wittering about something and I kind of zoned out."

I laughed until the pain in my side stopped me. "She has that effect on me too. Lovely lady – makes amazing cakes – but boy does she ever go on."

"And on! Talking of cake – she dropped one off this morning. Date and walnut, I think. Want some?"

"Yes! And tea. Proper tea. That stuff they served in hospital was not right on any level."

"Coming right up." Helen leant down and kissed my forehead.

"What was that for?"

"Just because. It's so good to see you home. We've all been so bloody worried." She began to cry softly, and I felt suddenly guilty. This whole thing must have been hell for my family and friends.

"I'm okay, sis. I'm going to be okay." We looked at each other for a moment, and I felt the tension ease. "Now – get me tea and cake! I'm gagging for it here."

Richie lay down on his bed and pulled me over to him. "Sit on my face. I want you to grind your sweet cunt into my mouth. Take what you need."

I straddled his head and lined myself up with his mouth. I could feel the juices running from my hole, making my thighs wet, I was so turned on by him.

"That's it. Give it all to me." He put his hands on my hips and moved me slightly so that he could push his tongue up into me without having to crane his neck.

I eased down onto his face and felt his tongue working inside me. "God, that feels so good!"

Richie made a sound that let me know he was enjoying what he was doing. He dug his fingers into my hips and rocked me so that he could taste the length of my slit. Then he lifted me off him slightly. "Need to come up for air, babe. Fuck – you taste every bit as good as I thought you would."

I felt my skin tingle as he purred the compliment. "You've thought about eating me out?"

"Of course. Lying here, listening to you enjoying yourself next door – what's a guy to do?"

"What else did you think about?"

"*Turn around. I want you to play with my dick while I make you come with my mouth.*"

I swivelled around so that I was facing the other way, and settled down on Richie's face again. I heard him moan with approval as his mouth pressed against me and I felt the contact like a shock through my pussy. I leant forward and grasped his cock with my right hand. It was hot and hard, but the skin felt silky in my palm. He raised his hips slightly to let me know what he wanted me to do, and I watched as a drop of clear liquid oozed out of him and ran down towards my fingers.

"*Please, Tori – I'm going out of my mind here!*"

I bent over and licked the top of his penis; as his taste filled my mouth, I felt his tongue flicking against my clitoris. My orgasm slammed into me, leaving me squirming and gasping for breath.

"Tori – Tori – wake up! Are you alright?"

"What?"

"Are you in pain?"

The aftershocks of my dream-induced climax were still racing through my body; one thing I wasn't feeling at that moment was pain. Just frustration that my sister had woken me up. "No. I'm fine. Why did you wake me up? It's still dark."

"You were groaning. I thought you were hurting."

I looked over to the cabinet that was next to my bed; the baby monitor that Helen had set up was blinking innocently at me. "Thanks for that."

"What? What do you mean?"

"Nothing. Go back to bed. I was just dreaming, that's all."

"Oh." Helen stood up straight and her brow furrowed. "Sorry. I just thought …"

"I know – thank you – I really appreciate it. Sorry – you know I'm grumpy when I wake up."

"Okay, honey. Can I get you anything? A drink? Do you need more codeine?"

"No – I'm all good. Go back to bed. See you in the morning."

Helen kissed my forehead and went back upstairs. I lay in the dark, wide awake now, staring up at the ceiling. My insides were still throbbing from the effects of the dream. What the hell was going on? I could remember experiencing an orgasm like that before, but the dreams that went with it had never been so vivid. And I hadn't thought about Richie Callahan in years – so why now? It had to be the drugs I was on. When I was in the hospital, the morphine made me think all sorts of things – my sister, Esther, says it made me violent. I was glad when they were able to switch me to codeine and paracetamol; at least I stopped seeing things that weren't there.

Next morning, my sister, Rose, arrived to take over from Helen. She made breakfast for us and sat on my bed eating porridge. "How did you sleep? Helen said you had a restless night."

"Oh. No. It was okay. Just having some odd dreams."

Rose smiled and raised an eyebrow. "Helen mentioned something about that. Odd, moany dreams?"

"Leave off. I can't control what my brain is doing when I'm asleep. I think it must be the drugs."

"Sounds interesting. Do tell."

"Rosie – I'm not going to discuss my erotic dreams with you, so forget it."

"But you will admit that they're erotic? I knew it. When Helen said she'd heard you moaning and groaning, I had a feeling it wasn't because you were in pain. Look – there's nothing to be ashamed of. We all have them. Do you need anything from upstairs – you know – anything?"

"Rosie – I can hardly move. I'm not exactly in any shape to get busy with my battery-operated boyfriend." I sighed at the thought of it. It might ease the boredom if nothing else.

Rose nodded, picked up our breakfast things and went into the kitchen. I heard her go upstairs and a few minutes later, she returned with the pink, satin bag that held my favourite vibe. She smiled knowingly and put it in the top drawer of my cabinet. "Just in case you feel the need."

"How the hell did you find that?"

"You hide yours in the same place that I hide mine. Knicker drawer. You've got quite a collection in there. I liked the satin bag, so I figured it might be your favourite."

I was blushing so much that I could feel the heat radiating off my skin. "Thanks. I … ugh … just, thanks."

Rose kissed my forehead and grinned. "No worries. Now – I think we need to get you ready for a shower. As soon as the healthcare worker gets here, I'm going to get her to give me a hand. You'll feel better."

She was right – I did feel better. It was a bit of a palaver getting me in and out (thank god, I had that wet room installed in the ground floor extension when I moved in) but once we'd fixed the waterproof things over my legs, and got me on a shower seat, it was fairly easy. I can't tell you how good it felt to wash my hair and let the water soak my skin. It felt like it had been an age. They'd wheeled me into a wet-room several times in the hospital, but this was my shower, my shampoo, my shower gel. And when Rose and the nurse helped me dry off, it was with my towels. You really appreciate the little things when you've been without them for a long time.

When I'd got settled back in my bed, I looked out of the window. The rain had stopped, and the sun was trying very hard to break through the cloud. And there was a man in my garden. He was standing with his back to me, pruning the overgrown shrubs against the fence. "Oh – that must be Margaret's son. Helen said he was going to come and do the garden." I watched him for a minute – he was wearing a tee-shirt that showed off arms that were nicely muscled and decorated with a variety of coloured tattoos. His khaki cargo pants hugged a very nice bum. "Mmm – the view suddenly got a lot better."

Rose looked out of the window and laughed. "Well, if the view just gets too much to cope with, don't forget what I put in your top drawer." She ruffled my damp hair. "I'm going to make coffee – I'll go and see if he'd like some."

I turned to look out again. The sun had come out fully now, and I could see steam rising off the garden path. The man in the garden stopped and began to pull off his tee-shirt. "Hello! Diet Coke break moment." His bare back was decorated with yet more tattoos – a fine pair of wings that covered his shoulders and extended down his back, disappearing into his cargoes. A fairly big part of me wanted to find out where they ended. I heard Rose's voice as she joined him in the garden. She stood next to him while he pointed out what he was going to do and she was nodding enthusiastically. When she turned to come back into the house, he turned too, giving me my first view of his front. His abs and chest were swoon-worthy, but that wasn't what had grabbed my attention. I recognised him. He was the guy I'd been having dream-induced orgasms about. I hadn't seen him since I'd left uni eight years ago, but I'd know him anywhere. The guy pruning my bush (ooh, matron) was Richie Callahan.

Rose came back in a couple of minutes later with a cup of coffee and another slice of Margaret's cake. "He seems nice. And your view really has improved, hasn't it?" She waggled her eyebrows and winked at me. "His name is Rich. Says he knew you at uni."

"Yes. He went by 'Richie' then. Richie Callahan. How come I didn't know he was my neighbour's son?"

Rose took a sip of her coffee and looked out of the window. "Honey, since you've lived here, how often have you been here in the daylight? You work too hard."

"That's a fair point. I haven't even thought about work."

"Well, don't start now. You've got to concentrate on getting better first." She looked out of the window again; Rich was bending over, gathering the branches and leaves that he had cut off a wayward forsythia. The outline of his very fine butt was visible against the fabric of his pants as he bent over. "Concentrate on that. It'll give you sweet dreams." She winked at me again and drained her coffee mug. "Shout if you need me. I'm going to cook some meals to put in your freezer."

"Okay. I think I'll watch some TV. Rose?"

"Yeah?"

"Thank you."

"You are very, very welcome, little sis."

"Turn around. I want you to play with my dick while I make you come with my mouth."

I swivelled around so that I was facing the other way, and settled down on Richie's face again. I heard him moan with approval as his mouth pressed against me and I felt the contact like a shock through my pussy. I leant forward and grasped his cock with my right hand. It was hot and hard, but the skin felt silky in my palm. He raised his hips slightly to let me know what he wanted me to do, and I watched as a drop of clear liquid oozed out of him and ran down towards my fingers.

"Please, Tori – I'm going out of my mind here!"

I bent over and licked the top of his penis; as his taste filled my mouth, I felt his tongue flicking against my clitoris. The sensation travelled through the whole of my lower body, and I felt his fingers spreading me so that he could get deeper. I sucked the tip of his cock into my mouth, and he pushed up with his hips, thrusting into me until he brushed the back of my throat. I felt powerful as I held him; I knew that he was desperate for my touch and the knowledge thrilled me. He spread his thighs and undulated his hips. I could see his balls moving in his sac, and I reached for them with my free hand. He groaned with pleasure, so I pulled my mouth away from his penis and bent lower to suck one of the hot globes into my mouth.

"Oh – yeah! Tori – yes!" Richie spread his thighs even wider.

I grasped his cock, pulling down the foreskin and rubbing at the tender, sensitive underside, then I transferred my mouth to his other testicle. The effect I was having on this gorgeous guy was making my head spin. I felt Richie's fingers push into my aching hole and I reared up onto my knees. I felt the first waves of pleasure begin to travel through my pussy as my orgasm began to build.

My body jerked with the power of the climax that had shot through me, and I woke up. "Fuck! What the hell is wrong with me?" I said the words out loud before I remembered that my sister could hear everything through the baby monitor. A few moments later, I heard her coming down the stairs. "Sorry – I didn't mean to wake you up." I felt so embarrassed. "Maybe you should turn that darned thing off."

Rose fussed around my bed for a bit, making sure everything was where it should be, then she sat on the edge and looked at me. "I'm not turning it off. What if you need me in the night?"

"I know, but ... god, this is so embarrassing."

"There's no need to be embarrassed. Your brain is just trying to make sense of something. Do you want to talk about it? I mean – what are these dreams about? When I have them, they're always really weird."

"Weird, how?"

She pulled her *I'm thinking* face and looked me in the eye. "Sister pledge open?"

"Agreed." That simple word meant that we promised to keep whatever we said between ourselves. We wouldn't even share it with Esther or Helen.

"This needs hot chocolate. I'll be back in a bit." She returned about ten minutes later with two, steaming mugs of Cadbury's finest and a packet of Bourbons.

I hit the button on the remote control and raised the head of my bed so that I was sitting up. "Thanks. That smells good. So – what sort of dreams make you come in your sleep?"

Rose savoured her chocolate for a moment then nodded. "Okay. Promise me you won't think I'm a weirdo?"

"I already think you're a weirdo, Rosie."

"Fair point. Well – whenever I have one of those dreams, I'm usually dreaming that I'm masturbating."

"What's so weird about that?"

"In public."

"Oh. Wow. That is a bit out there. Do you ever consciously fantasise about doing stuff in public?"

"What? No! I'm not a pervert."

"I never said you were. But fantasies usually have little to do with what we actually want."

"Yeah. I know. I guess that sometimes my mind might stray that way when I'm enjoying some *personal time*."

I laughed at her coyness. "And what does Mark think about you having *personal time*?" My sister's husband was the PDA king; I didn't think for a minute that Rose needed to make up for any lack in the bedroom.

"He likes to watch." As soon as she had said it, I could see the colour rising up her neck and spreading to her cheeks. "What I mean is … well … yeah."

"And do you like having him watch?"

"Yeah. I do. It makes me feel powerful. When he can't control himself, and he does it too. It's hot. I love to watch him make himself come."

I pictured my good-looking brother-in-law lost in erotic pleasure. "I get that."

"You do?"

"Yeah. Mark is hot. I told you that when you first started going out."

She smiled broadly. "Yes, you did."

"And maybe your love of watching and being watched is what causes your dreams."

"Maybe. I'd never really thought about it like that. But that would make sense. Okay – your turn. Tell me. What's been tossing your salads in these dreams of yours?"

I thought for a moment about where to start. "Well, do you remember I had that crush on the guy next door in my first year at uni?"

"Vaguely. Go on."

"I haven't thought about him for years. It was all too embarrassing, to be honest."

"Why? What did you do?"

"Nothing. But the day before I came home, he told me that he'd often heard me call out his name when I was having some *personal time*."

"Oh my god! Well – if what I've heard over the baby monitor is anything to go by, then you are pretty loud."

"Yeah. Thanks for that. Anyway – that's not all."

"What? You didn't?"

"No. I didn't. But he offered. He said I should go into his room to experience the real thing."

"And you ran into your room and locked the door?"

"How did you know that?"

"I've known you for your whole life, baby sister. But I don't get it – dreaming about locking yourself in your room shouldn't really get you going enough to climax."

"Yeah – well – in the dreams I take him up on his offer."

Rose laughed, but not in a way to make me feel bad. "That's great! Long may it continue – it's putting some colour in your cheeks, anyway."

"There's something else – something which is going to complicate things a little."

"What? You haven't started things up with Callum again, have you? That man is a total loser – you're better off without him."

"What? God, no!" My most recent relationship disaster had ended about a month before I got blown up. Callum Roberts had emptied my bank account and sold my jewellery to pay gambling debts. I kicked him out with the help of my sisters, who packed his stuff into bin bags and threw them out on the street. He paid me back most of what he owed me, but there was no way I'd have him back – no matter how good he looked in the shower.

"What then?"

"That guy from college – he was here yesterday – doing the garden."

"What?" Rose stood up and gaped at me. "You're telling me that that tattooed hunk offered you a ride around his amusement park and you turned him down?"

"He wasn't tattooed then – or quite so hunky – he's bulked up."

"Even so. Well – this makes things a lot more interesting. He clearly remembers you – and wants to help you. We need to get him in here next time – to say hello."

"Oh no – no, you don't – I'm never going to agree to that. In case it's escaped your notice, I'm not exactly at my best at the moment."

She gave me that look – I knew it so well from childhood. She'd want me to do something, I'd say 'no', and she'd give me that look that said she knew she would win me over eventually. "We'll see."

"No – we won't. Now go back to bed and let me sleep."

"Okay." She chuckled as she gathered up the empty mugs and folded the end of the packet over the remaining biscuits. "Sleep tight. Sweet dreams. Really sweet dreams, baby sis. But try to keep it down –

I need my beauty sleep." She kissed me on the forehead and left me alone.

The next couple of days were fairly uneventful. My sisters came and went, the healthcare worker came every day, and I couldn't believe how much being at home was helping with my recovery.

A physiotherapist came and gave me some exercises to do. "You're doing so well, Tori. We need to start getting you out of bed. You've probably got enough strength in your arms to use the wheelchair now. Fancy giving it a go?"

The thought of fresh air and a change of scenery made me say 'yes', and with the help of Esther and the physio, I was showered, dressed in clean sweats and sitting in my wheelchair before I quite knew what had happened. Esther wheeled me out of the house. Someone had built a ramp over the step at my back door. "When did this happen?"

Esther eased me down the ramp onto the concrete path that led to the garden. "Just after you came home. We had a bit of a job getting you in, so Sean and his dad came over to build it. It's not permanent – as soon as you're on your feet again, it can come right off, and you won't even know it was there."

Sean was Esther's husband. He was very handy with a power-drill; he and my other two brothers-in-law had helped me a lot when I moved into my house. Helen's husband, Rob, is a plumber, so my ancient pipes and water-tank got taken care of very quickly. "Everyone's been so kind."

"That's because everyone loves you, hun."

"It's not just friends and family – it's people I don't know as well – Margaret next door has been baking like Mary Berry since I got home. Some kids down the road picked some flowers from their garden and brought them over. Sainsbury's delivered a whole bunch of really lovely shopping, and I have no idea who sent it. Then there's Margaret's son, Rich. He's doing my garden for me."

"I noticed it was starting to look a bit tidier. He's doing a good job."

"Yes, he is." I looked around at my small patch of garden. I hadn't done any more to it than keep it under control since I moved in, but it was starting to look like a garden. Rich had cleared the borders (I really enjoyed watching him do that sans shirt) and pruned all the shrubs so that they were neat and tidy. He'd also planted some things on the empty trellis – a honeysuckle and a clematis were happily winding their way over the wood lattice. I wheeled myself over to admire them; then I heard Esther greet someone.

"Hey – you're out of the house – how great is that?"

I turned around and there he was; my friendly, neighbourhood gardener was standing beside me. "Hi – I – uh – hi."

He smiled at me, and the memory of all those dreams came flooding back, making me blush. "Hi, Tori. It's great to see you. Do you remember me? From uni?"

"Yes – of course – Richie Callahan."

"I go by Rich these days. Richie made me sound like a child-star." He nodded and smiled. "Do you like the climbers?"

"Oh – yes – they're lovely. I don't know what to say – everyone's been so kind – you must let me pay you for your work."

He shook his head and put his hand on my shoulder. "No. This is all on me. When mum told me that her neighbour had been hurt in that suicide bombing, I just wanted to do something to help you. She's really fond of you, you know? And then, when I found out who you were, well, anyway, I won't accept anything from you. Except for the odd cup of coffee."

"I can't believe you remember me. Uni seems like a lifetime away now."

"Are you kidding? I lived next door to you for a year. I'm sorry I was such a jerk the last time I saw you." He blushed slightly and looked at his shoes.

"No need to apologise. I was pretty jerksome myself." I smiled up at him, and it felt like something had been resolved. "Now – how about that coffee? If you help me get back in the house, I'll get my sister to put on a fresh pot. There's some of your mum's stellar apple cake to go with it if you'd like?"

"Oh, now you're talking. That was always my favourite. I love her marmalade cake too. And the lemon drizzle. Actually – I just love my mum's cakes."

"That makes two of us. She's been so kind." I felt my throat hitch as I said that. "Everyone's been so kind."

He started to push me towards the house. "I guess that when someone has been injured by an arsehole doing something stupid, the rest of the non-arsehole population feel the need to make up for it. Or something."

"That was actually quite erudite."

"Why, thank you, ma'am." He pulled at an imaginary forelock. "Good to know that philosophy degree wasn't a complete waste of time."

"How did you go from that to landscape gardening?"

"Well, I discovered that a third-class philosophy degree only really qualified me to ask, 'do you want fries with that?' and after a month or so of not being able to wash the smell of chips out of my hair, I decided that there had to be more to life. I got an apprenticeship with a garden designer, and the rest is history. I love it. Wouldn't do anything else now. What do you do?"

"Not a lot at the moment. But when I'm not recovering from bomb-blasts I work in the city. Investment banking."

"Oh – that sounds interesting." His voice told me that he didn't think it was the least bit interesting.

"It isn't. I hate it. This thing has made me re-evaluate things a little. I'm not sure I'm going to want to go back to it. But I'll cross that particular bridge when I come to it. I've got to get back on my feet first."

"You'll get there. And they're such pretty feet." He laughed and pushed me up the ramp and into my kitchen. "I think this is your stop."

"Oh – yeah! Tori – yes!" Rich spread his thighs even wider.

I grasped his cock, pulling down the foreskin and rubbing at the tender, sensitive underside, then I transferred my mouth to his other testicle. The effect I was having on this gorgeous guy was making my head spin. I felt Rich's fingers push into my aching hole and I reared up onto my knees. "Oh god, yes! I want you inside me like that. I'm so empty, I ache."

Rich pulled his fingers out of me and flipped me over onto my back. "Oh, I'm getting to that. But I want to explore first." He gripped one of my ankles and lifted my foot, cupping it in his hand. "You've got such pretty feet." He dipped his head and sucked my big toe into his mouth.

I felt the soft pad of his tongue swirl around the digit, and it sent a shiver of pleasure straight towards my aching pussy. "Rich – please – I want you – now! It's torture."

"Let me do something about that." He pushed my legs apart and positioned himself between my thighs. I felt the head of his gorgeous cock nudging against my wet entrance. "Okay? Do you want this?"

I felt nearly out of my mind with wanting it. I could feel my inner muscles clutching in readiness to take him. "Yes! I want it. Give it to me."

He pushed forward, and I felt myself stretch to take him. "Oh, god, it's been so long. You feel amazing."

"Why did you make me wait so long? Oh, fuck, Tori, your pussy feels incredible."

"Fuck me. I want you deep inside me. Your cock feels incredible too."

He rocked his hips and burrowed deep into me. I could feel his pubic bone press against mine and his balls slapping against my upturned buttocks. It was a frantic mating that churned my insides, turning my legs to water and robbing me of my breath.

"Oh god, Tori – I'm gonna come!" Rich pushed himself up on his elbows and thrust into me as hard as he could.

"Yes – wait for me – I'm nearly there too."

"Can't. Sorry. I'm already there." He went rigid above me, and I felt his cock throbbing deep in my channel as he poured himself into me.

His orgasm made me tip over the edge, and I joined him, crying out as my inner muscles began to pulse, pulling at him, milking his cock until he had nothing left to give me.

We lay together, waiting for our breathing to steady. When I shivered in his arms, he pulled the duvet over us and settled his arm around me, pulling my head onto the pillow of his chest. He stroked my hair gently and kissed the top of my head. "I'm so glad that finally happened."

"Me too."

"Does this mean you've stopped running from me?"

"I guess it does."

The warmth of late spring gave way to the heat of summer. I still had the pins and a frame on my left leg, but I was getting about on crutches now, and my sisters were only staying over a couple of nights a week. The garden was finished and looked amazing; Rich had somehow managed to create something that looked like it belonged in Italy rather than Kensal Green, and I was making the most of having a shady patio to sit on. The dreams had stopped. I was taking minimal painkillers now, and I suspected that those two things were linked somehow. I was a bit sad about it. My drug-induced dreams were probably the most erotic things I'd ever experienced. And yes – I am aware of how sad and boring that makes me sound.

My boss came to see me. It was the first time anyone from work had visited me since I'd been home. A couple of them came once or twice when I was in the hospital, but unlike the many people who had been helping me, and who were now close friends, they had given me a wide berth for about three months. As soon as I saw Henry Sallis's bloated face, I knew what he was here to talk about. "How are you doing, Tori? We've all missed you."

"I'm doing really well, thanks, Henry."

"You'll soon be back to your old routine, then?"

I couldn't decide whether the tone of his voice was telling me that he wanted me back or whether he was hoping I would say 'no'. So, I decided to string him along for a bit. I knew that I was entitled to six months on full pay and another six months on half pay. The first six months was coming to an end, but I could live easily on half-pay. I owned my house, thanks to some very clever investments, and I wasn't exactly living it up at the moment. "I hope so, Henry. I really do."

I also hoped that my tone of voice didn't give away the fact that I had decided not to go back. My near-death experience had forced a much-needed re-evaluation of what I wanted to do with my life. I had concluded that working so hard that I never saw my house in daylight was not what I wanted anymore. I wanted to spend time with the wonderful people who lived on my street, and I wanted to enjoy the fabulous garden that Rich had created for me. No – I would string out my employer for as long as I could. When my six months on half-pay were up, I'd go back to work for a week or so and then quit. I had no idea what I was going to do, but something would turn up.

When Henry left, I manoeuvred myself outside to sit on my patio. My sister had got a handy little trolley for me, so I loaded it up with a tall glass of G&T and my kindle, and trundled it, and myself out into the late evening sunshine. I was enjoying re-reading Diana Gabaldon's wonderful story of the time-travelling nurse who falls in love with a braw Scotsman after travelling back to the eighteenth century. I sighed as Jamie told Claire that he was still a virgin and that he was glad she wasn't. *"Reckon one of us should know what they're doing."* I laughed softly and took a sip of my drink.

"What are you laughing at?" Rich was standing on the lawn about six feet in front of me, hands in pockets, his muscular arms more than filling the sleeves of the thin sweatshirt he was wearing.

I smiled warmly at him. I'd missed seeing him around the place since he'd finished my garden. He was coming about once a week now, just to water things and make sure everything he'd planted was still alive. "Jamie Fraser. The woman that wrote this book expected us to believe that a gorgeous, six-foot, kilted man was a virgin on his wedding night." I laughed again. "I suppose it was a different time."

Rich walked over to where I was sitting, picked up my glass and took a sip of my drink. "Mmm. Can I get myself one of these?"

"Yeah – gin and tonic are in the fridge. There's a lime out on the work surface, and there's ice in the freezer. Help yourself."

I watched him walk into the house. The sight of that butt, which was encased in tight denim tonight, was never going to get old.

"Stop ogling my arse." He turned and winked at me, then turned back and wiggled that very fine arse at me before going into my house. When he returned a few minutes later, he was carrying a glass that clinked with ice-cubes and a bowl of peanuts.

"Where did you find those?" I was pretty sure I didn't have peanuts in the house.

"Brought them with me. You never have any decent snacks." He put them down on the small table I was using before dragging one of my garden chairs over to sit next to me. He waved his hand in the general direction of the garden. "It's all looking very good."

"Yes, it is. I'd never have managed to get it looking like this – but it's just what I wanted. Thank you."

"You're welcome. I was a bit worried about the shrubs – it was too late to prune them, really, but I wouldn't have been able to do any of this if I hadn't cut them back. They're recovering well."

"Yes, they are."

"And so are you. You look better every time I see you."

"Yeah – I'm getting there. I've had a lot of help."

He took a long sip of his drink and scooped up a handful of peanuts before pushing them into his mouth. I watched him chew and swallow, then he picked up his drink and downed it in one. He took a deep breath and looked at me. "You know – I want to tell you something."

"Colour me intrigued." I felt very relaxed around him now – the weeks he had spent working on my garden had shown me a very different person to the arrogant guy who had lived next door to me all those years ago. "Go on."

"I still kick myself over that last time I spoke to you in the hall outside our rooms."

"There's no need – I got over it pretty quickly."

"No – you don't understand. I was a jerk. But I was only a jerk because I didn't know what to say. I'd fancied you all year. The first time I heard you calling out my name, I came in my boxers." He sighed heavily and ate some more peanuts. He picked up his empty glass and looked at it with disdain before picking up my glass and drinking the remains of my G&T. "There you were – standing there looking so bloody lovely, and I say something that makes you think I'm a total ass-hat. I'm sorry."

I laughed and picked up my empty glass. "Make me another drink, and I'll forgive you." In truth, there was nothing to forgive. We were both different people back then. "To be honest, I'm glad you did. It wouldn't have been nearly so nice getting to know you again if you hadn't been such an ass-hat first time around."

"It's been nice?"

"Get me that drink."

He got up and disappeared into my house. The sun was starting to go down, and my garden looked lovely in the early evening light. It was also starting to get cold, so I put my kindle and the bowl of peanuts on the trolley and started to trundle it back towards the house.

"Let me get that." Rich came out of the house empty-handed. "I was just coming out to check if you wanted to come in – it's getting a bit cold." He took over control of the trolley and walked slowly so that I could keep up. "When are the pins coming out?"

"Not sure. I've got some on the inside that are never coming out. I'm going to be one of those people who sets off alarms in airports." I laughed and manoeuvred myself up the ramp into my kitchen. "But it could have been so much worse."

"Yeah – it could."

"I could have carried on working myself into an early grave, never tasting your mother's amazing baking, never getting to know my wonderful neighbours, and never having a fabulous garden. Thank you, Rich. I do love it."

He smiled and parked the trolley in the corner of my kitchen. "You're welcome, lovely lady." He walked to me and put his arms around me very gently, pulling my head onto his shoulder.

I returned his hug the best I could without dropping my crutches and inhaled deeply. His smell was familiar – but surely, I imagined that? "You smell nice."

"Thank you." He pushed his fingers into my hair and stroked my scalp in a way that made me relax against him even more. "So do you. I like your shampoo. You smell of roses."

"It's my favourite. When I was in the hospital, everything smelled of hibiscrub. When I came home, I promised myself I would never smell of it again."

"Good job."

"Thanks."

We stood like that for a couple of minutes; me hugging him with one arm and him holding me close while massaging my scalp with his strong fingers.

"Tori?"

"Yeah?"

"Have you got a boyfriend?"

"No."

"Do you want one?"

"Are you offering?"

"Yes."

"Okay."

Four months later

God, it felt good to hold her. She was asleep on my shoulder; we'd started to watch a movie, but she'd fallen asleep about half an hour in. I continued to watch it, but in truth, I was content just to have her sleep on me – safe, warm and relaxed. I'd worn her out with a walk along the beach. We'd watched the late autumn sun set into the sea and then walked back to the cottage we had rented. I'd made beans on toast for us, which she ate hungrily. That made me content too. I was caring for her, and it made me happy.

I looked down at her legs. The frame had come off ten days before and this little holiday was to celebrate her freedom from it. I'd watched her heal and taken great pleasure in being a part of that process.

I thought back over the last ten months. That dreadful morning when the suicide bomber had caused chaos during morning rush-hour was still very clear in my mind. I'd been stuck in traffic as a result and was three hours late to a job. I hate being late for anything. When I got home that night, the news coverage showed the names and faces of the victims, and I recognised Tori straight away. Then mum told me that she was her neighbour and I asked how I could help. When mum said that Tori's garden could do with a little TLC, my mind was made up. I still shuddered when I thought about how I'd propositioned her at college – I was nuts about her but didn't have a clue what to do about it. And like all stupid young men, I went down the sleazy road because I didn't know there was an alternative.

But that didn't matter now. I'd fallen in love with her all over again and, by some miracle, she felt the same way about me. I looked down her body, and I felt the first tingle of arousal. We hadn't had full sex yet – god knows I wanted to – but I didn't want to hurt her. We'd done lots of other stuff together; I'd given her countless orgasms with my tongue and my fingers, and she had done the same for me. She'd never told me she didn't want sex – in fact, for the last few weeks, she'd said she thought she wanted to give it a try. But I was so worried about causing her any more pain; she'd suffered enough.

She shifted against me, and I felt her body stiffen. She was dreaming. Her breathing changed and I watched as her nipples hardened under her tee shirt, standing proud through the thin fabric. She moaned in her sleep and my cock hardened in response. She was so fucking sexy. I eased her off my shoulder and lay her down on the sofa. She moaned again, but she didn't wake up. I lifted the hem of her tee-shirt and exposed the lacy cups of her bra. Her nipples were straining against the fabric, so I pulled one cup aside, exposing the rosy nub to the cool air of the room. I captured it between my lips and sucked the sweet, puckered flesh into my mouth. I swirled my tongue around it, warming it as I sucked.

"Rich?" Tori's sleepy voice broke my concentration. "What are you doing?"

"I'm sucking on your beautiful tit. You were moaning in your sleep, and I just couldn't resist taking advantage of you."

She chuckled beneath me and reached behind herself to unfasten her bra. She pulled her tee shirt over her head and then dropped it and her bra on the floor. "Well, don't let me stop you." She shifted slightly, getting comfortable on the cushions. "And I have two of those, you know?"

I grinned at her and latched onto her other nipple, sucking hard and rolling it with my tongue. My cock was straining against my jeans, so I reached down and unzipped them. I was so hard for her.

"Rich?"

"Mmm?"

"Take me to bed."

I pulled my mouth off her nipple and knelt up so that I could look at her. "Okay. You were asleep before I woke you up – it's been a long day."

"That's not what I mean."

My heart started to pick up speed as I processed what I hoped she was saying. "Really? What do you mean?"

"I want to try – you know – what we've been doing has been amazing, and I definitely don't want to stop. But I want more. I want you. Can we try?"

"Absolutely!" I took a deep breath to try to stop myself sounding like a desperate teenager. "I mean – if you're sure?"

She giggled and looked down at the bulge in my boxers that was poking out through my open fly. "I'm sure. Help me up?"

I couldn't help myself – I came over all caveman and picked her up. I swung her into my arms and kissed her mouth. "Whatever you desire, my lady." She laughed as I carried her the short distance to the bedroom – we had chosen this little cottage because it was a bungalow – so no stairs to worry about.

I laid Tori on the bed and turned on the bedside lights – I wanted to see her – I wanted to remember everything about what we were going to do. She let me take off the rest of her clothes, and she lay back on the pillows. "You're so beautiful."

She looked down at herself and went to cover up the scars on her left side where she had been burned so badly. "I'm still really self-conscious."

"I know. But you don't need to be. I've seen every inch of you – kissed every inch of you – and every inch is beautiful." I took off my clothes and went to join her on the bed, but she stopped me.

"No – stay there." She got off the bed and stood in front of me. "I want to see you." She began to run her fingers over the skin of my chest, drawing around the lines of my tattoos. "I love your ink." She walked around me and began to repeat the process on my back. I felt her fingers travel down the length of the wings I have inked on my back. "These are my favourite. When I first saw you take your shirt off in my garden, I wanted to know where they ended." Her fingers splayed over my buttocks – the wings covered my entire back, the tips of the wings curled under my ass. Her fingers were caressing the curves of my butt now, and my whole body was so aroused by her touch, I felt as though I might catch fire. "So beautiful." She walked around me again and ran the backs of her fingers over my belly and down towards my straining cock. She curled her fingers around my shaft and leant towards me, capturing one of my nipples between her lips.

"Fuck! Tori – that's so hot. Don't stop." Our restricted lovemaking had led to many long explorations of each other's bodies. With Tori, I had discovered that my chest is a real erogenous zone for me. I love it when she sucks my nipples. "Use your teeth."

She did as I asked, pulling my hard, little nub between her teeth. It felt incredible, and my cock twitched in her hand. "God, I love that – they're so sensitive - I think I might get them pierced."

She made a sound of approval without taking her mouth from me. Then she stood up and licked her lips. "I want to see that." She sat down on the bed, and I helped her swing her legs up and round so that she was lying flat again. "But now, I want you. We're not stopping this time. I'm ready."

I knelt beside her on the mattress and reached for her. "I'm so hard for you, baby. I don't think I'm going to be able to last very long once I'm inside you."

"I get that. And it might be a good idea to make this a bit of a quickie – just in case my leg starts to hurt."

"I won't hurt you, Tori. So, if you have any pain, you must tell me, and I'll stop."

"I promise."

"So, here's the plan. I lick your gorgeous pussy until you're nearly there."

"I like that plan."

I arranged her legs in the position that I knew she could hold without pain and I went to work. I adore eating her out – she makes this cute, whimpering sound when she's getting close. And she tastes amazing. I love to get it all over my face. I pressed her pussy lips apart with my fingers and licked that deep pink inner skin. She jerked when I ran the tip of my tongue over her little clit, so I sucked it into my mouth. She started groaning and moving her hips in small circles, so I licked her entire length before putting two fingers into her tight, little hole. I love the way it feels – it's like hot, wet silk. She gripped my fingers with her inner muscles, and I nearly came at the thought that my cock would soon be enjoying that sensation.

"Rich – please – don't stop!" She was moving her hips a lot now, and I knew from the sounds she was making that she was getting pretty close.

I gave her pussy one, last lick then I moved up her body until we were face to face. "Are you ready?"

"So ready." She reached down and curled her fingers around my cock.

"No – oh – I'll come if you touch me. Sorry." I felt so stupid.

She laughed softly and let go of me. "Looks like you're driving, then."

I looked into her eyes and then kissed her deeply, pushing my tongue into her mouth. "Okay. I'm driving." I smiled at her and the enormity of what we were about to do made my heart clench. "Are you comfy?"

"Yes, Rich. I'm comfy. Now just put your dick in me – I'm going crazy here."

I took hold of myself and lined up the head of my cock with her hole. One, easy thrust and I was in. "Oh, fuck! You're so … oh, fuck that feels good!"

"It does. God, I've wanted this for so long." We lay still for a moment, just looking at each other. Then she moved her hips a little and put her hands on my back. "You can move. I want you to move."

I couldn't hold on anymore. I started to thrust into her in long, deep strokes.

"Yes – oh god – Rich – that's it – that's what I needed." She was writhing beneath me and making the sounds that told me she was close to orgasm. "Fuck me! I want your cock all the way inside me."

I pushed all the way into her; I was going to come inside her, and the idea of that was one of the most erotic things I'd ever experienced. I felt her inner muscles clench around me and she cried out. I managed to keep thrusting into her while she came, then I couldn't hold it any longer. One last thrust and I held myself deep inside her as I came so hard I saw stars. I covered her mouth with mine, groaning into her as the last spasms went through me. The kiss gentled until we were just touching each other's lips, but I was still shuddering from the aftershocks. I held myself on my elbows above her. "I love you, Tori."

"I love you too."

"That was so worth the wait." I couldn't help the grin that spread over my face.

"Agreed. Maybe there is something to be said for delayed gratification." She laughed and wriggled under me. "Can you move? I need to straighten my leg."

I pulled out of her reluctantly, then moved us into a spoon, holding her from behind. We pulled the covers over us, and a few minutes later, I heard her breathing slowly as she fell asleep. And at that moment, I knew that it didn't matter what life threw at us, we were going to be okay. She had survived something horrific, and that incident had, in a roundabout kind of way, brought us together. I'd been given a second chance with this girl, and I wasn't going to stuff it up this time. I was going to hold on tight – tonight and always.

What makes up a person? Is it a body; arms and legs, the ability to walk or run? In the last ten months, I've learned a lot in answer to that question. A person is a body and a mind — but a person is also the love of the people around them and the way we respond to that love. I didn't know that before. I'm thankful that I was given the opportunity to find out.

WATER

Cancer
Scorpio
Pisces

♋

Cancer

Emotion, diplomatic, intensity, inquisitive, intelligent, changeable

*D**ear Michael,*

It's been a long time since we last saw each other. As I approach the sunset years of my life, a life which has been both wonderful and sad in equal measure, I feel the need to write to you. I don't know if you'll ever read these words, or if you do, whether they will mean anything to you. Someone wiser than me once said that some things are better left unsaid, but I disagree. This needs to be said. My only wish is that I had said it to you all those years ago.

Michael, I love you. I have always loved you. You were my sun and my moon; the first thing I thought about when I woke and the last thing I thought about before sleeping. I dreamed about you – in fact, I still do. In my dreams, you are young and beautiful, and my hair is golden, not silver as it is now.

I remember everything about you. Your scent haunts my memories; sometimes I will conjure up the memory of it and my heart contracts, as though the room has suddenly been drained of air. Every memory I have of you is precious – I keep them all locked away where no-one can find them. My memories of you are for me alone.

Do you remember the day we met? I do. I remember it as if it were yesterday. You were wearing navy trousers that were worn at the knees and a red shirt that had been washed too many times. When we shook hands, I noticed that yours were dry and calloused. You told me that you were working for the summer in the box factory; a poor use of those talented hands, but I understood, probably better than anyone else in the room on that humid, June evening. We moved in circles of privilege, you and I, but we were both imposters. Included for our ability, rather than the name we were born with or the amount we stood to inherit.

These days, I grow tired of the fake people who move in those circles. I have little tolerance for them and their games of one-upmanship. I still adore music – especially the music we shared during that wonderful summer – but enduring the pretentious, mindless noise that must accompany the experience of it makes me tired. These days, I only hear the beloved strains of Finzi from my gramophone, and it is a poor substitute. Like my memories of you; clear as a recording, but with none of the warmth and life of the real thing.

I wonder where you are now? I wonder who you are with. Did you marry? Have children? I hope you did. I hope you found a beautiful girl and that she made you happy. I wish that, almost as much as I wish I could have given it to you myself.

I must confess something to you. I hesitate to do it, because once it's written, it cannot be unsaid. But you deserve to know the truth. You have a son. You gave me a son. I called him Michael. He looks like you; he has your fair hair and slightly crooked smile. I love him so much. He has been raised with love; Donald never suspected, even though Michael is my only child. In all our long marriage, I never conceived again.

I wish I had been braver. I wish I had not sent you away. I wish … if wishes were horses, then beggars would ride. I know you didn't understand why; you were twenty years old and love was king. I know you couldn't forgive me for letting you go; it is my dearest hope that now, with the benefit of time and experience, you can at least afford me that, for I find I need it in my old age. Past hurts and pain weigh heavy on my aged heart, and I have no wish to carry them with me to the grave.

I will write again when memories of you come to the surface. They have been doing that more often of late. It is as though the strength of will I had to keep them buried is dissipating; like the strength of my body as I head towards my final journey.

Forgive me, Michael. I love you. There has never been anyone else in my heart.

Yours, always

Katherine

Michael Preston looked at the letter once more. It had been written by his grandmother, Katherine Preston, at some point before her recent death. It wasn't dated, but she had written it before the death of his father. It was written in her usual, green ink and he knew which pen she had used to write it. It was placed in an unsealed envelope that just said, 'For Michael' on the front, so he had opened it, thinking that perhaps she had left a message for him. Clearing the house had fallen to him as he was now the owner. He was the last of the Prestons; the only child of an only child, so any instructions about what to do with his grandmother's innumerable possessions would be welcome.

"Well, shit." He sat down heavily on the bed where his grandmother had slept. The bed she had shared with her husband, Donald, and the one on which his father, Michael Preston Senior had been born. If what the letter claimed was true, then Donald wasn't his grandfather at all – some unknown man named Michael was. Her words came back to him: *I wish I had been braver.* Katherine Preston was the most formidable, brave woman he'd ever met. She had taken on the care and upbringing of her only grandchild when her son and his wife died within months of each other. Michael Junior had been only thirteen years old when it happened. The bottom dropped out of his world when his father's coffin was lowered into the grave so recently dug for his mother. Everyone said it was a tragedy. Katherine held back her tears, put her arms around his shoulders and got on with the job of raising him as best she could.

Now she was gone too, and Michael was alone. At thirty-two, he'd spent most of his time concentrating on making a name as a photographer, and he was doing alright for himself. He didn't have time to sort this house out right now, but he knew that he would do it as one, last sign of respect for the woman who raised him. She had secrets. Would the house offer up any more?

He took the letter with him as he climbed the stairs to his room. He hadn't lived here since his early twenties, but his bedroom remained unchanged, and he had been sleeping here since the day before his grandmother's funeral. He intended to read the letter again, which he did just before he fell asleep. As his eyes began to close and his breathing slowed, he heard her voice echoing through his semi-consciousness. *I wish I had been braver. I wish I had not sent you away. I wish … if wishes were horses, then beggars would ride.*

The dream came, as it often did, but this night it was somehow clearer, more painful. He had loved a Catherine too, just like his real grandfather. He'd shortened her name to Rina. He had loved her, and he had let her go.

"I don't understand, Michael. I love you. You love me. Why are you ending this?" Rina's voice sounded pained, and he couldn't bear to look at her because he knew her stricken face would break him.

"Yes. I do. But you have an amazing career ahead of you. I don't want to hold you back."

"Bullshit!" She turned on him, and he had no option but to look at her. "This is all about you. You've been offered that internship, and you don't want any obstacles. Is that all I am to you? Is that all our love means to you?"

He couldn't look at her. "I'm sorry. I can't do this right now."

"You can't? Then perhaps I should just leave. That way, you won't have to deal with it at all." She disappeared into the bedroom of the tiny flat they had been sharing for a couple of months. A few minutes later, she reappeared, carrying a suitcase. She removed the cheap ring that had been all they could afford, and left it on the mantelpiece; then she walked towards the door. "Are you going to say anything?"

He looked up at her, and his heart felt like someone was squeezing it. There was so much he wanted to say. He wanted to beg her to stay, to ignore what he'd said. But he didn't. He wasn't brave enough. He just shook his head and looked away.

Rina opened the door to leave and, as she did, a version of Katherine's words came out of her mouth. "One day, you'll wish you were braver. One day, you'll wish you hadn't sent me away."

Michael woke with a start, his heart hammering in his chest and his breath sawing in and out of his lungs as he gasped for air. He sat up and looked at the clock on his bedside table; Three fifteen. "Okay, I'd like to thank the academy and Marley's ghost for that little masterpiece." He tried to calm his breathing and got up to get a drink of water. He stood in the kitchen and sipped at a bottle of Evian, but his heart wouldn't calm down. "Alcohol. I need something to drink." He walked to the cabinet in the dining room where his grandmother had kept the booze, and started to look for something decent. "Sherry, port, marsala. God, did she ever drink anything that wasn't sweet?" He pulled the many bottles out of the cabinet and put them on the dining room table. "Cherry Brandy, apricot brandy, Advocaat? Yeeuk!" At the back of the cabinet was a rather fine crystal decanter. He took it out and sniffed the contents. "Bingo! Scotch. And if I'm not mistaken, a rather good one." He reached for a tumbler from the back of the top shelf of the cabinet and noticed an envelope – rather like the one he had found earlier – wedged among the crystal. *For Michael.* He poured himself a glass of whiskey and sat down to read the letter.

Dear Michael,

I've been thinking about you a lot today. I'm sure an old woman shouldn't feel such emotions at the memory of a lover, but I can't help it. When I think about you, my mind is twenty-three again, and my body responds of its own accord.

Michael hesitated. Did he want to read about his grandmother's erotic memories? He knew the answer to that question should probably be no, but curiosity got the better of him. After taking a swig of what turned out to be a very good single malt, he returned to the faded letter in his hand.

I find my mind wandering back to that summer. You and me; the barn, your kisses, your sweet body as I undressed you. In my mind, I can still see every inch of you. I can still run my hands over your soft skin and tangle my fingers in your hair. I can still taste you. Your body made me wanton; I never desired to take a man's member in my mouth before, and I never wanted to again. But your body was mine, and I wanted to taste every part of it.

"Jeez ..." The thought of his grandmother sucking a cock made Michael stop for a moment. "TMI, grandmother dearest." But after another swig of whiskey, he found he couldn't leave it unfinished.

I felt honoured to be your first. I think it made me fall in love with you, even more, to know that you had known no other woman's touch. I only wish that I could have been your last as well. The thought of you sharing your sweet body with another woman makes my heart hurt, but the thought of you never experiencing that joy again is worse somehow, so I hope you did. But for those fourteen, glorious days, you were mine. And every day since, a little more of my heart has chipped away as our time together disappears into the distance of time, getting further away as every day passes.

I hope you were loved in the years after we said goodbye. I hope your life was happy. I wish I had been braver.

Yours, always

Katherine

Michael put the letter down on the dining room table and took another drink from his glass. Reading this new instalment of his grandmother's story wasn't going to help to get rid his own ghosts. He poured himself some more whiskey and started to go through the drawers in the sideboard; perhaps there were some more clues hidden in there. He found more letters, filled with pain and regret; Katherine had truly loved this Michael and regretted her decision to leave him behind. It just made him think more about Rina. What was she doing? Was she married?

He reached for his phone and did a google search for Catherine Murray. She had been studying fine art when he knew her, so she was probably doing something creative now. The search came back with a couple of results; a paediatrician, a freelance journalist and many people on Facebook, none of which were his Rina. With a heavy heart, he decided that her surname was probably not Murray anymore, so he had no idea where to start. Both of those facts made his heart hurt even more.

The alcohol was beginning to kick in now, so he climbed back up the stairs to his room and lay down on his narrow bed. Just before sleep came back to him, he saw Rina's face. He saw her sweet mouth as she wrapped her lips around his cock. Despite his sleepiness, his hand crept down towards his hardening penis and, as he took hold of himself, he imagined it was Rina's mouth on him, Rina's hand caressing his balls. He came suddenly, before he had time to take a breath, and he cried out her name as his seed spilt into his boxer shorts. A dreamless sleep overtook him then, and he slept soundly until his phone rang, just before nine o'clock.

"Mike? Sorry, did I wake you up?"

Michael heard the voice of his old school friend, James Hammond, and squinted at the clock on his bedside table. "What? Yeah – but it's okay. I needed to get up anyway. I've got a lot to do today. Good to hear from you, man."

"Yeah – long time no see. I got your email about coming to appraise your grandmother's stuff. I've got some time this afternoon if that's any good to you?" James worked for his father's auction house, and they dealt in quality house clearance as well as some sales of fine art and antiques.

"Oh – yeah – that would be amazing – thank you. I'll be here all day, so come as soon as you can. I'll text you the address."

After making himself a pot of very strong coffee, Michael started to sort through the huge, oak dresser in the dining room. There was a complete dinner set of Masons china and some Chinese pieces, but most of them were damaged. There was a large vase with weird pictures of fish that were scratched into the surface of the clay. Michael thought it was ugly, but something in the back of his mind told him that it might be valuable. He turned the pot upside down to see if there was a mark. He turned it to the light. "Martin Bros, London Southall, 3-1898. Wow. That's actually pretty cool."

As he turned the vase to put it back on the shelf, he noticed that something had fallen out. He picked up the folded card. It was a photograph of a group of young people. He spotted his grandmother's youthful face straight away; her trademark blonde curls were instantly recognisable. She was laughing at the camera, standing in the centre of the group. A man was standing next to her with his arm around her shoulders. He was holding up his other hand to obscure his face and the man behind him had him in a bear hug. They were all having a really good time.

On the reverse of the photo, his grandmother had written: *Oxford Festival, July 2nd – 16th 1953*. There were several names written as well, and Michael scanned along the line until he got to *K. Preston*. The next name, the one of the man with his hand in front of the camera was *M. Fisk*. Could this be Katherine's Michael? He did some internet research and discovered that the Oxford Festival of the Arts had been part of the Festival of Britain celebrations. It had included young musicians and artists from Oxfordshire in concerts and exhibitions. Katherine had been a talented clarinettist. She had mentioned the music – and her beloved Finzi especially – in that first letter. Did this mean that Michael had been a musician too?

He was just about to start another internet search when he heard James' voice coming through the open kitchen door. "Hello, the house! Mike – are you home?"

"Yeah – I'm here – come on in." He hugged his friend as he came through the archway into the dining room. "God, it's great to see you, man. How long has it been?"

"Too bloody long, mate. We need to do some serious catching up over a large quantity of ale!"

"Well, let's get this over with, and we can make a start on that."

They started in the dining room. Michael showed James the Martin Brothers vase. "I think this might be worth something?"

James picked up the pot with the strange decorations and turned it over to look at the mark on the base. "Oh yeah – this is good – we can auction this for you. I'd estimate about twelve to fifteen hundred."

"Really? Wow. Go, Grandma."

"Don't you want to keep any of this stuff?"

"Not really. I've picked out a couple of things, but I want to completely re-design the place before I move in."

"You're going to live here, then?"

"Yeah. I can do my job from pretty much anywhere, and living in London is starting to get me down. Plus, this one room is almost as big as my whole flat. I can have a studio here."

James nodded and walked into the sitting room. "I get that. I'd want to live here too – this place is amazing. I'd want to keep all the original features, though. All this art deco? You'd be mad to rip it out."

Michael joined him in the sitting room. "You may be right. I suppose I'm just so used to it; I don't really see it anymore."

"Well, take a fresh look, my man. Don't you dare change those light fittings." He walked over to the fireplace to study the painting that hung over it. He took it down and blew the dust off. "You want to keep this too." He held the painting up for Michael to see. It was a landscape of a ripe wheat field with poppies. At the end of the field was a barn.

"That was always my grandmother's favourite."

"She had a good eye." He pointed to the signature in the bottom left-hand corner of the canvas. "This is a Fisk. His work is starting to go for serious money. I wouldn't part with this for all the tea in China."

"Did you say, Fisk? Michael Fisk?"

"Yep. Royal Academician. Died about five years ago. I like this." He took the painting over to the window to look at it in the light. "Great condition considering it's been hanging over a fireplace."

"We only ever used this room on high days and holidays. The fire was hardly ever lit."

"Good thing too. If you really want to sell it, I'll be very happy to auction it for you."

Michael walked to his friend and took the painting from him, studying it in the light coming through the bay window of the sitting room. *I find my mind wandering back to that summer. You and me; the barn, your kisses.* "No. You're right. I should hold onto this one. I like it."

"They've got some of his stuff in the Ashmolean. You should go and have a look."

"Yeah." Michael felt a smile start at the corners of his mouth and spread to the rest of his face. "I'll do that. I might go tomorrow."

He dreamt about Rina again. This time, they were in the barn at the end of the wheat-field. Rina was laughing as she led him into the sweet-smelling interior of the old stone building. She turned around and began to undo the buttons of her shirt as she lay back on the hay. "Come here."

He went to her eagerly, lying beside her on the hay. "I want to kiss you." He pushed her back onto their soft bed and covered her mouth with his, pushing his tongue into her, to stroke and caress her. She tasted so good – so familiar. "I've missed you so much."

"I've missed you too, Michael. Why did you send me away?"

"I don't know. I really don't know. It seemed to make sense then."

Suddenly, the hay bed where they were lying began to melt away, replaced by stones. Rina sat up clutching her chest, blood pouring through her fingers. She looked down at the gaping wound then looked up to face him. "What have you done? Why?"

He looked down to see that her still-beating heart was in the palm of his hand. "I'm sorry! Rina! Please!" He held out her heart, trying to give it back to her, but she was getting further away as every second passed. He reached out to her again, but it was too late. She was gone.

Michael came awake with a scream. He sat up, sweating and gasping for breath. He looked at his shaking hands, half expecting to see them covered with Rina's blood, but they were just white and damp with sweat. "Christ!" he rubbed his hands over his face to try to shake the image of the nightmare. It had started so beautifully; he had never made love to Rina in a barn, but it would have been a sweet dream. But he understood what his brain was trying to tell him. He had made a massive mistake letting Rina go. Reading about his grandmother's lifelong regret had re-opened this old wound, and now, he had no idea how to heal it.

The Ashmolean was fairly busy for a Thursday afternoon; several parties of school children and tourists were milling around. Michael asked the lady at the entrance where to find the Fisk paintings, and she nodded and marked the gallery he needed on a floor plan leaflet. "Level 3M – Modern Art. Room number 62. Take the lift over there." She smiled at him and gave him the floor plan.

"Thanks. That's great." He made his way to the third floor and followed the signs to the Modern Art gallery. There weren't many people in there, so he was able to walk around the room and look at the paintings without having to wait. He recognised the first of his grandfather's paintings without needing to read the name on the information plate. It was another picture of the barn. This time, it was a winter scene, the ground and trees covered with snow. The colours were glorious; he had somehow captured the colour of the sky just before it is about to snow. Michael read the information plate then. *Study of a barn in winter by Michael Fisk R.A. Oil on canvas. 1958. One of three known studies of this subject, painted between 1956 and 1958.*

He walked slowly along the line of five paintings by Michael Fisk; all landscapes of the Oxfordshire countryside. Except for the last one, which made him take a step back. It was a portrait of a man who looked extraordinarily familiar. The man was looking out at the viewer, his blue eyes smiling. In the background, which was probably his studio, there was a painting on an easel; his grandmother's painting of the barn in the summer wheat field. On the desk in front of him was a clarinet and a half-written letter. It was loosely painted, but when he squinted his eyes, he could just make out the first two words. *Dear Katherine.*

He stood back to look at it again; then he stooped to read the information plate. *Self-portrait with clarinet by Michael Fisk R.A. On loan from The Fisk Trust. A rare example of portraiture from this artist, it remained in his private collection until his death. Oil on canvas. 1957.*

"It's a great painting, isn't it? It's one of my favourites up here. We are so lucky to have it."

Michael turned to see that the museum volunteer who was looking after the room had come to stand beside him. "Yes – it's wonderful."

The woman in the museum uniform looked at him and her brow crinkled. "Say, are you related to Fisk? This painting looks an awful lot like you."

Michael shook his head. He had no desire to get into the family bombshell that he'd recently discovered. "No – I don't think so – it's just a coincidence. But you're right; I do look a bit like the guy in the picture."

The woman smiled and nodded. "Well, you're not alone in thinking he's pretty special. Everyone who comes in here ends up spending some time with him." She smiled wistfully and let her eyes settle on the peaceful face in the painting. "He's never lonely." She shook her head and laughed. "Listen to me! I'm spending far too long with these paintings – I'm starting to think of them as real people."

Michael smiled her. "I don't think that's a bad thing. And it's nice to know he's got people looking after him."

"I suppose you're right. I can't get over the likeness though." She looked back at Michael and lifted her hand, resting her fingers against her chin. "Our good lady doctor would love to see you."

"Who?"

"We have a lady – she's a doctor at the Radcliffe – kids' doctor I think. Anyway, she comes here the first Sunday of every month, regular as clockwork. She told me he looks like someone she used to know. Spends at least ten minutes in here."

Michael thanked the woman and took a photo of the painting with his phone. He needed to get home and google Catherine Murray again; he was sure that one of the results that had come up when he'd searched before had been a paediatrician. The museum volunteer said that the portrait's regular visitor was a kids' doctor at the John Radcliffe. Could it be too much to hope that this was his Rina? That she had come back to Oxford? And did he just think about his grandmother's house as 'home' in his thoughts? He smiled at that realisation and made his way back to the lift.

When he got home, he made some tea and settled in front of his laptop to find Rina. It didn't take very long at all because she was the paediatrician whose name came up third from the top of the search results. He pulled up her details on Linkedin and there she was; his Rina, smiling out at the world, looking every bit as lovely as she had when they were together. He thought about requesting to be added to her contacts, but somehow, that didn't seem appropriate to him. When he made contact with her again, it needed to be face to face. Whatever twist of fate had caused this sudden desire to link with her again, their reunion deserved something better than a *hi, what are you up to* over the internet. And if the woman at the museum was right, then he knew where to find her next Sunday.

The next nine days dragged for Michael. He had builders in to quote on renovations on the house - a new kitchen, creating an en-suite bathroom for the master bedroom and installing a new boiler and central heating system. But, just as James had suggested, all the original 1930s floors and fittings were going to stay. The house was a gem, which he was only just realising, and he needed to keep as much of it as possible, while also making the house suitable for living in the twenty-first century. The plan was to get the work done and move in within four months. The large conservatory would be cleared of its dead plants and rattan furniture and would be re-fitted as his photography studio. The light pouring in from all angles through the South-facing glass structure made it an obvious choice. He put his London flat on the market and started to make decisions about how much of his grandmother's furniture to keep.

When Sunday morning finally dawned, he was ready. He was standing on the steps of The Ashmolean, waiting for it to open, armed with a flask of coffee, a Sunday Times and a fully charged e-reader. When he got to the Modern Art gallery, he spent a little time looking at the self-portrait before sitting down to wait.

"You came back." It was the woman he'd seen on that first visit. She was smiling at him encouragingly. "I had a feeling you might."

Michael didn't know what to say to her. "Yes. I think I might know the lady you were talking about. I haven't seen her in a very long time. It would be good to see her again." That sounded quite credible; better than the truth, anyway. *I've just found out that my grandmother had an affair with the guy in the painting and that he's my grandfather. Reading her letters to him has made me regret letting my ex-fiancé go, and I think she is the woman who comes to look at the painting. I need to see her again, so that's why I'm here.* Yeah – that didn't sound like something that needed to be shared with a total stranger.

"Well, I should have told you she doesn't normally get here until early afternoon. She's a Friend of the Museum, so she comes here for lunch. She always comes up here afterwards. Why don't you go and have an explore? If you give me your mobile number, I can text you if she gets here before you get back."

It sounded like a good idea. And he had never really looked at the Ashmolean's vast collection. So, he thanked the woman, whose name was Jenny, gave her his number and went off to explore.

It was just after one o'clock when he returned to the Modern Art gallery. Jenny greeted him warmly as he took his seat to wait. After a couple of hours, he was beginning to think that Rina wasn't going to show. He was just about to get up to leave when he heard Jenny greet someone behind him. He heard their conversation - comments about the weather and the food in the restaurant. But Jenny didn't mention that he was there, and he was glad for that. He needed to see Rina before he decided whether to speak to her. He knew it was cowardly, but that was how it had to be.

She walked around the room, gazing at the paintings on display. He watched her. She looked the same – a little older, her hair was shorter, and she was wearing glasses. But he would have recognised her in a heartbeat.

When she came to the Fisk paintings, he heard her whisper something that sounded like hello you.

Michael could tell by her body language that she didn't intend to linger; it was now or never. He stood up and walked the short distance to where she was standing. "Rina?"

She turned around and, when she saw him, her eyes flew open in shock and she put her hand up to cover her mouth.

"Rina – it's so good to see you."

She looked at him for a moment, then looked back at the portrait. "Goodbye, Michael." She turned around and walked quickly out of the gallery.

Michael wasn't sure if she'd been talking to him or the portrait. He looked over to Jenny, who shrugged her shoulders and looked sympathetic. "Guess she wasn't happy to see me." He wasn't angry. He realised that the overwhelming feeling that was hitting him now was sadness. He thanked Jenny for her help and made his way home, stopping to buy a bottle of Glenfiddich on the way. There was a very good reason that he had buried the memories of Rina for so long; allowing them to come to the surface was painful. Excruciatingly painful.

The Scotch burned as the first mouthful made its way down his throat. "Come on, idiot. Don't mope. Do something constructive." How long had he been talking to himself? He looked around the sitting room where he had set up a desk. The bookshelves that were built-in to the walls either side of the fireplace drew his attention. He hadn't been through them yet. Perfect – just what he needed to take his mind of what a waste of time today had been. He started pulling out volumes to check them - some old and valuable, some old and worth nothing. When he pulled out a battered copy of The Rubaiyat of Omar Khayyam, an unsealed envelope fell to the floor. With a sigh, and after replenishing his glass of whiskey, he moved to sit on the cushioned seat that followed the curve of the bay window.

Dear Michael,

This will be the last time I write to you. My heart is so heavy tonight that I feel it could break. My son, Michael, our son died today. His lovely wife, Maria, died six months ago and I think he just gave up. I would like to give up too, but my grandson needs someone to look after him. I am all he has in the world now, so I must be strong for him.

So, at last, a letter he could date. The day that his father had died, his grandmother sat down and wrote this letter to say goodbye to the love of her life.

I feel guilty somehow that on this night the only person I want to talk to is you. I have so many regrets about my life. So many things I would have done differently if I had the chance. But our son was the one thing I wouldn't want to change. The circumstances? Yes. I would change things so that we could have raised him together, but I wouldn't have gone through life without knowing that I had a part of you with me; that I had nurtured that part of you within my own body. But now he's gone, and I feel that my one reason for carrying on has gone too.

Michael felt her grief pouring out from the green ink and the faded paper. He remembered how she was when he first moved into this house after his father's death; she had loved him, but she was distant. As he grew to look more like her lover, it must have been very hard for her to look at him. But she never gave the slightest clue that she was hurting.

I can't give up, though. That is a choice I can't make. Perhaps I'm being punished for making the wrong choice all those years ago. So, this is what I choose; I will move on, I will look after my beautiful grandson, and I will stop wishing that I could go back and change things with you. There is a line in The Rubaiyat:
> *"The Moving Finger writes; and, having writ,*
> *Moves on: nor all thy Piety nor Wit*
> *Shall lure it back to cancel half a Line,*
> *Nor all thy Tears wash out a Word of it."*
I have tried to cancel out the lines of my life without you. My tears have not been able to wash out a single word of what I said to you on that last day. It's time to accept that and to let you go.

Goodbye, Michael. I will always love you and want you, but I can't do the things I need to do now while you haunt my dreams and fill my heart. I know you are successful now; we bought your painting of the barn — our barn — it hangs in my drawing room. I'm glad for you. It eases my pain a little to know that you have found your place.

I will fold my memories of you away with this letter.

Your Katherine

Michael sat back in his seat and felt the tears start. His grandmother had lived with the pain of regret for almost all her adult life. He saw how it ate at her; he'd thought her cold, distant, a product of her stiff-upper-lip generation. But now he knew that she had loved once with a passion and that the memory of that love had stayed with her for the rest of her life. She had given it up for him, folded it away with this last letter on the day he had become her responsibility.

He took a large gulp of whiskey and refolded the letter before putting it back between the pages of the book. Perhaps he should try to fold away his regrets about Rina with it. He knew that wasn't going to happen anytime soon – the sight of her horrified face and her hasty retreat had only deepened the wound that the letters had opened. He batted away the tears with the back of his hand, but they kept coming.

A ringing sound pushed through his self-pity. He had to stop and think what it was; it wasn't his phone. It rang again, and he realised it was the doorbell. "Who the hell?" He looked at his watch – it was almost nine o'clock. The ringing started again, so he shambled to the door and opened it.

"Hello, Michael." Rina stood on the doorstep.

"Rina! How did you know where to find me?"

She walked past him into the house and waited for him to close the door. "A good guess. I know your grandmother passed away. And you were at the museum today. So, there was a good chance I'd find you here."

"You knew about my grandmother?"

"We kept in touch. I met her a few years ago when the Friends of the museum negotiated with the Fisk Trust to have the portrait. She was a patron."

He hadn't known that. He hadn't known anything about the artist, or his grandmother's connection to him, until a few days ago. How could there be something so important in his family history that he didn't know anything about? "I only just found about him. I found some letters my grandmother had written to him. He was my real grandfather."

Rina blew out a breath and raised her eyebrows. "I figured that one out the moment I saw the portrait. You say there were letters? Are they something the Trust might be interested in?"

"What? God – no. They're private. She never sent them. They were like some kind of catharsis for her. She loved him all her life. They're full of regret and pain. I'd never let anyone else see them."

"Sorry. Of course. That was insensitive of me." She took her glasses off and rubbed her eyes; then she looked at him again. "You've been crying. I'm sorry – I've clearly come at a bad time. I'll leave you alone."

"No!" The word came out before he could stop it and he reached for her, grabbing her wrist and pulling her towards him. "Please, stay. I really want to talk to you."

She looked a little uncertain, but she didn't pull away. "Alright."

He led her into the sitting room and sat her down on the sofa that faced the fireplace. "Would you like something to drink?"

She nodded and eased back in the seat, fixing her gaze on the painting. "Do you know what the significance of the barn is? Katherine would never tell me."

Michael poured Rina a glass of whiskey and sat down next to her. "Yes, it was explained in one of her letters. It's where they used to meet to make love. It looks like neither of them ever got over it. They met during the Festival of Arts in 1953 – my grandmother was a talented clarinettist."

Rina considered what he'd said for a moment and took a sip of her drink. "Why did they split up?"

"Katherine was already married to Donald Preston. Things were different then, I guess. If they'd run off together, it probably would have ruined them both."

Rina looked at him, studying his face. "Why were you crying?"

"I've been reading her letters; it's what made me think of you. So much regret, I hardly know where to begin."

"Hers or yours?"

"Mine." He looked at her and tears started to fall again. "I regret everything about what I did to you. I'm not expecting you to forgive me, or anything, but I need you to know that I was an idiot. I should never have let you go."

Rina stood up to leave. "It's late. I have an early start in the morning."

"Oh – yes, of course." Michael stood up and couldn't help the feeling of sorrow that washed over him. She was leaving. There was so much more he wanted to say, and he wasn't going to get the chance. He didn't blame her, but he wished more than anything she'd give him the chance to explain. He took her empty whiskey glass, putting it next to his on the coffee table. "It was lovely to see you, Rina. I'd like to see you again, but I'll understand if you don't want anything to do with me."

She looked at him for a moment, then took one last look at the painting over the fireplace before turning towards the door. "What are you doing on Tuesday?"

"What? Oh – um – nothing, as far as I know."

"I'll pick you up at ten o'clock. There's something I'd like to show you."

She was there at exactly ten o'clock. Michael smiled as he watched her pull up in his driveway; she had always been spectacularly punctual for everything they ever did together. He left the house before she had a chance to get out of the car, dodging the raindrops as he hurried to open the passenger door.

"You must have been looking out for me." She smiled at him as he fastened his seatbelt. "You always used to do that."

"And you're bang on time. You always used to do that." He looked at her and felt something familiar but long-forgotten; peace. She gave him a sense of peace, just being in the same space as her. "Shame it's raining though."

"I think it's going to clear up later." She put her car in reverse and pulled out of the driveway.

"Where are we going?"

"It's a surprise." She flashed him a smile before putting her eyes back on the road and concentrated on driving to wherever it was they were going.

The conversation between them was a little strained, to begin with, but it soon eased. It would have been very easy for Michael to forget the years that stood between them, and the animosity that had developed because of his stupidity. When she laughed at something he said, his heart leapt in his chest as he looked over at Rina. "I've missed you."

She looked at him momentarily before turning to face the road again. There was a distinct blush of colour to her cheeks, but she didn't say anything.

"I'm sorry. I shouldn't have said that. It was all my fault that you went, so it was my fault that I missed you. But I did."

"Thank you." She took a breath and gripped the steering wheel. "I appreciate you saying that."

The conversation ceased, and Michael looked out of the car window as the Oxfordshire countryside sped by. The rain had eased up a little, but the fresh smell of rain on green things was flowing into the car through his open window. When the car came to the crest of a hill that looked down into a picturesque valley, he realised where they were going. At the bottom of the hill, nestled between two sloping fields, was the barn. "Is that *the* barn?"

Rina smiled at Michael's obvious delight. "It is. I thought you might like to see it."

"But how do you know about it?"

"Michael Fisk bought it in the 1970s. It was going to be demolished, so he bought the two fields and the barn. He renovated the barn. It's in the hands of the Trust now. They rent it out to the farm that used to own it." She parked on a wide verge about a hundred yards from the barn. "I've always loved it. But now I know its significance, I think I love it even more."

Michael walked to stand next to her and took in the view. "I know this view so well. This must be the spot he stood in to paint it." He was overcome suddenly with how important this was to his history. "It's beautiful."

Rina looked up at him; it was obvious that he moved by the vista, and something inside her began to melt. She had never stopped loving Michael. "I missed you too." Before either of them could say anything else, the rain began to fall again; a heavy, summer shower that arrives suddenly, the fat drops bouncing when they land. "Oh! Let's get inside." She took off at a run towards the barn, grabbing Michael's hand to take him with her.

The barn smelled of sweet hay and the sound of the rain amplified on the red, metal roof. Michael shook the water from his hair and pulled off his damp sweater, shaking it off as well. "Bloody hell! What a storm!"

Rina laughed and pushed her wet hair off her face. "Good job it's not cold out there." She ran her hands over her bare arms, shaking the water from her fingers. "We'll dry off pretty quickly in here." She looked over at him, and her heart clenched.

"Did you mean what you said? About missing me?"

She dropped her head. "Yes. I missed you. I still do."

Michael moved to stand in front of her. "Rina … I …"

"Shut up Michael."

"I'm sorry." He made a move to step away, feeling the full weight of sorrow land in his belly. He gasped as Rina grabbed his wrist and pulled him back towards her.

"I want you to stop talking, put your arms around me and kiss me."

Michael opened his mouth with surprise and looked at Rina's lovely face. It hit him then; here she was, the reason he had never really connected with any other woman. "I'm so sorry, Rina. I wish I could go back and change everything."

Her mouth curved into a sly smile. "So, are you going to kiss me, then?"

He didn't need any more encouragement. With a laugh, he dipped his head and sealed his lips over hers. She tasted the same, and his mind began to race with something he couldn't name.

Rina felt the familiar caress of Michael's mouth on hers, and she felt herself relax. This was how it was meant to be. She thought fleetingly about the last time a man had kissed her; it hadn't felt like this. In fact, of all the men she'd ever kissed, including the one she had recently divorced, none of them had felt like this; like home. As she pushed her tongue into Michael's mouth, she heard him groan as he deepened their contact.

He pulled back slightly, breathing heavily, and rested his forehead against hers. "God, Rina. I don't want to stop."

"Then don't."

"No – I mean ..."

"I know what you mean, and I don't want to stop either. We're too old to play games, Michael. I'm going to go over there and lie down on the hay. I want you to join me."

"Oh. Okay." He'd forgotten how direct she could be; she'd often been the initiator in their love-making, and he'd forgotten how much he liked that too. He watched her walk towards the pile of hay that sat in the far corner of the barn.

She turned to face him and began to undress. "Well?"

"Oh yeah. I'm in. I just want to watch you for a while though."

Rina smiled and raised an eyebrow. Then she continued to remove her clothes, and it was one of the sexiest things he'd ever seen. When she was naked, she turned to face him. She felt no shame at all, in fact, displaying her body to him made her feel powerful. And the effect she was having on him magnified that.

Michael walked the short distance to the hay pile, pulling his shirt over his head as he went. Shoes and socks, followed by trousers and underwear joined the heap of clothes that Rina had started. Then he was holding her again, and this time it felt so much better because it was skin against skin. "I don't have any condoms."

She reached for her discarded jeans and pulled a small, square packet out of the pocket. With a grin, she got on her knees, looking up at him as she took his erect cock in her hand.

"You thought we might do this?"

"No. I knew we would do this. I had no intention of leaving here without becoming reacquainted with this." She stroked his cock and placed a light kiss on the crown.

Michael shuddered as her lips made contact with the sensitive skin of his penis. "Oh, god, Rina! If you suck me, I'm not going to need that condom." He was stunned by how quickly his body had responded to her; like water following a worn path; he felt pulled towards her. "Lie down – please – I don't think I can stand up for much longer." It was true; his legs were shaking, and he was aching with the need to touch her.

Rina lay back on the hay. It was prickly against her aroused skin, and she wriggled to get comfortable. She reached for her lover, but he shook his head and pulled her thighs apart, exposing her sensitive flesh to his gaze.

"How have I gone so long without you? Without this." Keeping eye contact with her, he put his mouth on her and began to lick in long, slow strokes.

Rina jerked against Michael's mouth as he began to tongue her in earnest. "Christ! I'd forgotten how good you are at that." She began to rotate her hips against him, forcing him to go deeper. "Yes – like that." She licked one of her fingers and ran the moist tip around one of her hard nipples, and she closed her eyes to enjoy the sensations that were rocketing through her system.

Michael watched her teasing her breast while she ground herself against his mouth. He hadn't seen anything so arousing since – well – since the last time he had made love to her. Her taste flooded his mouth, and his body responded to it like he'd been plugged into the mains. He reached up, and Rina took his hand, twining their fingers together as she rode his face. He lifted his other hand from her thigh and pushed two fingers into her. She was open and ready for him, but he was going to make her come with his tongue and fingers before he fucked her.

Rina opened her eyes when she felt Michael's fingers pushing into her. It felt so good to have him there, tonguing her clit and fingering her hole. How many times had she fantasised about him? He was her favourite masturbatory stimulus. She blushed with shame when she remembered how many times he had also been the one she thought about when she was having sex with someone else. She shook her head to clear that feeling. "You owe me for all the years you deprived me of this. All the time we could have been together. You have a debt to pay, Michael Preston."

Michael lifted his head, and she could see his lips glistening with her juices. He licked his lips, savouring her taste and looked at her, his eyes burning with lust. "And I intend to repay you. With interest. If you'll let me." He reached for the condom, ripping open the packet and rolling the thin latex over his erection. He was painfully hard. He wasn't going to last once he was inside her. "Open your legs. I'm going to fuck you, and it's going to be quick, coz I'm about to come just from eating your pussy."

Rina grinned and rolled over onto her stomach before getting up on all fours. "Well, if we're going for a quick fuck, do it this way. I want to feel every part of your beautiful cock, so fuck me deep."

She had always talked dirty, and it turned him on like lighting the blue touch-paper. As she flared her hips, lifting her ass to his view, he felt a surge of adrenaline go through him that probably would have knocked him out if so much of his blood hadn't been diverted from his brain to his dick. He positioned himself and pushed inside her. The sensation of her warm, tight pussy pulling him inside and gripping like a fist, made him see stars. "Oh, god, Rina! I've needed you all this time. I just tried to tell myself I didn't." The admission came out of his mouth before he could stop it, accompanied by a groan of deep pleasure.

Rina pushed back against him and reached down to tap her finger against her clitoris. She felt wonderfully full of him, and the muscles of her sheath clenched around his stiff member. Her insides were tingling as if her impending orgasm was growing from her whole cunt, not just the tiny bud of her clit. She had only ever felt that with him. "I've needed you too. So much. I'm not letting you go again. Even if I have to tie up to keep you from leaving."

Michael groaned and laughed at the same time. "You're not going to need to do that. But I wouldn't object to it now and again. I always used to enjoy it."

"I remember." And she did. She tied him to their bed the first time after they had watched a porn movie together. Michael had been so aroused that she made him come by letting her hair fall over his cock and balls. She felt her pussy start to spasm in warning; she was going to come very soon. But she wanted to see him as she did. "Pull out. I want you under me. Now."

Michael did as he was told. Pulling out of her was not what his body wanted to do, but he still had just enough brain function to hear her request and act on it. And besides, he loved to be ridden. He lay down on the hay, spreading himself for her. "Jesus – this stuff is prickly!"

"I know. Now shut up and let me fuck you." She climbed over him and positioned herself to take his cock. As she eased down on him, they both groaned. "God, Michael, I love your cock." She started to rise and fall, slowly at first, working herself on him to find the right depth and angle of penetration.

Michael tried to hold off his orgasm for her, but he couldn't. The sensation of her tight, wet sheath milking him and the sight of her glorious body writhing on him was too much. "I'm coming, Rina!" He pushed his hips up and cried out as he emptied himself into the condom. "I tried to hold on. Sorry." He was breathing heavily; his mouth open as he tried to pull air into his lungs. "God, Rina. That was incredible." He looked down his body at her; she was still rotating her hips on him, bringing herself to orgasm. The semen he had poured into the condom was beginning to leak out, pooling on his pubic hair. He reached down and pressed his thumb against her swollen little clit, rubbing her as she bounced on his still-hard cock. He felt it begin - a throbbing, squeezing sensation.

Rina threw her head back and cried out in triumph as she pulled her orgasm from him. She pushed down on him, grinding against his pubic bone. She looked down at Michael. He was the only one she had ever felt so brazen with; the only one who made her feel it was okay to take what she needed from a man. She had come here with every intention of seducing him. Her first thought had been to make him realise what he'd been missing all these years and then walk away – as he did all those years ago. But her body wasn't going to let her do that. He was hers, and this time, he wasn't going anywhere.

The hay was too uncomfortable to stay on for much longer, so they dressed quickly, grinning at each other like naughty children. Michael pulled Rina into his arms and kissed her gently. "We've got an interesting time ahead of us."

She looked up at him and pulled a piece of hay out of his hair. "Yes. I suppose we do. I'm not expecting anything from you."

"Good." When she looked queryingly at him, he continued. "That means I have endless scope to surprise you. I know I have a lot to make up for. And I'm not expecting things to go back to how they were before, well not straight away, anyway. But I've been given a second chance with you, and I'm not going to throw it away. My grandmother's letters made me realise what a stupid arse I'd been with you. Can you give me another chance?"

Rina nodded and bent to pick up her shoes. "I can. And I already told you what I intend to do if you try to run again." She looked up towards the door of the barn and smiled shyly at the couple who had just walked in. "Oh – hi – we're just leaving – sorry." She blushed as she realised that they must have guessed what she and Michael had been doing.

Michael turned around, but there was no-one there. "Who are you talking to?"

"What?" Rina finished putting on her shoes and looked up again. "Oh – they were just here – a couple. They were holding hands and smiling at us."

"Well, they're not there now. They must have hightailed it when they saw what we'd been up to." He couldn't help the grin that spread across his face.

"That's just weird. They were right there."

"What did they look like?"

"Um – I don't know – guy had a red shirt, girl was really pretty, blonde curly hair, yellow dress."

They left the barn holding hands. Michael spotted a patch of moon daisies growing near the entrance. "Oh – those were my grandmother's favourite. Hang on a minute." He bent to pick a small bunch of the cheery, white flowers then ducked back into the barn. Laying them on the hay where he and Rina had made love, he whispered, "Thank you, Katherine. Rest in peace."

"Come on, Michael. I'm hungry. For food, as well." Rina's voice came through the open door of the barn as a soft breeze picked up and swept over the hay pile, scattering the daisies.

Michael got to the door and saw Rina standing in the sun. "My queen, I will feed you with pleasure. Food, as well." As her laughter blended with the sounds of the house martins that were nesting in the eaves, he took one, last look inside the barn. He saw them then; not quite a shadow, but not quite real either. A guy in navy blue trousers that were worn at the knee and a red shirt that had been washed too many times. He was holding hands with a pretty girl in a yellow dress. She was holding a bunch of moon daisies and, as Michael turned to face them, the young man waved, and they both disappeared. He shook his head and looked again. Had he imagined that?

"What's the holdup?" Rina walked up behind him and put her arms around his waist.

"What? Oh – nothing. I thought I saw something." He turned in her arms and kissed her on the mouth, opening her lips with his tongue. "Come on. Take me home. I think we've probably got a lot to talk about, and then I want to make a start on repaying that debt." He kissed her again, and let her lead him back to the car.

"I did tell you it was a usurious debt, didn't I?"

"Just tell me where to sign."

Scorpio

Transient, self-willed, purposeful, unyielding
For Bee

Being a vampire has its advantages. As one of the undead, I've already done the one thing that most folks are scared of. For me, that particular rite of passage happened when I was twenty-four and was the result of an infection that could have been cured if it had happened twenty years later. But then, I would have just lived and died, and that would have been it. As it is, I lived, died, then lived again, thanks to a small blood donation from the priest who came to give me the last rights. I hadn't wanted to see him, but my mother (god rest her soul) was a devout Catholic, so the priest was sent for.

It doesn't happen as it does in the movies. I was pretty out of it for those last few hours, so I wasn't too sure what he did to me. I just knew, when I woke up a few days later feeling full of the joys of spring, that something had happened. The priest – who it turns out wasn't a man of god at all – told me what he'd done. I could have killed the bastard.

So, I expect you're wondering what all those advantages I was talking about might be? Well, I look pretty good considering I'm over a hundred years old. I'm virtually indestructible; there's almost nothing that I can't come back from. I can tell you that beheading hurts like bloody hell, but it's not fatal. I can eat, drink, smoke or inject anything that takes my fancy. I can ignore those god-awful warnings they're putting on fag packets these days, and my weekly intake of alcohol would probably give most regular men a bad case of alcoholic poisoning. I'm not worried about undercooked chicken, eggs infected with salmonella or nitrates in bacon. And neither should you be; your life is too bloody short to live without full English breakfasts (or full

Irish, in my case) and a regular supply of KFC and Nandos, preferably consumed in front of the TV and accompanied by copious amounts of beer.

But – I hear you say – what about all those pesky vampire problems like silver and sunshine and crosses and shite. Well, I think it's probably past time that all that was put straight once and for all. Apologies to fans of Anne Rice, Charlaine Harris or the woman that wrote those fucking awful Twilight books, but the classic picture of a vampire in literature is a bit off. Here are the facts:

Fangs – no, don't have them. They would be cool, though. I don't have yellow eyes or skin that shines like diamonds either, for which, I am eternally grateful.

Supernatural strength – no, I don't have that either. I never could run very far, and I still can't.

Sunshine – not a problem. I get sunburned more than the average person, but that's down to my Irish complexion. I always did.

Silver – I prefer gold, but I can wear it, no problem.

Crosses, holy water, churches etc. – I'll lump all that shite together for you to save time. Religious symbols, buildings, relics of any flavour have no effect on me whatsoever. Other than revulsion, but I pretty much had that going on before this whole undead thing happened.

Mirrors, photos, and all that – I can see myself, no problem at all. Sometimes I wish I couldn't.

Turning into a bat – no – that never happens – that would just be really, really, stupid now, wouldn't it?

Drinking blood – yes, I do have to do that. I wanted to do it a lot when I first became a vampire – I used to crave it, but as the years have gone by, it's not much of a thing anymore. I only need it if I'm injured. And any blood will do – human tastes the best to me, but it's not that easy to come by, so I usually have to make do with rodent of some description.

So, you're probably thinking that this whole vampire gig sounds pretty cushy and where can you get some of it? Well, let me tell you the truth. I'd happily give it all up and become mortal again for a damned good fuck. I haven't had an erection since I died. Yes – you did hear that right – vampires can't get it up. We are indestructible, immortal, eunuchs. I still think about sex, I watch porn (though I really should stop that – apparently, it rots your brain) and if I see a gorgeous woman, my body remembers wanting it. But I can't do anything about it. It's fucking horrible.

I have a friend called Fergus. That's not actually his name – I'm not good with names – I called him Fergus once, and it stuck. He's never corrected me, but he's Italian, so I think the likelihood of his name being Fergus is pretty small. He's also very old. He remembers when Italy was all different little states instead of one country, and god only knows when that happened. Anyway, this friend, Fergus, knows a lot about vampire stuff. I ask him for advice sometimes. Those times usually turn into three or four days of heavy drinking. The last time, we both woke up, stark bollock naked and covered in something sticky, in the middle of the monkey enclosure at London Zoo. I never did find out what the sticky stuff was, but I was washing it out of my arse crack for days.

Anyway, Fergus is usually pretty good for information, so when I come across something, I don't understand I usually call him. It was Fergus who told me how the whole thing with the blood works. I must have drunk some of the priest's blood shortly before I left this mortal coil. When my heart stopped beating, the blood went to work, regenerating all my insides, and then I came back to life. I woke up as a completely healthy, impotent version of my old self. You'd never know unless you tried to take my pulse. I don't have one of those. My heart doesn't beat either, and blood doesn't move around my body, which is the reason none of it can be redirected to my cock when I feel horny. I've met female vampires; they have the same problem. A man can fuck them, but they don't really feel that much. Although, one did tell me that she could still have an orgasm if she rubbed away at her little clitoris for long enough. I wish that worked for males as well. When I first changed, I rubbed myself sore and had blisters on my hands from trying to get it going, but nothing worked. They say you never really appreciate what you have until it's gone. I'd say that was very true. I gained so much when I became a vampire, including an endless life. But I lost the one thing that would have made that endless life worth having. If I believed in god at all, I'd join a monastery – it would make things so much easier.

Vampires tend to live alone. We get into stupid fights if we live together for too long, and it also makes the moving around a bit easier. I never live anywhere for more than ten years; longer than that and people around you start to notice that you never seem to get any older. It was more than fifty years since I'd last lived in the city of my birth and I was heartsore from missing it. So, I packed in my job at that shitty call centre and got on a train, then a ferry, then a bus back to Dublin. One of these days, I must learn to drive a car. I could never steer a horse and cart, so I've given driving a bit of wide berth up to now.

I rented a bedsit over a shoe shop in Drury Street. It was small and smelled funny, but it was cheap and suited me for now. I got a job in another shitty call centre (those things are a godsend for people like me – they never check your background or anything) and got on with the job of living. News of my arrival soon spread through the vampire community and it wasn't long before I'd found myself a fine drinking partner. His name is Gunther. He's German, but he's alright. He told me he got a bit carried away on the night the Berlin Wall came down and ended up drinking some girl's blood mixed with tequila, just before he fell off the wall and broke his neck. I told him you should always stay away from that Mexican shite. Even I won't drink tequila.

I'd been back in Dublin for about a year and a half, and things were going well. I was managing some stealthy visits to the family; told them I was a distant cousin from Limerick. It was nice. My great, great, great (possibly one more 'great') grandson is a doctor. I'm very proud of him. It all feels like a very long time since I had anyone I could call family. I had to leave them behind – it was something that the priest insisted on. As far as my mother, wife and infant son were concerned, I was dead and buried in a pauper's grave in Perrystown. I was enjoying being home – even though the city has changed so much since I was last here – and thinking that I would try and stick it out for a little longer than ten years. Maybe try some of the ageing makeup that Fergus uses when the time comes.

One night, I was walking back from the pub where I'd been drinking with Gunther when I smelled something bloody gorgeous. I couldn't name it – it was like every delicious thing you've ever smelt in your life, crossed with something like flowers and candyfloss. My nose picked it up straight away and, for reasons I couldn't explain, I was drawn to follow it. I followed it all the way down Grafton Street and around the college. I had to stop when I got to some locked gates, but I didn't want to. I wanted to follow it forever. It was making me light-headed, like the best drugs you've ever had. I was out of my mind on it after following it for that long. I must have looked like my mother's ginger tomcat after he'd been at the catmint.

I tried to find a way through the gates, but there wasn't one. I could have gone over, but they were very tall, and I felt very high, so it probably wasn't a good idea. I started to walk back towards home when I felt something like a jolt in my body. It felt as if someone was thumping me hard in the chest and then it happened – my chest thumped back. My heart was beating. I started to sweat, and my mouth was watering in warning that my stomach was about to empty itself, which it did a few moments later. I was bent double, heaving for all I was worth, as the remains of my liquid supper hit the pavement with a sizzle.

I staggered back to my place. I didn't know what to do, or who to call. Fergus would be asleep, and he gets mightily pissed off if I ring him in the middle of the night, so I decided it would wait until the morning. The internet isn't great for real facts about vampires, so, even though I Googled like my life depended on it, I couldn't find anything about what might have happened to me out there. I felt different. My heart was beating, very slowly and I still didn't have a pulse, but every few minutes or so, it would thump away in my chest and the sound was like thunder in my ears.

I was feeling a bit light-headed again, so I lay down on my bed. I must have fallen asleep because the alarm woke me up to go to work. I tried ringing Fergus, but it went to voicemail, so I left a message saying I really needed to talk to him, then I had a shower, got dressed and made my way to the call centre. What else could I do? At least it would take my mind off it.

We're not allowed to use our phones when we're working, so I waited until my coffee break to check if Fergus had got back to me. There was nothing from him, so I finished my cup of coffee (or whatever it is that passes for coffee from that bloody machine) and went back to my desk.

"Are you okay, Daniel? You look a bit pale."

I looked up at the shiny face of Chantel Jeffries, the girl who works in the cubicle in front of mine. "Oh, I'm just fine thanks." *Tickety-fucking-boo, love,* "And yourself? You're looking pretty as a picture today, Chantel."

The girl blushed and started telling me about some new thing she was doing with her eyebrows, and I tuned out. Then I noticed something odd. She was a very pretty girl, and I was looking at her like a man looks at a pretty girl. And I felt something stir in my underwear as a particularly hard thump resonated in my chest. What the …?

"… I watched a video on YouTube. I think it looks really cool. What do you think, Daniel?"

"What?" Oh god, I hate it when girls ask me questions when I haven't been listening. Something about eyebrows. Quick, think of something, you eejit. "I think they look great. Just great. In fact, I think you could probably go for a bit more if you liked. Your face could take it."

"Really? Wow – thank you, Daniel!" She leaned over the partition and kissed me on the cheek. "I love working with gay guys – they always give the best fashion advice."

I may have neglected to tell you about that. I'm not gay, but girls find that easier to accept than the truth. They don't flirt or try with me if I tell them I'm only attracted to other men. There have been some over the years who have taken that as a challenge. I remember one, particularly dedicated girl in Rome who sucked my unresponsive cock for over an hour in an attempt to get me going. She said she'd converted gays before that way, though from what I know of homosexual men, she didn't do any such thing. It was probably a straight man who'd hit a dry patch and used it as a way to get a no-strings blow job. Can't blame the fella really.

"Oh, you're more than welcome, sweet thing." I smiled at her as effeminately as I could and tried to concentrate on the job at hand. It's not a dream job, cold calling people who don't want to be bothered. I get sworn at a lot. You get used to it. I like it when someone, usually an old person, keeps me on the line for ages, just because they're lonely. I get that. I get lonely sometimes. I'm supposed to take advantage of those situations – get them to sign something over or allow me to take control of their computer, but I don't have the heart for it.

I went out at lunchtime for a smoke and checked my phone again. Fergus had left a message saying that he was out all day but I could call him after nine, so I set the alarm on my phone and lit another cigarette. My heart chose that moment to give me a kick so hard it nearly pushed me off the low wall I was sitting on. I felt sick again, and suddenly, the cigarette tasted like acid in my mouth. I threw it down on the ground and trod it out with my shoe. What the fucking hell was going on with me?

I wanted food – real food. I told you that I can eat what I want, but usually, I'm not that bothered. I prefer my meals to be at least forty percent proof. But my stomach growled at me, so I went off in search of something tasty. I was just finishing off my second meat and potato pie when I smelled that smell again. It wafted past my nose, then disappeared before I could catch it and follow it. My heart thumped twice in succession, and I felt that half-forgotten sensation in my bathing-suit area again. I looked down at myself. I was sporting a semi. It went down before I had the chance to think about doing something with it, but it had definitely been there. I needed to talk to Fergus.

Nine o'clock finally arrived with a ringing of my phone. It wasn't the alarm, though; it was Fergus. "What is the matter, my boy? You sounded so stressed out in your message."

I sat down on my bed and rubbed my hand over my face. "Oh, Jayzus, Fergus, I don't know what the fuck is happening to me."

"Tell me. I'm listening."

"My bloody heart has started beating. Not all the time. Just every now and again, it hits me like I've stuck my fingers in a light socket or something."

"When did this start, Daniel?" He sounded far too calm for my liking.

"Last night. And there's something else. I got a bit of an erection."

"A bit? How much of a bit?"

"I don't know, enough to notice, but not enough to be dangerous – what does it matter how fucking much?" I heard him sigh over the phone. "I'm sorry, Fergus. I'm just going out of my mind here. I don't want to smoke anymore – they taste disgusting. And I just ate real food because I was hungry. I was actually hungry. I can't remember the last time I ate food because I was hungry."

"Anything else?"

"Isn't that enough? My whole world is going to shite here, Fergus, do you have any idea what's happening to me?"

"Can you think of anything unusual that happened before this began?"

"What sort of thing? Like freak weather? Is this because of a meteor shower or something?"

"No, Daniel. It's not because of a meteor shower. Think. Did you notice something strange? Any odd smells or anything?"

I was just about to say no when I remembered. "Oh – yeah – there was something. I smelt something amazing. I couldn't put my finger on it, but it was incredible. I followed it as far as I could, but I lost it. Come to think of it; the thumping started as I was walking home after that."

"Daniel, I need you to listen to me very carefully. I will say this only once."

"This is no time for quotes from eighties sitcoms, Fergus."

"Sorry. But I do need you to listen very carefully."

"Okay. I'm listening."

"I think you may have scented your mate."

"My mate? I thought that was just made up? You mean, those things really exist?"

"They do. You are blessed if you can find her. I have read that there is only one mate born for every one of us. The chances of meeting them are very slender. I can't even begin to think of the odds. It must be billions of billions to one."

"About the same as winning the national lottery since they added those extra numbers, huh?"

"Probably."

"So, what do I do about it?"

"You could choose to do nothing about it."

"What would happen then?"

"If you don't find her, the effects of the scent will wear off eventually. You will go back to how you were, and you will have missed your chance."

"My chance at what, Fergus?"

"I'm not sure. I've heard stories. But if one smell of her got your heart beating again, who knows what more could do?"

"Right. Yeah. Okay. Thanks, Fergus."

"Daniel? My name is Piero. I'd like it if you stopped calling me Fergus."

"Piero? Okay. Right. Thanks, Fergus."

He ended the call, and I put my phone on my bedside table. I felt overwhelmingly tired all of a sudden, so I decided not to fight it. I got undressed and went to the bathroom to brush my teeth and take a leak. As I stood there, pointing Percy at the porcelain, my heart gave an almighty thump which sent me sprawling on the floor, clutching at my chest. I watched as my piss continued to flow all over the floor and I gasped for breath. Not the usual, shallow inhale that I only need if I'm going to speak. This one felt like it went right down to my toes and, when I'd filled my lungs, my heart gave another thump.

When I managed to stop shaking like a leaf, I realised something else. I was lying in a pool of piss. Since I've been a vampire, whatever has come out of my body has been pretty much in the same condition as it was when it went in. I don't digest the food I eat or absorb the liquid I drink. I can get drunk if I drink enough alcohol to embalm a baby elephant, but that's about it. I don't truly understand how it works, but I eat and drink because I enjoy the taste and the sensation, not because my body needs it. So, when I take a piss, what comes out is usually a pretty disgusting mixture of whatever I've had to drink; not urine. But what I was lying in now, was a pool of yellow, unpleasantness. My kidneys had done something for the first time in about ninety years.

I cleaned myself up and got into bed. I felt cold. That was new too. Something fucked up was happening to me, and I had no clue what it was. After putting another blanket on the bed as well as virtually every item of clothing I owned, I finally managed to get to sleep.

"When are you coming?"
"Soon. I just need to find you."
"Are you going to hurt me?"
"What? No! Why would I do that?"
"Aren't you angry with me for making your heart beat again?"
"I'm not angry. I'm a bit confused, but I'm not angry."
"Does it hurt?"
"A bit. It's like someone is kicking me. But I've survived a heck of a lot worse."
"I'm sorry. I didn't want to cause you pain."
"It's alright, ma mhuirnín, it's not that bad."
"When are you coming?"
"Soon. I just need to find you."
"Hurry. Time is short."

I woke up, sweating and gasping for another breath. I rarely dreamed, and this one was just fucking weird. That voice – it was like someone was pouring warm honey in my ear. I sat on the edge of my bed, shivering as the sweat cooled on my skin, my heart thumping a slow rhythm in my chest. I looked at the clock, thinking it must be nearly time to get up anyway, but it was only midnight. I knew there was little chance of getting back to sleep, so I pulled my sorry carcass into the shower. I was freezing cold, so I stood under the hot water for as long as I could to warm up.

I probably need to clarify the whole feeling cold thing. I'm usually room temperature; I don't have any way of maintaining a regular body temperature, so if you touched me, I'd feel cold to you. But I don't feel it. To me, I just feel normal. So – if I'm feeling cold, it means something has changed. Another thing to add to my list of fucking weird things that have been happening to my body. Maybe Fergus was right; that smell was my mate and getting a whiff of her has woken me up somehow. I had no idea, but I knew I had to do something, or I was going to go crazy, so I dressed up in my warmest clothes and headed out into the night.

I walked around the streets where I'd picked up the scent before. There was nothing; the trail had gone cold. And it was going even colder as I stood there, trying to decide what to do. I sighed and headed back towards my bedsit, my freezing hands deep in my coat pockets. I was about a hundred yards from my door when it hit me. The scent was so strong that it nearly knocked me off my feet and, when I got a lungful of it, my heart started beating so fast, it sounded like it was applauding in my chest. The coldness I'd felt eased a little, and a slight sheen of sweat broke out on my upper lip.

I had to follow it. I didn't have any choice. If you're of an age, you might remember a TV ad from the 1970s; two scallywags catch a waft of delicious gravy (yes, *Ah, Bisto!*) and follow it. You can see the smell as a gravy-coloured cloudy line in the air. Well, as I stood there, listening to the percussion section that had started up in my chest, I could see the trail. It looked like a sparkly stream of air going off into the distance in front of me. My feet seemed to make the decision, and I took off as fast as they would carry me. They took me over the river, and I found myself in Jervis Street. Outside the Leprechaun Museum.

"Oh no – you're not getting me like that – I know there's no such thing as leprechauns." I looked around at the deserted street. The scent trail seemed to end here. I felt my newly awaked heart slow down as the disappointment hit. Had this all been some elaborate joke? Did someone have a bottle of *attractovamp* or something to trap me? I waited for a minute, expecting someone to jump out and shout "Surprise!" but nobody came. I was alone, in Jervis Street, in the middle of the night, feeling like I'd just lost something precious.

"Is that you, Daniel?" A voice came through the night and made me turn around. It was the landlord of TP Smiths, a bar on the other side of the road. "If you're hoping to catch sight of the little people, they're only open ten till six." He chuckled to himself as he emptied a bucket of water onto the pavement. "Do you want to come in for a swift one?"

I had nothing better to do, and my feet had run out of steam, so I followed Tom Brannon into the dimly-lit bar. My nose was still full of that gorgeous scent, and I shook my head to try to clear it as I closed the door behind me. Pubs are strange places when there's nobody drinking in them; like schools without children or shops without customers, they seem to cry out for someone to help them do what they were designed for. I can be quite philosophical when I choose, or when I'm depressed, or when there isn't enough alcohol flowing around my system to dull the thoughts. It was a case of the latter right now, and I fully intended to take advantage of Tom's hospitality to do something about it. "Very civil of you Tom. How have you been?"

Tom went to the bar and poured us both a large tot of whiskey. We clinked our glasses together and downed the delicious liquid in one. He refilled our glasses and tilted his at me. "Here's to your good health, Daniel. Now – what brings you out this way at this hour?"

I sipped at my liquor, savouring the flavour. "You were right. I was looking for leprechauns."

Tom laughed and refilled his glass. "Well – I have to tell you, you look like you've seen a ghost or something. Are you feeling unwell?"

I nodded. I wasn't sure what I was feeling, but *well* definitely wasn't on the list. "I'm okay. Just feeling a bit out of sorts, that's all."

"I know what would cheer you up." He walked to the foot of the stairs that led up to the flat where he lived and shouted up at whoever was upstairs. "Niamh, love! Is there any of your mammy's soup left from tea time?"

A voice that sounded vaguely familiar came down the stairs. "I don't work here anymore, Da."

"I'm aware of that, love." He looked at me and raised his eyebrows. "Kids." Then he turned back to the stairwell and resumed the long-distance conversation. "I only asked as you've not long been home and you can save me the walk to find out for myself. So, be a love and check for your daddy?"

I heard a harrumph from upstairs, and Tom came back to the bar. "My Mary's secret soup will put a smile on your face. I'm sure there's some left. Niamh will bring it down in a minute or two."

"That's very kind of you, Tom. You needn't go to any trouble." I raised my glass to him, and we drank in silence for a couple of minutes.

Footsteps coming down the stairs were accompanied by two, distinct, glorious smells. One, I guessed was Mary's secret soup. The other made my heart thump and sweat break out on my skin. Just then, the most beautiful creature I'd ever laid eyes upon walked into the bar carrying a tray with a bowl of soup and some buttered bread. She put the tray on the bar then looked at me. Her eyes went wide and her mouth opened in shock. "It's you."

I looked behind where I was sitting, half expecting to see someone standing there that she recognised.

Tom looked between the two of us. "You know Daniel?"

She looked flustered, and I didn't have a clue what to say so I just smiled at her. Then I reached over to shake her hand. "Hello, Niamh. It's good to see you." When the skin of her hand touched mine, I felt like a bolt of electricity went through me. Every hair on my body stood to attention, and so did my cock. I was very glad for the heavy overcoat I had put on.

She looked at me like she couldn't quite believe what she was seeing. She let her hand linger in mine for a moment, then she pulled it back and looked at her father. "Yeah – Daniel comes into Neary's sometimes."

Neary's in Chatham Street. That would explain why I'd smelled her around Grafton Street. But not why she had apparently walked in the wrong direction to be a hundred yards outside my home. I hadn't been in there for a while. The last time I popped in there for a drink, it was full of loud Americans, and it put me off a little bit. She hadn't been there then; I would have remembered a face like that. I was desperate to ask her all sorts of questions – not least of all what she had meant by it's you. But Tom was looking at us both, waiting for some kind of explanation, so I had to think on my feet. "The soup smells lovely. Thank you, Niamh."

"You're welcome." I don't know if it was my imagination, but when she said that, I was hit by a wall of that scent. "Well, if that's all, I'll say goodnight." She looked at me again, and I could tell she had questions too.

"Are you working tomorrow, pet?" *Please say yes, please say yes.*

"I am. I'm on at six."

"Oh, that's grand. I might see you."

"Okay. Goodnight then." She turned to Tom and kissed him on the cheek. "Goodnight, Da."

Tom hugged her and kissed her back. "Night, princess. Sweet dreams."

She looked at me again. "I think they will be."

I watched her go up the stairs, leaning over in my seat until her ankles disappeared from my sight. I straightened in my seat and looked at Tom, shrugging my shoulders to explain why I had just perved on his daughter as she left the room. "That's a very pretty girl."

Tom looked at me suspiciously for a moment, then he smiled and clapped me on the shoulder. "She is indeed. And if you've got any intentions where she's concerned, then you'll be a gentleman. Or I'll skin you alive." He smiled as he said it, but I knew he was serious.

"Understood." Right at that moment, my cock was throbbing in my jeans, and my mind was filled with all sorts of intentions, none of which were gentlemanly. But I didn't fancy being flayed by Tom Brannon. I know how much that hurts and how long it takes to heal from it. "I was thinking of maybe asking her out, but I didn't know she was your daughter."

"You can ask her. Just be a gentleman if she says yes, that's all." A moment's silence, then he nodded towards the cooling bowl of soup in front of me. "Now, eat your soup before it goes cold."

I did as he instructed. It was very good soup. Mary's secret, whatever it was, warmed my belly and reminded me of something my mother used to make. I hadn't thought about that in a long time. After finishing the soup and cleaning the bowl with the bread, I bid Tom a goodnight and made my way home. I wasn't working the next day, so I went back to bed, just as the birds were starting to sing and the sky was showing signs of dawn.

"It's you."

"Yes, I found you."

"I'm a little bit scared of you."

"There's no need, ma mhuirnín. I'm not going to hurt you."

"How do you know?"

"I just do. I know that hurting you would be hurting myself. You're a part of me."

"I know too."

"Sleep now."

"Yes, anamchara."

God, I slept like the dead; well, the undead anyway. The dreams were good, and I woke up feeling, quite literally, more alive than I had done in decades. My heart was beating steadily, and my body seemed to be warming up by itself. TMI warning; when I went to the loo, it was clear that things in my body were working. I'd forgotten how disgusting that whole digesting food thing is.

I ate some breakfast because I was hungry. Then I started the serious job of deciding what to wear when I went to see Niamh later. After trying on every item of clothing I own (which, to be fair, didn't take that long), I went out to buy a new shirt. I hate buying clothes – life was so much easier when my mother or my wife made everything that I wore.

I felt like a teenager getting ready for his first date with a girl. I didn't want to appear too keen, so I set off for Neary's, resplendent in my new, purple shirt, just after seven. The place was fairly quiet, so I was able to take a seat at the bar. I smelled her before I saw her; that glorious haze of pure delight that seemed to be made for my nose alone came wafting towards me as she came up from the cellar through the trap door behind the bar.

When she looked up, she saw me and smiled. She was in front of me in two, short steps. "Daniel! You came!"

"Yes." I kicked myself for stating the bleeding obvious, but my tongue was hogtied at the sight of her.

"What can I get you?"

"Oh – yes – a drink." I tried to calm my breathing (I was breathing?) and managed to mumble an order for a pint of Guinness. I watched her pour it. She drew a heart shape in the foam before shutting off the tap; then she put it in front of me with a smile that turned my stomach to water. "Thank you, Niamh. That's grand."

"I get off at eleven. Do you want to go for something to eat?"

"What? Oh – yes – yes, please – that would be great." I was feeling like an idiot in front of her, but I was helpless to do anything about it.

"Cool. Just sit tight, then."

What else could I do? I was rooted to the spot watching her. I also had a mother of an erection, so moving was off the table until I managed to do something about that.

Just after ten o'clock, she came around the bar carrying her coat and bag. "Mikey is going to cover for me – we can go now if you like?"

Five minutes later, we were sitting in a quiet booth in the Pizza Stop, and my tongue was refusing to work again.

"You look great. I love the purple shirt." She smirked a little bit when she said that, so I guessed she was being sarcastic.

I looked down at the offending garment. "I panicked. I didn't know what to put on. I didn't want you to think I'm a slob."

She laughed at me and did that thing girls do with their hair when they're flirting. "I'm flattered."

We made small talk until our food arrived, then I plucked up some courage from somewhere to ask the question that had been burning in my mind since the night before. "Can I ask you – what did you mean when you saw me and said, 'it's you'?"

She looked down at her food, and a huge waft of her scent came over to me. "You'll think I'm crazy,"

"No – believe me – I won't. I've got some pretty crazy stuff going on here myself."

"Right." She looked a little confused, took a bite of her food, then looked at me. "Okay. I've been dreaming about you. For years, actually. About once a week, you'd be there, front and centre, my knight in shining armour, or whatever."

I felt a little bit hard done by; I'd only been dreaming about Niamh since her scent started to do whatever it was doing to me. But, to be honest, I didn't dream about anything much before then. "I don't think you're crazy. I've dreamt about you too."

Her face brightened. "Really? You're just saying that, surely."

"No. Though I have to admit, it's a recent thing for me. I have to ask you, though, why were you outside my bedsit last night?"

"What? Where's your bedsit?"

"Drury Street."

She blushed a little bit, and it made her look beautiful. "You're just going to laugh at me."

"We've already established I won't do that."

She pulled a face that said she didn't believe me. "Something told me to go there. I don't know what it was – and I don't hear voices, honest – but something was pulling me there. I didn't know it was where you lived." She looked down at her food again. "But – just a minute – how did you know I was there? Did you see me."

"Well, no." Now it was my turn to be embarrassed. "You're going to think I'm nuts, but I smelled you."

She looked a little shocked and tucked her nose into her armpit to sniff herself.

"No – I don't mean like that. You have a scent; it's gorgeous. I followed it a couple of times. That's how I came to be outside your dad's bar last night. I followed your scent."

She sat back in her seat and looked at me. "So, what are you, a bloodhound or something?" She chuckled and took a bite of her pizza.

I thought about lying. I probably should have, but being with her was like truth serum. "No. I'm a vampire."

She stopped chewing and looked at me. Her eyebrows went up, and she laughed. "Right. And I'm a werewolf."

"I know you're joking about that because there aren't any of those in Dublin. They stay in the mountains." I wasn't laughing, and I was willing her silently to take me seriously for a moment. "I don't know what you are; I just know that, since I first caught a whiff of you, my body has been coming alive slowly. I think you might be my mate or something." I wished that last bit hadn't come out of my mouth before I finished saying it.

She looked like she was going to choke on her drink. "Your mate? Really? Okaaaaaay … Step away from the crazy person."

I'm not sure what happened then. Something snapped inside me, and I grabbed her hand. She tried to pull away at first, but I got eye contact with her, and she seemed to relax, almost like I'd put her under some kind of spell. "Look – I know it sounds nuts, but you know there's something strange happening here. You just told me that you've been dreaming about me for years. How do you explain that?"

She shook her head slowly, without taking her eyes off mine. "I don't know. I can't."

"I'm not lying to you, Niamh. In fact, I'm beginning to think that I can't lie to you. I had no intention of telling you the truth tonight, but it just came out."

She looked unsure, but she didn't pull her hand out of mine. "Well, I suppose if you can't lie to me, that would make you different to every other man I've ever been with."

"How many men have you been with?" I didn't intend for that question to come out quite so bluntly, but something instinctual was riding me, and I couldn't stop it. "Tell me who they are, and I will end them." I felt the change in my face, then. I felt my eyes change because my vision went sharp; in the dim light of the pizza parlour, I could suddenly see every detail, every hair on her head, every pore in her skin. And then something sharp dug into my bottom lip. I raised a finger to feel what was happening to find I had fangs – real, fucking sharp fangs that had come down in place of my canine teeth.

"Jesus!" Niamh pulled her hand out of mine and sat as far back in her seat as she could. "What the fuck was that?"

"I don't know." I shook my head, trying to clear it somehow, but I knew I still looked as scary as hell. "I'm sorry. Honestly, that's never happened before. It was just when you said you'd been with other men. I don't know – I came over all cave-man."

She sat forward and looked at me closely. "Your eyes – they're different. And I saw those teeth come down. This is either the most elaborate practical joke in the history of practical jokes or ..."

"Or I'm telling the truth."

"Yes."

We were silent for several seconds, but it felt like an age. "I can hear your heartbeat. It's slowing down a little bit now – it was racing a minute a go. And your scent changes when you're scared. I don't want to hurt you, Niamh. I don't think I could, even if I wanted to. This protective thing I've got going on right now is completely involuntary."

"Can you walk me home now? I need to think about what you've said."

"Of course." My heart sank, but I took a little comfort in the fact that she had asked me to walk her home, which I did. I kissed the back of her hand when we reached her door. "I'm in the bedsit above the shoe shop if you want to see me again. I want to see you, but I won't force you. I'll leave the ball in your court."

She nodded and wished me a shy good night. I watched her disappear into the bar and stood there for about ten minutes, drawing the last of her fading scent into my lungs.

I didn't hear anything from her for three days. Three, whole days and nights of fucking hell. I walked to Neary's a couple of times and looked through the window. I caught sight of her but didn't go in. I told her the ball was in her court and, like everything I said to her, it was the truth. My body was starting to go back to its old, dead self and I had a creeping feeling of desolation coming over me. I rang in sick for work and, on the third day, they told me not to come back. That's the problem with zero hours contracts; if you can't go to work, they'll soon find someone who can.

Fergus was no help. I rang him a couple of times, and he just kept saying that the decision had to be hers – that if I forced her into something, I'd never be able to live with myself. I knew he was right, but it hurt like bloody hell, feeling her slip away from me and knowing that I was missing a chance at something – though I had no idea what.

I was trying desperately to get drunk. I'd already downed a whole bottle of cheap whisky and was about to start on the second when I smelled Niamh. The scent got stronger and stronger and, just as I thought I would suffocate with it, there was a frantic banging on the door. I opened it, ready to say something apologetic or pathetic.

Niamh looked at me, and before I had the chance to say anything, she pushed past me into my room. "Where's your computer?"

"I … what?"

"I've found some stuff on the internet. It explains everything!"

"There's nothing on the internet about real vampires, Niamh."

"Yes, there is. You just need to know where to look!" She walked around my room, and it was as if the sun had come out in there. She spotted my laptop and sat down at it, typing furiously.

I went to stand behind her to see what she was doing. She had found websites that I hadn't been able to and, as I watched, I saw what I can only describe as the Facebook of Supernatural beings begin to scroll on the screen.

"Right – I'm logged in. I've been talking to this guy called Mateus."

When she said she'd been talking to another man – and another vampire at that – I felt the eyes and fangs thing happen again. A low growl came out of my mouth as I stood behind her.

Niamh looked over her shoulder at me and laughed. "I love that whole protective thing you've got going, but you can relax. Mateus is mated to a woman called Eleanor. They've been together for nearly two hundred years."

"Two hundred years? Is she a vampire too?"

"No. Read this."

A message from this Mateus filled the screen, so I crouched down by Niamh's chair to read it.

Hi, Niamh

I'm so glad you got in touch with me. Please don't be frightened about what is happening with you and your Daniel. From what you have described, I can say that there is no doubt that a mating is well under way. For Daniel, it has reached a critical stage. He will need to complete the bond with you in the next couple of days, or the instinct will disappear. This should not be something you undertake lightly, however. There are many advantages to being mated to a vampire, not least of all a life that will be as long as his. But it must be something you want to do; you cannot change your mind once the bond has taken – if you do, he will die.

You told me about your dreams of Daniel. I think you already know in your heart what you want to do – if you wished to abandon him, then you would not have gone to the considerable difficulty of finding me and asking for advice. But the decision must be yours. So, make it with the greatest care. Just know that it is a very rare thing for a vampire to find their mate. When they do, the relationship is always significant and right for both parties. Eleanor would be the first to tell you that it won't always be perfect, but she would also tell you that it is worth it.

Let me know what you decide. If you are sure you want to go ahead, go to him. Once he holds you in his arms, he will know what to do.

Yours in fellowship

Mateus

I sat back on my heels and let the information sink in. Niamh had read this, and she had come to me. Dare I hope that she was prepared to give this bonding thing a go?

"Well? What do you think?"

"I think I'm hoping that you being here is a good sign."

She smiled, and it made my heart quicken. "It's a very good sign. I knew the first moment I saw you. I just thought it was a love-at-first-sight thing – and I have to admit that I was totally freaked out by the vampire stuff – well, you would be, wouldn't you? But I've spent the last three days thinking about nothing else. And all this information just makes sense."

"Yes, I wish I'd been able to find that myself. I still find computers a bit confusing. Remember, I was born before most people had even seen a telephone."

She grinned at me. "I can teach you." She reached up and put her arms around my neck.

"Niamh. I don't want you to do this because you feel you have to. If you walk away, I'll just go back to my old self, and I will understand completely if you want to do that."

"I don't want to do that. If I bond with you, we will both become something new. I've found out so much in the last couple of days, and it all just confirms what I thought the first moment I saw you. You're mine, Daniel, and I have no intention of letting you go." She leaned forward and placed her lips very gently on mine.

The sharp points of my new fangs elongated as my cock stood to attention. Niamh tasted incredible, and her kiss made me feel like I had something fizzy going through my veins. "This is your last chance to change your mind, *ma mhuirnín*."

She didn't reply. She just turned and walked towards my bed, pulling her sweatshirt over her head and kicking her shoes off as she did. She turned to face me, and she was blushing. "I haven't done this in a while. So just go easy, okay?"

I couldn't help the laugh that escaped my mouth. "I can guarantee that it's been longer for me."

"No, Daniel – I'm talking more than a year."

I pulled my shirt over my head and walked to her, putting my arms around her and feeling her skin against mine for the first time. "Niamh – you clearly didn't get all the information from that website. Until you started to wake me up, I hadn't been able to get hard since before I died."

"What? And when was that, exactly?"

"June fifteenth, nineteen twenty-five. I was twenty-four."

She looked shocked for a moment; then her smile turned feral. "We're the same age. Sort of." She reached behind her and unfastened her bra. I watched it fall to the floor; then she took off her jeans and socks.

My beautiful mate was standing naked in front of me, and I was completely overwhelmed. Like a child who's just been given the biggest, most amazing box of chocolates, I didn't know where to start. "Lie down." It came out as a growl, and I barely recognised my own voice. I watched her sit on the bed and slide to the centre of the mattress as I removed the rest of my clothes, then I had no choice but to let instinct take over.

I landed beside her on the mattress and covered her mouth with mine. Her scent and taste sang in my head, and I felt almost drunk from it. She came to me; she didn't shy away or cry out. My brave girl. My hand moved of its own volition, first to cup her firm little breast, then it travelled down to where she was moist and swollen. I touched her there and she gasped. As I cupped her pretty mons, the words of an oath spilt out of my mouth. "I give myself to you, heart, blood and body. What I am is yours. I pledge to love and honour you until death parts us. My life is in your hands. Do you accept this gift?"

Her eyes dilated, and her mouth went soft. She nodded. "I accept your gift and offer you one in return. My heart, blood and body are yours. You are my mate." She turned her head and offered her neck.

The information from Mateus had been correct. As I held her in my arms, I knew what to do. When my fangs sank into the soft flesh of Niamh's neck, I felt something indescribable. Her blood tasted fucking amazing. Human blood is always sweet, but this was something else; like a really good wine or port. Something made me think of the last time I'd taken wine at Mass a very long time ago, but I knew that what I was experiencing with Niamh was a true communion. My body and brain tuned into hers and I could hear what she was thinking.

"Oh god, that … didn't hurt. It feels so good. Oh, fuck, I think I'm going to come!"

Her body started to writhe under me. I positioned myself between her legs and thrust myself inside. It felt incredible; not only because it had been decades since my cock had last been buried in a woman, but because this was *my* woman. This was my mate. My teeth were embedded in her neck, I was balls-deep in her, and she was writhing beneath me. I'd hardly started to move when she came; had my bite done that? I groaned, and my mind was suddenly filled with images of all the filthy things I wanted to do to her.

"Yes – oh, god yes – I want you to do all that to me – all of it!"

"I can hear you, Niamh. Tell me what you want."

"What? Daniel – I think I just heard you in my head."

I couldn't speak because my mouth was still latched onto her vein. *"Yes, ma mhuirnín. I can hear you too."*

"That is so hot." She was rotating her hips now, forcing me to penetrate her as deeply as possible. "This feels so good, *anamchara*."

"I love it when you call me that. I am your soulmate. This is real." I was going to come inside her. I had a fleeting thought that perhaps I should have checked whether vampires need to wear condoms, but it was drowned out by everything else that was rioting through my brain. Then there was something else. I knew, as clearly as if someone was reading me instructions, that as I came inside my mate, I had to give her some of my blood. That was what would complete our bond and keep her with me forever. I felt that long-forgotten sensation starting with a heavy feeling in my balls and a tingling in the tip of my cock. When the sensation travelled down my cock, I knew there was no going back, and I knew what I had to do. I pulled my mouth off Niamh's neck and licked at the wound I'd left. The sight of my mark on her made me growl. "Oh, god, Niamh, I'm going to come."

"I know. I can feel it."

"When I do, I need you to have some of my blood."

"I know. My mouth is already watering for it. It's all I can think about. Hurry, you're so close."

I sank my fangs into my wrist and held it over her mouth. My blood was a deep red, not the black it had been since I was made into a vampire. I watched it drip between her open lips, and her tongue came out to lap at it. Her eyes closed and she moaned with pleasure. The sound of my mate moaning, the sight of her delighting in the taste of my blood and the sensation of her tight little cunt clenching around my cock again was enough to tip me over the edge. I grabbed her hands with mine, cried out her name and I emptied myself into her; as my blood slipped down her throat, my seed flooded her body, and she came again.

We lay there, gasping for breath for a couple of minutes. I was still holding her hands over her head; our bodies fused together as we both came down from it. I was breathing – really breathing and my heart was beating in a steady, normal rhythm. I felt my fangs begin to recede and I lifted my head to check the wound on Niamh's neck. It had stopped bleeding, and, as I watched, it healed over, leaving only a tiny scar. I knew somehow that my blood had done that. And I knew that, as long as Niamh took my blood and seed at the same time, she would be with me. "I love you, Niamh. I know we've only just started, but I just know it. You're mine."

She kissed my hair and sighed against me. "I know too. And, at the risk of sounding like a Disney princess, I think I've always been in love with you. That's why I never really got serious with anyone else – none of them lived up to the guy who came to me in my dreams."

I laughed and let go of her hands so that I could go up on my elbows to look at her. "That does sound a little bit like something from a dreadful romance film."

"Make me a cup of tea?"

"Your wish is my command, my lady."

We drank several cups of tea, wrapped around each other on my sofa, and I couldn't get over how good it tasted. It was as though all my senses had suddenly become stronger. The tea tasted so good, I could feel the blood moving through my veins, and everything was different. My eyesight was clearer; my ears were sharper, even the sensation of my shirt against my skin was somehow more intense. "I feel different."

She looked at me, then reached for her bag and pulled out a handful of printed sheets. "There's some information on here. You feel different because you are different. It says here that you're a different kind of vampire now. You breathe, and you have red blood. You've got heightened senses, and you're stronger."

"I'm a vampire superhero?" I chuckled and flexed my fingers, watching as the muscles moved beneath my skin. "I certainly feel like one. Though when I was inside you, I felt like a god." I leaned forward and kissed her. "I'm never going to able to get enough of you, you know?"

"Just as well you don't have to then." She flashed me a smile that made my balls ache. "Now – about all that filthy stuff you imagined while we were fucking. I'm up for all of it."

I felt myself blush with embarrassment when I recalled the flood of pornographic images that had played in my brain when I was inside her. "I just blushed. That's a first too."

"Don't be embarrassed. I was putting some of those images into your mind."

"You were? Well, that would explain the vibrator. I've never fantasised about using one of those before."

"Did you like it?"

I launched myself at her. "Oh yes. Please tell me you have one of those in your bag as well."

"Sorry. I'll bring it next time. We'll just have to make do with fingers."

"And tongues." I was desperate to taste her. I got up, lifted her in my arms (which felt extraordinarily easy) and carried her back to my bed. We both shucked off the tee shirts we had put on, and I watched her slide back until she was sitting against the pillows, propped up against the headboard.

"Is this what you want?" She opened her thighs and displayed herself to me. Her pretty little pussy was still wet and swollen, like some exotic marine creature.

I could smell her wonderful scent, plus something else, something new, coming from her. "I want to taste you."

"You're not going to get fangs again, are you?" She dropped a hand to cover herself, and looked anxious for a moment."

"I don't know. I can't feel them. I promise I'll stop if I do." I began to stroke her skin gently, moving up her legs from her ankles to her knees. Her scent grew stronger and I watched her relax as she eased into my caress. "You're mine, *ma mhuirnín*. Forever." My fangs didn't descend, so I moved forward and started to lick the slick skin at the top of her thighs, easing my way up towards the prize my mouth ached to enjoy. I pushed her legs further apart, pressing her thighs against the pillows and I watched as her little hole opened as I split her. "There she is." I kissed around her pussy lips, nipping gently at her with my human teeth. I could smell her blood and hear it pumping through her femoral artery. "Next time I have my fangs out, I'm biting you here."

She shuddered under my hold. "Yes. I want that. Oh, god, I want that. I want your mouth on me, now."

My body jerked at her command. I wasn't going to be able to refuse her anything, was I? I was good with that. Putting my hands under her buttocks, I pulled her towards me. She was on her back in front of me, and I had my thumbs either side of her pussy, spreading her open for me. As soon as my tongue made contact with her wet flesh, I was lost. "God, you taste like honey down here." Unable to stop myself, I pushed in and started to eat her like the starving man I had become.

She was trying to wriggle, but I held her still. "Daniel! Please!"

"Keep still. Take what I'm giving you. If you try to wriggle again, I'll tie you down."

She made a sound that was almost like purring. "Oh, fuck, I really want you to do that." She started to rotate her hips, rubbing herself on my mouth, nose and chin.

I was drenched in her scent, and it was driving me wild. "You want that?"

"Yes." It came out on an exhale, and I could see the desperation in her eyes. She was so aroused I could feel it throbbing through her body, and I could hear her blood pounding in her cunt.

I reached for the shirts we had discarded and used them to tie her wrists to the bars of my headboard. When she was held fast, I ran my tongue down the side of her face before covering her mouth with mine. I pushed my tongue into her mouth, and I felt the vibration of her moan in the back of my throat. "If you say 'stop', I promise I will."

She nodded to let me know she'd understood, and watched me as I kissed down her sweet body. Her lovely little breasts were thrusting up towards me, her dark nipples hard and aroused. I sucked one into my mouth, and the taste of her skin was like her scent; spiced honey and addictive as any drug. I sucked at her, rubbing my tongue against the hard, little nub, making her writhe and moan. I took my time, torturing her with pleasure, then I repeated it all with the other nipple. By the time I'd given those beautiful tits the attention they deserved, I was almost out of my mind with wanting her. I kissed a trail down her midline and pushed my tongue into her navel. Her belly had a soft swell to it that was so feminine. I ran my tongue under the silky curve and nipped lightly at the skin there.

"Daniel. Please, I'm desperate for you to touch my clit!"

"Patience, love. I've not been this close to a woman in over ninety years. Let me get my bearings." I loved teasing her. In truth, I had got my bearings the minute I first put my cock inside her. I didn't need a road-map with her; I knew her body as well as my own from that first moment.

"Daniel Connolly put your mouth on me right now."

It was like a clarion call. "That's not fair. I was enjoying myself. And I can't even stop you from commanding me by gagging you." My smile gave away just how annoyed I wasn't as I moved to place a long, wet lick along her slit.

"I think I'd like you to gag me some time."

I had my mission; I'd been called, and I could do nothing but answer. I pushed my tongue into her hole, swirling it around to taste the heady mixture of her juices and the cum I had left inside her. She was wriggling again, pulling on the loose knots I'd used to tie her wrists. I reached up and released her hands. "Touch me while I lick you."

She reached down and pushed her fingers into my hair, directing my movements and forcing me into deeper contact with her aroused skin. "Oh, Daniel. Yes. Please – fuck me – I want you in me now."

I couldn't refuse her. Whatever she wanted was hers if it was in my power to give it to her. "I want you on top. I want you to ride me." I lay back on the bed; my cock was heavy against my belly, and it was throbbing, pulsing with the beat of my heart. My balls felt heavy and I reached down to cup them, unable to stop the involuntary movement of my hips as I rotated them.

Niamh licked her lips and bent over me. She lifted my cock with her hand and leant down to suck the head of it into her mouth. I felt her tongue swipe across the slit, and I knew she was tasting me. "You taste so good. I want more." She went back for more, sucking and swiping me with her tongue.

I thought my head was about to explode. "Niamh! Please! If you want me to fuck you, you'd better climb on me now because if you keep sucking me like that, I'm going to come."

"Poor baby." She slung one leg over my body so that she was straddling my hips. "Do you want to come?"

I wasn't able to say anything, so I just nodded while I tried to pull some air into my lungs. I reached for her and put my hands on her hips while she held my cock, positioning the head so that she could slide herself onto it.

She flexed her hips and took me in one, easy movement. Her pubic hair mashed with mine as she ground herself against me. I watched her as she began to gyrate above me, moving her hips in a small circle, taking me with her. She cupped her breasts with her hands, pinching her nipples as her eyes closed and her head went back.

I pressed my thumb against her clit as she rode my cock and I watched her fall apart. She cried out, swearing in Gaelic. I felt her inner muscles clench as her orgasm took her over and she fixed her eyes on me. Her blue eyes had a new light in them, and they seemed to glow in the dimness of my room. She spoke then, and her voice had a new timbre. "You are mine. Your body and blood are mine. Your seed is mine. Give it to me now."

I did as she commanded. I felt my balls draw up into my body and then my cum shot out of me and flooded her. Her inner muscles milked me as my orgasm seemed to trigger hers again and I felt like we were floating together. I pulled her down to my chest and wrapped my arms around her, kissing any part of her I could reach as we came down from what we had just shared.

She stayed there, her head on my chest, her pussy still holding on to my cock. Her breathing started to slow, and I could hear her heartbeat easing back to normal as well.

I stroked her hair and then moved my hand down to her back. "Can you hear my heartbeat?"

"I've got my head on your chest, so yes."

"How does it sound?"

"Like music."

"I know. It's singing your tune. I can hear yours too. I can hear your blood flowing through your veins."

She sat up and looked at me. "Really?"

"Yeah. I can hear everything that's going on in your body. I can hear your gut telling you that you're hungry."

"I am a bit. What have you got to eat?"

"Not a lot. I've had a bit of a liquid diet for the last couple of days."

"We could go out for something."

"Yeah. In a bit. I just want to hold you for a while."

She lay back down against me, and I thought she might have fallen asleep, but then she spoke again. "Am I a vampire now?"

"I don't think so. I think you need to be dying for it to work like that. And my blood is red now, so I'm not sure it would work at all."

"My voice went all funny."

"Your eyes changed too. They were glowing blue."

She chuckled against me, and I felt it right down to my toes. "I put on the blues and twos."

"You did." I kissed the top of her head, "And it was glorious." I held her to me, and the enormity of what had just happened hit me. I had a mate. I'd become some kind of super-vamp, and I'd just had a sexual experience that was so far removed from any of the brief, nightclothes-on-light-off fucks I'd had in my old life, that I didn't even know how to describe it.

After a few minutes of holding each other like that, she lifted herself off me. As my wilting cock slipped from her body, we both watched as a pool of our combined juices oozed out of her and pooled on my belly.

I put the tip of my index finger into the wetness. "In all of that information you found on the interweb, was there anything about whether or not we can make babies?"

Niamh nodded and smiled. "We can. It's my choice. Apparently, I can command you to make me pregnant."

"Oh." My eyebrows went skywards, and I felt myself smile. "Well, I'm glad I don't have to use a condom." I reached for the box of tissues from the side of my bed and handed them to her. "Clean me up, then."

"I will command you to do it one day. But not for a long, long time."

"Good plan. Maybe wait until your Da is too old to beat the crap out of me."

She laughed, then her eyes went wide. "Oh, my god. My Da. How are we going to explain this to him?"

"We're not going to. As far as he's concerned, I'm going to court you like a gentleman. Then we're going to get married, and, with the help of a little makeup and subterfuge, we'll just get blissfully old together. Then we'll move on and live somewhere where nobody knows us, and it will start all over again."

"Is that how it's been for you, all these years?" She looked sad, and I could feel it in my own body.

"Yes. But it's going to be so much better now because I'm not alone anymore."

"No, you're not. I'm so glad you found me, Daniel."

"Me too, *ma mhuirnín,* me too."

Pisces

Fluctuation, depth, imagination, reactive, indecisive

"**M**iranda!" Gabriel Brant, Captain of the Space Explorer Typhon, ejaculated against the glass wall of the shower enclosure in his private bathroom. The woman whose name he had shouted as he came was his soon-to-be ex-wife; Miranda Bouvier-Brant, chief engineer of SE Typhon, who had moved out of their shared quarters a month ago. Since then, his morning showers had included solitary sex inspired by memories of the love of his life playing on a continual loop in his brain.

He hadn't wanted her to move out, and he did not want to sign the divorce papers that had arrived in his virtumail inbox last night. He loved his wife, and he had no clue what had gone wrong with their marriage. They stopped connecting somehow, stopped talking, stopped making love. He had tried to talk about it, but he was never any good at talking. And the less he talked, the cooler she became, until that morning when she'd said she didn't want to live like that anymore. As she walked through the door, he tried to talk to her again, but he just didn't have the words.

He'd always been the same. Ask him to talk to the SE Council or give a lecture about the benefits of fission jet propulsion to a class of cadets; then he was a regular chatterbox. But put him in a situation where he needed to tell Miranda how he was feeling and his brain went lights-out. It was a miracle he'd ever managed to woo her in the first place. She was the most beautiful woman in their trainee cohort at SE Central, and he had fallen for her at first sight. Their first date was set up by a couple of mutual friends who were fed up with listening to them mooning over each other. He remembered everything about that night; her clothes, her hair, and how it had ended with the most incredible sex he'd ever experienced.

"You look really beautiful tonight, Miranda."

She giggled and took a sip of her wine. "Thank you, Gabe. I think that's the most words I've ever heard you say to me in one go." She took another sip of wine. "You look beautiful too."

Gabe blushed and drank some of his beer. "I don't find it that easy to talk."

"You didn't seem to have any problems in the debate today. You were very eloquent."

"Thank you. I can talk about things; I just find it hard when it comes to … you know."

"Feelings?"

"Yeah. Feelings. I never know what to say."

He showed her how eloquent he could be with his body when he took her home.

"Would you like to come in for coffee?"

"I think coffee is overrated."

She laughed and opened the door to her quarters. "I agree. I can think of lots of things I'd rather do with you than drink coffee."

"Such as?" He tried not to sound too desperate. He had longed for this woman since he first laid eyes on her and now, here he was, in her room and she was looking at him like she felt the same. He couldn't remember who moved first – maybe they had both moved at the same time – but a moment later, he was kissing her as though his life depended on it and she was tearing at the buttons of his shirt. He pulled his mouth from hers for a moment. "I don't normally do this on a first date."

"Neither do I."

"I think I wanted you the moment I saw you."

"Me too. Now stop talking and come with me to the bedroom or I'm going to get on my knees and suck your cock right here."

He needed no more encouragement. He let her take his hand and lead him out of the tiny living room of her quarters into an even tinier bedroom. "I don't have any condoms – I wasn't expecting …"

"I have some. Now get undressed. Please." The polite interjection sounded a little like an afterthought. Was she used to ordering men around in her bedroom?

The thought that she might be made Gabe's cock stand even harder. He took off the rest of his clothes and helped Miranda remove the last of her underwear. He could smell her arousal as the soft, heady scent of it filled the warm air of the tiny room. He got onto his knees and helped her step out of her panties then lifted them to his face, inhaling her glorious scent. He groaned as she filled his lungs and nose.

"Gabriel Brant is a panty-sniffer. Who would have thought it?" She sounded pleased with her discovery, and she reached down to run her fingers through his hair.

"Well, if you want salacious info to use against me, here's something else. Gabriel Brant is also a pussy-licker." He moved his head forward and pressed his mouth against the soft, wet skin of Miranda's pussy. He opened his mouth and pressed his tongue into her, licking around her hole as he grabbed hold of her buttocks and pushed her as against his face.

Miranda felt her knees weaken at the sudden onslaught. *"My god, Gabe, don't stop. Fuck! You're good at that!"* She rotated her hips a little, forcing his mouth to make contact with her clitoris. *"There. I want it there."*

As Gabe licked at the sensitive little bud of flesh, he felt Miranda's legs start to shake. She was going to come soon. He reached down to fist his aching cock and began to rub himself, lost in the taste and scent of her.

"Take your hand off your dick right now. It's mine." She spoke the words as an order that she clearly expected to be obeyed. *"Stick your fingers in me. I want to feel full of you when you make me come."* She shuddered as she said that and fell against him.

Gabe did as she had commanded. He pushed two fingers into Miranda's clenching cunt and hooked his fingers, making a 'come here' gesture inside her.

She cried out and threw her head back. *"Yes! O, god, yes!"*

Gabe continued to finger and lick her until her internal muscles stopped clenching and her moans quieted to soft gasps. When she had stopped moving, he sat back and smiled up at her. Then he looked down at his cock; it was hard against his belly. *"Now — what are you going to do about this?"*

Miranda licked her lips and nodded her head in the direction of the bed. *"Sit on the bed. Feet on the floor."*

Again, he did as he was told. He sat on the edge of her bed, his feet flat on the floor, and leaned back on his elbows. His cock sprang up, a drop of clear fluid oozing from the tip that cooled the heated skin as it ran down towards his inflamed balls. *"Suck it. I want your mouth on me."* Now it was his turn to give an order.

Miranda fell to her knees between his legs and took hold of Gabe's erection in her right hand. *"This is a beautiful cock."* She put out her tongue and licked at a newly-formed drop of the pre-cum that was oozing freely from his piss-hole now. She ran her tongue over the moist head of his cock before taking it into her mouth.

Gabe pulled in a deep breath as he watched his cock disappear into Miranda's mouth. He felt the tip brush the back of her throat and he pulled back a little. *"Easy. Go easy."* He was breathing heavily as she began to suck him in earnest and he felt the tell-tale tingling in the tip of his cock that warned him his orgasm was close. But he didn't want to come in her mouth. He had tasted her sweet pussy and felt her internal muscles with his fingers. He wanted to bury his cock inside her and fuck her till he came. *"Where are the condoms. I want to come while I'm buried in your cunt."*

Miranda pulled away from him and smiled slyly, licking her lips. "Top drawer." She pointed at the nightstand that was built into the bed frame. "I want that too. I want to ride you and watch you come apart."

Gabe reached into the drawer and found what he needed. He opened the packet and put the thing on as quickly as he could, then he lay on his back on Miranda's bed. "Ride me. Sit on my cock and do what you like. I'm not going to last very long."

Miranda mounted the man lying on her bed. He was a gorgeous specimen and, even though she had already enjoyed a knee-trembling orgasm thanks to his skilled mouth, she felt her pussy watering again at the sight of him. She took hold of his sheathed cock and positioned herself over it, easing down until he was held completely within her tight channel. She felt a delicious stretching sensation as he filled her and she knew this wasn't going to be a one-night stand. This cock was hers. "Oh, my god! You feel so good. So right."

Gabe tried to control his breathing to slow the progress of the orgasm that was threatening to break. The tingling sensation had spread down to his balls now and, as he watched Miranda moving up and down on him, he knew he had reached the point of no return. "Yes! Oh, fuck! Miranda! I'm coming."

Miranda bent over and captured his mouth with hers. She kissed him hard, pushing her tongue into his mouth as he thrust up into her, moaning and writhing. When he went still, she broke the kiss and stroked the side of his face. "I have a feeling we're going to be doing this again before too long."

They married three months later. They'd been together for ten years. He was now in charge of SE Typhon, and Miranda was chief engineer. It seemed that the higher they both climbed up the promotion ladder, the further apart they became. Whenever Miranda wanted to talk about where their relationship was going, he'd panic and silence her with kisses. She always responded to his body; they seemed to speak a language of their own in bed, but in the past year or so, she had pushed him away when he tried that trick. Fairly soon, they weren't talking, and they weren't having sex either.

How many times had he tried to talk to her? Clearly, not enough. And now he was paying the price for being tongue-tied; the only woman he'd ever loved was sleeping in a single crew member's quarters two floors down from the captain's apartment they had shared since coming aboard Typhon two years ago.

It probably didn't help that they were stuck on board this ship. Typhon was tasked with observing M74 – a spiral galaxy in the Pisces Constellation – and they were going to be there for at least another year. If they were back on Earth, he could try to get her to remember why she'd fallen in love with him in the first place by taking her to the places they'd visited together. But what could he do when they were stuck out here? You might be able to get divorce papers sent from Earth in the blink of an eye, but you couldn't just pop back for a weekend.

Gabe finished getting dressed and looked at himself in the mirror. "You bloody fool." He felt his heart sink even further down until that sick feeling settled in the pit of his stomach again.

He was pulled from his self-pity party by a call coming into his personal communicator. Picking it up, he saw the worried face of his First Officer. "What's the problem, Bridget?"

"Sir, the main navigation system on Eros is down."

"Have you instructed E2 to fix it?"

"Yes, Sir. He's been trying since twenty-three hundred hours last night, without success."

"I'm on my way." Gabe heaved a sigh and made his way towards the main deck. Eros was one of a pair of small craft orbiting Typhon, which housed deep space telescopes. Eros and Aphrodite, like Typhon, were named after the characters of a Greek Myth. In the story, Aphrodite and her son, Eros, were trying to escape the monster, Typhon. They ran to the water and were transformed into fish, which became the constellation of Pisces. The pair of observation craft were maintained by human simulants; robots who looked exactly like real people but didn't need things like food and sleep. Aphrodite was maintained by A1, a dry-witted, black woman who called everyone Cher. The current occupant of Eros was E2. E1 had been lost when a small meteor struck the tiny craft. The crew of Typhon thought it would be hilarious to order the replacement to look like Brant and it was a running joke amongst them. E2 was an almost perfect copy of Gabriel Brant with one exception; E2 could talk to anyone. He could quote poetry and make people laugh. That was a running joke too.

When Gabe reached the bridge, he could see E2's eerily familiar face on the viewer screen. "What's going on out there, Two?" The shortened version of the simulant's name was used commonly among the crew.

Two looked serene as he replied. "I apologise, Captain, but I am unable to reset the navigation system on my own. Would it be possible to send Lieutenant Bouvier-Brant to help me? I estimate that I would need her assistance for approximately seventy-two hours."

Brant thought about the request for a moment. Miranda was going to hate the idea. But perhaps some time away from Typhon might be good for her. And anyway, they had to get Eros up and running again. Two was not able to lie, so if he said he needed help, then he did. "I'll arrange it. Expect the Lieutenant in the next ten hours." It took three hours to get to Eros, but he knew he might need a little time to persuade Miranda that she really needed to go.

"Sir, shall I ask Lieutenant Bouvier-Brant to come to the bridge?"

"Thanks, Bridget, but I think I'd better handle this one." He walked down two levels to the crew deck and, after taking a deep breath, knocked on the door of her quarters. He could hear her moving around in there, but she didn't answer, so he knocked again. "Miranda? Are you there? I need to talk to you about something."

More movement and a crash of something falling on the floor, then the door opened just enough so that Gabe could see into the dim interior and Miranda's face looking up at him. "Gabe – I told you I don't want to talk about it anymore." She sniffed, and her eyes were red.

"It's not about that. I need you to go to Eros to help Two reset the navigation system." He looked down at her lovely face, and his heart clenched. "Miranda – have you been crying?"

"Leave it, Gabriel." She wiped her hand over her face and opened the door fully. "Come in. You can tell me about Eros while I'm getting dressed."

Gabe followed her into the tiny room and closed the door. "You know, there is probably a much nicer cabin free on the Officers' Deck; you are a Lieutenant, after all."

"This is fine." Miranda wrapped her hair in a towel and pulled on a pair of trousers. "Tell me what's happened. Why can't Two handle it himself?"

"The nav system needs a complete reboot. Two said he'd need you for about seventy-two hours."

She nodded and began to rub her hair dry. "Right. Yeah, if the main computer needs rebooting, then it is a two-person job. And we'll need to monitor it for a couple of days – you often need to do several restarts after it updates itself."

"So, you're okay with going?" Gabe couldn't quite believe this was going to be so easy.

"Why wouldn't I be? Three days in the company of your conversationally unchallenged doppelganger; what's not to like?" She threw her towel on the bed and started to brush her still-damp hair with angry strokes. "I'll pack and go. Tell the shuttle crew to get ready to take me."

"Thank you. I'll do that. Let me know how it goes."

Miranda stepped through the airlock into the small anti-room of SE Remote Eros. She switched on the oxygen circulatory system and waited for it to make the air breathable; Two didn't need oxygen to function, so the reserves of the precious gas were kept for occasions such as these. When the light turned from red to green, she took off her helmet and stepped into the main control room of the little spacecraft.

"Welcome, ma'am. It is good to see you again." Two was waiting for her by the main console. He smiled and walked towards her, his hand outstretched.

Miranda took his hand and shook it. "Thank you, Two. It is good to see you as well." She looked at his face; so familiar, yet completely strange at the same time. Gabe was a very good-looking man – tall, muscular, an almost perfect face complete with dimples, green eyes and a head of thick, black hair that made her want to run her fingers through it. It had been love at first sight for her. Two was a perfect copy of her estranged husband and looking at him filled her with an overwhelming sadness. "Fill me in – what's been going on?"

Two walked back to the main console and brought up the system schematics on the screen. "I've stabilised the system. We can reboot it whenever you're ready."

"Good. Can I just take a shower first? The ride over was a bit hot."

"Absolutely. I'll show you to your quarters."

"No need – thank you – I know where it is." She retrieved the small bag she had brought with her from the ante-room and walked the very short distance to the cabin that was reserved for human visitors. After a quick shower, she returned to the control room. "Right. Let's get down to it."

An hour later, they were watching Eros' onboard computer come back to life; lights flashing and code scrolling on the screen as the operating system restarted. The need for two people was a failsafe; on an earlier mission, a replicant had decided that the most logical thing to do would be to reprogram the main computer to deny oxygen to the crew who weren't essential to the running of the ship. The two-person re-set had been implemented shortly after that. "The update has started." Miranda sat back in her seat and watched the main screen of the console. "All we can do now is wait. It will probably take a couple of hours."

"Can I make you something to eat, ma'am?"

"Thank you, but I can do that for myself. You're not my servant, Two."

The simulant smiled and nodded. "It would be my pleasure to do such a small thing for you. Let me see what the shuttle dropped off when you arrived."

Miranda watched him walk towards the anti-room and go into the airlock. The familiar form of the replicant made her chest feel tight. She missed her husband so much, but the life they were living before the breakup was not what she had signed on for. He had always been a man of few words, but since they moved to Typhon, he had become a man of almost no words. And the words he did say were about work, never about her or their relationship. She had just reached the point where she couldn't do it anymore. She felt tears burning her eyes and dashed them away with the back of her hand.

"I was very sorry to hear about you and Captain Brant."

She looked up to see Two holding out a paper tissue. She took it and blew her nose. "Thank you. News travels fast, then."

"A1 told me."

"I had no idea that you talked about things that happen on Typhon." In truth, she was a little shocked that Two knew her marriage had broken up; even more, surprised to hear that he felt sorrow about it. "Do you often swap gossip with A1?"

"It's important that we keep up to date with things that might affect the running of Typhon and the two remote ships. I apologise – I can see that I shouldn't have mentioned it – please forgive me."

Miranda looked up to look at Two properly. His face showed all the signs of emotion, but she knew it was just programming. He couldn't feel sorrow, or joy, or love, or hate. He was just responding to input. "There's nothing to forgive. I overreacted, so I am the one who should be apologising. Now – what delights did you find for my supper?"

The simulant smiled broadly. "On the menu today, we have a very fine mushroom risotto."

"Did they send any wine?"

"I do believe they did."

"Lovely. Will you keep me company? I hate eating alone."

"That would be my pleasure, ma'am."

Gabriel Brant watched Two offer his wife a tissue. It was the first time he'd seen her cry in years and it made his heart clench that he wasn't with her to offer comfort. The camera from Eros' communicator gave him a good view of everything that was happening in the control room. He turned up the volume coming from the communicator's microphone so that he could hear what they were saying. He felt a momentary pang of guilt; that he was intruding in some way. But something was driving him to watch and listen.

Two put a plate of food and a glass of wine on the small table in the centre of the control room. "Here we are, ma'am. Your supper and a glass of wine."

Miranda walked to the table and sat down. "Thank you, Two. This smells very good."

"I agree. My olfactory sensors are registering that the food is very good." He sat down opposite Miranda and watched her eat. "It is very pleasant to have some company. Perhaps we could play chess, or a card game when you have finished eating?"

"That would be very nice, thank you. I love to play chess – Gabe and I used to play sometimes."

Gabe felt a wave of sorrow wash over him. He remembered the last time he and Miranda played chess. The game had remained unfinished, pieces scattered, as she climbed onto his lap and rode his cock until they both came. That was a long time ago. Bringing his attention back to the screen, he watched Miranda pick up her empty plate and glass and take it over to the small sink at the side of the control room. She made herself a cup of coffee and returned to the table, where Two had set up a chess board.

"If you don't mind me asking, why do you have a chess board? You don't exactly have frequent visitors to play with."

"A1 and I play over the communicator sometimes. It is good for synapse development."

"Yes – I sometimes forget that you have organic elements in your CPU. I suppose that is what gives you the ability to make decisions that aren't always based on logic." She took a seat at the table, choosing to play black. Gabe had guessed that she would do that – she always liked to play black – be on the defence from the start.

"Indeed. Sometimes, logic alone would lead me to make decisions that could be disastrous for the crew of Typhon." Two sat in the other chair and moved one of his pawns forward.

"Do you ever feel any – I don't know – emotions?" Miranda moved out one of her knights – her favourite opener.

"I experience different processing algorithms, depending on the nature of the input. I suppose the way I respond could be interpreted as emotion. I did, for example, experience something you might identify as sorrow when I heard about you and Captain Brant."

Miranda sat back in her chair and looked at her strange companion. "Thank you. It's been a very difficult time."

Two moved another of his pawns out into the centre of the board without looking at it. Gabe knew that he had taken Miranda's first move and created a program to follow the most likely outcome. "I don't wish to appear forward or inappropriate, but if you would like to talk about it, it would be my pleasure to listen. I can assure you that whatever you choose to tell me will go no further than this room."

Gabe had another, sudden pang of guilt. Two was offering Miranda the seal of the confessional, and he was listening in like a grubby eavesdropper. His hand hovered over the button to disconnect, but something in him wanted to hear what she had to say. They hadn't been able to have this conversation face to face, so hearing her tell her side of the story to Two might give him some much-needed insight.

Miranda took a long drink of her coffee and considered for a moment. "You know? I think I would like to talk about it if you don't mind. I haven't got anyone on the crew I can confide in. Gabe was my go-to guy for all that kind of thing. I suppose talking to you would be the next best thing."

"I am aware that I resemble your husband. Does that make this awkward?"

"No," she shook her head and finished her coffee. "In fact, I think it makes it easier."

"Do you want to finish our game first?"

"No. I want to talk. Thank you."

"It is my pleasure to help you, ma'am."

"Right. Where to start?"

"The beginning. Start at the beginning. Tell me how you met and fell in love."

"Well, that's easy, because those two things happened at the same time. We met at SE Central when we were cadets, and I fell in love with him the first time I saw him."

"What does it feel like? To fall in love?"

"It's like every cell in your body is filled with champagne or something fizzy. You can't sit still, and you live for the next time you're going to see him. Gabriel Brant was the most beautiful man I'd ever seen, and my whole body responded to the sight of him."

"I'm trying to process that. I have read much about human sexual desire, but I find it difficult to understand."

Gabe remembered when the replacement simulant had been ordered. It is possible to have a system installed that allows the machine to perform sexual acts, but the thought of something that wore his face doing that had been too much to think about, so he had put a very large 'NO' in that box on the order form. Watching the conversation developing between Two and Miranda now, he was very glad about that.

Miranda chuckled. "Believe me; it's no easier to understand when you can process it. Sometimes the body just wants something that it knows isn't good for it. Speaking of which, I don't suppose the shuttle dropped off any whiskey?"

"I'll go and have a look." Two got up and left the room.

Gabe watched Miranda clear the chess game away. As she bent over to put the box back in the low cupboard, her trousers stretched tight over her bottom, and he felt his cock stir. "Dammit. Oh, Miranda." He felt pathetic and stupid; wanting so much to beg her to come back to him, but having neither the words or the necessary proximity.

Two came back with a bottle and glass. "This was in the food package." He poured a shot into the glass and handed it to Miranda. "To your good health, ma'am."

Miranda raised her glass, "*Slàinte.*"

Two looked at her for a moment, and Gabe knew he was searching for information about what Miranda had just said. "*Slàinte* is a word literally translating as "health" in several Gaelic languages and is commonly used as a drinking toast in Ireland and Scotland."

"Exactly." She lifted the glass to her lips and tipped the contents into her mouth, savouring it for a moment before swallowing it. "Mmm, that's not bad." She reached for the bottle and poured herself another shot.

"I'm glad it meets with your approval. Though I do not understand why you would use such a salutation. Your personal record states that you have no connection to Ireland or Scotland."

Miranda laughed loudly. "I guess you know everything, huh? Birthday, favourite movie, et cetera."

Two looked confused for a moment. "January 26th, but the information about your favourite movie is not available."

"But you knew my birthday. Which is more than Gabriel Brant ever did."

Gabe felt like a hot knife had been thrust into his chest. Her birthday had been the day before she moved out of their apartment. He had never been able to remember it, and even when his calendar reminded him, he rarely did anything about it. Miranda always said she didn't mind. She said that having him in her life was like every birthday and Christmas she could ever want. How could he be so stupid? He loved her, didn't he? Why couldn't he show her that now and again?

"I'm very sorry to hear that your husband didn't wish you a happy birthday. I understand that it is something that is celebrated on Earth." He looked to the side as if he was trying to remember something. "With cake. And gifts."

Miranda took another mouthful of whiskey and swallowed it quickly. "I could have done without the gifts, but a sticky cake and a birthday kiss wouldn't have gone amiss. Or, maybe a birthday cake and a sticky kiss." She giggled, showing that the alcohol was starting to take effect.

"Tell me more about what drew you to Captain Brant. If we know that, then perhaps we can calculate why you felt you could no longer stay with him."

"Yes. You're right." She settled herself and sipped her drink." Well, it was purely physical to start with. He's a very good-looking man – well, you know that – you look at him in the mirror."

"I rarely look in the mirror, but I understand what you are saying. My recognition software tells me that his face has pleasing proportions and I know that females find tall stature in males attractive."

"He has very pleasing proportions in other places too."

Two looked to the side again, then nodded. "You are making a veiled reference to the size of his genitalia."

Gabe sat forward in his seat, the primitive part of his brain wanted to hear what Miranda had to say about his body.

Miranda raised her glass to toast the air. "I am indeed. That man has a cock that I want to worship."

"You want to? Present tense? You still have feelings for him, then."

"Of course, I do. I'm still in love with him. But he just stopped talking to me. He was never the most verbose man, but when we did talk, it was good. And he could put his tongue to other uses that made my knees weak, but in the last year or so, he hasn't used it for that either."

"You are referring to oral sex." Two's head moved to indicate he was searching for information again. "Oral sex, sometimes referred to as oral intercourse, is a sexual activity involving the stimulation of the genitalia of a person by another person using the mouth (including the lips, tongue or teeth) or throat. Cunnilingus is oral sex performed on a female." He looked back to Miranda. "So, Captain Brant is skilled in cunnilingus?"

"Very skilled." She sighed, "But as I said, there hasn't been much of anything in the last year or so. I don't know what happened. When we took up residence on Typhon, everything just started to tail off; conversation, sex, everything."

"My recognition software tells me that your appearance is very pleasing. Why would Captain Brant neglect your needs so blatantly? My systems conclude that the logical course of action would be to enjoy a mutually satisfactory relationship with you to the benefit of both parties. What he has done is illogical."

Miranda looked at Two and tears began to fall again. "You know, it's just as well that Gabe didn't allow you to be created with the sex add-on. If you had it, I'd probably be climbing you like a tree right now. I want nothing more than for my husband to realise that what he's done is illogical and to claim me back like some knight in shining armour. But he's not going to do that. I just have to accept it and move on."

Gabe had heard enough. He felt sick and ashamed; how could he have treated this wonderful woman so carelessly? He felt tears prickling his eyes as he shut off the communicator and returned to his empty apartment.

Miranda woke with a headache and a dry mouth. She had drunk far too much whiskey the night before. After a quick shower, she went out to the control room. Two was standing at the main console of the computer, watching the update code scrolling on the screen. "Good morning, Two."

The simulant turned around and smiled at her. "Good morning, ma'am. Did you sleep well?"

Miranda ran a hand through her damp hair. "I did, thank you. I heard the airlock in the middle of the night, but apart from that, the whiskey knocked me out."

"I apologise for waking you with the airlock. I was disposing of some waste." He walked towards the small kitchen area and poured a cup of coffee from the pot he had brewed for her.

"Oh, thank you. That is JUST what the doctor ordered." She took the steaming mug and inhaled deeply. "This smells good. You've made it just how I like it. Don't tell me, that's in my personal information as well?"

Two nodded and gave a brief smile. "I am glad it is to your liking. I will prepare some breakfast for you; then the computer will be ready for another re-set."

Miranda watched her strange companion as he prepared food for her. "Two – is everything okay with you today?"

The simulant looked at her, his expression blank. "All is well with my systems, ma'am. What made you ask?"

"I don't know." She took a sip of her coffee and shook her head. "I think I must be very hung-over. For a moment, you looked – I don't know – different somehow. Forget I mentioned it."

"That would be my pleasure, ma'am."

They re-set the and cleared the breakfast things away. Miranda made a call to Typhon to let them know that things were going to schedule and that she would probably be able to leave Eros in about twenty-four hours. "Thanks, Bridget. It's been quite nice. A change of scenery was long overdue."

"Good. I'll let the Captain know that it's going to plan."

"Yeah – thanks. Don't mention about the change of scenery thing though. I don't want to give him anything else to stress about." She signed off on the communicator and turned around to see that Two had set up the chess board. He'd set up the pieces as they had left them the night before. "Oh - that's a good idea."

Two smiled at her. "Yes. I thought we could finish our game while we wait for the next update to complete." He pulled the chair out for her and waited for her to sit down.

The chess game went the way it always did; Miranda had Two in Check, but she'd been so busy getting her Queen into the right position that she hadn't noticed her opponent moving his Rook and Bishop into place to put her in Check-Mate. She sat back in her chair and laughed as she tipped over her King in defeat. "You play just like my husband."

Two smiled broadly. "I was just following the most logical path. It is a sequence of moves that are used very frequently in the game."

"Oh." Miranda looked down at the table. "That would explain it. I guess I'm not a very good player?"

"Not at all, ma'am. You play very well. And I believe that if you chose to play white from time to time, you would find it easier to win."

Miranda laughed loudly. "Now, you sound like Gabriel too. He always used to say that to me."

"So why don't you try it?"

She got up and walked to the kitchen area to get a glass of water. "I suppose I'm just not brave enough to make the first move." She felt the weight of an unspoken sadness in her belly, and she fought the need to cry. "I think that probably applies to quite a lot of things in my life."

Two got up from his seat and walked to where she was standing. "I understand that it is normal for humans to offer each other an embrace when they are upset. Would you like me to put my arms around you to comfort you?"

Miranda went into his arms easily. It had been so long since she had been hugged, it felt wonderful to be sharing that simple embrace with someone, even though he wasn't a real human being. She rested her face against Two's shoulder; it felt so familiar and comfortable. She could feel the hard plate of the simulant's chest underneath his shirt, but he was warm and solid. "I must be imagining things. You even smell like Gabe." She sniffed and wiped her nose with the back of her hand. "I guess I just miss him. I miss this." She moved closer so that he could hug her more tightly.

"We didn't finish our conversation last night. You told me how you fell in love with Captain Brant, but you didn't tell me why your marriage has ended. It would help me to understand more about the complexities of human emotion if you felt able to share that with me."

Miranda looked up into the familiar green eyes. "How do your eyes work?"

Two looked confused for a moment then he nodded. "My ocular sensors work in the same way as yours. They take in light and process the input into an image. Why do you ask?"

Miranda shook her head and laughed lightly. "I just noticed that your pupils dilated a little when you asked me to share my experiences with you. I had no idea that the eyes of a simulant were so advanced. The light levels in here haven't changed; I could almost imagine that you were feeling emotion, or perhaps a physical pain."

"Alas, no. My physical form is designed to be as close to the real thing as possible to make humans feel at ease. Perhaps my systems performed that simple task to make it appear that I was empathising with you?"

"Well, it worked." She pulled out of his embrace and reached for the whiskey bottle that she had placed on the shelf above the sink the night before. After pouring a glass for herself, she walked back to the table and sat down. "Join me. I can give you lots of information to help you better understand the complexities of human emotion."

Two sat in the chair opposite Miranda. "I appreciate your assistance."

"No problem." She took another sip of her drink. "So, what would you like to know?"

"You told me how you fell in love with Captain Brant, and I think I understand a little about how that works. Would I be right in thinking that you feel that you don't have complete control of your feelings and actions when you are falling in love with someone?"

"Yes, you'd be right about that. Sometimes, it feels as though everything in the world is happening simply because you want and need to be with someone. I remember a day – it was about a week after we had gone on our first date – Gabe was due to do a test flight of a new fighter. I didn't want him to do it; I'd worked on the schematics, and something just didn't feel right. There was a bad sandstorm, and he wasn't able to take off, so we spent the whole day in bed." She stopped speaking and smiled at the memory.

"Your husband is a skilled lover? You told me that he is well-proportioned and that he is skilled at performing cunnilingus. Was sexual intercourse also satisfactory?"

"It was more than satisfactory. He could make my body sing. We just fit together. I can't describe it any other way."

"So, this day, when he should have been flying the test, made you feel that things were working in your favour?"

"It was more than that. The next day, Gabe was off rota, so another pilot took the flight. The jet exploded as it took off. I just knew that it was meant to be."

"I remember."

Miranda looked up, her eyebrows pulling together in confusion. "What?"

Two nodded. "Let me clarify. I have an account of that incident in my memory bank. The young pilot was killed, and the design of the fighter was changed completely. The new design was called Meteor 3; it is still in production."

She looked a little wary, but she nodded. "Yes. That's right."

"Tell me more about how you felt this relationship was pre-destined in some way. My logic processes do not allow for such a belief."

Miranda got up and refilled her glass. She leant against the sink and looked at Two. "Well, there is no logic in how people fall in love. It just happens. It takes you by surprise, and you can't switch it off. I fell for Gabe, heart, body and soul. I gave him a part of myself, and he gave me part of himself in return."

"Did it hurt? To lose a part of yourself in such a way?"

"No. It didn't hurt. Not until he started to withdraw that part of himself that he had given to me. Then it hurt. It left me feeling … empty."

"Do you think Captain Brant knows that he made you feel this way?"

"I don't think so, no. He's so occupied with running Typhon; I really don't think he notices anything unless it's presented to him in a report." She was aware how bitter she sounded, but she needed to express the feelings that were filling her heart so much, she could barely breathe. "If he would only take a little while, every day, to tell me what I am sure he still feels, then I don't think I'd be sleeping in a single cabin."

"Have you said that to him?" Two's voice was calm. It was as if he was asking about the weather or how to make a cup of coffee.

"No. I haven't. I suppose that after all these years together I feel that he should know what was wrong without needing to be told."

Two got up from his seat and walked to face her. "Forgive me for saying, ma'am, but that is illogical. I am designed to behave and respond like a human being. I could not process something as complex as how you are feeling without any input on the subject."

"Are you saying that it's my fault? That we drifted apart because I didn't tell him that his increasing distance and coldness towards me was killing me? That kind of thing has a physical effect. He should have bloody well noticed that something was wrong with me and asked. If he'd just taken one minute to consider my feelings, I'd have happily given him his fucking input." Tears were falling fast now, and she felt hot and sick. "When the computer needs to be re-set again, come and get me. Until then, I'll be in my bunk."

Two respected her wishes. He placed a tray of food outside her door when it was time for her to eat, but she didn't take it, even though he knocked softly and told her it was there. He removed the tray when he heard her shower running.

Miranda walked out into the control room, her hair damp and her clothes rumpled as though she had slept in them. "Two, I have to apologise for my behaviour last night. I shouldn't have reacted the way I did."

Two looked a little confused for a moment and seemed to be accessing information. He looked directly at her and smiled. "There is no need to apologise. You didn't say anything unpleasant to me. Did you sleep well?"

"I drank enough whiskey to knock out a rhino. Have you made some coffee?"

Two walked to the coffee machine and poured a cup of the dark liquid for her.

Miranda took the mug and lifted it to her nose. "You used a different blend today?"

"I followed the instructions. Is it not satisfactory?"

"It's fine." She took a drink and smiled. "Is the computer ready for a re-set?"

"It has already been done, ma'am."

"What? I thought all the re-sets needed two pairs of hands?"

Two held his hands up and looked at them. "I do not understand that comparison."

"I mean – I thought that two people were needed to re-set the computer."

"I was able to perform the last re-set without your assistance. It is all working properly now. You may request a return journey to Typhon whenever you are ready."

Miranda looked closely at Two's face. He looked as calm as ever; his face showed no emotion and his appearance was, as always, immaculate. She looked into his eyes; when they created him, they hadn't got the colour quite right. Gabe's eyes were green, but if you looked very closely, they were flecked with a blue so bright, it was almost turquoise. Two's eyes were a plain green. Miranda shook her head – how come she hadn't noticed that last night when they were standing so close together? "Well – thank you for looking after me so well. It was oddly cathartic to talk to you."

"It was my pleasure, ma'am." The simulant put out his hand to shake farewell.

Miranda looked at Two's hand and shrugged her shoulders. "After last night, I feel I want to hug you. Would that be alright?"

Two smiled briefly. "Of course. If it would please you, ma'am."

Miranda stepped forward and put her arms around Two's neck. She felt the simulant's arms come around her, hugging her tentatively. She inhaled deeply, hoping to get a calming dose of Gabe's familiar scent, but today he smelled different. She sighed. Perhaps she had been longing so much for her husband's embrace that she imagined his scent on the manufactured skin of Two's body. "Thank you, Two. I enjoyed our chess game. Perhaps we can play again over the communicator?" She stepped back and looked at his eyes again. There was no change to the size of his pupils, no indication that he was feeling anything at all, even though he was smiling at her.

"Yes, ma'am. I would like that very much."

The ride back to Typhon was a bit bumpy. The pilot looked across the cockpit to where Miranda was holding on to her seat. "Sorry for the turbulence. It's been the same for a couple of days now."

"Really? I thought you hadn't been out since you brought me to Eros."

"What? Oh – no – we had to fly some stuff out to Aphrodite last night."

"Stuff? What kind of stuff?" Miranda laughed at the lack of technical language. The shuttle pilots were usually so efficient.

"Supplies. For repairing a break in the outer shield. These storms knocked a small hole in it."

"I'll bet A1 was happy about that." Miranda laughed; she knew the acerbic simulant of old. "I expect she gave you chapter and verse about the poor design of the remotes."

The pilot looked uncomfortable and shifted in his seat. "It was another pilot. But he said she was a bit rude, yes. I don't really understand how a simulant can be rude."

"She was programmed that way." Miranda looked out of the window of the cockpit. "We're nearly home." The familiar shape of SE Typhon loomed in front of them and, moments later, they began their descent towards the airlock that would end her small foray into freedom from the rigours and routines of the ship that had been her home for the last two years. She sighed. "I'm not sure I'm ready to go back yet."

But she did go back. The shuttle docked, and ten minutes later, she was making her way to the bridge to report back to Gabriel that the mission had been a success.

Bridget greeted her with a hug when she stepped onto the bridge. "Hey – welcome back. I hear it was all a great success."

"It was. Where's Gabe?"

"In his quarters, I think. I haven't seen him since just after you left. He's been laying low – giving orders from a distance – you know how he is."

"Yes. I do. Thanks – I'll go and find him." Miranda wanted nothing less than to go and find her estranged husband, especially after her candid conversation with Two, which had brought so many things to the surface. As she was leaving the bridge, she noticed an abandoned pile of clothes; a plain uniform and one of the paper-thin armoured plates that the combat soldiers wore over their chests. She fingered the fine armour. "What's this doing here? Have we been attacked by pirates again?"

Bridget looked up from the computer display she had been studying. "Not that I know of. Perhaps the Captain was testing it out for some reason?"

"That's probably it." Miranda tried to sound calm, but she had a growing sense of unease. She walked the short distance to the apartment she had shared with her husband and was glad to discover that the scanner still accepted her hand to let her in. The room was in darkness. "Dammit, Gabe. Where the hell are you?" She left the officer's deck and took the stairs down to her quarters. A shower and a change of clothes would make her feel better. But when the door slid open, the lights were on and she knew straight away that Gabe was waiting for her. She pressed her hand to the scanner to close the door and she looked at the tiny room that had been her home since she moved out of their shared apartment. "Hello, Gabriel." She put her bag on the floor and turned to look at him.

"Miranda. I'm so sorry."

She walked up to him, made a fist, pulled back her arm and swung it as hard as she could. Her fist made contact with Gabe's nose, and he doubled over in pain, clutching his face. She also doubled over, clutching her hand to her chest, pain radiating up her arm. "Fuck!"

"You broke my nose!" Gabe straightened, and she watched as a steady stream of blood ran from his nostrils, down over his lips and chin, staining the front of his crisp, white shirt. "What did you do that for?"

Miranda straightened too, flexing her fingers to make sure that nothing was broken. "It was you. You bastard!"

"What – what was me?"

"Yesterday on Eros. That was you. I heard the airlock the night before – you came to Eros and took Two's place. What did you do with him, anyway?"

"I asked him to stay in the airlock."

Miranda looked at the bloodied face of her husband for a moment; her anger was boiling now. "You tricked me! I would never have said all that if I'd known it was you."

Gabe walked to her and grabbed her upper arms. "Well, I'm glad you did. I know this is all my fault – because I'm a stupid, selfish son-of-a-bitch. But you didn't tell me what you were thinking. I always depended on you telling me, because I'm fucking useless at all that feelings shit. But you stopped telling me. And I didn't have a fucking clue what was going on. But you talked to that simulant – and I'm glad you did."

"You listened in to our conversation on that first night?"

Gabe hung his head in shame and nodded sheepishly. "I did. And I just wanted to be there with you. I wanted to hold you and tell you I still love you. Okay – it was a bloody stupid idea, but I know now. Please, Miranda – you still love me, and I still love you. I know this isn't going to be fixed over night, but can we at least try? Please – come home."

"Okay – I'll admit that I didn't tell you how I was feeling. But what difference would it have made? You didn't ask me. You didn't notice that something was wrong. You're not going to change. And I just can't live like that anymore."

"Miranda – tell me what you want."

"You know what I want."

"No, I don't. I'm not good at knowing what you want. I need you to tell me. I need you to make the first move."

Miranda shook her head at the reference to their conversation after the chess game. "You're un-fucking-believable, do you know that?"

"I'm starting to get the picture. Now, tell. Me. What. You. WANT."

She looked at him for a moment then lifted her eyes to the ceiling, breathing deeply. "What do I want? I want my husband back. I want my life with my husband back. I want the man I married back."

"I'm right here, Miranda. I haven't gone anywhere."

"Yes, you have! As soon as we set foot on this godforsaken ship, you started to withdraw from me. You were never one for long, deep discussions, but you stopped communicating altogether. And you stopped wanting me. You haven't so much as touched me in months. That hug you gave me on Eros was the most contact we've had in I don't know how long. And you were pretending to be someone else!"

Gabe looked at the floor, and his shoulders dropped in defeat. "I don't have anything to say to defend myself. I've been stupid and selfish – everything you said. I've never been able to express myself – you know that. But you and me? We worked. We worked because you led the way. You told me what you wanted from the start. You stopped doing that, and I was lost – I didn't have a clue what to do. And the further away you got, the more lost I became."

"So, this is all my fault, then?"

"No! That's not what I'm saying! I'm saying that I NEED you. I'm rudderless without you. Please, Miranda!"

She shook her head in disbelief. "Gabriel – you run this ship – you tell hundreds of people what to do every day. Are you seriously expecting me to believe that you've let things between us get this bad because you didn't know what to do about it?"

"Yes." The single word was almost a whisper.

"So, whatever I tell you to do, you will?"

"Yes." Gabe fell to his knees in front of his wife. "Anything."

Miranda considered her options for a moment. Then she inhaled deeply through her nose and looked down at Gabe, and her lip curled. "This is what I want. I want you to get up and go back to your quarters. I want you to sign those fucking divorce papers because no matter what I want, you're never going to change."

Three days later, Gabriel Brant resigned his commission on Typhon and began the long journey back to Earth. Miranda didn't wave him off. He left the signed divorce papers on her desk and waited as long as he could, but she didn't show. As the huge Space Explorer grew smaller in the porthole of the transporter ship, he felt as though his heart would break. She was right. He was a pussy, and he deserved no-one's respect. The Admiral had tried to persuade him otherwise, but his mind was made up.

After a short sabbatical to re-acclimatise himself to a life where day and night weren't virtual constructs, he took up a post at SE Central. Training new recruits was a heck of a lot easier than running a ship, and the little house he bought a few miles from the base suited him. It had a small garden and room for his piano. He'd missed all of that when he was in space. But now he was missing something far more important than a patch of lawn or a collection of wood and metal. He was heartsore for Miranda.

He hadn't heard from his wife since he left Typhon; he'd received a letter from his divorce lawyer about a month after he came home, but he didn't open it. He didn't need to read the whys and wherefores of the end of their marriage. The letter had gone, unopened, into his file of certificates and papers. He thought about throwing it onto the first bonfire of Autumn leaves that he had in his new garden, but he decided he'd better hold onto it.

Gabriel lost track of time. Every day was the same; get up, shower, dress, travel to work, teach, eat, come home, sleep, rinse and repeat. So, when a familiar face stepped into his office one Friday afternoon, he was both surprised and delighted. "Bridget?"

His former second-in-command smiled warmly at him before greeting him with a hug. "Hello, old friend. Long time, no see."

"When did you get in? God, it's so good to see you." He hugged her back. He'd never been a hugger – any more than he was a talker – but he was so glad to see her.

"We just got out of debriefing."

"God, has it really been a year? Did everyone come home? Or did some sign on for another term?"

"A couple stayed. But she came home." There was no need to clarify who she was. Bridget knew there was only one person from the Typhon crew that Gabriel was truly interested in.

He tried to steady his voice so that he didn't sound too pathetic. "How is she?"

"She's fine. She's trying to pretend that she doesn't want to come to see you. But you didn't answer her letter, so she's being brave."

"Letter? What letter?"

"The one she wrote you? Her lawyer should have put it in with the letter saying the divorce was on hold."

"What? I didn't receive any … hang on a minute. Oh shit! I didn't even open it. I thought it was the divorce and I didn't want to read it."

Bridget nodded and smiled. "Well, I suggest you read it now. And if you want to see Miranda, she's staying in the Officers' hostel. Room 10." She pulled him into a brief hug and left, closing the door behind her.

Gabriel grabbed his briefcase and raced out of his office a couple of minutes later. On the stairs, he met a female student who was on her way to see him. He groaned inwardly when he saw her; she had been visiting him every other day or so on some pretence of needing help with an assignment or something, but he recognised a predatory female when he saw one.

"Captain Brant! I was just coming to see you."

Gabe passed her on the stairs, taking them two at a time. "Sorry, I'm rushing home. My wife has just returned from Typhon, and I really need to see her."

The girl looked shocked and put her head over the bannister to watch him fly down the stairs. "Your wife? I thought you were divorced." She managed to sound surprised, disappointed and whiney all once.

Gabe looked up at her and grinned. "No. Not divorced. It was just a trial separation. But I'm hoping the trial is over." He felt completely energised as he left his office building. A short journey on an auto-tram and he was bounding up the steps of his small house. He knew exactly where to find the letter, and he ripped into the envelope in his hurry to read it.

Dear Gabriel

I have asked the lawyer to put the divorce on hold until I return to Earth. When I get home, I would like us to try again — maybe get some couples counselling, if you feel the same. I still feel that moving out of our apartment was the right thing to do. We were going nowhere and only growing further apart. But talking to Two (and to you, pretending to be Two — I still haven't forgiven you for that) made me remember what it was that made me fall in love with you in the first place.

When you left Typhon, I was both glad and sad. Glad for you, because being hemmed in on that ship was killing you. I tried to tell you so many times, but you never heard me. But sad too — mainly for myself — because I couldn't see you every day. I hear that you have got a teaching position at the Academy. That is the best news (I gave a tiny squeak of joy when I heard) because you are a natural teacher.

Your students are very lucky to have your expertise, knowledge and experience at their disposal.

I really hope that you will want to talk when I come home. I'm going to finish my term, but it will be my last off-world. I would like to secure a teaching position at the Academy too. I have made some enquiries with the Engineering department, and it sounds promising.

In the meantime, I hope that you will spend some time finding yourself again — play the piano and grow things in your garden. And perhaps you will remember why you fell in love with this neurotic, possessive woman.

Yours, always
Miranda

Gabe ran up the stairs of the Officers' hostel. The room list in the foyer told him that Room 10 was on the second floor. When he reached the second-floor landing he was panting; not just from the exertion but from the emotions that were cascading through his body now that he was mere feet from the woman he loved. He forced his breathing to be steady, standing outside the door for a couple of minutes to calm himself before knocking.

Miranda opened the door, and her breath caught in her throat when she saw her husband standing there, looking for all the world as if he was about to burst into tears. "Gabriel! What are you doing here?" She knew that was a stupid question the moment she had uttered it.

"Hello, Miranda. I came. I had to. I ... I'm sorry."

"Sorry? What for?"

"Can I come in?"

"Oh. Yes. Of course." She stood aside and let him come into her room. These were Officer's quarters, but they were almost identical to the rooms she and Gabe had lodged in during their training. "Can I get you something to drink? Coffee?"

"I didn't come here for that."

Miranda's face fell. So, it was as she feared; he didn't want to talk. He had left her letter unanswered because he didn't see any future for them. "Okay. Say what you came here to say. I don't want to draw this out any more than we have to."

"That came out wrong. Oh, fuck it — I'm no good at this. I only just read your letter, Miranda. I thought it was the divorce and I didn't open it. I've longed for you. I want to try again. What I mean is — I think coffee is overrated."

Miranda smiled at his reference to their first date, and she blushed when she remembered how that had ended. She looked around at their familiar surroundings. "You do?"

"I do. And as much as I'd like to re-enact our first time in a dorm bed, we need to talk. And I want you to come home with me. To our home. Please." He had winged that completely, but he felt pretty pleased with how it had come out, and he looked at her hopefully.

They took the short auto-tram ride back to the small house that Gabe had called home for the last nine months or so. When they walked up the front path, Miranda looked at the pretty garden with its mixture of flowers and vegetables. "You've been gardening."

"I have." Gabe couldn't help the smile that broke out on his face. "You were right – I need to do that. Being on that ship was the worst thing possible for me. And you were right about something else, too." He opened the front door and ushered her inside. The first thing anyone saw when they walked into the small house was the baby grand piano which dominated the first reception room.

"Your piano! You got it out of storage!" She walked quickly to it and ran her fingers lovingly over the keys. "Play something for me?"

"I will. Later. But I've got stuff I need to say to you. Can I go first?"

Miranda smiled warily. "Okay." She moved to sit on the couch. "I'm listening."

"Good." Gabe began to pace in front of the fireplace. After he had gone back and forth half a dozen times, he stopped and turned to look at Miranda. "Right. Here it is. I love you. I never stopped loving you. I really don't know what happened up there, but I was feeling you move further away from me and I didn't know what to do about it. When you moved out, I couldn't understand why. Then I heard you talking to Two, and I understood. I remembered what we used to be like. I want that again. I want to be your man again. Do you think we can try? Can you forgive me?"

Miranda stood up and put her arms around him. He was agitated from sharing all that with her, and she could feel his distress coming off him in waves. As she pulled his head down to her shoulder, she heard the first, shuddered sob. "Gabriel – my darling – please don't cry. I've done enough of that for both of us." She lifted his face away from her so that she could look at him. "You're the only one I've ever really wanted. You broke my heart up there – I didn't know what I'd done wrong."

"You didn't do anything wrong – it was me …"

"It was both of us. I should have talked to you. We're as bad as one another."

He faced her, wiped the tears from his eyes and looked at her. He lifted his hand and began to run his fingertips over her soft cheeks as if he was seeing her for the first time. "I love you so much."

She smiled at him and brushed the last of his tears away. "I love you too. Now, please kiss me. I've wanted you to kiss me since I opened the door to you."

They reached for each other at the same time, and Gabe covered Miranda's mouth with his, sighing with a mixture of relief and desire as her familiar taste filled his mouth. His hands followed their favourite path down her back to cup her buttocks, pushing her against his hardening cock. He felt her relax against him, so he broke their kiss and picked her up in his arms before heading towards the stairs that led to his bedroom.

Miranda squealed with delight as she was lifted into Gabe's strong embrace. When he put her down in the bedroom, she looked around quickly. "You got our bed out of storage too?"

"It made me feel like a little bit of you was still here." He put his arms around her once more and pulled her soft body as close to him as he could. "And now you're really here. A part of me can hardly believe it."

"We've still got a long way to go. We're going to need time to get back to where we were."

"I know. And I'm prepared to wait. If you don't want to do this, then I'll understand."

Miranda laughed and cupped the swell of his cock with her hand. "What? You expect me to wait for this?" She laughed again and undid his trousers, letting his erection spring free. "Oh no. I want you to fuck me into the middle of next week. And then I'm going to want you to do it again.

Gabe grinned at his beautiful wife. "That would be my pleasure, ma'am."

And it was.

Miranda stretched like a lazy cat, nestled in the warmth of the bed she shared with her husband, Gabriel. He was sleeping beside her, his black hair over his eyes as he snored softly. Miranda thought about their life together – so much had changed since she returned to Earth all those months ago. She felt a little flutter low in her belly and smiled.

"Good morning Two." The fluttering started again and she felt Gabe's warm hand as he laid it over her belly.

"I think he likes the name." He pushed up onto his elbows and smiled at his wife.

"I think *she* just likes to hear my voice. And yours." She raised her hand and pushed the hair out of Gabe's eyes. "So, you'd better say good morning to your firstborn." She couldn't help the smile that spread across her face. *Two* had been a bit of an accident. In the weeks that followed her return to the marital home, they had made love in every way imaginable; gently, passionately, voraciously, desperately. She had forgotten to get her birth control shot renewed, and they had made Two. Once the shock had worn off, they were both delighted; Gabriel had been strutting around like a prize turkey-cock telling everyone that his beautiful wife was carrying his baby.

Gabe sat up properly and ran the palm of his hand over Miranda's belly again. He felt the little kick and grinned. Leaning down, he kissed the skin just below her navel and spoke quietly to his baby. "Good morning, Two. We're so excited about you." His eyes glossed over for a moment then he kissed his wife's belly again.

Miranda wriggled as the kicking continued. "She likes that."

Gabe moved so that he was kneeling between her legs and he began placing wet, open-mouthed kisses on the soft swelling of her belly. "Good. Do you like it?"

"Oh yes." Her reply was breathy, and she moved her hips a little under his caresses. "Gabriel – god – that's really turning me on."

Gabe grinned against her skin but didn't break contact. He started to lick a slow, wet path down towards her pussy. He knew she was aroused because he could smell her tell-tale scent; it was a mixture of the ocean and something musky. His cock hardened in response. He used his fingers to part her outer labia then he placed his mouth over her clitoris, sucking it gently and stroking it with his tongue. He looked up at Miranda. She had her eyes closed, and she was pinching one of her nipples between her thumb and forefinger as she squirmed in his hold. "Do you want me to fuck you?"

"Yes." She was panting a little now. "Yes, please. Do it. I want your cock in me." Gabe had always been able to turn her on, but since she found out she was pregnant, she had become almost insatiable. She hadn't been troubled with sickness, other than a little nausea during the day, and she felt better than she had in years. If being pregnant was always going to feel this good, then she could easily imagine a *Three* and a *Four*.

"That would be my pleasure, ma'am." Gabe enjoyed aping the voice of the simulant. They had role-played the night on Eros several times, with the crucial difference that Two had discovered he did have the sex add-on after all. One of their most kinky sessions had involved her giving him step-by-step instructions. She guided him through tying her to the kitchen table, licking and fingering her pussy, using a vibrator on her clitoris, pushing a butt-plug into her anus and finally fucking her with his cock until she begged him to stop. He was fairly sure that this particular session was when she had conceived, so the baby was nick-named *Two* in honour of the simulant who had indirectly brought them back together.

"Please, Gabriel. I need it." Miranda was reaching for him, her face was relaxed, and her eyes were hooded with arousal.

He moved up her body and captured her mouth in a searing kiss. She pushed her tongue into his mouth, and his body snapped to attention. He moved into position between her thighs and his cock found its goal. He pushed into her, and they sighed together as he penetrated deeply. "Miranda! I need you so much – I need you all the time."

"I know. I need you too. I need this. I think I'd go crazy without it now."

"That won't happen. I'm not going anywhere. And neither are you." He punctuated his statement my slamming into her and holding himself still, pressing her into the mattress. "Your place is here with me." He dipped his head and sucked on her bottom lip. Then he grinned mischievously. "And my place is here with you, keeping your horny cunt satisfied."

"God, this pregnancy has turned me into some kind of nympho." She grinned back at him and reached down to place her palms on his buttocks. "Now, get to it, soldier. My horny cunt is in desperate need of your attention."

Gabe began to move his hips so that his cock rocked in and out of Miranda's pussy. His mouth quirked into a smile and he started to mimic the simulant again. "Ma'am, my systems are struggling to process the input from my genitals. I think I am feeling something new. What might it be?"

Miranda grinned – she loved this little fantasy. "Two, I believe that what you are feeling is lust."

"What should I do about that, ma'am?"

"What does your CPU say that you should do?"

Gabe thrust his hips so that he was inside her fully. "My CPU is producing random output. It would seem that all my processing capabilities have been diverted to my genitals. I just want to do this." He moved in a steady rhythm, in and out, deep then shallow. "Is this satisfactory?"

"Oh yes." Miranda gripped Gabe's waist with her knees, pulling him closer to her, forcing a deeper penetration. "Yes. Oh, Gabriel! Fuck me and don't stop!"

He kissed her mouth, stroking her tongue with his. This was the signal that the play had ended and he was no longer pretending. He groaned as the sensation of her pussy gripping him filled his whole body. He was going to come soon. He knew by the sounds that she was making that her orgasm was close too, so he continued to thrust rhythmically into her, concentrating on keeping the momentum going until she came.

"Gabe – oh – yes – like that – there – I'm going to – oh fuck!"

He felt her climax begin and he pressed into her. He couldn't hold back anymore, and he let himself go, spilling his seed deep inside her. "Miranda!" He always cried out her name when he came. He always had – even when they were apart if he made himself come, he would cry out her name, dedicating his orgasm to her. They all belonged to her. They always had.

"Gabriel." She replied, holding him as they both came down from the high they had shared. "Thank you."

"What for?"

"Everything."

"You're welcome, ma'am.

Acknowledgements

This book feels a bit like a magnum opus – not because it's good, but because it took a long time to write. It was a lot harder to create twelve different scenarios than I thought it would be and, as I explained in the foreword, it didn't quite go to plan!

I would like to thank my dear friends Jay and her husband, G. They read each one of the stories as I wrote them and gave me feedback to help me improve them. G also gave me some very honest information to help me write from the male perspective. As several of the stories are written in the first person by a male character, this helped make them sound more realistic, so I'm very grateful for G's candour.

As with the other books I have written, there are characters I like more than others in here. I think my favourite is Daniel – my charming, Irish vampire made me smile as I was writing him. My other Danyell – from Leo – is also a favourite. His confession that he is a 'pillicock' (an archaic form of 'pillock') made me warm to him. I didn't realise that I had used the same name twice until I was editing the stories. I thought about changing one of them, but I decided to leave them as they are.

I'm looking forward to revisiting and developing Leah and Pej's story from Aquarius. I have an idea for a series where characters from the various Stations take on the jackals and find their redemption and freedom.

Thank you for reading. I'll hopefully have more for you soon.

About the author

Cate Tyrrell has been writing for many years; poetry, short stories and factual articles. This is her third book. Her first two books, *37 Songs* and *Parallel Lines*, were well-received and she is currently working on the first book in a series of paranormal romance stories.

Cate reads voraciously. She loves good romance books and paranormal romances. Her favourite authors are J. R. Ward and C. D. Reiss. Like most writers, she leads two lives. During the day she is a teacher (and unrepentant computer geek) but at night, and during the school holidays, she is a writer. She also sings in a choir and loves music – it will probably always get an honourable mention somewhere in her stories.

She lives in a small, Gloucestershire town and dreams of being able to give up the day job so that she can write full-time.

Follow Cate on Twitter: @catetyrrell
Facebook: @catetyrrell
Website: www.catetyrrell.com
Email: catetyrrell@catetyrrell.com